OVERTURES

Anita Burgh is the author of *Distinctions of Class* (shortlisted
for the Boots Romantic Novelist of the Year Award), *Love
the Bright Foreigner*, *The Azure Bowl*, *The Golden Butterfly*, *The
Stone Mistress* and, most recently, the bestseller *Advances*.
She was born in Gillingham, Kent, and is the mother of
four grown-up children.

ALSO BY ANITA BURGH

ANITA BURGH

OVERTURES

PAN BOOKS
In association with Macmillan London

First published 1993 by Macmillan London Limited

This edition published 1994 by Pan Books Limited
a division of Pan Macmillan Publishers Limited
Cavaye Place London SW10 9PG
and Basingstoke
in association with Macmillan London Limited

Associated companies throughout the world

ISBN 0 330 33311 9

1 3 5 7 9 8 6 4 2

A CIP catalogue record for this book is available from
the British Library

Typeset by CentraCet Limited, Cambridge
Printed and bound in Great Britain by
Cox & Wyman Ltd, Reading, Berkshire

For my daughter Kate, with love

We – are we not formed, as notes of music are,
For one another, though dissimilar?

P. B. SHELLEY (1792–1822)

PRELUDE

1982

From the foot of the hospital bed, Kitty watched the patient intently, and glanced at her watch. If the woman was going to die, she hoped she would do so quickly.

She pulled her coat closer about her. Was it the night-time temperature of the ward, or the circumstances, or her thoughts that were making her so cold? She could not remember ever being chilled like this, not even in Sweden. For the icy feeling had burrowed deep inside her until she felt frozen to her marrow.

She was tired, mind-numbingly so. She had dropped everything to fly here, and now she was, she knew that her first reaction – not to come – had been the right one.

'Would you like some tea, Miss Lawrence?'

Kitty swung round at the sound of the voice.

'That would be kind of you,' she said to the buxom, plain-faced nurse. 'No sugar,' she added, smiling this time, a bright, accomplished smile which was not reflected in her eyes.

Holding firmly to the steelwork at the foot of the bed, she turned back to watch the patient who lay neatly under sheets that barely moved, her breathing so shallow that it was almost as if she were already dead. Kitty was looking at a stranger. It must be this illness, this place which had drained the woman of the person she once had been. Or was it even her? She only had the nurse's word for it. How long had it been since she had seen her last? How many years? And people changed . . .

'Hope that's not too much milk?' the nurse said in a whisper so loud she need not have bothered.

'It's fine,' Kitty replied automatically, not even looking at the tea.

'I'll put it on the locker. You can sit here.' The nurse was already putting a chair in place near the head of the bed. 'There, if she wakes up she'll see you immediately,' she said kindly.

'I'll drink it here, Nurse.'

'Sister, actually.' The sister smiled with the patient resignation of one who often had to make the correction.

'Sorry, Sister. I'd rather stand,' Kitty said quickly. 'The plane – I've been sitting for hours,' she added in hurried explanation, conscious of a rising panic that she might be expected to sit close to the patient, even to touch her.

'Of course. Nasty, uncomfortable things, aeroplanes,' the sister said in a comforting tone and handed Kitty the cup and saucer. She took a sip and managed not to grimace at the over-milked taste. 'Are you all right? Sure you wouldn't be better off sitting?' the sister asked, noting the cup shaking in Kitty's hand.

'No, I'm fine. Just desperately cold. How do your patients survive in these temperatures?'

'I'll move the chair for you,' the sister said, aware that the ward was kept at a constant and comfortable temperature, but suddenly understanding. It was easy for her to forget when dealing with death on a daily basis that most people were afraid of it, and of being too close to it.

Kitty sank on to the chair placed at the foot of the bed. She held up the tea. 'I'm sorry bothering you. I don't really want it now.' The sister took the cup and saucer. 'Is she . . .' Kitty nodded her head to the shape in the bed, finding she couldn't quite say what she wanted to.

'A real fighter this one. Last night,' the sister shrugged and bent down and this time really whispered, 'last night it was touch and go. But you know, Miss Lawrence, the human body is a wonderful thing. She's a long way to go yet but . . . well, quite honestly I wouldn't be surprised if she pulled through.'

'Oh, I see,' said Kitty, aware of a flicker of annoyance that she had come all this way for nothing.

'But then . . .' The sister heaved her well-padded shoulders. 'Who knows?'

There was a sudden slight movement from the bed. The sister bustled to her patient, felt her pulse, stroked a wisp of hair away from her forehead and bent close. 'Who's got a visitor, then? Isn't that a nice surprise?' She straightened up. 'Just a few minutes, we don't want to tire her out, now, do we?' she said briskly, and made way by the bedside for Kitty.

Slowly, nervously, Kitty rose from the chair to stand beside the patient's head. The lamp which shone down was shaded an eerie blue, its muted light accentuating the shadows on the emaciated face.

'Is that Lana?' The woman spoke in the hoarse rasp of a voice which had been unused for some time. She wearily waved a hand so thin it looked like a bird's claw. Kitty recoiled from the hand as it waved, reaching for contact, reminding her of the searching tentacles of some sea creature. 'Lana? At last. What took you so long, my darling?'

Kitty's hand inched towards the beckoning one, to touch it, finding pity winning over distaste.

'It's not Lana, it's Kitty . . .'

The woman's eyes snapped open with surprising suddenness. Kitty was stared at by eyes of startling blue.

'What are you doing here?' Her voice was accusing, her hand dropped back dejectedly on to the covers. 'I don't want you. Who sent for you? I want Lana.' The voice had become wheedling. Kitty put her own hand back safely into her pocket.

'I don't know where Lana is,' she said.

'Then find her. You can do that for once, can't you?' She was breathless with the effort of speaking.

'I'll see what I can do.'

'And hurry.'

'It might take time.'

'I haven't got time.' The patient sighed with exasperation.

'Don't talk like that, please. Of course you've got time . . .' Kitty tried to sound encouraging.

'Don't bloody well talk to me like those dumb-cluck nurses. I'm not a child!' The exertion needed for such a long sentence made her begin to cough, the thin body was racked with the effort and arched like a bow from the strain. Kitty looked frantically into the gloom for a nurse. 'Water . . .' The hand rose again, waving impotently in the air. 'Water . . .'

Kitty leaned forward, put her arm awkwardly round her and lifted her into a near-sitting position with ease, for she weighed little. Kitty sat on the bed, supporting her with her own body, and with the other hand she held the spout of the feeding-cup to the patient's mouth. She sucked hungrily at it and then, exhausted, slumped back on to the pillow, trapping Kitty's arm. A thin sheen of sweat covered the woman's face. Kitty knew she should sponge the sweat away, but also knew she could not. Gingerly she inched her arm from under the other's body.

She looked down to see the blue eyes gazing at her, pleadingly.

'Get me out of here, Kitty. Get me somewhere private.'

'I will, I promise.'

'And find Lana.'

'I will.'

'Come back when you've found her.' And the eyes shut as if in sleep, but Kitty knew it was in dismissal.

Kitty picked up her handbag from the floor where it had dropped and without looking back walked quickly towards the lighted office where she could see the sister and two other nurses sitting at a desk. Both nurses were knitting busily.

'You off then, Miss Lawrence?' The sister stood up as Kitty appeared in the open doorway.

'Yes. She wants a private room. How do I arrange that?' Kitty spoke quickly.

'I didn't realize she was unhappy here with us.' The sister bridled noticeably.

'It's nothing to do with any of you, Sister. I doubt if she'd be satisfied anywhere.'

The sister sucked in her cheeks in remonstration. 'I'll tell the day sister, she'll arrange for her to be moved to the private wing. Do you want the same consultant to attend to her or do you have your own choice in mind?' There was still the ice of disapproval in her voice.

'No, I'm sure he's the best.' Kitty's response seemed to placate the sister momentarily for she smiled suddenly.

'I don't appear to have a contact number for you, Miss Lawrence – just in case, you know. We have your agent's but that's only available during office hours.'

'I'll give you his home number. I shall be away.'

'You're not stopping, then?'

'No, I don't think it's necessary. Just send any bills to my agent – he'll deal with them.'

Kitty looked back into the darkened ward. 'Well, that's all I think,' she said, in the way of one who wants to be going but is unsure how to extricate herself. 'Thank you, all of you.' She managed to produce one of her slick professional smiles and turned to go.

'Miss Lawrence.' The sister put out a restraining hand. 'I'd feel happier with a telephone number where we could contact you direct. She could go at any time – tonight, even – one never can tell with cases like this.'

'Oh no, Sister. She won't do that. You've got my mother for some time yet.' Kitty turned into the corridor. They heard her high heels clicking on the heavy-duty linoleum, and they waited for the swish of the ward door closing.

'Well, there's a cold cow if ever I saw one.' The staff nurse spoke for the first time.

'Doesn't she care?' the student nurse asked. 'Why, her mother's such a sweet, uncomplaining soul.'

'Fancy swanning off with her mother this ill.' The staff nurse made a tutting noise in time to her clicking needles. 'My heart goes out to that poor woman.'

'I don't know, staff. I've seen a lot in my time. She was upset out there, shivering and complaining of the cold – mild shock, I'd say. We never know the full story, do we? What's gone on between people in the past to make them the way they are? People always behave in a certain way for a reason, I've found.' The sister nodded her head as if agreeing with her own wisdom. 'Right, staff,' she said more briskly. 'Now our VIP's gone, I'll be off on my rounds.' She picked up her large black torch, flung her cape over her shoulders and left the office.

'I still think she's a cold bitch for all that,' the staff nurse said, picking at her teeth with the point of one of her knitting needles.

'And did you clock that coat? I could never like anyone who ponced about in a fur coat. That shows how unfeeling she really is.' The student nurse shuddered.

The chauffeur-driven car slid to a halt outside the mansion block of flats. Kitty was out of the car and across the pavement before the driver could open the door for her. Nor did she thank him or say goodnight, which was unusual for her, he thought, as he sat back behind the wheel.

Kitty took the lift, gilded and elegant but old and agonizingly slow, to the top floor. She let herself into her flat, the hallway was lit, she hoped that meant that Jenny was up and waiting for her. But the drawing-room was in darkness. She flicked on the lights, kicked off her shoes, and crossed to the well-stocked drinks tray where she poured herself a large Scotch which she downed in one. She hurried back to the hall, taking off her coat as she went. In the large, blindingly white and airy kitchen, she searched under the sink and took out a black bin-liner. She folded the mink coat and stuffed it unceremoniously into the bag. She unzipped her smart black dress and added it to the coat. She tied the top of the bag tight, opened the back door which gave on to the fire escape and put the bag with the others waiting to be collected.

In her bedroom she stripped and, naked, walked into the bathroom. For ten minutes she scrubbed herself under the cascading water of the shower. Only then did she feel warm again. Only then did she feel clean.

ACT ONE

1959–1963

1

Mike Lawrence strode along the road in his thick, crêpe-soled shoes. He always walked quietly even in normal shoes for he was light of foot. It annoyed Amy, his wife, out of all proportion. 'Creeping Jesus' she called him when he came up behind her and made her jump. Not that there was anything he could do about it, one was born with one's footfall and that was that, he would explain, and his explanation annoyed her equally.

He paused at the bend in the road, as he often did, just for the pleasure of seeing his home and knowing it was his.

It might be special to him but to anyone else it was an ordinary house, one of the thousands built in the twenties before the Depression had snapped its jaws shut on developers. It stood in an avenue of some two hundred similar properties, equally loved and tended by their owners. But to Mike, Number Fourteen always looked that little bit neater, tidier and better cared for.

A small green gate with a latch led up a stone-flagged path between two small lawns surrounded by Mike's standard rose bushes. The downstairs and upstairs bays had pristine white net curtains hanging at the windows, whose frames and sills he repainted every four years, completely burning off and sanding down – he'd never been one to skimp or make things easier for himself. He thought he preferred the green – Nile Green, it said on the can – and cream to last year's black and white. The black gloss had been a mistake, not to be repeated, for it had shown every speck of dust, every bird's dropping. Green was better.

Over the panelled door was a small, oval, stained-glass

window featuring an orange sun rising or setting – he'd never been sure which. Amy was all for removing the pane, which she thought old-fashioned, and changing it for a frosted glass one, a demand Mike had so far resisted. The bell, when pressed, which was not often, chimed – Westminster chimes they were called.

The house was pebble-dashed. He regretted this, for the covering was beginning to lift in places, needed constant attention and was the cause, he was sure, of the small damp patch in the bedroom over the porch. Try as he might, he had not been able to eradicate it. But there it was, pebble-dash he'd got and there was no use complaining about it.

To the side was a shared access with Number Twelve, the edges cement, the middle grassed – exactly centred to show where Twelve ended and Fourteen began. Mike had seen houses with such arrangements where one neighbour cut his grass and the other let his grow. And although Frankie in Number Twelve had never been known to handle a mower, Mike wasn't petty, and cut the grass for both of them. Amy said he shouldn't, that he was doing the idle sod a favour for which he showed no appreciation. But Mike did not mind. He liked things tidy.

He walked up this approach at the top of which were two garages, semi-detached like the houses they served. There was no car in the Lawrences', but one day . . .? Mike was nothing if not an optimist. This side entrance, making the house semi-detached, made Number Fourteen superior in both Mike and Amy's eyes, for most of the Avenue was terraced.

He reached the gate, a gate of a man's height made of planked wood and as carefully painted as the front of the house. Its number and a '*No hawkers or circulars*' notice were screwed to the top. He lifted the latch and pushed hard. The gate always stuck despite his taking it down, planing the edges, changing the hinges, keeping everything well oiled. He had become used to it sticking and, in fact, had grown quite fond of it, and no longer tried to correct it. At least it always gave Amy warning of his return since his feet didn't.

He crossed the yard – which Amy preferred to call a terrace – and passed under the pergola he had built, heavy with climbing roses. First he inspected the small patch of lawn where the grass was so smooth and unpolluted with weeds that it looked like the finest green suede. His dahlias, each carefully staked, were his pride and joy, and each had to be inspected for mould or parasites. Then it was the turn of the vegetable patch. He only checked his garden at this stage for he did not want to dirty his working clothes. He would have his tea, change, and then, the light permitting, he would potter about the garden he loved. Not an inch of space was wasted, he'd even covered the old Anderson shelter with turf. In spring it was a fine show of crocus and snowdrops. Satisfied that all was fine, he retraced his steps. He wiped his shoes carefully on the outside mat, repeated the procedure on the one inside the back door and called out, 'I'm home.'

There was no reply, there often wasn't. He looked beside the kettle for the note that would explain where Amy and his daughters were. He read that this evening they were at the dressmaker's.

More expense, he thought with sadness not irritation. Sadness, because he had always vowed that whatever made his wife happy he would provide. And he had, even when it had meant hours of overtime, time he would rather have spent in his garden. But no matter what she wanted and he gave, it did not make Amy happy.

At first her ambition had been for this house and its contents to be the best in the Avenue, for herself to be the best dressed, for her children to be the smartest and prettiest. In the past five years she had turned her energies and thwarted ambitions totally upon their daughters. Amy had decided they were to be dancing stars – no matter the cost.

Ah, the cost! When he had been just an assistant, oddly, it had been easier to cope. Now he was the manager of the store there was no overtime to augment his income, he was expected to put in the extra time out of devotion.

There was a saucepan on a low heat on the gas stove. He took an oven-cloth, removed the plate that was set on the top and placed it on the oil-cloth which covered the table. He carefully washed his hands before lifting the saucepan lid. Good. Shepherd's pie with mushy peas, his favourite. The table was set for him with knife and fork and OK sauce which he spread liberally over the top of the potatoes.

As he ate he thought of Amy. She reminded him of a dragonfly, the way she darted about with apparently inexhaustible energy. He thought she must be like one of those exotic birds in the tropics he'd read about – brightly coloured, small, always active.

They had met at a dance just as Europe was accelerating into war. She was a trainee hairdresser, he an assistant in the Co-op. She hadn't wanted to be a hairdresser, she'd longed to be a dancer, but her strait-laced, chapel-going parents had put their foot down, imagining that all the sins of Sodom and Gomorrah would await their daughter on the stage. They were none too happy about the hairdressing either, regarding any artificial adornment as sinful – but it was the lesser of two evils. Mike had loved Amy at first sight but so had many others for she had a neat figure and a pretty face framed by a mass of golden curls. His campaign to win her had been a long one. From his first day at work he had saved a good portion of his wage. He had always known why he saved – he knew that one day he would fall in love and he wanted to be in a position to offer his bride the best. And to Mike the best was a house with a bathroom, miles away from the tin-bathed terraces of his youth. In Amy he had found a soul-mate for she saved too and she knew exactly what she wanted – a house on Mulberry Avenue.

The war might have put back their plans. A conscript's wage did not leave much over, but women were desperate to try to look their best in such austere times, and Amy worked harder than ever and continued to put money in the bank.

They had married in July 1941, sooner than either had planned, but Amy wrote that she was pregnant by him and Mike managed to scrounge a forty-eight-hour pass so that he could do the right thing. Her period started on their wedding night.

Mike did not mind. He had her now. When he was away from her he'd worried that someone else with larger savings than he, maybe even with a flash car, might come and pinch her from him. Amy was not so pleased at being hurtled into marriage. She had wanted things 'nice' right from the start of her married life and now she was going to have to make do.

For four years they served their time in bedsits and then a rented flat. It had not been a happy period in either of their lives. He had wanted to start a family; she had refused. Mike had felt real panic as he had seen his pretty wife turn miserable and dejected as they moved from one type of rented accommodation to another. But the savings account, helped by the bonus of his gratuity payment, had grown, so that by 1946 Mike was able to buy his Amy's dream – 14 Mulberry Avenue.

On a May morning the key to the house was theirs, and they stood in their semi, with its panelled bath, separate WC, and fitted dresser in the kitchen.

'What do you think, then?' Mike asked her, smiling proudly.

'I'm chuffed as hell. Imagine, at last, us in Mulberry Avenue.'

'We'll get some wallpaper, do the living-room up really nice.'

'No, the hall first.'

'But why? The living-room's in real need.'

'More people see the hall, that's why. Then downstairs – front room first of all.'

'If that's what you want, Mum,' Mike said, puzzled, but then much about his wife puzzled him.

'Don't call me "Mum", it's common.' She moved swiftly into the kitchen with the grace of the dancer she would never be, opened the back door and looked at the garden.

'Flowers. I want flowers, hundreds of them, so I can have the house full of them – great vases cascading with flowers,' she said dreamily.

'Whatever you want, my girl.' He stepped forward to take her in his arms, hopefully to kiss her. 'You know what they say? New house, new baby . . .' He grinned at her.

'Oh, Mike, whatever next? Can't you think of anything else? We've tea-chests to unpack.' And she'd skipped lightly past him in the way she had and he followed after her feeling huge and gross, which she often made him feel. But he was right – one year later, after a very difficult pregnancy and birth, their first baby arrived, followed two years later and after a far easier birth by the second, both born in the bow-fronted bedroom where they had been conceived.

Ah, yes. Those were happy days, Mike thought as he picked up his empty plate and crossed to the sink where he carefully washed and dried it, replacing it in the tidy china cupboard. He walked along the narrow hallway, up the carpeted stairs – fully fitted, no stair rods to collect the dust. He smiled when he saw the large copper pot full of dahlias on the landing window-sill – he let her pick them, as many as she wanted. In the neat bedroom he took off his office suit and hung it carefully in the double wardrobe of pale walnut. He stroked the fine wood and was puzzled why

Amy should want to throw it out in favour of fitted cupboards.

After he had changed into his gardening clothes he went out to his vegetable patch. He began to tie up the newer shoots of the runner beans and knew that no matter how much thinking he did about the happy part of his life he could no longer keep the bad part at bay, the niggling fear that kept him awake at night while Amy slept unconcerned beside him. Worry that sometimes turned his guts to water and made him wonder how long he could go on.

He did not have enough money – that was his problem. There were the school fees, for Amy had insisted the girls attend a private school and he had been in full agreement. Then the bewildering array of uniform such establishments demanded, and the extras – the piano lessons, the horse-riding. On top of all this, there were the dancing lessons for both daughters, four times a week – two in class and the other two private. Then there were the dressmaker's bills for the costumes for the dancing school's twice-yearly concerts. There were tap shoes and ballet shoes and leo-tards and tutus without number.

Mike resented none of this. He had two beautiful and talented daughters, it was his duty to give them every possible chance in life.

If only Amy wasn't wanting the fitted wardrobe in their bedroom, and the fitted kitchen, and a new carpet in the front room. He always knew what Amy wanted, and was expecting him to supply, for suddenly magazines would appear left open at the relevant pages showing someone else's lovely kitchen or bathroom or bedroom. Samples of fabric and carpet would appear too – that's how he knew what was expected of him.

This time he had no idea how he was going to pay for the new carpet and fittings. He'd already taken out a second mortgage on the house and that had all gone on redecorat-ing it from top to bottom, a new three-piece suite, a dinner service – which they only used at Christmas – a mass of clothes for his three ladies and a new radiogram. The borrowed money was all spent and the interest payments were a mounting burden.

He should have been able to explain all this to Amy but he could not, for several reasons. If he confessed he would feel he was letting her down. If he let her down he would feel a failure. If he failed her he knew what her reaction would be. One of the things he loved about Amy was her charming childlike quality which had always made him feel protective towards her. But there was a downside to this: when thwarted, she could have tantrums, like a child.

'Dad, where are you?'

He looked up from the row of spinach and his face lit up. Coming up the path towards him were the two people who made everything worthwhile. First Lana, blonde hair flying as she ran, her blue eyes, replicas of her mother's, shining with excitement, her pretty face aglow with the joy of living. And not far behind, walking not running, taller by far more than the two years between them, came Kitty. Her hair was dark brown to Lana's blonde, her eyes hazel like her father's, her face serious. It was a face which would be handsome rather than pretty in adulthood. Kitty was more thoughtful, quieter, less exuberant than her sister, and Mike knew she was the one he needed to protect.

2

Lana was a constant source of irritation to Kitty. She knew she loved her for if anyone was unkind to her, Kitty would step in like an avenging angel. But liking her was a problem.

Kitty could not remember a time when she had felt differently. She had been told that when her sister was born she, at two, had been like a little mother to her – fetching and carrying, rocking her pram, bottle-feeding her when their mother's milk had dried up. It had to be true, for her father had told her so and she had never known him to lie. But it was a truth that amazed her.

There was one certainty in Kitty's life: she loved her father. She loved everything about him – his face, his bearing, the way he dressed, his voice, his smile, his laugh. She admired his intelligence and his gentleness, his honesty and his tolerance. Most important of all she felt safe with him, sure that he could, and would, always sort out any problem. She trusted him.

The same could not be said of her feelings for her mother. Kitty loved her even if she was afraid of her but she did not trust her. Kitty's trust in her mother had been irretrievably damaged when she was only three. It was Christmas Eve and it was snowing. Amy had held Kitty up to the window to see the snowflakes falling.

'If you listen very carefully you can hear the bells of Santa's sleigh,' Amy had said.

Kitty strained her ears to listen, her small mouth open with concentration.

'I can. I can. I can hear the bells.' She turned to face her mother, face alight with excitement.

Slap! Her mother's hand lashed across her face.

'Don't you bloody lie to me,' she'd said, dropping Kitty unceremoniously on the floor. Kitty had cried – not so much because the smack had hurt as because she did not understand what she had done wrong. She *had* heard the bells. She soon forgot the incident but not the legacy – her mother had destroyed Kitty's trust in her.

Lana was her mother's favourite. Not that Kitty wanted for anything; each child received the same material things. Amy's preference showed in the expression on her face when she looked at her younger daughter, in the tone of her voice when she spoke to her, in her inability to reprimand her. Mike had remonstrated with her but it did no good.

'She's me, you see,' Amy explained. 'Not only does Lana look like me but she thinks like me. She wants all the things in life I wanted.'

'But Kitty's part of you too, even if she looks like me,' Mike had argued with her one day after Amy had been particularly sharp with Kitty and he had decided to get to the bottom of the problem.

'Which part?' Amy snorted.

'It's almost as if you don't like her.'

'What a stupid thing to say.' Amy started to peel a potato with abrupt movements.

'Is it? You were never the same with her, not even when she was little. I know you had a hard time having her and you were depressed after she was born, but you didn't stay depressed, did you?'

'No.' She threw the peeled potato into a saucepan of cold water.

'So, what is it? Tell me, Amy. I'm only trying to help you both.'

'I don't know what you're going on about, I really don't.' Her lips taut with irritation, she picked up another potato and dug the peeler hard into the flesh.

'She's a nice kid and I'm afraid you'll make her withdrawn or jealous of Lana.'

'I doubt if she even notices what *I* think of her. It's you she's all over, always has been.'

'Because she doesn't have your love, that's why.'

'Don't talk such old cobblers, Mike. Honestly, you give me the pip at times.'

'I feel I have to speak up. Sometimes it's as if you're the child, not Kitty . . . sometimes you're just plain . . . well . . . petty.'

Amy swung round from the sink and faced him.

'Petty? Me? You're a fine one to talk – this whole flaming conversation is petty. You want the truth, right, I'll give it to you.' Angrily she wiped her hands on her pinny. 'I don't like her because she doesn't like me. She's a superior little cow, she always has been. And what can you, a man, understand? Did you suffer the agony I went through when she was on the way?'

'No, but you can't blame her—'

'It was as if that was to be the way of it. She gave me hell from before she was born and she's been sneering at me ever since.'

'Amy, love, this just isn't true.'

'Don't you bloody lecture me. I know who loves me and respects me. My Lana, that's who. You're welcome to Madam Kitty.'

'Amy—'

'If I'd had her in a hospital instead of at home I'm sure I'd have thought there had been a mix-up. She doesn't *feel* part of me and that's that.'

'But Amy—'

'Oh, Mike, do me a favour, go and dig your flaming vegetable patch and leave me alone.' And Amy turned back to her peeling and Mike went to his vegetables and the subject was never mentioned between them again.

At this stage Kitty certainly did not seem to notice Amy's withdrawn attitude to her. Since she had never known any different, she accepted it as normal.

Kitty was sitting in her room. It had taken until her twelfth birthday to get a room of her own away from Lana. Originally the box-room, it was so small that even with only herself in it, it appeared crowded. Her father had ingeniously managed to create space for her possessions. He had built a small desk in the window recess and cupboards with sliding doors and two large storage drawers beneath her bed. Kitty had chosen the colour scheme of dark blue and white.

It was an austere room, and tidy for a child of her age. Her books stood in order of category on a shelf above her bed. Work in hand was arranged neatly on the desk. Clothes were always hung up immediately they were taken off. There was only one ornament – a modern Staffordshire cottage her father had given her. Over the door was a small print of a Toulouse Lautrec poster, sellotaped on, bought with saved-up pocket money.

There were no dolls or toys from her past. When she had given them all to Lana she had been told how kind she was, but she had given them simply because she had no further use for them.

Kitty was fiercely protective of this room. She cleaned it herself so that her mother need never enter, for she loathed anyone else, even her father, to come into it.

Lana's room, once Kitty had quit it, had been redecorated. The whole room was a pink and white froth of frills, bows and ruching. On the bed, covered by a satin quilt stitched in a complicated design of cabbage roses, were scattered lace-trimmed pillows shaped like hearts. The dressing-table was skirted in pink organza and on it was a white and gold triple mirror so that Lana could see her prettiness from every angle. The wardrobe was full to overflowing with clothes as frilled as the room. There were dolls on shelves and dolls on a button-backed chair, not for playing with but arranged charmingly in groups. Pictures of Elvis Presley, cut from magazines, were pinned on the wall. It was a strange room for a child of ten. It was as if she could not wait to grow up and her mother was aiding and abetting her.

Lana welcomed visitors to her room. Kitty could have come in any time she wanted – but she didn't.

It puzzled Lana why Kitty felt this way about her, for she was sure she had done no wrong. And the puzzle deepened when she knew everybody else loved her so much.

'Why don't you like me, Kitty?' she would ask. Usually Kitty did not reply but one day she'd said, 'I'd like you if you stopped breathing.'

To oblige, Lana did – she went pink, red, blue and a horrid mottled purple colour which Kitty watched with rapt amazement. But then, fearing she might have gone too far, she hit Lana hard between the shoulders. 'Breathe, you fool!' she yelled.

Lana gulped air down with relief. 'I wish you'd make your mind up,' she said, once she had recovered.

Kitty's dislike of her made Lana feel unhappy when she thought about it, so she decided it was better not to think about it, to continue as if she was Kitty's favourite person in the whole world. After all, she reasoned to herself, alone in her pink and white bedroom, she did not *need* Kitty's love. There were plenty of others willing to smother her with it. But Kitty's feelings were like a blot on Lana's otherwise perfect exercise-book.

'Mum, I've decided I don't want to do dancing any more,' Kitty said as they sat round the dining-table eating their traditional Sunday lunch.

'What on earth do you mean?' Amy asked, surprised.

'I hate it.'

'What nonsense. You love it.'

'But I don't. I never have. I hate tap dancing, the noise – it drums through my head.'

'I'd agree with that,' her father said, smiling at her as he remembered the endless concerts he had sat through, the thudding of the children's feet as they had blundered in ragged lines about the stage for adoring parents.

'You love ballet.'

'I like the music, I don't like the dancing. And in any case I'm going to be too tall – I might just as well give it up now.'

'Yes, you'll probably be too tall. But that's no fault, you could end up a Bluebell Girl with your long legs,' Amy said brightly, for to be a member of such a troupe would have been a hopeless dream for herself at five foot three.

'I don't want to be a Bluebell Girl – I can't think of anything more boring.'

'Just listen to your grumbling. No wonder you look such a sourpuss all the time. More trifle, Lana?'

'If she doesn't want to do it then there seems little point, Amy,' Mike said, his mind racing with relief as he worked out how much money he'd be saving.

'I'd prefer extra piano lessons instead,' Kitty said, immediately drowning his hopes.

'Now that *would* be a waste of money. You know what Miss Coleridge thinks of your piano playing. Why, you only just managed to scrape through your Grade 3 exam. You could never earn a living at that and that's for sure.' Amy patted her lips with her paper napkin, which she insisted on calling a serviette.

'I'd like to get better and I like the music. I know I'm not good but just to be able to play a little —'

'Rubbish. Your father and I haven't lashed out all this money on your and Lana's careers to throw it all away now.'

'But don't you understand, Mum? I don't want to be a dancer. That's your dream, not mine.'

Faster than the eye could register Amy's hand struck out and slapped Kitty hard across the cheek.

'Don't you be rude to me, my girl. You'll do as I say.'

Kitty stood up, fighting tears, determined not to give her mother the satisfaction of seeing her crying.

'If you do give up can I have your shoes?' Lana asked from the other end of the table.

'Don't be silly. You've got such dainty feet they'll never
grow big enough to fit those boats your sister wears.' Amy
began to pile the plates noisily.

'I'm going to my room,' Kitty said.

'Can I help you with the washing-up, Mummy?'

'What a little angel you are. No. You run along and do
your homework. Kitty can help me.' Amy smiled triumphantly at Kitty.

Mrs Flynn sat at the upright piano, her large bottom
squeezed between the wooden arms of the piano stool, her
slippered feet pumping the pedals. The piano was in the
corner of the dance studio and she was playing as she had
done every work-day and every Saturday morning for the
past fifteen years. She played without thinking, she played
without listening, her fingers finding the keys like homing
pigeons coming in to roost. She thumped out a regular
beat, as loud as possible, to be heard by the sixteen young
girls as they went through the tap routine devised for them
by Camilla de Souza in preparation for the summer concert
at the local Empire.

The noise was deafening as the girls, several of them too
overweight for this occupation, concentrated their minds
into their feet. The heat in the room was high from the
sweating bodies and the effort. Dust rose from the floor in
puffs, in time with the pounding shoes. The smell of the
dust filled the air, mingling with the BO from the older
girls.

'One . . . two . . . three . . .' Camilla shouted, pacing up
and down in front of the troupe like an inspecting general.
'One . . . two . . . three . . .' she clapped in time with Mrs
Flynn's rendition of *California Here I Come*.

In the front, as befitted the best pupil in the school,
danced Lana. Her long blonde hair was in a pony-tail, her
pretty face alight with a wide smile showing her perfect

white teeth. Behind her tapped the three next best dancers, then a row of five, then of seven, so that they formed a triangle with Lana the apex. Kitty danced in the back row with the older girls, placed there because anywhere else her height made everything look untidy.

The students were dressed identically in their practice uniform of red skirt, black fish-net tights and round-capped red shoes tied with flopping red laces which made all their feet look bigger than they were. Their skirts carried the school's logo, a semi-quaver and *De Souza Dance Academy* in italics embroidered beneath it. No girl was allowed into class improperly dressed, Camilla was strict about that.

Camilla de Souza was slim and dressed in a black leotard and tights, a shawl round her shoulders. She wore long dangling earrings which jingled musically as she moved – not that anyone could hear over the sounds of tap. She was fifty, but with heavy make-up and in a good light could pass for early forties. Her eyebrows were black, heavy and arched as if she was always elated about something. Her lips were full and painted scarlet as were her long nails. Her artificially black hair was pulled severely back into a bun and shone like lacquer from the oil she used on it. She looked Spanish, which was what she intended, especially since Flamenco was her speciality. She liked to be thought exotic. The truth was, Camilla had been born plain Gwen Roberts in Swindon, not Seville.

Camilla always referred to her 'studios', but the use of the plural was misleading. There was only one – this room. It had originally been a greengrocer's and the shop and the store-room had been knocked into one. The small kitchen at the back had been turned into a changing-room with a basin in one corner and pegs on the wall. The lavatory was outside.

The studio was painted cream with two strip-lights. One wall was covered in mirror glass with a barre running the full length. Against the other wall was Mrs Flynn's piano and a row of chairs for any parents who cared to watch the classes.

'Kitty, how many times do you have to be told? It's one two, glide, one two three. Look.' Camilla turned her slim form so that her back was towards the class and demonstrated the steps. 'And smile all of you, can't you? It's supposed to be fun. If Lana can smile, why can't the rest of you?'

Amy sat on the side-lines and smiled to herself in satisfaction.

After the class was over the children, their red shoes tap-tapping noisily, moved off to the changing-room. Amy asked for a private word with Camilla, who diplomatically suggested to Mrs Flynn that perhaps a cup of tea might be a good idea before the intermediate ballet class arrived. Mrs Flynn hauled her huge behind from the vice-like grip of the wooden arms of the piano stool.

'What can I do to help you, Mrs Lawrence?' Camilla asked as she sank gracefully on to the seat beside Amy.

'Two things, really. The first is Kitty. She says she's fed up and doesn't want to dance any more.'

'I've been expecting this,' Camilla said, folding her hands elegantly on her lap, admiring her slim fingers with their perfect nails as she did so. But even as she admired them her heart was sinking at the prospect of losing the revenue from one of her pupils.

'Expecting it?'

'Yes, by twelve they've usually long since had enough, unless they want to make a career in dance. They want to spread their little wings and seek out new interests and excitements.'

'I'm sure it's just a phase,' Amy said, sure of herself. 'She'll come round. It's just that I wondered if perhaps we should drop one lot and concentrate on the other – ballet or tap. Doesn't really matter.'

'Oh, but it does, Mrs Lawrence. It's apparent in Kitty's

work that her heart hasn't been in it for a good year now. You can't make someone dance, they've got to want to, to hurt for it.' Camilla sounded quite breathless with emotion.

'I can make her,' Amy said shortly.

'But what would be the point? She's an adequate little dancer but she won't get better, no matter how many lessons she has. She'd never make a professional. No, Mrs Lawrence, it's best to let her go.'

'But I'd set my heart—' Amy said in the whining, wheedling voice that invariably got her what she wanted from Mike.

'But Kitty obviously hasn't, has she?' Camilla smiled, she hoped charmingly and sympathetically, at this pretty but pushy mother whom she did not like. Camilla was suspicious of such saccharine prettiness and had often found that beneath the floss lurked a somewhat shrewish nature.

'Can she sing? She's never shown any inclination to. I have a friend who would be happy—'

'Don't encourage her to.' Amy held up her hands as if in horror. 'It'll blast your ear-drums. She joined the school choir but she was asked to leave – too loud, you see, she drowned the others and they didn't like it. I told her to stop showing off and tone it down a bit, but did she listen? Does she ever?'

'She always strikes me as a serious child. Maybe she has no artistic leanings – there's nothing wrong in that, Mrs Lawrence.'

'Books, books, books, that's all she's interested in. Shut up in her room on her own. Hates anyone to go in there,' Amy added, darkly.

'What was the other thing you wished to discuss with me? Two things, you said.' Camilla steered the conversation away from further discussion of Kitty, a girl she liked and had often felt sorry for. She knew that the right thing to do would have been to tell the parents years before that they were wasting their money on the girl's lessons. But Camilla's financial position did not allow for such fine ethics. Yet talk of hiding away in her room only made her feel more sorry for Kitty. Any intelligent and very sensitive child, as she knew Kitty was, would want to hide from such an empty-headed mother.

'My Lana.' Immediately there was a change in Amy's expression. Just saying her daughter's name made her voice change, it was softer, bursting with pride.

'Well, we've no worries there, Mrs Lawrence. I'm sure Lana will be a success – unless, like her sister, she tires of it.'

'She won't do that, I'll see she doesn't.'

'She's a lovely dancer and is developing a good presence with it, even if she is a little on the small side.'

'She'll grow – it's early days. I watch her diet carefully,' Amy said defensively, for she herself was somewhat worried by Lana's petite size. 'But is she getting on fast enough? That's what I wanted to ask you.'

'She's only *ten*, Mrs Lawrence. You can't rush things.'

'I was wondering if she wouldn't be better off at a stage school. She'd get it all then, wouldn't she? Elocution lessons, singing, acting, as well as dancing. She could be an all-rounder.'

'She would. But it's too soon. I mean . . .' Camilla was floundering here; to lose two pupils at the same time would be a disaster. 'If it's elocution and drama lessons you want, I can easily arrange those for you.' She'd give Sarah Selling, her out of work actress friend, a call. Sarah would fall over herself to give lessons and Camilla could take a cut. Stupid of her, she should have thought of this before. Already she was rewriting her little brochure in her mind to include these new activities. She might even get Miriam, her failed opera singer friend, interested. At this rate she might need bigger premises. Camilla's cheeks turned pink with excitement at the new project opening before her.

'But at a *proper* school she'd get to know of auditions for the *real* stage, was what I'd been thinking.'

Camilla bridled at this. Her qualifications might be more suspect than the parents realized – she had no diplomas to put on the walls. For a consideration the previous owner had left her own framed credentials, and Camilla had hung up her ballroom-dancing certificates, a combination which so far had fooled most of the parents since no one ever bothered to study them carefully. But she liked to think that the stage show she put on twice a year at the Empire was as good a recommendation as any.

'I rather think this is a real school, and I'm rather proud of my shows.'

'Oh, come off it, Miss de Souza. I'm surprised you've got away with it as long as you have. You're not a qualified teacher and never have been. I know you've been hood-winking everyone, including the authorities. That's why you are so cheap for a start.'

At this Camilla forgot she liked to sit like a Degas drawing of a ballerina in repose and slumped in her chair, feeling quite weak and dizzy not knowing exactly what to say.

'That apart – go on, you needn't worry, I won't let on, you're a good teacher and that's all that matters. But with a girl like Lana, with her talent . . . well, I have to think to the future. Do what's best for her. At a stage school she's going to know what auditions are available, what's going on on the London stage. We don't get to know down here, now do we?'

'I do,' Camilla said, sharply pulling herself together. 'I read *The Stage*. I'm always on the look-out.' She did read *The Stage* avidly but, if she was honest, more for opportunities for herself than for her pupils.

'Haven't had much success then, have you?' Amy said sniffily.

'It's not so easy, Mrs Lawrence. There's a lot to be

considered. I'm against any child being forced too quickly. It can lead to damage later – a little girl can so easily lose interest, *if pushed too hard*.' She purposefully emphasized these words. 'What's worse, if care isn't taken, we can damage their little bodies.' Camilla might not have the necessary diplomas but she understood dance and she understood the wear and tear that could ensue.

Amy was not listening. She was busily searching in her handbag. 'Here it is. Look, the Philbert School of Drama and Dance. See, they take boarders from eight.'

Camilla read the cutting with difficulty, she needed spectacles for reading but, feeling they did not fit her image, used them only in the privacy of her apartment.

'But what about the rest of her education?'

'She'll get it there of course. It's run like a proper school.'

'But the expense?' Camilla said first. Then, 'But she's so young. And so small . . .'

'So you keep saying,' Amy said acidly.

'But it's in Cambridgeshire, that's miles away, and so damp and cold in winter.'

'If it will help her career no sacrifice is too much.'

'I've never heard of this establishment, Mrs Lawrence. One of the good London schools . . . well, that would be a different kettle of fish.'

'It's new. That's to their advantage. They've got to prove themselves.'

'You sound as if you've made your mind up already, Mrs Lawrence.'

'Oh, I have, I was just telling you really.'

3

'Bloody hell, Amy! Do you think I'm made of money?' Mike stood in front of the fireplace and looked at his wife's reflection in the mirror above it.

'I'm fully aware you're not and more's the pity.'

'I've done my best. We've got a lovely home.'

'I'm not talking about this house. I'm talking about all the other things – clothes, better opportunities for the children. A car.' Amy spoke in a voice of studied reason.

'Fat chance we've got of ever getting a car, what with the school fees and the dancing lessons and now this.'

'Exactly. You don't earn enough.' Amy, while looking smug, still managed to look pretty, Mike thought.

He swung round to face her, his eyes full of hurt and, for him, anger. 'And what am I supposed to do? Go to the bosses, say this store manager should earn more than everyone else because he's got a nagging wife who's not satisfied?'

'I'm not nagging. No one can ever accuse me of that – I'm just pointing out the facts to you, even if you don't like hearing them.'

'Then what do you expect me to do?'

'You could get another job in the evenings.'

'Jesus, woman. I'm exhausted enough when I come home. I haven't the energy to do another job. In any case the Co-op wouldn't like it – it wouldn't look good if a manager was moonlighting.'

'Oh, we mustn't upset the Co-op, must we?' Amy said in a sing-song voice which made Mike want to hit her. He turned away, shocked at himself. He caught his face in the mirror, saw a sad-faced, middle-aged man with grey at his temples, and felt defeated.

'I don't know what's happened to you, Amy, what's

making you like this,' he said, the puzzlement of years heavy in his voice. 'We were so happy, once.'

'Once! That's it, isn't it? Once!'

'But look, love.' He softened his tone, wanting to placate her. 'You've got everything you ever said you wanted – even the built-in wardrobes. Another year we might run to a car. But not with this. Not with this expense.'

'You don't care, do you? You've got a daughter with remarkable talent – everyone says so – and yet you don't want to put your hand in your pocket to see her get on.'

'It's not that simple. If I put my hand in my pocket what would I come up with? Nothing. I'm as proud of her as you are – maybe even prouder. Because I'm proud of what she does, not what I want her to do.'

'And what does that mean?'

'Quite honestly, Amy, I don't think it's about whether she's happy or whether it's what she wants. It's what *you* want. You want her success for yourself.'

'And what's wrong with that?'

'Everything, if you must know. Have you talked to her about it? Does she want to go? To leave home, a little kid like that? It's unnatural.'

'No, I haven't discussed it with her. I didn't want to raise her hopes.'

'Don't give me that, Amy. You never consult her about anything.'

'She'll want to do it.'

'Yes, probably. She'll do it to please you. She likes to please, and you know that and you work on it.'

'Well, I never expected to hear such spite from you, Mike Lawrence.'

'It's the truth.'

'No, it's more than that. You want to keep her all to yourself . . . you don't want her out there in the world, admired by others. You're jealous, Mike. Jealous of your own daughter.'

'That's a disgusting thing to say, Amy. As well you know. You'd risk anything to get what you wanted, wouldn't you?'

'For her, yes. Because she isn't going to end up like I did, in a hairdressing salon talking to stupid women, pretending you like them when you despise them.'

'And what have you done to feel so superior to them?' He laughed shortly, feeling he'd caught her out there.

'Produced Lana. That's what I've done. She's a rarity, a true rarity.'

'She's a little girl who likes to dance, Amy – like thousands of others. You fill her head with dreams but, realistically, what chance has she got?'

'Fat chance with you as a father. But I'll fight for her – she's not going to end up like me, married to a no-hoper like you—'

'You bitch. You ungrateful bitch—' He spat the words out. He rubbed his eyes with the back of his hand as if to wipe away the thought aching in his mind that everything he'd done for her, with her, had been taken, but with no love given in return.

'I'll get a job. I can go back any time with my hairdressing skills. Any salon in town will have me. I might set up on my own – working from here – going into people's homes – I might make more that way . . .'

Mike looked at her with despair. When she had an idea there was no stopping her, he might just as well try stopping a train. He turned and walked from the room.

Kitty was sitting on the stairs, her long legs bunched up so that her chin rested on her knees. She looked at her father with her hazel eyes full of pity for him, and he looked away, finding her expression unbearable. He turned abruptly and walked out through the kitchen to his garden. There might be enough light left to do some weeding.

Kitty sat for some time staring into space. Why did he let her mother get away with everything? Why didn't he stand up to her? Shout at her? Why always turn his back and walk away? She wouldn't. She slid down the few remaining stairs on her bottom, jumped up and entered the living-room where her mother was unconcernedly folding the laundry on the dining-table as if oblivious to the fact that she had destroyed yet more of her husband's self-confidence.

'Were you asking Dad about the acting school for Lana?'

'What were you doing listening?'

'I couldn't help it. I was coming down the stairs. The door was open.' She picked up an apple from the bowl on the sideboard – utility furniture which she knew her mother longed to be rid of. 'Doesn't he want her to go?'

'No. Says he can't afford it. Here, help me fold this sheet.' Amy gestured with one end of the sheet to Kitty who took it in her hand while her mother took the other end. Kitty walked backwards until she was standing in the doorway.

'Maybe he can't.'

'Rubbish. He's got savings. I know he has. Too mean to take them out of the bank, that's what.' They both pulled on the sheet, tautening it, flapping it to straighten the cloth.

'You won't have my lessons to find now,' Kitty said amicably, walking towards her mother now, giving her her sheet end. Amy placed the folded sheet on the table, picked up another one and the ritual began again.

'That's true. But what about the piano lessons you said you wanted? I mean, fair's fair.'

'I can do that at school. I could practise at home, if we had a piano.'

'If pigs could fly at the moment . . .' Amy said. 'Still. It would pay in the end, wouldn't it? Something second-hand shouldn't cost too much.'

'No, not too much.'

'You ask him, he's none too pleased with me.'

'Perhaps I could get a Saturday job – in a shop or

something. Then you need not give me any pocket money either.'

'You'd do that for Lana? Honest?' Amy looked at her daughter with new eyes.

'Why not? She's the one with talent, not me.' Kitty shrugged her shoulders as if she did not care. She did. She was excited, for in one stroke she could see two things she desperately wanted looming on the horizon. A piano of her own and no Lana. Then she'd feel less irritated – she always found it an uncomfortable emotion. But, best of all, she'd have her father all to herself.

'You talk to him. You try and persuade him. Tell him it's the best thing for Lana. He might listen to you.'

Mike did listen. He looked at his solemn-faced elder daughter as she outlined her plan to get a Saturday job to help pay for her sister's fees and he was deeply moved.

'There'll be no need for that, Kitty, though it's a grand gesture and one Lana should know of. But I can't have you working – not at your age. I don't think it's even legal. No. I'll find the money from somewhere even if it takes time.'

It did take time. It was a year later that he finally told his wife he had arranged things so that Lana could go away to school. At least he'd had one little triumph, he'd kept his daughter at home until she was eleven.

The following morning Amy strode briskly to the call-box on the corner of Mulberry Avenue. She was well supplied with penny pieces. She dialled the operator and gave the number of the Philbert School in Cambridge-shire. The conversation was short and to the point. An appointment was made for September – the new term. That night in bed she rewarded her husband with her body – to his delight, for Amy rarely allowed him near her these days.

One person in the Lawrence household had not been informed of the new arrangements which were to change her life – Lana. When she did hear she shocked everyone.

For the first time in her life she screamed and cried and threatened and stamped her feet in terrified rage. She did not want to leave home, she was not going to leave home, no one could make her.

Kitty felt strange and also guilty. If she hadn't talked to her father this scene would never have happened. She looked at her pretty younger sister and saw fear in her eyes. Suddenly she experienced a wave of new emotions. She wanted to comfort Lana more than anything else. She crossed the room and tentatively put her hand out to touch her sister but then drew it back sharply as if she'd had a change of mind.

'Lana, don't cry,' she said awkwardly, her arms hanging by her sides, her hands feeling large and useless. 'Don't, please.' She took a step closer. 'If you don't want to go you don't have to, nobody can make you. Lana, please . . .' She stopped searching for other more reassuring words. 'I love you, Lana, —' she heard herself say.

Lana wiped her eyes with the back of her hand. 'You do?'

'Yes. And I hate seeing you so unhappy. Oh, Lana.' Then she stepped forward and took hold of her sister in a tight hug. 'I don't want you to go . . .'

It would have been impossible to say who was the more surprised by Kitty's sudden change of heart. Lana clung to her and began to cry again and this time Kitty's tears mingled with hers as they held each other, rocking back and forth in mutual comfort.

Kitty might have changed her mind but Amy had not. Both Kitty and Mike worried for Lana who now seemed unable to stop crying. She could not eat and began to lose weight. She took no interest in the clothes that Amy bought for her or rapidly ran up on her Singer sewing-machine. When she was fitting these new clothes Lana stood silently, like a doll, as Amy pinned and tucked, chattering blithely as if unaware of her child's distress.

To placate her, and hopefully to arrive at the school with a non-weeping daughter, Amy agreed to let Kitty travel with them to the school. She was not being truly altruistic, it would be a long journey and she did not relish the idea of returning alone. Such a journey seemed likely since the Principal of the school had suggested that, given the distance from their home, they should bring a case with the essentials for Lana. If the interview was a success she could stay and the rest of her luggage could be sent on.

'You can have my room, if you like,' a wan-faced Lana said to Kitty as they stood on the steps of the large house near Cambridge, waiting for their mother to finish saying goodbye to the owners of the school.

'No. We'll keep it just as it is for when you come home for the holidays.'

'I don't mind you having it. It's not fair on you in your tiny room.' Lana smiled bravely, though she looked suspiciously close to tears again.

'You don't have to worry. I like my room. It suits me.'

'Do you still love me?' Lana asked anxiously.

'Don't be silly.' Kitty gave her a shove.

'I need to know you do. It's important.'

'I hate all this sloppy talk.' Kitty looked intently at her shoes.

'Please . . .'

'Oh, all right. A bit.'

'You're not jealous of me getting this chance?'

'Me? Good heavens, no. I hate dancing, you know I do, and I could never act for toffee.'

'I'd hate you to be jealous.'

'Well, I'm not. In any case I got a piano out of it, so I'm fine.' Kitty laughed but she was aware as she did that it sounded hollow and wondered if Lana heard it too.

From the top step in front of the school, Lana watched her mother and Kitty trudge along the drive to the main road and the bus that would take them to Cambridge to catch the train home. She waited, small and alone, until they disappeared from view. She felt her throat constrict as she fought against the bout of weeping that threatened to engulf her. She didn't want anyone to see her crying. Quickly she walked down the steps, across the gravelled drive and the flat lawn opposite. She did not want to join the others yet, she needed time alone to come to terms with what was happening to her. She had delayed facing it, telling herself that it would not, could not happen to her, that her parents would change their minds, that the school would burn down, even that the train bringing her here would crash. Since none of these things had happened she had to accept she was here. She wiped her eyes with the back of her hand as tears began to fall. She sat down on a stone bench beside a large pond and stared at the metal-coloured water. She had heard Mrs Philbert refer to it as 'the Lake'. But it wasn't, it was a pond. She wondered why grown-ups exaggerated so and pretended things were grander than they really were. A bit like the house. In the brochure it had been referred to as 'a mansion steeped in history'. Lana wasn't sure what a mansion was or should look like, but she was fairly certain that this wasn't one. It was far larger than their own house in Mulberry Avenue, certainly, but it was no bigger than the vicarage where she and Kitty had attended Sunday school classes. Creeper covered the grey stone walls and framed the windows in a living pelmet of greenery which made it look as if the house was hiding. Six wide stone steps led up to the heavy front door behind which was a porch with a fawn, white and blue tessellated floor.

A second glass-panelled door opened into a hall made dark by the abundance of stained pitch-pine on the walls and ceiling. A large metal hat-stand stood against one wall. The sides were formed like two rampant stags at bay, their antlers intertwined at the top for hats to hang on. At their feet deerhounds snapped, and here, receptacles for shoes were cunningly provided between the animals' splayed legs. In the centre was a sculpted bear, head flung back, mouth agape in a silent snarl, paws joined to hold the sticks and umbrellas which slotted into its stomach. Over the hat-stand metal plants trailed in a convoluted tangle – a memorial to the Victorian ironmaster's craft, and a dust-collector of monumental proportions. It petrified Lana the moment she set eyes on it.

Four spacious rooms led off this hall. On the right-hand side at the front was the schoolroom, with desks, a black-board and a large cupboard. At the back was the dining-room, with twelve chairs set round a large mahogany table. There was a glass display cabinet filled with a hundred tiny stuffed birds, and a heavy sideboard, as intricately carved as the hat-stand, with a mirror set in the back. Two large, rather gloomy paintings of dead game-birds completed the contents of the room.

Across the hall and at the back of the house was the studio, a bare room with parquet floor and french windows leading into the wild back garden. A large gilt mirror hung on one wall and along two sides of the room ran a barre. A baby grand piano was the only furniture.

At the front and overlooking the pond was the Princi-pal's study where the interview had taken place and which was also the Head's sitting-room and private sanctum. It too was filled with Victoriana, bric-à-brac which Amy had thought a load of rubbish. The chairs decorated with antimacassars were overstuffed with horse-hair and were fiendishly uncomfortable. The many small tables looked as if they were about to collapse under the weight of ornaments and silver-framed photographs. It was a room for an elderly person. The incumbents, in their mid-thirties, stylish and handsome, looked out of place.

'Do you think I should go and talk to her? She looks so sad, poor little thing,' Portia Philbert said, as she stood at the window watching the small figure who still sat looking at the water.

'Leave her a bit. She probably needs some time alone,' Portman Philbert replied, as he filled his pipe from an antique tobacco drum on his desk.

'Ghastly woman, the mother, didn't you think?'

'Quite. Still, her money's as good as anyone's.' He prodded the tobacco down.

'If the cheque doesn't bounce.'

'It won't. She's too ambitious for the child to allow that to happen. We might have trouble with money from her in the future but not now.'

'Why in the future?'

'Because she can't afford us, it's as simple as that. But she's the type who'd scrub floors to give the kid a chance.'

'I'm not sure if that's commendable or not.' Portia stared at the wan-looking child as she spoke.

'Most decidedly not. Poor Lana will be thanking her mother for this for the rest of her life, if I'm any judge of human nature.'

'She's got talent, though.'

'You're the judge of that, not me. But she seems very amiable.'

'I liked the look of the elder one, didn't you? Pity we couldn't have had both of them. Still, six is a nice number.'

'Eight would be better.' He puffed contentedly on his pipe.

'Do you think she's been called Lana after Turner?'

'Probably. It's the sort of name a stage-struck mother lumbers her child with.'

'How dreadful! Look, she's coming. I do hope she grows a bit. She's terribly small for her age. I'd best go and meet her.'

Portia slung a paisley shawl round her slim frame and, with the grace of the ballet dancer she had once been, walked hurriedly from the room.

'Nice walk?' She met up with Lana as she crossed the lawn.

'I was watching the water – there's a fish in there.' Lana averted her face so that Portia should not see her tear-stained cheeks.

'There were dozens once, when my grandmother lived here, but the herons eat them,' Portia said brightly. She wondered if she should put her arm around Lana, she was sure the child had been crying. But Portia was never sure what to do in situations like this for she was the type that did not like her own emotions to be seen and felt she should respect others' need for privacy.

'Why didn't they eat them when she was here?'

'I don't know.' Portia laughed. 'Perhaps they were afraid of her, I was.'

'Were you?' Lana forgot her tears and looked at Portia with surprise. She had not known that adults could be afraid of anything.

'Gracious yes. She was very tall and thin and looked like a witch and had a fearful temper. If you did the smallest thing wrong – whoosh, she was shouting and banging her stick.' Portia spoke quickly, again noting the tear-streaked face and wishing she could help.

'Was the hat-stand hers?'

'Yes, horrible thing. But it's so big and heavy we can't move it. It used to give me the creeps when I was young.'

'Really?' Lana said, and felt much better about it.

'Would you like to meet the others now? They've been unpacking.'

'Will you be there?' Lana looked alarmed.

'If you want.' Portia finally put out her hand and Lana grabbed it and held on so tightly it almost hurt.

Lana was to sleep in a room with the two other pupils who were closest to her in age.

'This is Pat,' Portia said, and Lana said hello to a rather overweight but pleasant-faced girl of eleven who grinned broadly at her. 'And this is Avril.'

'Hi.' Avril was pretty and had the sweetest smile. She was even blonder than Lana and was far taller and more willowy than any other twelve-year-old she'd met. Lana immediately envied her height.

'Tea in an hour. Help Lana with her unpacking, won't you, girls?' And with a swish and flick of scarves, Portia had gone and Lana felt betrayed.

Lana clicked open her case and smiled shyly at the others, though her stomach was churning with nerves as they gathered round her as if to inspect her possessions.

'You come far?' asked Pat.

'Yes. From Kent.'

'I've been there, when we went to Dover to catch the ferry,' Avril said.

'You been abroad?' Pat asked in an impressed manner.

'Often.'

'Gosh, you are lucky. I'm dying to travel,' Pat said in a voice rigid with envy but softened by longing.

'Are you both new?' Lana screwed up the courage to ask.

'I was here last term,' Avril said.

'What's it like?' Pat asked.

'It's fine. Old Port's a bit of a pain – he's always got hangovers, that's why we christened him that. So lessons are a bit hit and miss, though I don't mind that at all.' Avril laughed, and Pat and Lana joined in. 'Portia is divine. She's so good. She really makes you want to dance.'

'My mother saw her dance at Covent Garden, said she was fantastic,' Pat volunteered.

'So tragic.' Avril sighed.

'What's tragic?' Lana asked.

'Don't you know? Gracious, I thought *everybody* knew.'

'I don't,' Lana stated truthfully.

'She was in a dreadful car crash – smashed her legs. She's fully recovered, but of course her dancing days are over.'

'But she doesn't limp,' Pat said, as if doubting the tale.

'The strength for dancing has gone from her legs. She couldn't rely on them. What was so awful was it was all old Port's fault. He was driving.' This last was said with everyone in a huddle and Avril whispering.

'How can she even *speak* to him, let alone live with him?' Pat said, wide-eyed with horror.

'Because she's a saint, that's why.'

'Was he drunk?'

'Probably.'

'Then why didn't he go to prison?' Lana was grateful to Pat for asking all the questions she didn't like to ask.

'Because . . .' Avril looked over her shoulder at the door. 'Because Portia said she was driving, that's why.'

'How do you know all this?' Pat's voice was heavy with suspicion.

'It was in all the newspapers.'

'What, that he was driving and drunk?'

'No, silly, but that's what everyone said afterwards. What do you want to be, Lana?' Avril asked, as if bored with gossiping.

'Me? I don't know. I don't really mind.'

'What do you do – sing? Dance? Act?'

'Only dancing. Tap preferably.'

'We don't do tap,' Avril informed her.

'No? I don't think my mum knows that.'

'Portia says tap will be out completely in a few years.'

'Does she?'

'Yes, she teaches us much freer modern-style dancing, you see, that and ballet, of course.'

'And you, Pat?' Lana asked.

'I'm not much good at anything. My last school expelled me for being a failure. So my parents sent me here as a last resort, I think. Wanted me out of the way, probably. I quite like acting – not that I'm any good at that either.' Pat giggled self-consciously.

'Poor Pat. Still, you've got us now.' Avril took hold of her hand and squeezed it. 'Doesn't anyone want to know about me?' She laughed. 'I'll tell you in any case. I want to be a singer – like Shirley Bassey.'

'Who?' asked Pat.

'Honest?' Lana asked, very impressed.

'If I get lucky, yes. I think you've got to have something to aim for. Of course, once I wanted to be a second Pavlova but these put paid to that.' She waved her long thin legs in the air. 'You're going to need more clothes than that, Lana,' Avril went on practically, looking at the small pile on Lana's bed.

'I know. They're being sent on later – I hope.'

'And you're going to need the elocution lessons they give, that's for sure.'

'Avril! That's not kind,' Pat admonished.

'But it's true, isn't it?' Lana smiled at them. 'I'd love to talk with a posh accent like you two.'

'And so you shall, my sweet.' Avril hugged her. 'Come on, everyone. Tea must be ready by now. That's one very good thing, Lana. The grub here is fantastic – not like my last school. Why are you called Lana, by the way?'

'After Lana Turner, my mum liked her.'

'Honestly?' Avril giggled and winked at Pat but Lana did not know why.

It felt strange when Amy and Kitty opened the front door and entered the house knowing Lana wasn't there. Kitty could not remember the house without her younger sister in it.

'She stayed?' It was Mike standing in the front-room doorway, his shoulders slumped in disappointment.

'You didn't expect her home, did you? I knew it would be fine and they'd want her,' Amy said, as she shrugged off her coat.

'I suppose I sort of hoped.'

Kitty put her hand out to her father. It was a shy gesture, they were not a tactile family. 'Still. We've still got Kitty here.'

'Mike, you do talk such rot. You sound as if Lana's left us for good.'

'Maybe she has, Amy. Maybe she has.'

'And what on earth does that mean?'

'She'll change. Maybe the Lana we knew will have gone for ever.'

For a week Lana was homesick. Nothing interested her. She did not want to eat, she could not sleep, even dancing held no interest for her. She felt heavy with a misery she was convinced would never go.

And then, one day, she awoke to find the sadness had disappeared and she could not think why she had been so wretched.

Lana was happy now but she was also tired. She had always put a lot into her dancing, but she had never worked

as hard as she did here. She knew she was being taught
well, so it was a satisfied tiredness.

From seven in the morning until nine at night Lana's
day was full. At first she had found the huge breakfast she
was expected to eat too much but soon she was tucking in
with the best of them.

'You burn up so much energy you need stoking up,'
Portia explained to them. This was in total contrast to Amy
who had watched her daughters' diet like a hawk, living in
terror of their putting on weight and ending their careers
prematurely.

None of them was keen on the fifteen-minute run they
were expected to do, no matter the weather.

'You must look after your lungs,' Portia lectured them
when they groaned at the prospect. 'It doesn't matter which
you choose to be – a singer, dancer, actress. Without strong
lungs you'll never succeed.'

The first lesson, after the run, was always dancing. 'See,
the run has limbered you up. Got the circulation going.
Moving will be easier now,' Portia told them, grinning at
their moaning. For an hour they did ballet or Portia's own
free movement dance class.

'Avril tells me you were disappointed we didn't do tap
dancing. If you want to continue with it, I can arrange a
teacher for you,' Portia said to Lana one morning.

'No, no. I always hated tap, I like your sort of dancing
best of all.' Lana had happily lied to please Portia and
glared at Avril for interfering.

Lana loved the drama classes even more than the singing
lessons. Portia described Lana's voice as sweet but in need
of strengthening. Lana was pleased but longed to sound
like Avril whose voice was clear and strong and whose face
seemed to change once she had begun to sing.

Lunch was followed by tuition by Portman Philbert in
English, French, maths, history, geography – all the lessons

a normal school would give, except that, in the absence of a laboratory, the only science taught was biology.

The lesson Lana looked forward to most, however, was Portman's drama class. Portia's class taught them stage movement and management and breath control, Portman concentrated on drama and Lana loved it. He was good at his job. He taught the class to project their voices. He made certain they understood the words. He showed them how to work at becoming the people they were acting.

Portman took the elocution lessons too. Lana was the pupil most in need of these, so the others tended to chat among themselves while Portman concentrated on refining Lana's flat vowels. By bedtime at nine, Lana was happily exhausted.

Sometimes on Saturdays the girls would be taken to the theatre in Cambridge, and the Philberts invited the performers they knew back to lunch on Sunday. Then the afternoon was spent in impromptu charades and stage gossip, of which none of them could get enough. Meeting professionals made them feel that they too were part of the stage world.

By sheer good luck Amy had found the perfect setting and the perfect teachers for Lana.

Until this time Lana had danced and sung well because that was what her mother wanted her to do. She had not minded what she did as long as it made her mother happy. But everything had changed. Now she worked as hard as she could, danced the best way she knew how, practised and practised her singing to give her voice the strength it lacked. She did all these things because she was in love with what she was doing and also because she wanted to please her teachers.

She loved the Philberts but she wasn't sure which of them she loved the most. She watched them and saw how much they adored each other and was happy for them. Lana began to learn how love could be, and it made her think of her own parents and their constant bickering. She was forced to realize that they were never like this. In public Portia and Portman rarely touched, they did not need to, Lana saw the looks that passed between them, and saw in their expressions the deep feeling they had for each other. And she had found a vantage-point where sometimes she would sit and spy on them as they kissed and caressed. And she liked the strange warm feeling, low in her body, which came when she did so. At night she would dream that one day such a love would be hers.

5

As Christmas approached, Kitty, very much to her surprise, found that she was looking forward to seeing Lana again; that, in fact, she had missed her. She volunteered to clean Lana's room ready for her first visit home – not that it needed it, Amy had tended it rather like a shrine since the day Lana had left.

Mike had gone to the station to meet Lana. He was nervous for two reasons. First, because he felt that she was far too young to be travelling alone. Amy had called him a fool and said that, at twelve next birthday, of course Lana was capable of getting off at the right stop. He also felt nervous because he feared that in the three months she had been away she would have changed.

She had changed, and she hadn't, was his conclusion after the first half-hour as they walked back through the damp streets to 14 Mulberry Avenue. She was taller, he was sure, and he told her so which pleased her enormously.

She was heavier as well, and although he did not tell her that, he thought she looked the better for it. And her voice had changed, she spoke more slowly as if wary of the words, as if she chose each word carefully before she said it. But, skipping excitedly along beside him, laughing up at him and his tired old jokes, telling him several times during the walk back from the station that she loved him – that was his Lana and no mistake.

As soon as they reached the house he had to relinquish her, for Amy took possession, ushering her away upstairs to her pink and frilly room. The door was firmly shut and Mike and Kitty had to wait a good two hours before they could talk to Lana again.

'And you're really happy?' Mike asked over the celebration tea of tinned red salmon and salad.

'Ecstatic, Dad.'

'My!' Mike laughed. 'You sound like an actress already.'

'And doesn't her voice sound real nice now, Mike?' Amy glowed with pride and when Mike put out his hand to touch his wife's gently, for once she did not snatch it away. It was for such moments that all the worry over money was worthwhile.

'Very ladylike,' he agreed.

'Which lessons do you like best?' Kitty asked.

'All of them.' Lana laughed. 'Well, not maths and creepy things like that . . . Best of all?' She paused, thinking. 'Portman's drama class, I think. He's wonderful the way he makes us understand the parts, how to get inside them and *become* the characters.'

'But what about your dancing?'

'Oh, I love that too, Mum. Portia is divine,' Lana said in a breathy voice which, to Kitty, sounded as if she had been running, but since she knew she hadn't she concluded that, along with the carefully rounded vowels, this was part of Lana's new voice. 'She's such a wonderful teacher. When she talks to us I think I can do anything. Sometimes, when I dance for her, I feel I'm floating.'

'And how's your tap coming along?' Amy asked.

'We don't do tap any more,' Lana said airily.

'You what?' Amy frowned. Kitty, sensing storm-clouds gathering, began to read the label on the Heinz salad cream bottle with apparently rapt attention.

'Portia thinks that in less than ten years there won't be any call for tap.'

'Oh, yes? And what about the chorus at the Palladium? What about the Bluebell Girls? Answer me that.'

'Portia says we are living through vast changes in the theatre. It will never be the same again. Why, we've already moved away from the old music halls, and we'll never go back to them. Portia says—'

'What's she know, stuck away in the Fens? Bet she hasn't seen the queues outside Chatham Empire every week. No one's told them they're finished, I'll bet.'

'Let Lana tell us what she's learned, Amy. This is interesting,' Mike said in his placating way.

Lana looked anxiously at her mother, suddenly aware that she had made her angry. 'I can do tap, I suppose, if I want. It's just . . . I thought—'

'It's not for you to think, that's our job. You just do as you're told. You're a dancer, of course you do tap – all dancers do tap.'

Lana paused as if wondering whether to argue the point. 'Yes, Mummy,' she finally said, and Kitty stopped reading the Heinz label.

'I've never heard such a load of old cobblers in all my life. What's this woman teaching you, then?'

'We do ballet, of course, and Greek movement and free movement. Portia *adores* Isadora Duncan, you see. She thinks dance should be a free expression, not regimented.'

'Oh, yes? How interesting.' Amy sat back and sucked in

her cheeks. 'And what if the chorus all decided to do some of this free expression with no choreography – they'd all crash into each other, now wouldn't they?' Amy grinned at her own indisputable logic.

'It *is* choreographed, Mummy. It's just that we're allowed to use free movement within that framework.'

Amy changed the subject, she was becoming bogged down by Lana's explanation. 'And what about auditions? You been to any?'

'Portia and Portman feel strongly about children being exposed to the real theatre too early. They're afraid we might peak too soon or that our expectations might be fulfilled too early and we might become disillusioned later, in our awkward teen years,' Lana recited, as if she had learned this by rote.

'But auditions are one of the reasons we sent you there,' Amy huffed.

'It's school policy.' Lana smiled sweetly.

'What the bloody hell are we sending you there for, then? Sounds to me we're wasting our money and that's a fact.' Amy pushed her half-eaten salad from her with an angry gesture. 'I think you're going to have to talk to them about all this, Mike.' Amy had gone quite pink with indignation and Kitty observed that her mother had a slight double chin which wobbled as she talked. She had not noticed it before but now she watched it with fascination.

'Now, Amy. Don't take on so. You mustn't let yourself get upset.'

'And how am I supposed not to be upset? We're being conned, Mike. That's the truth of it. And they call themselves teachers? We're going to have to find somewhere else for Lana to study.'

'No, you don't!' Lana stood up, pushing her chair back so that it wobbled, toppled over, and the fake leather seat fell out with a clatter which they all ignored. 'No, you can't.

You mustn't do that. I love it there. I'm so happy and I'm learning so much.'

'Not enough in my opinion,' Amy said.

'I work all the hours God gives as it is. I can't learn more than I'm doing now.' Lana's voice wasn't breathy and slow any more but fast and shrill.

'But the wrong things – free expression, bah! See how much you can earn from that! You should be having tap, singing lessons—'

'No, Mother, you're wrong. If I did that I could damage my voice at this stage. I'm happy working within the limitations Portia sets me. She knows best.' Lana was staring pointedly at her mother as if to warn her to say no more. 'As for tap dancing, I don't want to learn it. I never really liked it, I did it because it was what you wanted, Mother.'

'Well, you can do it again for me, can't you? It's tap or nothing or we'll search around for a more professional school,' Amy said smugly, convinced she was winning the argument.

'Then it will have to be nothing, Mother. I'm not going to any other school. I don't want to. You can't make me.' Lana's normally pale face was flushed with emotion and Mike thought how pretty it made her.

'We'll see about that.' Amy's mouth set in a determined line.

'You can send me elsewhere, sure. But you can't make me dance or do anything when I get there. I warn you. If I don't go back to Philberts' then I quit. I mean it. Now, if you'll excuse me, I've unpacking to do.' Lana turned, picked up the fallen chair and walked, gracefully but stony-faced, from the room.

'Well, I never! Cheeky little cow!' Amy said indignantly.

'It means a lot to her,' Mike said, secretly rather proud of the stand Lana was taking and wishing he had that sort of courage.

'She must know more about the subject now than we do,' Kitty offered, feeling as surprised as her parents at this untypical reaction from Lana. Maybe she wasn't such a goody-goody after all.

'And you can keep your oar out of affairs that don't concern you,' Amy snapped at her least-favoured daughter, who shrugged her shoulders with resignation and began to pile the dirty dishes one on top of the other. 'Leave that. A body can't think with all that clattering.' Amy waved her hands in irritation.

'Fine by me,' Kitty muttered, and turned to the door just as it opened and Lana reappeared.

'I'm sorry, Mum. I was very rude,' she said immediately. Kitty pulled a face, exasperated that Lana was still the same.

'That's all right, Lana, my pet. I expect you're overtired,' Amy said, a self-satisfied smile flirting about her mouth.

'Of course I'll do whatever you want me to do.'

'I knew you would,' Amy patted her younger daughter's hand. 'You know Mum knows what's best, don't you, my darling?'

Kitty left the room, preferring not to watch what she regarded as a sickening scene. In the kitchen she tidied up, more for something to do than to help her mother – she had long ago given up trying to please this complicated woman. She heard the dining-room door open and shut again, followed by her sister's light footsteps on the stairs. Kitty folded the tea-towel and turned out the light. She intended going to her own room but on the landing she paused outside Lana's door. She would have liked to go in and talk to her sister but felt awkward. She hesitated. She never went into Lana's room, and if she did so tonight she didn't want Lana to think it was just to gloat. The door opened.

'I thought I heard someone. Come in,' Lana invited, holding the door wide open. Kitty thought how confidently the invitation had been made. In an odd way it made her feel she was the younger sister. She frowned at this uncomfortable reflection. She sat on the bed and watched Lana continue with her unpacking.

'Why did you back down?'

'What do you mean?' Lana looked up.

'For the first time in your life, you stood up to Mum for what *you* wanted and then spoiled it by going back and apologizing.'

'I was rude.'

'You weren't, you were making a point.'

'Yes, but do I have the right to make it? They're paying, not me. And they've a right to expect to get what they're paying for.'

'I think you're daft.'

'Do you? It's often easier to agree.'

'What about your self-respect?'

'Who needs it, provided one gets what one wants in the end?' Lana burrowed back into her suitcase. Kitty looked puzzled, not quite sure what Lana meant.

'You've changed, and I don't know what it is.'

'Don't be silly, I'm exactly the same.'

'No, there's something different but I can't put my finger on it.' Kitty put her head on one side, looking at Lana, as if by studying her hard enough she might come up with the solution. 'Maybe it's just that you are more confident.'

'Maybe,' said Lana placidly. 'Do you think Mum would be upset if I asked if I might change my room round? I've never really liked it, it was just that she wanted it this way. Now I don't think it suits me at all.'

'I shouldn't think so.' Suddenly, for reasons she didn't understand, Kitty felt almost sorry for her mother – an unusual reaction. 'What's the school really like?' she asked, more to change the subject than from any genuine interest.

'As I said – wonderful. Honestly, Kitty, if Mother did move me I don't know what I'd do. It would break my heart.' Lana stood on the rose-patterned rug in front of the unused fireplace, which was decorated with a pink paper fan and paper roses, clutching a pile of vests and knickers to her undeveloped breasts.

'Gracious, you do look dramatic.' Kitty laughed. 'Relax, there's no chance of that happening. For a start, they couldn't afford the other schools' fees – this one is struggle enough for them. And she won't, because then she couldn't boast about you to her cronies.'

'She boasts about me?' Lana looked up with interest.

'All the time – to those who'll listen and to those who won't. All of them get an ear-bashing about how wonderful you are. No, she'd lose too much face if she took you away.' Kitty spoke with humour in her voice but it hadn't been so funny to see her mother constantly making a fool of herself, buttonholing acquaintances, boring them like the Ancient Mariner with her tales of Lana.

'How embarrassing,' Lana said, but with a smile that implied she did not find it so. 'Everyone?'

'Everyone.' Kitty nodded.

'Imagine how impossible she'll be when I'm a star.' Lana flopped down on to the pink velveteen dressing-stool.

'Are you going to be a star?' Kitty asked, amazement at such an announcement swamping any amusement she might have felt.

'Oh, yes. I feel it here.' And Lana pointed vaguely in the region of her heart.

'What sort of star?' Now Kitty could not stop herself from smiling. Other people became stars, not her kid sister. And conversations like this did not take place in suburban back-bedrooms with the would-be star clutching a liberty bodice to her breast. It all seemed so silly. She longed to laugh out loud but her sister's intense expression stopped her in time.

'I thought, of course, that it would be dance, but now . . . now it's the stage I love best. When Portman is teaching me I know I could play any part in the world. That he could make it possible for me.' As Lana spoke, Kitty noticed, she changed. Her face altered, seemed to become thinner, she looked older, not pretty, but animated and almost beautiful. 'When I'm working with him I know, I just know I can achieve whatever I want to do.'

'You'd best not tell Mum, then. She's set her heart on you becoming a Bluebell Girl.' Kitty laughed, embarrassed by such blatant emotion. Ambition like this was something she knew nothing about, nor understood. But she realized now what the change in Lana was.

'I've set my sights higher than a chorus line – even the Bluebell Girls. She won't mind what it is I do, once I'm famous.'

'That's true,' Kitty said, and wondered what it must feel like to be so totally confident of oneself and one's abilities. Having no ambitions of her own, not even knowing what she wanted to do when she left school in a couple of years, Kitty once more felt younger than Lana and once again did not like it. 'What's this man Portman like, then, to work such wizardry?' She laughed again as if to show she was still in control.

'Wonderful.' Lana sighed. 'Everybody's dream-man. Don't you remember him? He's tall, handsome, with a moustache, and his voice is divine – of course.'

'I hate moustaches. You used to, too. Sounds to me as if you've got a crush on him.'

'Me? Don't be silly. What would be the point when he's so in love with his wife?'

'He's got a wife?'

'Of course he has – you met her – the equally divine Portia.' Lana leaped up from the stool to continue her unpacking.

6

Kitty had been right. Lana returned to the Philbert establishment in the New Year.

It wasn't until her sister had left in a flurry of last-minute packing and dramatic kisses that Kitty realized that, in the three weeks she had been home, Lana had not once asked Kitty what she was doing, if she was happy, if she minded making the sacrifices necessary so that Lana could have her chance. Not once had she inquired how school was, how her piano lessons were progressing, or what she hoped to do when she left. Kitty also suddenly realized that despite that first-night row, Lana had left with reassurances from Amy that she need not do tap if she didn't want to and that her bedroom would be redone in a nice smart style in time for her return at Easter. Kitty found herself admiring such an achievement.

Mike had been elated at his daughter's return but soon found there was a distance between them, a distance created in three short months. Not only was Lana speaking differently, she was behaving differently too. Her manners, never bad, were now so impeccable that they bordered on the grotesque. The small house was not large enough for Lana's leaping up to open doors with a swish, or standing back and gesturing others past with a wide sweep of her arm.

Mealtimes, which normally were quickly over, with everyone concentrating on eating, changed. Lana made them take an interminable time, making polite, inconsequential conversation between the smallest mouthfuls Kitty had ever seen taken.

'Does she have to be so la-di-da?' Kitty asked, as she helped with the washing-up – Lana was not available to help, she was out on some urgent errand in town. When there were chores to do, Lana invariably found pressing engagements elsewhere.

'She's learning to be a lady as well, that's nice. You could learn a thing or two from her,' Amy said sharply.

Amy herself was in a muddle over the whole affair. She might appear proud but secretly she felt that Lana's behaviour was stupid and, worse, boring. They might shut themselves away in Lana's bedroom as they used to but it wasn't the same. Amy found herself enduring several lectures on clothes and décor generally. So often did Lana quote Portia's opinion on things that Amy had to bite her tongue to stop herself from saying what she really thought. She was wise enough to know that her daughter was so infatuated with these people that if there were any hint of criticism from Amy then Amy would be the loser. So it was Mike, in the privacy of their bedroom, who bore the whispered brunt.

'Who the hell does that bloody Portia woman think she is . . .?

'It's not natural changing a child like that. Making her into a woman before her time . . .

'Do you know what now? Her bedroom doesn't suit. Wants it changed. Says Portia says modern girls should have modern things . . .

'And what sort of name is *Portia* for a start? Bet she wasn't christened that . . .'

In the dark she would lather herself into a fine jealous rage until, most bitter of all, she burst out, 'I blame you, Mike. If you made more money we could send her somewhere half-way decent . . .'

Mike would lie silent, staring at the darkened ceiling, wishing he'd never heard of the Philberts, wishing he'd made a stand and not let Lana go, almost wishing that she had no talent and had remained safe with them. And, most of all, wishing he wasn't a man and could cry at the injustice of his wife's perpetual nagging.

Mike did not mind Lana's attempts to appear a sophisticated woman nearly as much as Kitty and Amy did. After all, he thought, a girl needed to know how to behave to succeed. No, what saddened him was the distance he sensed between them. Now he felt as if he was watching this pretty creature, his little girl, through a plate-glass window and that if he spoke she would not hear, would no longer react to anything he said to her. He feared that she did not need him and had gone from them for ever.

They waited for Easter with anticipation, all having resolved to be more tolerant and to try again, but they were not to see Lana until the summer. A month before Easter Mike received a letter from Portia asking if they might take Lana with them on a trip to Paris for which, Portia delicately indicated, the Philberts would be happy to pay.

None of this seemed right to Mike and he quickly said so. It was an odd sort of business they were running if, on the one hand, they took hard-earned money for Lana's tuition and, on the other, gave her a free holiday. If you asked him, it was a rum do. But then nobody did ask Mike, least of all Amy who, by return post, replied that they were very 'obliged' by the Philberts' interest in their little girl.

'She'll see the Bluebells first-hand,' Amy said, eyes shining with excitement. 'Imagine that.'

'She won't, she's too young to be taken to a nightclub, and in any case I don't think I want my girl in places like that.'

'Don't be stuffy, Mike. You wait – she'll see those girls legging it and, mark my words, we'll have heard the last of this giving-up-tap baloney.'

'She's too short,' Kitty said, feeling rumblings of jealousy for the first time. She longed to travel, longed to go to Paris, to see the paintings in the Louvre, to visit Versailles.

But, with money so tight, the chances of Kitty going anywhere were remote, so she said nothing.

Mike found himself reeling at the long list of things Lana needed for the trip. A free holiday it might be, but it was rapidly turning into an expensive one all the same. With a worried frown he wrote the cheque to cover the cost of the new clothes that Portia had kindly volunteered to purchase.

When Lana's letters and postcards began to arrive, bubbling with excitement and wonder, he smiled to himself and felt how worthwhile it had been. 'At least she appreciates it,' he said, putting down the latest postcard on the kitchen table and smiling with satisfaction.

'Of course she appreciates it. Lana appreciates everything we do,' Amy said defensively. 'We should thank our lucky stars we've got a child with so much talent to spend our money on. Odd she hasn't mentioned the Bluebell Girls yet, isn't it?'

When the summer holidays came, and with them Lana, Kitty found herself quite maliciously pleased that her sister was barely half an inch taller.

For two years the Lawrence family settled into this new routine. During that time, apart from when Lana went to Paris, Kitty had felt no jealousy or resentment at the advantages her sister was given. This was due in part to her father but also to her own logical character.

Mike tried to make things fairer for Kitty. If a new dress was bought for Lana he made sure Kitty had one too. If he could not run to a trip to Paris he could at least take her to London, where they had visited the sights. In the evening he had taken her to the theatre and afterwards for a slap-up supper in one of the new steak houses.

There was no space in Kitty's bedroom for any alterations on the scale of the upheaval in Lana's. But all the same he'd had Amy make a new bedspread and curtains and he bought Kitty one of the new-fangled angle-poise lamps which she could truthfully say she preferred to anything else.

Mike was willing to continue paying the extra for her music lessons, hard though it was to find the money, but it was Kitty herself who gave them up. No one could be more honest with herself than Kitty, she knew she did not have the talent to be a pianist. She could read music and she could play to amuse herself, and that was what interested her. Some of Mike's happiest moments were when Amy was out. Then he would persuade Kitty to perform and would sit in the half-light listening as she played him some Chopin – his favourite – and dreaming of how life could be without the constant pressure of finding money. They could only do this when Amy was out for she did not share their love of classical music. If Kitty wanted to curry favour with her mother she had only to play a selection from *Annie Get Your Gun* or something by Ivor Novello and Amy was as sweet as pie.

When she was alone in the house Kitty would sometimes sing to herself as she played – she knew the words of some of Ivor Novello's work, and at school she had learned old English folk songs. She liked to sing and felt happy when she did but she never let anyone hear because, as Amy had pointed out, no one else enjoyed the sound she made – 'caterwauling', her mother called it.

Admittedly Amy took more interest in Kitty now that Lana was away. She talked to her more and even asked her about her day. It didn't alter anything, though; Kitty loved her father but had little time for her mother.

However, one day in the summer after her fifteenth birthday something happened which caused a change in Kitty. Resentments began to surface, and attitudes changed. Afterwards she always thought of it as 'the Locket Day'.

Her mother had two lockets. One was of heavy gold, embossed with an intricate design of lovers' knots and flowers, its chain of equally heavy gold, more like a man's watch-chain than a woman's necklace. When the clasp sprang open there were two pictures inside, one of Kitty with a lock of her straight dark brown hair, and on the other side Lana with a curl of her white-blonde hair. The locket had belonged to Kitty's grandmother and to her great-grandmother before her, and had been handed down to the eldest girl of each generation.

The second locket was silver, also embossed but more simply with a Celtic cross, which Mike had bought Amy on their honeymoon in Scotland. Inside were two snapshots of them taken on their wedding day. This locket had no tradition as yet.

On that eventful day Kitty had gone in search of Lana, who was home on holiday, to see if she wanted to join her to walk up to the High Street to meet some girls from Kitty's school. She heard voices from behind the half-open door of her mother's bedroom.

'No, Lana my pet, you can't borrow it for a party. I'm sorry, but there it is.'

'But why not?'

'Because it's too valuable, that's why. Gracious, the chain alone is worth hundreds.'

'It's so pretty.'

'Yes, it is, isn't it? One day when you're older then you can borrow it. And one day, when I'm dead and gone, why, it'll be yours to wear whenever you want.'

'Oh, please, Mummy, don't say things like that. I don't want it if you've got to die first. I want you to live for ever.'

'You're so sweet. I'll try, my love.' Amy laughed and was kissing her fair-haired daughter when her dark-haired one pushed the door fully open.

Amy and Lana were sitting on the lilac candlewick bedspread, the modest contents of Amy's jewel-case scattered on the cover. The sun was slanting through the bay window lighting Lana's head, making it even fairer.

'You can't do that. It's mine. That locket goes to me.' Kitty stood in the doorway, her face distorted with anger. 'It's mine,' she repeated defiantly, as if saying so ensured that it was.

'If it's anyone's it's mine. I'll do what I want with it and leave it to whoever I want, so there, madam.' Amy spoke coldly and her expression, soft when she had been looking at Lana, became stony as she looked at Kitty.

It was in that moment that Kitty saw everything and wondered why she had been so stupid. She saw that that was how her mother always looked at her, realized how her mother's voice changed whenever she spoke to her. Kitty suddenly became aware of the huge gulf in her mother's feelings for her, a gulf which could never now be bridged.

'But I'm the eldest.' She took a step into the room, her hand outstretched as if she was about to seize the locket. Amy snatched it from Lana and began to wrap it in its tissue-paper.

'It's got nothing to do with who's the eldest.'

'It has.'

'How could it? I had a brother, no sister. What put that nonsense in your head?'

'Nan said. Nan told me, she said she was the eldest . . .'

'Well, Nan was wrong.'

'She wasn't. She understood . . .' Frustrated, Kitty stood in the doorway, not knowing how to proceed in staking her claim. The irritation she normally felt for her sister disappeared, to be replaced by much more complicated emotions.

Until then she had not minded about the money spent on Lana – she was the one with talent and deserved the chance, she had told herself. And she had decided to give up her dancing classes, no one had made her. In any case she did not want to leave home. She liked her school, even though she was not over-popular, but then she wasn't unpopular either. She was one of those pupils whose passage through school was not to be marked by prowess at games, or on the stage, or by great academic achievement. She passed her exams in the middle range, she was always in the reserve team, and while she had friends she spent time with and sometimes met on Saturdays for a cappuccino coffee or a milk-shake in the new Italian ice-cream parlour, she had no great intimate to confide in. But then, she did not need one, for she had nothing of an intimate nature to confide.

It was as if, after the locket incident, Kitty had become fully aware that her life had set into a series of ruts. The very predictability of her life began to instil in her feelings of discontent which had not been there before. Even when she passed her exams she felt no satisfaction with the results. When she mastered a particularly difficult piece of music she only found herself wondering why she bothered. She wanted to do something with her life but she did not know what it should be. She wanted to go places, but she did not know where.

Even her feelings for her father began to change. She still loved him, nothing would ever alter that, but despite this she began to find herself viewing him dispassionately. She saw a weak and tired man whose jokes were old and boring, whose strict routines were irksome. She always knew where to find him at any time of day – his habits never varied – knew how he would react to a situation, even, most times, the very words he would say. All this had once meant security to her, but now that feeling was turning into an irritation with him, and with the sameness of everyday life with him.

Kitty was not normally bad-tempered and had usually

hidden any ill-feeling or anger by the simple expedient of
going to the privacy of her room. Now she did not bother
to hide it.

'Trouble with you, young woman, is you need a boyfriend,' Amy had said one day when Kitty had flown off
the handle about nothing in particular.

'That's just the sort of reaction I'd expect from you,'
Kitty had shouted as she slammed the door behind her.

She spent more and more time alone in her room. There
she read books and played her classical music on the new
electric automatic record-player her father had bought her,
with the sound turned down so as not to annoy her mother.
She began to feel sorry for herself and to resent her sister –
more for knowing what she wanted to do than for anything
else – and longed to know, to have a pointer, that would
tell her what she was to do with her life. Or was she
doomed to live like this always, to feel this uncomfortable
discontent gnawing away inside her?

7

That it always rained on market day in Rochester was a
local joke, and today was no exception. It was half-term
and Kitty mooched idly around the stalls. She enjoyed the
market, watching the people, listening to the barkers'
improbable sales patter. She found her way to the crockery
stall, where the best sales pitch of all was made, and joined
the crowd standing in the drizzle, her navy blue school
mackintosh belted tight, and wearing one of her mother's
headscarves.

'Call me a nut cutlet, call me St Nick, call me what you

like, I'm here to make you happy. You happy? You there' –
he pointed at Kitty, who reddened at the unexpected
attention – 'what are you, deaf or somethink?'

'Yes. No. I mean . . . I'm happy . . . I suppose.'

'Suppose? A pretty girl like you and you *suppose*? Good
God, girl, what're the fellows in this town thinking about?
If I didn't have me own trouble and strife I'd meet you after
and then you wouldn't suppose no more, that's for sure!'
He winked exaggeratedly at the crowd and leered, and they
cheered, and Kitty felt herself going redder and redder. 'So
what have we here – as I was saying, not a quid, not fifteen
bob not even ten but . . .'

'Kitty? It is Kitty, isn't it?'

Kitty groaned inwardly that anyone should have been
here to see her discomfort. Slowly she turned.

'Miss de Souza!' she said with genuine pleasure.

'I thought it was you. I thought, who's that poor soul
that dreadful man has picked on, and then I was almost
sure it was you. But you've changed, so I couldn't be totally
sure.'

'Changed? Me?'

'Gracious yes, you're a woman already. And so wonderfully tall – I do envy you, a good height is such an asset.
Shall we have a coffee or are you too busy?'

'That would be lovely. I'm not doing anything – my
mother asked me to get some material for a dress but I
couldn't see anything I liked.'

'And how is your mother?' Camilla de Souza asked, as
they fell into step and made their way to the café by the
Cathedral Gate.

'She's fine,' Kitty said noncommittally.

'Still determined young Lana should become a star?'

'Why, yes.' Kitty laughed, for there had been amusement in Camilla's voice.

They entered the low-beamed café. It was not too busy,

so they were able to sit on wheelbacked chairs at a table in the window from where they could watch the people coming and going beneath the Cathedral Gate.

'I love this place and all the copper and brass. I like to think that perhaps Dickens himself might have had a coffee here. What do you think?'

'I've never been here before,' Kitty replied. She and her mother usually went to the ABC restaurant further along the road.

'A pot of coffee for two and a selection of your delicious cakes,' Camilla ordered from the waitress. 'So how long is it since we talked?'

'I'm sixteen now, so it's four years.'

'Gracious, how time flies. So dear little Lana is fourteen, though I suppose she's no longer little either.' Camilla picked up the menu to study it with care.

'Oh, she's still little.'

Camilla looked up. She smiled, having picked up the trace of satisfaction in Kitty's voice.

'So she's not to be a Bluebell Girl, after all.'

'Not unless they start taking midgets.' Kitty smiled back. 'She claims she's five foot one but I think she's fibbing that last inch.'

'It's a shame, she was a good little dancer. Still, I'm sure your mother has found other talents for her to pursue.'

'She sings – it's quite a nice voice really, I suppose.'

'But you don't like it?'

'Well . . . it's a bit sugary-sweet, if you know what I mean. And she's very keen on acting.'

'Really? That does surprise me. Is she still at the stage school?' Camilla moved the flower vase and ashtray to make space on the table for the cups and coffee pot.

'Oh, yes, she wouldn't leave it for anything. She's very happy there. Thank you,' Kitty said as she accepted her cup.

'Which of these sinful confections takes your fancy?'

Camilla held out the plate of dainties, as Amy called them. Kitty chose a chocolate éclair. 'I was very worried when your mother insisted on sending her there, you know. You get the oddest people setting up in my business. But I made a few inquiries and everyone I spoke to had nothing but praise for the Philbert couple.'

'Mum's not too happy, she doesn't think they push Lana enough. I think she imagined Lana would be a West End star before she was thirteen.'

'Then I'm glad they didn't. Quite often a child performs well and then burns herself out and you never hear of her again. People like Petula Clark and Julie Andrews are rare, you know, the way they keep going. But even stars like them could still disappear without trace.'

'I see,' Kitty said politely, but with little interest in the fate of young stars.

'And you, my dear? What are you planning to do?'

'I don't know. Perhaps I'll teach.'

'What subject?'

'Oh, no, not that sort of teacher. Infants are more my line. I don't think I'm bright enough to go to university.'

'Strange. I always thought you were. Still . . .' She looked at Kitty intently as if checking she had not made a mistake. 'Maybe you lack confidence, my dear. Or perhaps you haven't been encouraged?' Camilla raised an eyebrow questioningly.

'Or something . . .' Kitty laughed but coloured with embarrassment and began to take a keen interest in her surroundings.

'Yes, well . . .' Camilla said vaguely, regretting now that she had obviously confused the girl. 'Yes, decisions on one's future are always difficult. And time does fly so,' she added inconsequentially.

'Yes,' agreed Kitty, unsure.

Camilla suddenly signalled for the bill. 'I must be making a move, I've a little soirée tonight.' She stood up.

'Of course.' Kitty followed.

'I wonder.' Camilla stopped and turned to face her. 'Perhaps you would like to come? Just a small group of friends, we meet for the odd musical evening. Say seven-thirty at my place?'

'Thank you, Miss de Souza. I'd like to very much.'

Kitty was the first to arrive and Camilla was still flitting about, putting the finishing touches to the room. A dozen candles glowed, the one standard lamp, in the corner by the record-player, had its shade swathed in a red chiffon scarf to diffuse the light. Camilla was placing large squashy cushions, with bright jewel-coloured covers, at random on the floor.

'There.' She looked about the room, 'Pretty, isn't it? People relax better on the floor. Now, I'll just powder my nose. But first . . .' In a twirl of long taffeta skirt, a black lace mantilla thrown nonchalantly over her shoulders, Camilla crossed swiftly to the record-player. She selected a record and placed it carefully on the turntable. 'Something for you to listen to while I'm elsewhere. Do answer the door for me, won't you?' And with a skip she was gone.

Kitty lowered herself on to one of the cushions as the music began. 'Un bel di . . .' The soprano's voice soared and Kitty sat bolt upright. She felt her spine tingle, she saw the hairs on her arm stand up, she felt all her senses come alive. She suddenly wanted to cry. She had not known that such a sound was possible.

'What was that?' she asked Camilla as the music faded away and a new aria began. She jumped up and ran to the record-player. 'May I?' she asked, already pressing the button to make the stylus lift. 'I've never heard anything so lovely.'

'That was Maria Callas. Have you not heard her before?'

'I've occasionally listened to opera on the radio – when

my family were out.' She smiled. 'But I can't have heard her, I'd never have forgotten a voice like that.'

'The purists say she's not as good as everyone says.'

'They what? Honestly, Miss de Souza, I don't think I've ever heard a purer, more moving sound in my life. I felt it devouring me.'

Camilla laughed at Kitty's excitement. 'Then play it again.'

Carefully Kitty replaced the stylus and once again the voice floated through the tiny room, filling every space, carrying Kitty with it.

'What's it mean?' Kitty asked.

'Over here somewhere, I've a . . .' Camilla began to run her finger along the spines of books on the small bookshelf.

'Ah, here it is. *Madam Butterfly*, Puccini.' She leafed through the book. 'So handy, this – it has the English translations of all the great arias. Do you sing?' she asked, as she handed the book to Kitty.

'No. Everyone complains when I do. But I like to sing to myself when no one is listening.'

'Don't we all?' Camilla smiled. 'Why, in my bath I'm certain I'm as good as Callas any day. Ah, the bell . . .' And in her quick but fluid way of moving Camilla was out of the door and down the stairs, while Kitty replaced the stylus and followed the words of the short aria in English.

Camilla returned with three people, and Kitty regretfully stopped the record as introductions were made.

'Kitty, this is Simon Whittaker, Miriam Headly and Bracken Sills. Everyone, this is Kitty Lawrence who used to be a pupil of mine until she wisely decided she didn't want to dance.' Camilla laughed as everyone shook hands. 'She's in a bit of a trance – she's just heard Callas for the first time.'

'Lucky you. That first time is a magical moment, perhaps never to be repeated,' Simon said. He was an elderly, bearded man wearing a shapeless, discoloured sweater over matching corduroy trousers, with sandals on his socked feet. Judging by the crumpled state of his clothes, the fact that jumper and trousers matched was probably more by accident than design.

'Oh, no, a record can only ever be a poor second. Nothing surpasses hearing a great diva live for the first time,' Miriam admonished him. She was short and so fat that she appeared to be as wide as her height, but she was rather pretty despite her weight. She was blonde, and wore a floating garment in tinselly material which looked like a large bag in which holes for her head and arms had been cut.

'Miriam used to sing, didn't you, my darling?' Camilla said encouragingly.

'Only in the chorus, I regret.'

'But only because you weren't ambitious enough, and too sweet to push yourself forward,' Bracken interrupted. She was a tall, thin woman wearing black trousers and jacket which reminded Kitty of a soldier's battledress. Her face was very white and her eyes very black, the lashes coated thickly with mascara. Her dark hair was cut short like a man's and greased smoothly to her scalp with brilliantine which made it shine as if polished.

'Drinks, everyone?' Camilla appeared with a tray on which stood a large bowl full of a red mixture with fruit bobbing about on it.

'Mulled wine. You're a wonder, Camilla. Just what one needs on a filthy night like this,' Simon said enthusiastically.

Kitty gingerly accepted a glass mug of the drink and sipped it apprehensively. Even though she had not expected it to be warm, she liked the sweetness and the taste of cinnamon.

They sat on their cushions and drank the wine, and then more. A good dozen glasses had been ladled out, but after an hour, and much surreptitious glancing at her watch,

Camilla announced that the others must have got held up
in the traffic. Everyone kindly agreed, even though they
were fully aware that traffic jams were unlikely on such a
night.

'Then I think we should eat before it's all ruined,' Camilla
fluttered.

The food arrived – just in time in Kitty's case for apart
from the éclair she had not eaten all day. She never
normally drank and was beginning to feel a strange light-
headedness. They ate, still sitting on the cushions, and
Kitty found it difficult to juggle plate, glass, knife and fork,
napkin and bread roll. But the others did not seem bothered
when they dropped things, evidently they were used to
eating cross-legged on the floor. Kitty could just imagine
what her mother would have said about these
arrangements.

The wholemeal flan with its vegetable filling was heavy
and indigestible but Kitty chewed it stoically, washing it
down with the red wine which Camilla had now served
them and which, to Kitty, tasted like vinegar. With a brave
smile she accepted another slice of flan.

The talk was all of books she had not read, music she
did not know and actors and actresses she had never heard
of. She sat silently, absorbing it all, thinking what interesting people these were and how much they knew.

Camilla referred to the pudding as a 'little compote' but
Kitty identified it as stewed apple with rather too many
cloves added. By now she was feeling relaxed and not the
least bit shy, which was unusual for her, and she was soon
busily chatting away.

'Right, everyone!' Camilla stood up, her bright-coloured
skirt swirling about her as she did so. Her face was alight
with excitement as she clapped her manicured hands for
order. 'Time we sang for our supper,' she said gleefully.

The relaxed and pleasantly drowsy feeling left Kitty in a
flash. Her eyes looked nervously from left to right as she

kept her head rigid, but she seemed the only one to be put
out by this announcement.

'Each of us gives a little performance, it's a tradition, my
dear.' Camilla smiled encouragingly at her. 'You can do
whatever you like – recite a little poem, tell us a story, do a
dance, even.' She laughed at this as if it was inordinately
funny but Kitty felt her stomach churning with horror at
the prospect.

'I'll go first.' Bracken stood up, delved into her trouser
pocket and produced a piece of paper. She coughed importantly, stood with feet apart, took a deep breath and
launched herself into a long poem. At least, Kitty thought
it was a poem. There was no rhyme and little rhythm. Kitty
did not understand the love it referred to – a secret love, a
forbidden love – and was even more confused when it
became obvious that the narrator was a woman writing to a
woman.

As Bracken finished, Miriam blew noisily into her handkerchief. 'So beautiful,' she said, her voice catching with
emotion. 'Such clarity . . .' She blew again.

'Who's next?' Camilla asked after a silent interval while
the others contemplated the work they had just heard and
Kitty was wondering if she might ask for another glass of
wine.

'Me?' Miriam lumbered to her feet, smiling brightly, all
previous emotion gone as if a slate had been wiped clean.
She too stood with feet apart, flexed her shoulders and
stretched her neck as if setting her body into a new stance.
She looked about her in a manner which commanded
perfect quiet, took a deep breath and began to sing.

Miriam had a loud voice, the loudest Kitty had ever
heard, the closest she had ever been to. The voice
rebounded about the room, crashing into walls, bouncing
off one and into another, the sound covered them, deaf-
ened them. It was a powerful voice but also, Kitty was sure,
off-key, and so not a particularly lovely sound. But it

seemed she was alone in this opinion, for the reaction of the others was rapturous and everyone begged for an encore.

After that it was Simon's turn and he played the jew's harp, which Kitty had not heard before, and which she liked. Then Camilla danced a tarantella to a record. It was wonderful and they all clapped in time. After that Camilla needed to quench her thirst and bottles of white wine were opened. Kitty was sufficiently fuddled to accept another glass.

'What about Kitty? What's Kitty going to do?' It was Miriam asking.

'I doubt if Kitty wants to perform.' Camilla stepped forward rather protectively.

'That's not the rules, Camilla. You know the rules, whoever attends must contribute,' Bracken insisted.

'But poor Kitty . . .'

'I don't mind.' Kitty was as surprised as Camilla to find herself standing on her feet, swaying somewhat, smiling broadly from ear to ear and feeling she was game for anything.

'What will you give us, my dear?' Miriam smiled up at her kindly.

'Have you got a piano? I'll play for you.'

'Sadly not up here, just the one in the studios,' Camilla replied.

'Then I'll sing.' Kitty seemed determined to shock herself rigid. 'I'll sing . . .' She paused, thinking, her mind completely blank. Then, 'I'll sing this.' She picked up the book that Camilla had given her earlier that evening. She rustled through the pages and taking a deep breath she launched herself, unaccompanied, into 'One fine day'.

Kitty had never sung music like this before, music that burrowed into her brain and took over her mind, controlled her emotions. She gave herself to the sound she was making, she felt as if she was leaning into a great billowing sail. It was as if someone else inside her was singing, as if she had nothing to do with it. She was lost in the music and as she came to the end she felt a sadness that it was the finish.

There was total silence. Kitty giggled nervously, thinking she had made a fool of herself, fearing that the wine had done something to her ears, deceiving her into thinking she had made a beautiful sound.

'Kitty, my darling, I did not know . . .' Camilla was on her feet, rushing over to her, arms outspread. 'I had no idea.'

'The child's got perfect pitch.' Miriam was shaking her head in amazement, her mouth twisted into a strange attempt at a smile.

'I don't believe she'd only just heard that for the first time.'

'But she did, Bracken. Didn't you, Kitty?' Camilla assured them.

Kitty nodded her head, unable to speak, feeling dazed, the sound she had made still echoing in her head.

'But she sang it nearly perfectly, as if she had studied it,' Bracken said, her voice heavy with cynicism.

'Some people can do that,' Simon offered. 'A friend of mine only has to hear a tune once and he can play it.'

'The voice is somewhat different,' Miriam pointed out coldly. 'And it wasn't perfect, let's not get too carried away with excitement.'

'Oh, Miriam, don't spoil it. I think Kitty's got a remarkable voice,' Camilla said, but Miriam, looking suddenly angry, had turned away and was intent on studying a small watercolour.

'I think there's a bit of screech there, wouldn't you say, Miriam?' Bracken interjected hurriedly, glancing anxiously at Miriam's back.

'And a shallow lower register.' Miriam swung round to face them, looking more in control of herself.

'But if taught . . .' Camilla began.

'Sing it again,' Miriam ordered.

'Again? Are you sure?' Kitty giggled nervously.

'Yes, Miriam's right. Try again, Kitty. See if you can do it a second time,' Bracken commanded.

'One minute. Have you the score?' Miriam asked.

'Yes, here somewhere.' Camilla scrabbled feverishly in a pile of sheet-music and emerged waving a score triumphantly.

'Right.' Miriam settled herself with the music.

Kitty looked about her, the light-heartedness slipping away from her, making her nervous this time. Feeling almost sick with apprehension, she looked at the corner of the room, concentrated on the chiffon-covered lamp. She closed her eyes and this time sang without referring to the book she still held.

'That was even better, wasn't it?' Camilla clutched her hands together as if to stop them waving about.

Miriam slumped heavily back on the cushions when Kitty had finished the second time. 'It was good,' she said reluctantly.

'It was that all right, clear as a bell,' Bracken said. 'I feel I am in the presence of something quite extraordinary,' she said dramatically, but without looking at Miriam.

'My dear, you have a wonderful talent.' Simon was smiling at Kitty kindly.

'Do I?'

'You must know you have,' Miriam snapped at her.

'No. I never sang before, only to myself. Everyone said I sang too loud.'

'What do we do?' Camilla asked. 'I feel almost weak with excitement.'

'She has to have lessons,' Bracken said firmly.

'Would you, Miriam? You're the only singer I know,' Camilla asked.

'Of course. I will – I'll do my best with her,' Miriam said, not looking directly at anybody.

Kitty felt herself blushing.

'Could your parents manage for you to have lessons, Kitty?' Camilla asked. 'I mean, you know, financially?'

'I don't know. I could ask. It's a bit difficult, with Lana . . .'

'Bah! Lana's had her chance. She's not got a talent like this. Yours is something unique.'

Kitty glowed at the compliment. She continued to glow as more were heaped upon her. She was floating on a great cloud of happiness as the little group excitedly discussed her and her future. It was midnight when the party finally broke up.

'I've been privileged tonight, Kitty. One day, when I listen to you at Covent Garden, I shall tell people I was one of those who discovered you,' Simon said as he kissed her hand in a courtly fashion.

'Oh, go on . . .' Kitty pushed him gently with embarrassment, giggly from all the wine she had drunk.

She made an unsteady way home. She put the key in the lock and tiptoed in, expecting her parents to be in bed. But there was a light shining under the dining-room door. She opened it, smiling happily at her father who was sitting at the dining-table struggling with a long line of figures.

'Dad, listen to this.' And she leaned against the sideboard and sang for the third time that night. When she opened her eyes it was to see her father looking at her with a stunned expression, a trace of a tear in the corner of his eye.

'What do you think?' She grinned at him.

'I knew you had a nice voice, I'd no idea you could do that.'

'Neither did I, not until tonight. I heard a recording of this singer, Dad – Maria something. I'd never heard a sound like it and suddenly I knew it was what I wanted to do. I'll do anything, anything, Dad, to sing like her.'

'Oh, Kitty. I'm so pleased for you.'

'And I met this opera singer – well, she only sang in the chorus and I don't think she's very good but she's agreed to give me lessons – I'm to let her know what you say.'

Mike looked down at the figures and an expression of weariness flitted across his face. But when he looked up he was smiling broadly.

'Of course you must have lessons. What sort of father would I be if I didn't help you?'

'Oh, Dad. I knew you would. Isn't it exciting?'

The door burst open. 'What on earth was that row?' Amy demanded, standing in the doorway in her nightie, her hair in rollers.

'That was our Kitty. She's found her voice,' Mike said proudly.

'Well, I suggest she unfinds it – God-awful racket at this time of night. What will the neighbours think?'

'I'm going to have lessons, Mum. Dad says I can.'

'Oh, yes, and where's the money for that coming from?' demanded Amy, hands on hips, and Kitty felt the happiness of the evening oozing away from her.

8

Lana was being sick for the fourth time that morning. She felt there could be nothing left in her to bring up, but still her body heaved, her shoulders shuddered, her brow was drenched with sweat.

'Oh, God, you're not still honking?' Avril stood in the doorway of the lavatories and shouted at the one booth with its door shut. 'Come on, do. Portia says if you're not in the wings in five minutes you can't audition.'

Lana wiped her forehead with a handkerchief already

sodden with perspiration and slumped against the white lavatory. 'I can't go on,' she said, her voice husky.

'Of course you can. Don't be so wet.'

'I couldn't sing. I've hurt my throat.'

'Of course you have, silly. Come out here. Portia's sent some of her magic throat lotion down for you.'

Lana stood up, weakly unlocked the cubicle door and shuffled out.

'God, you look a mess. Quick, wash your face, swig some of this.'

Obediently Lana splashed water on to her face and then sipped the pleasant, soothing mixture of honey and lemon Portia always carried with her. She coughed and then coughed again as if checking that her vocal cords were still there.

'Come on. Put on some lipstick and powder. Try and look half-way decent,' Avril ordered bossily. 'And stop making such a fuss. It's taken us long enough to persuade Portia this is a good idea – don't spoil it for everyone. It's only a cruddy pantomime after all.'

'Yes, but it's a start.'

Avril snorted.

'We have to start somewhere. How did you do?'

'I'm to come back tomorrow. I'm in the chorus – no problem. But tomorrow they're auditioning for the village maiden – I'm determined to get it. Perhaps you'll get chosen for one of the Babes, you're short enough.'

'And Pat?' Lana asked, ignoring the jibe about her height. Everyone joked about it, seeming unaware that it upset her.

'She's out but she didn't seem to mind. She's gone home for the weekend. She lives near here.

'Right, you look fine now. Come on.' Avril took her hand and virtually dragged her from the lavatories, along the dark green painted brick corridor and up the iron staircase at the end. She finally pushed her towards the wings where a small band of girls of their own age waited their turn.

How Lana ever managed to put one foot in front of the other to walk on to the stage she would never know. The stage had not seemed so large when she had sat with the others in the auditorium watching the auditions. Now it stretched in front of her like a football pitch. Shyly she made her way to the spotlight and stood miserably in its hot light.

'Name?' A voice barked from the darkness beyond the orchestra pit.

'Lana . . .' She coughed. 'Lana Lawrence.'

'Dancer? Singer?'

'Both,' Lana squeaked.

'What did you say? Speak up, can't you?'

'Both,' she said, as loudly as she could manage.

'Sing first.'

'I thought . . .' She looked down at the pianist. 'I thought I'd sing "Silver Dollar".'

From somewhere sound came. Once she started it was easier, she found to her surprise. Her pretty voice soared, she remembered all the lessons Portia had given her to project her voice, to make it sound far stronger than it really was. She finished and stood awkwardly in the light as she heard a whispered conference out there in the darkness. It seemed to go on for ever, far longer than the others had had to endure.

'Sorry. You're too short. Come back next year,' the disembodied voice yelled. 'Nice voice, though. Next year,' it added, as if to make amends.

'But my dance,' Lana said, emboldened.

'I said – too short.'

Lana turned and walked despondently towards the wings. The stage manager stood there holding his clipboard with the list of names. He was pushing the next girl on to the stage.

'Bad luck, love,' he said kindly. Lana smiled gratefully at him. 'You've got a nice voice there.'

'Thanks.'

'You'd best grow a bit, hadn't you? Mind you, parts of you seem to be growing nicely,' and he put out his hand and stroked her breast, his hand lingering over her nipple. 'Look me up?'

'Yes,' she said, blushing ferociously. 'Thank you,' she added.

Portia came rushing up to her. The stage manager made himself busy.

'Lana, I'm so sorry. You got so close. Did you register how long they took to make up their minds?'

'It seemed an age.'

'Exactly. You almost did it and on a first audition too, that's wonderful.'

'But I didn't, did I?'

'Avril's only just done it and I've lost count of the auditions she's had – against my advice,' she added.

'I'm a better dancer than her,' Lana said, suddenly bitter at the unfairness of it.

'Yes, but she's taller for the chorus – they're all big girls.'

'But I'm small – I could have been a Babe.' She began to cry.

'I know, darling, but you know what it's like if your face doesn't fit.' Portia squeezed Lana's hand encouragingly, and dried her tears. This was why she hated these wretched auditions when they weren't old enough to accept the rejection, when everything seemed unfair.

'Look, Lana, I've got to stay in town overnight to be with Avril tomorrow. Pat has gone home and the seniors want to stay on,' Portia said when Lana had finally dried her tears.

'I know.'

'Do you think you could get back to the school by yourself?'

'Of course, I'm not a kid,' she snapped.

'No, of course you're not,' Portia said soothingly, realizing that disappointment was the cause of Lana's uncustomary flash of temper. 'Here's your fare. I'll call Portman to collect you from the station.'

'Don't bother. I can get the bus from the coach station. Bye, then. I'll see you tomorrow.' She turned to leave. 'Wish Avril luck from me, won't you?'

'Yes, I will. Take care, don't speak to any strangers.'

In a way Lana was relieved to be travelling back to school alone. She didn't have to speak to anyone, she could sit and go over and over again in her mind what had gone wrong. She had so set her heart on getting into that pantomime, it had Sylvia Chance in it, one of her favourite singing stars. She had allowed herself to dream how she would make friends with Sylvia, get her to help her, get her to insist she should be in her next West End musical comedy. It was all so unfair, she thought, looking out of the coach window as it carried her back to Cambridge. She had sung well, far better than those she had heard before she had to rush to the lavatories. And the others' dancing hadn't been up to much. She should have got a job, not be returning as a failure. What was she to write to her mother? She had foolishly written about the audition as if it was in the bag. That wasn't entirely her fault, though. Portia had made it sound as if she would walk it, that she was good enough, certainly their best. Stupid Portia, it was all her fault.

Her coach was held up by roadworks at Royston and was late arriving at the bus station. She had missed the connection that would take her direct to the village, there would not be another for two hours. She caught a bus which would take her three-quarters of the way, she would walk the rest.

She was in the middle of a field when the storm broke, and she trudged on dragging her case through the pouring rain. Still, she thought, as the rain soaked her, that stage manager had liked her. 'Look me up,' he'd said. What did that mean? She had not liked the way he had touched her breast, that was rude. Still, it showed one thing, he obviously didn't think she was a kid.

Across another field. Only one more and then the long drive. She was exhausted and drenched by the time she reached the front door. She pushed it open and went in. The hall was silent. A clock chimed in the distance. She took off her hat and hung it up on the grotesque iron hat-stand. Wearily, she began to undo the buttons on her coat.

'Let me help you.' Portman was standing behind her. She turned to face him. 'My, what a poor little soaked thing you are.' He finished undoing the buttons, slipped the coat from her shoulders and threw it on to the floor.

'Thank you, Portman.' Lana smiled wearily.

He felt her shoulders. 'A little damp,' he said. 'Best take your sweater off.' Like a small child she obediently held up her arms as he lifted her jumper over her head. 'How's the rest of you, then?' His hands ran across her breasts. Surprised at his touch, she tried to break away, but the hat-stand was in the way. 'We shouldn't take any chances, should we?' Portman said, his voice strangely husky. Her vest followed her jumper into the corner of the room. Portman was feeling her legs now, his hands stroking her stockings, his hand on the inside of her leg inching up. 'Damp, damp, just as I thought.' She tried to speak, to tell him to stop, but no sound emerged. Gently he undid her suspenders and rolled down her stockings. 'Now, do we need this?' He was looking at her closely as he put his arms around her and undid her brassière. He removed it slowly and Lana stood rigid with terror. She wanted to lift her arms to cover her breasts but they felt like lead and would not move. He bent forward and sucked gently at one nipple and then the other. He raised his head and looked at her intently, his face so close she could smell the whisky on his breath. She averted her face, but he put his hand up and made her look at him.

'You don't mind Portman doing this to you, do you, my little one?'

She wanted to cry out that she did, that he was frightening her.

'Please, say you like it. Make me happy,' he whispered softly, his eyes pleading with her, his hands gently teasing her nipples.

'I like it,' she replied obediently. She didn't want to hurt his feelings and, she told herself, fighting to calm down, it was dear old Port, he would never mean her harm, and in truth, she quite liked this feeling as he played with her breasts. 'Yes, I do,' she repeated for it was obviously what he wanted to hear.

Then his mouth returned to her breasts but this time he was sucking urgently, pulling at her red-rose nipples, gnawing her, and the pleasant feeling disappeared and Lana heard herself making a strange mewing noise from pain and fear. As he continued to take her breast in his mouth he began to remove her panties. His hand was stroking her gently, as his mouth continued to devour her. He looked up at her. 'This is nice, isn't it, little one? Say it's nice.'

'Oh yes, oh yes!' Lana gasped, her legs suddenly weak as she stepped back and crashed into the arms of the great iron bear of the hat-stand. Portman held her wedged against it, the intricate ironwork pressing deeply into her flesh adding to the pain. He unzipped his trousers, his fingers constantly massaging her.

'This is going to hurt, my darling, but wonderfully so,' he said as he guided his penis towards her. Gently, so gently entering her. He caught hold of her shoulders. 'Now!' he shouted and he thrust hard into her, tearing her, and she cried out, and the pain passed and he was riding into her as the iron arms of the great bear held her. And he was laughing and Lana, confused, laughed too, there didn't seem much else she could do.

9

'What will Portia say about us?' Lana asked as she lay in Portman's vast Victorian bed in which his grandmother had been conceived and died. Warily, she watched him sitting on the side of the bed, pouring himself a large whisky. He had just made love to her again. She was sore and very muddled. She knew that what had happened was wrong and yet it was Portman who had instigated it. How could she have told him of all people to stop? But even more confusing was her realization that there had been moments when she had found herself enjoying what he did to her, and if she enjoyed them and he obviously did, was that very, very wrong? She reached out tentatively and stroked him, and the muscles in his back twitched involuntarily at her touch.

'One thing you're going to have to learn, my little sparrow, is that if you take a lover of my age he isn't as insatiable as you.' He was laughing as he patted her bare rump.

'I didn't realize I'd taken a lover, I rather gathered I'd been taken.' She smiled up at him, all innocence and unsure what he meant by 'insatiable', a word she thought was used for people who ate too much.

'I'll tell you one thing, you were just about the easiest seduction I've ever enjoyed.'

'That's not a nice thing to say.' She pouted.

He drank the whisky in one and immediately poured another.

'You drink a lot, don't you?'

'Yes, and I eat too much and I fornicate too much.'

'What does fornicate mean?'

'What we've just done and will do again and again.'

She frowned at his reply, she was not sure if she wanted to do this often – certainly not the painful bits; she wouldn't mind him doing the pleasant things to her, though. 'You didn't answer my question.'

'What question?' he asked, circling her bare nipple with his finger, making that strange feeling slide through her body so that she found she could not keep still.

'What's Portia going to say?' she asked, though now she found herself less interested in the answer as he began to play with her other breast.

'Oh, she won't mind. She'll be pleased for me, she knows how I yearn for young flesh.'

'She won't be cross with me?'

He stopped playing with her and sat up. 'Cross? Why should she be cross?'

'Well, lots of wives would be . . .'

'Wife? Portia? Don't be a clot – she's my sister . . .'

'But, I thought . . . I mean . . .'

'You mean we act like lovers?'

'Well, yes . . .'

'Because we are, silly.'

'Lovers?' Lana was sitting bolt upright, her mouth slack with surprise.

'It's called incest, sweetie. There's a lot more of it about than you realize. But what a laugh, you thinking we were married. Portia will love that.' He laughed out loud, rocking back and forth on the bed.

'But you never said, everyone thinks—'

'Why should we say anything to anyone? It's nobody else's business what we do. But you mean that the other pupils think the same? I don't believe it. God, you're all so stupid.'

'No, we're not. You've the same name and you mooch
about together all the time. And all of us have seen you
necking at one time or another.'

'Where?' Portman asked, suddenly serious.

'When you walk in the spinney we can see you clearly
from our rooms. And if you stand on the second shelf in
the linen cupboard you can see into here quite easily if the
curtains aren't pulled,' Lana informed him matter-of-factly.
'I often saw you kissing and stroking each other, but you
always turned off the light and I thought that was all there
was – now I know it wasn't.' She giggled at the memory.
Portman leaped from the bed, crossed quickly to the
window and pulled the curtains closed.

'What did you do that for? There's no one else here.'

'They'll be back soon.' He walked back to the bed and
stood looking down at her. 'Look, sparrow, this actually is
quite serious. Don't tell the others what I've told you, will
you? Let them continue to think Portia and I are a married
couple, there's a pet?'

'Why?'

'Because . . .' He stood naked, frowning. 'It could get us
into a lot of trouble and you wouldn't want that to happen,
would you?' He sat on the edge of the bed again and once
more began to play with her breasts. 'And best not to say
anything about us either, you don't want to make the
others jealous, do you? And you wouldn't want to get
Portman into a fix, now would you? You know, you not
being sixteen.'

'Oh, no. I won't say a word to a living soul.' She crossed
her heart, the last person in the world she wanted to hurt
was Portman.

'Especially your mother.'

'I wouldn't breathe a word, especially to her,' Lana said,
knowing that if she said all the right things he would stop
looking so worried. The foreplay continued, and already
Lana was learning that if she reacted too quickly Portman

would enter her again – she liked this bit, she did not like it
nearly so much when he put his thing inside her, it hurt –
so she lay mute beneath his caresses. The door opened and
Portia glided in.

'What a pretty picture,' she said, smiling at them both
and at the frightened expression on Lana's face, 'can
anyone join in?' Portia laughed as she threw her stole on to
the carpet and quickly began to unbutton her dress. Lana
tried to hide her nakedness with the sheet and covered the
shame on her face with a pillow, which made both the
others laugh.

In the following weeks Lana learned a lot. The other two
were willing to reward her for being in their bed. Within
days she had her own room away from the others. Portman
made up some excuse that she had mild asthma and needed
more space – at first the other girls accepted it without
question. She had extra tuition too – just her and Portman.
Sometimes they had a lesson, sometimes they made love.
Lana didn't mind so much now, it didn't hurt any more,
and sometimes she even enjoyed it. She was not so sure
when Portia joined them, for the things she wanted to do
to Lana embarrassed her in a way that Portman didn't. But
Lana said nothing, how could she? All she wanted was for
these two people she had learned to adore to be happy.

It was not long before problems with the other girls
began. Lana became less popular and her fellow pupils
were occasionally spiteful with her. Portman and Portia
thought they had been careful enough but as a sort of
disguise they were both stricter with Lana in class than
they had been before. They had no way of knowing if the
others had guessed at the relationship that had developed
under their noses, or whether they were jealous because
Lana had been given her own room, or perhaps because
she suddenly had more and better clothes than the others.

But what was really upsetting the other pupils was that Lana was pushed forward for auditions over them. She was never successful, though, which filled her classmates with considerable satisfaction. It was always the same – her height was against her.

They were even more put out to find that Lana's failures, surprisingly, did not bother her. Unknown to them, she had decided she did not want to be in any chorus, she did not want to play a minor role as a child, restricted by law to a certain number of performances a week. She knew now, deep inside her and aided by the Philberts' constant reassurances, that she would succeed, and she wanted to burst suddenly on the world as a ready-made star. She knew something that even Portia did not know. Portman was writing a play – a musical comedy – just for her.

The Philberts were clever with her in a way that she was too young to understand. But it was that very youth they played on. She was rewarded. Little presents began to appear – small ornaments for her room, pieces of jewellery, clothes. Occasionally she would find a note from Portman with a pound note inside and then another from Portia with even more money. She never mentioned this, presuming the one did not know what the other had given her. But of course they knew, they discussed everything about Lana with each other. On the one hand they used and abused her body and on the other they treated her like their little child. In Lana's mind the sexual acts became intertwined with the nice presents and the words of encouragement they gave her, so that finally she became addicted to both of them.

As Christmas approached, the idea of leaving Portia and Portman for the holidays filled her with misery. She could not bear to think of being away from them for three interminable weeks.

'Let's write to my parents and pretend we're going somewhere cultural and you want to take me, like we did on the Paris trip. They agreed to that. We could say we're going to Italy or something? My mother would agree. Oh, please write.' Lana was standing in front of Portman's desk, jumping from one foot to the other with impatience.

'But my little sparrow, we have family too. We've got to go to them.'

'You don't want me.' Lana's bottom lip trembled.

'Darling, don't say such things. Of course we want you – always. But we've got to go – our mother is very poorly, this might be her last Christmas.'

'What if you meet someone else?' Lana looked at them.

'Hush, dearest. Don't even say such a silly thing. How would we replace you?' Portia stroked Lana's long blonde hair.

'We'll make it up to you afterwards, promise. We'll buy you the most stupendous present, won't we, Portia?'

'We most certainly will.'

'And just think how much we'll all be needing each other when we return. Sometimes, Lana, anticipation can add the most delicious element to an affair.' Portman smiled at her.

10

An influenza epidemic had decimated Camilla's classes to such an extent that she had decided to cancel the rest, since she did not know from one day to another if anyone would turn up for them. It was a bitterly cold December day and, having done her shopping, Camilla decided to call in on Miriam Headly for she was longing to know how Kitty was progressing with her voice coaching.

Whenever Camilla thought of Kitty it was with a warm

glow of satisfaction. Many children had passed through her hands and her dream had been that one day she would discover a great star. She had had hopes of seeing Lana's name in lights, to be able to say she had started her on her way, but since she had heard that Lana now saw herself as an actress rather than as a dancer she very much doubted it. There was a young girl called Priscilla Constance whom she could almost allow herself to think might, just might, make it as a dancer. But now, the one she knew without doubt would succeed was young Kitty. Odd that it should be in a field outside her own expertise but she could, in all honesty, say that it was in her home that the star had been discovered. She could just imagine herself being interviewed on *This Is Your Life* when Kitty became the subject. She knew exactly what she would wear and what she would say – she had practised it often in the bath.

She turned into Sebastopol Road, peering short-sightedly at the numbers on the doors. Sixty-four, here she was. She could hear the sound of a piano and Miriam's voice, presumably demonstrating a scale, wafting down from what she fondly called her music-room but which, in truth, was a back-bedroom with a piano in it. Camilla did not ring the bell, she did not want to disturb the class. Instead, she put her hand into the letter-box and fished about for the string with the spare key attached. That was one of the nicest things about Bracken and Miriam. 'Drop in whenever you want. Just let yourself in and help yourself,' they often said to people. And, unlike many who offered such invitations, they actually meant it. So Camilla knew, as she quietly unlocked the door, that she would not offend anyone by creeping in.

'Your turn now,' she heard Miriam order. One note on the piano was played to give a key, and Camilla stood still in the hall, literally entranced, as she heard the beautiful sound of Kitty's voice soaring with ease up a scale.

'And again,' Miriam ordered, and a higher note was plucked. The voice climbed effortlessly.

'And again.' The voice rose still higher.

'And again.' Up and up. Camilla frowned. Kitty's voice sounded harsh and strained as she forced herself to scale heights it seemed she could never reach.

'I can't do it,' Kitty gasped, her speaking voice sounding quite hoarse.

'Of course you can. Call yourself a singer!' Miriam said, most unpleasantly in Camilla's opinion. 'Remember what I said. Remember that little voice-box in there. Vibrate those cords.'

Camilla dropped her shopping bag on the floor, turned towards the stairs and mounted them quickly. She might not know much about singing but she knew a lot about muscles and the importance of easing a pupil into using parts of her body never used before. By now she was pounding up the stairs and, without stopping to knock, burst through the door.

'Stop this!' she shouted.

A surprised Miriam looked up from the keys of the upright piano. Kitty, who was standing with one hand on its top, twisted round with an equally astonished expression.

'What the hell is going on here?' Camilla demanded. 'What on earth do you think you're doing, Miriam?'

'Coaching Kitty, as requested by you and her father.'

'Ruining her, more like.'

'I beg your pardon?' Miriam hauled her large, cumbersome square frame off the piano stool. She need not have bothered, for her legs were so short that standing did not add to her dignity, if that was what she was hoping for. 'And what do you know about voice production, might I ask?'

'I know enough to know you never strain a body.'

'A body, yes,' Miriam said, as if a body was not quite nice. 'A voice is different.'

'It's no different.'

'And when did you become an expert, Camilla? Answer me that.'

'She shouldn't be straining her vocal cords, I know that. Any fool knows that. Does your throat hurt, Kitty?' Camilla asked.

'Well, yes, it does.'

'Just today?'

'No, ever since I started. It aches a bit all the time now.'

'How *could* you, Miriam? You're jealous, aren't you? Jealous of Kitty's voice. You're trying to wreck it—'

'You watch what you're saying, you jumped-up bitch. I could sue you for what you've just said . . . implying I'm no good at my job.'

'Do that, Miriam. You'd lose because it's the truth. Just because you're a failure you can't bear the thought of someone else succeeding. How many lessons have you had, Kitty?'

'This is my fifth.'

'Right, Miriam. A cheque, please, for the full amount, to be made out to Kitty's father. You've been cheating these poor innocent people.'

'I've never cheated anyone. How dare you—'

'Cheque,' ordered Camilla, holding out her hand.

Reluctantly, Miriam dragged her voluminous handbag towards her. She wrote out a cheque and with even greater reluctance handed it to Camilla, who glanced quickly at it to make sure it was in order.

'Thank you,' she said politely.

'I've never liked you, Camilla. You're the fraud around here. I bet people would like to know about your lack of qualifications,' Miriam said defiantly.

'You do that, Miriam. See if I care. This child's future is more important than you or me.' Camilla stood, her slim frame erect, her dark eyes flashing with the anger she was feeling. She might not be Spanish by birth but in situations like this she was capable of looking more Spanish than many a native. 'Come, Kitty.' She turned her back abruptly on Miriam.

Kitty wavered in the doorway, unsure if she should be thanking Miriam Headly for her lesson or not. 'Happy Christmas, Miss Headly,' she said as a compromise.

'Don't you cheek me, miss,' Miriam said angrily.

In the hallway they retrieved Camilla's shopping and, each carrying a bag, walked hurriedly through the chill early evening along the length of Sebastopol Road.

'Come back to my place. I'll mix you a soothing drink,' Camilla suggested.

'That's very kind of you.'

'The least I can do. I feel responsible. Let's just pray that no irretrievable damage has been done.'

Kitty didn't answer, simply because she wasn't quite sure what to say. She thought that Camilla was making rather a drama out of things and wished she hadn't said her throat hurt. It didn't hurt that badly. And the scales – hard at first – were getting easier.

'What did Miss Headly mean about the people being interested in you?' she asked, to get off the subject of her voice.

Camilla did not answer immediately but glanced at Kitty with a thoughtful expression as if she was making up her mind what to say. 'I'm unqualified – no one knows,' she said in a rush. 'Miriam would like to ruin me. But I'd appreciate you keeping this information to yourself.'

'Of course I will. But you're a wonderful teacher, the best. All the qualifications and diplomas in the world couldn't make you a better one.'

Camilla stopped walking and turned to Kitty. 'Do you really mean that?'

'I do. I wish you could teach voice, Miss de Souza.'

'What a lovely thing to say. That's quite made my day.' Camilla fumbled with her key, for her eyes were suddenly annoyingly filled with water – must be the cold, she told herself. 'Please call me Camilla,' she added.

Camilla made Kitty a hot toddy of whisky, honey and lemon juice and crushed an aspirin into it too. 'Sip that slowly, let it seep over those poor damaged vocal cords,' she ordered.

'I feel better already.' Kitty grinned at her after a couple of sips that made her feel warm all over.

'I feel so wretched about you, I don't know what to do.'

'It's not your fault, Camilla.'

'But it is. I know Miriam, she can be a vindictive woman – failures often are,' she said sagely.

'But surely Miriam didn't really want to ruin my voice, did she? Why?'

'Jealousy. You'd be amazed what I've seen in my time. Glue stuck in the toe of a dance-shoe before a critical *paso doble*. The heel of a shoe sawn through so that it snapped on a triple turn and the poor girl broke her ankle, which put paid to her career. Spiteful people telling others the wrong train times so they missed the signing-in time for competitions. You'd be surprised, Kitty, the lengths some people will go to to stop others succeeding. Miriam was trying to stop you becoming the star she never had the talent to become in the first place.'

'That's all a dream, Camilla.' Kitty smiled.

'Don't you knock your dreams. That's how everyone starts – with a dream, with a goal that appears unobtainable. It's up to you to achieve it, to be willing to work hard enough, to push yourself to the limits, to have the sort of ambition that will stop for nobody and nothing.'

'And luck?'

'Never rely on luck alone. No one got to the top on that particular commodity,' Camilla said firmly.

'But what do we do now? I've no teacher . . .'

Camilla lit the gas fire and sat on her haunches for a while, gazing into the blue flame.

'What can you sing?'

'Not much. "I'll Gather Lilacs", "Greensleeves" and "One Fine Day" – at least, those are the only ones I know by heart right through.'

'Perfect. Absolutely perfect. I'll slot you into my Christmas concert – the local paper always reviews it and you never know who'll be in the audience. Come here tomorrow at three-thirty and we'll run through the numbers with Mrs Flynn – I'm not sure if she's up to Puccini, mind you, but we can give it a try. Oh, Kitty, this is most exciting!'

11

There was only time, the day before the actual concert, for one full rehearsal with all the company present. It took place in a church hall. The stage was too small and so the outline of the one they would be performing on was chalked out in the body of the hall. This meant that everyone not performing had to sit on the proper stage which led to two children falling off and the irate parent of one removing her child immediately, leaving a yawning gap in the Dance of the Sugar Plum Fairies.

From this point everything went from bad to worse – wrong sequences, forgotten lines and hopeless timing. It was just as well they could only have this one rehearsal for any more would have caused Camilla to give up in despair.

The concert was to take place on Sunday, the only day the theatre was not used professionally. Because they were amateurs and the proceeds went to Guide Dogs for the

Blind, the local council granted them a licence to perform on the Sabbath.

Kitty could not sleep the night before the performance. It wasn't nervousness which kept her awake but a bubbling excitement. Several times she turned on her light to check that the clothes she had chosen were still there, as, of course, they were.

Deciding what to wear had proved a problem. She had imagined herself in sophisticated black – long and slinky with perhaps, if she asked nicely, her mother's string of artificial pearls. When she had mentioned her dream her father had immediately objected.

'You're too young for black, my pet. Don't try and grow up before your time.' He smiled gently at her.

'You haven't got anything in black, and you needn't think there's any money to buy you a dress,' her mother had responded.

'What about that lovely blue dress with the full skirt you had last summer?' her father said softly, seeing the disappointment on her face.

'But it's a summer dress,' Kitty objected, not very forcefully.

'And you look pretty as a picture in it.'

'No one would know it was a summer dress – not unless you told them. You can borrow my gold locket if you like,' Amy volunteered.

'Thank you very much.' Kitty said, hoping her surprise had not sounded too obvious.

Just before she left for the theatre her father shyly gave her a box with a cellophane lid. Nestling inside was a single cream-coloured orchid. Aware of the cost, and knowing how short money was, Kitty had to fight back her tears.

She arrived early at the theatre for she was determined not to miss anything of the day, and so had left the house before Lana's return from school for the holidays. As a child Kitty had danced in Miss Camilla's concerts which had always been at the Empire – a large, cavernous theatre, which she found daunting. Unknown to her, Camilla had fallen out with the Empire's management, hence this concert was to be in the smaller Theatre Royal. The walls of the booking hall were covered with tiled pictures – scenes from Shakespeare, Kitty thought – the women's hair flowing in long tendrils, their clothes swirling about them as if moving. She studied them intently and dawdled through to the auditorium. In the doorway she paused and sniffed the air, remembering from the past the warm, musty smell of an empty theatre and liking it.

Already stage-hands were banging together the small amount of scenery Camilla could afford. Mrs Flynn was at her piano, still in carpet-slippers, running through the music for one of the senior dancers who was to do a ballet solo. The girl looked so wan and white-faced with nerves that Kitty wondered whether she would be capable of doing anything by this evening.

'Kitty! Kitty Lawrence! Don't just stand there, make yourself useful.'

Kitty swung round to find Camilla, clipboard in hand, wearing a dyspeptic expression, beads of sweat breaking out on her brow.

'What can I do?'

'Help with the little ones in the dressing-room and then get made up – there'll be an unholy squash later.' And almost immediately Camilla was off, racing up the aisle shouting someone else's name. Kitty had never seen kind Camilla like this before and put her sharpness down to nerves.

She asked for directions. They were in the communal chorus dressing-room, large and bare, its cream paint looking as if it had been applied many years ago. Children were running excitedly about the room, the noise was like bedlam. No one seemed to be in charge. A long wooden table ran down the centre of the room. On it stood a series of mottled mirrors with a couple of naked bulbs hanging above. A harassed-looking woman – one of Camilla's helpers – was single-handedly beginning to make up the whole cast.

'Can I help?' Kitty asked the woman.

'Would you? Could you brush hair and put the bunny rabbit ears on them?'

'How do I know which are bunny rabbits?' Kitty queried, looking around the room at children of assorted sizes and ages.

'Ask,' make-up snapped.

The general level of hysteria was not helped by Camilla's constant checking forays which only seemed to fuel the general sense of madness in the room. They had been joined by the wardrobe mistress – another of Camilla's friends – who knew nothing about being a wardrobe mistress, as she was at pains to tell them at regular intervals. This was soon shown to be true when Kitty, coming across a crying five-year-old, found that not only had she got her dancing pumps on the wrong feet, she'd been dressed as a slug when she should have been a ladybird.

'Good gracious, Kitty, aren't you changed? This will never do. It's twenty minutes to curtain-up, you know. Come on now, co-operate.' An irritated Camilla swept past an indignant Kitty. The wardrobe mistress then became equally annoyed when Kitty said she couldn't help any more.

Kitty had brought her dress in a big muslin bag she had sewn the night before. Carefully she checked it for creases; it was fine. She sat down to have her face done. Camilla's friend in charge of make-up dabbled in amateur dramatics and fancied herself more talented than she really was. Kitty found the application of the heavy make-up strangely relaxing but when she looked at the finished result she wasn't too sure of the effect. Her cheeks were bright red, as were her lips, and she longed to know why she needed two red dots in the corner of her eyes but didn't like to ask.

She changed into her dress in the quietest corner she could find. She had starched it twice so that the full skirt stood out, and when she moved it swirled and gave a glimpse of the equally full petticoat underneath. The make-up woman had loaned her a blue Alice band which toned with the dress. She pinned her corsage on to the bodice, stepped back and looked at herself in the full-length mirror.

'You look sweet, my dear.' Camilla appeared behind her. 'But the black shoes are wrong . . . and that corsage . . .' Camilla tutted as she fiddled ineffectively with the orchid. 'I'll find you some ballet shoes – red, I think, with that blue – and the ballerina length is perfect . . . the flower will have to go—'

'But it's a present from my father – I can't hurt his feelings.' Kitty frowned and readjusted the corsage and, for the first time, began to feel horrid inside, as if her stomach was floating free.

'Ah! Yes! Well!' Camilla spoke in a series of exclamations and Kitty's stomach churned.

'I think I'm going to be sick,' Kitty wailed.

'What nonsense. Of course you're not,' Camilla said airily. 'Don't tell me you're having silly nerves,' she added, totally oblivious to the fact that it was her own state of virtually uncontrolled panic which was setting Kitty off. 'Carry the orchid – far better.' And from her neck she untwined a long scarlet chiffon scarf, handed it to Kitty and stepped back to study the new effect. 'Perfect,' she said with satisfaction before rushing away to sort out another problem.

The whole company waited on stage. Camilla and the older children fussed around the smaller ones, putting them in their right places. From behind the heavy curtains they could hear the noise of the audience as they settled in their seats. The orchestra struck up. It was a ragged sound, not all the instruments seemed to be in the same key, but it was the best the local grammar school could provide. From her position in the back row Kitty was thankful she was to be accompanied only by a piano.

With agonizing slowness the big red curtain parted, the conductor pointed his baton and the whole group launched haphazardly into 'California Here I Come'. Kitty had been added to this ensemble at the last minute to give it some strength, for the little ones, not knowing the words, tended to stand about with mouths open and thumbs stuck in.

At the end the applause was tumultuous – not from critical acclaim but because the audience, which barely filled half the auditorium, was made up solely of loving friends and relatives.

Kitty had to wait until midway through the second half for her spot. She felt calmer now that she had been on stage. Back in the dressing-room she took off her dress and hung it up for safety, curled up on a bench in a borrowed dressing-gown and idly began to read a copy of *True Romances* which she had found there.

The evening plodded noisily on. There were successes and there were failures – more of the latter. Half the troupe of huntsmen dancing 'Run Rabbit Run' had turned left instead of right, crashed into the other half and scattered the bunnies. Camilla did the only possible thing; she stepped on stage, apologized, asked for the audience's indulgence and suggested they start again. The cheers for this number, when it was finally completed successfully, rocked the chandelier high above the stalls. The show continued: one ballet dancer fell over; an acrobatic dancer did the splits and literally split her leotard, and the curtain had to be pulled down on her; and one dancer inadvertently hit another while saluting snappily during the 'Military Two Step'. For all that, Camilla was quite pleased with the result.

Kitty had made sure that she knew nothing of any of
these catastrophes. Quite rightly, she felt that others' mis-
fortunes might unnerve her. So when her time came and
she waited in the wings she was calm. Her stomach had
relocated itself. She found she wanted to be out there, on
stage and singing.

The curtains closed on the previous act. The grand piano
was trundled on to the stage. Mrs Flynn was standing
beside her, but transformed. She wore a long black dress
with sequined bodice and neat patent leather pumps – no
slippers.

'Good luck, my dear – not that you need it,' she
whispered to Kitty, and gave her hand a squeeze.

As arranged, Mrs Flynn swept regally on to the stage
first. The applause for her faded, and, with a gentle push
from Camilla, Kitty stepped out into the bright lights. She
stood beside the piano, one hand resting gracefully on its
polished surface, the other holding her orchid and scarf.
She bowed slightly to the audience, nodded to Mrs Flynn,
and with the spotlight on her alone, began to sing.

When she finished the first song there was a momentary
silence. Her heart plummeted – they did not like her, she
had sung badly. And then the applause began, it built up
rapidly and a wave of it rolled from the darkened auditorium and over her and she felt herself warming to it,
glowing from it.

She sang 'Greensleeves' to the same reaction. Again she
bowed but the applause continued. She bowed once more
and held up her arms as if to quieten the audience and
turned to Mrs Flynn, who with a flourish of podgy hands
began the introduction to 'One Fine Day' which was to be
Kitty's finale. Camilla waited in the wings, clutching nervously at her neck. Singing it at her little soirée had been
one thing, but here? Could Kitty do it?

She sang. The cheers that followed were as loud as if

they came from a packed theatre, not one half full. Kitty stood beaming from ear to ear, bowed, and not knowing what else to do ran to the wings.

'They want an encore, go back,' Camilla hissed.

'I don't know anything else.'

'Then sing the aria again.' Once again Camilla pushed her and back she went, and they cheered louder as they realized she was to give them more. Kitty whispered to Mrs Flynn and launched herself once more into the Puccini. But this time it was different. This time she sang with all the emotion in her body for she was thanking them. When they had cheered her she had felt they loved her. This time when she finished tears were cascading down her cheeks.

There was only one act to follow – the Dance of the Sugar Plum Fairies. Then one by one all the acts returned for their final curtain call. Camilla caught hold of Kitty's hand.

'You go on last,' she ordered.

'Me? But you said . . .' Kitty hesitated.

'No. You were the star, you go last.'

And she did, and they stood and cheered, and Kitty felt she had never known such happiness. And then the whole company began to sing 'There's No Business Like Show Business', and it was Kitty who was leading them.

Backstage everyone was congratulating everyone else. The chaos was even worse now as most of the audience was pressing backstage to find their particular child. Kitty looked about desperately for her mother and father.

It was a pleasant experience to have total strangers approach her to congratulate her, to tell her how good she was. Then she finally saw her father standing to one side, a proud smile on his face. She pushed through the crowds to get to him.

'How was I, Dad?'

'I've never felt so proud in my whole life,' he said, beaming at her.

'Honest?' She would have liked to ask if he had felt prouder than when he watched Lana dance and sing, but she didn't. 'Where's Mum?' she asked instead, looking around her.

'She was heartbroken, Kitty.'

'She didn't come?'

'No, love. It was Lana. She came home, not well at all. Had to be put straight to bed.'

'Oh, I see.' Kitty turned away so that he could not see her disappointed expression. 'Still, you were here.' She smiled at him brightly, a shade too brightly, he thought.

'Shame it's a Sunday or we could have stopped off for some fish and chips. Never mind, another day.'

'Yes, I'll just get my things.' She turned away. A minute ago she had felt she was flying. In the dressing-room a party was already underway. Quietly she picked up her bags. She was no longer in the mood to celebrate.

12

'You know Mum. She said I had a fever and to go to bed, so here I am.'

'You don't look ill.' Kitty was sitting on Lana's bed, both were sipping hot chocolate.

'Dad says you were marvellous.'

'Oh, you know Dad.' Kitty grinned.

'Don't get too good, will you? One star in the family will be quite enough.' Lana said this smiling her beautiful smile so that it would have been impossible to do anything but agree. 'How's old de Souza?'

'She's fine. She's always asking after you.'

'That's nice. She's a good teacher, I've come to realize. Far better than we ever gave her credit for.'

'Dad wouldn't have agreed with you tonight. He said half the concert was chaos.'

'Oh, those concerts. They always were, don't you remember? But then she's not a director, is she? She's a teacher. She fires one up. That's what a teacher should do – just like Portman and Portia do.'

'Still loving it there?'

'Absolutely.'

'You seem different again. You always seem to have changed when you come home.'

'Me? How?'

'I don't know, more assured somehow. More grown up.'

'It comes to us all,' Lana said dramatically, and then laughed.

'No stage work yet?'

'No. We don't bother much now with auditions. I don't want to play child parts and yet I always seem too young for anything else. At least I grew an inch last year – I'm five two now, you know.'

'I doubt if you'll grow much more now,' Kitty said pragmatically.

'Oh, I know. But I'm not bothered. Look, don't tell *anyone*, will you? No one knows this. Not even Portia. But Portman is writing a play for me. I shall arrive with a bang. An immediate star.'

'Isn't that a bit unrealistic? Everyone has to start at the bottom.'

'Not necessarily. Not with the right vehicle. And Portman will write the most divine one for me – he knows me so well, loves me. It can't help but be a success.'

'I see.' Kitty looked about the newly decorated room, all modern lines and primary colours, and wondered if she hadn't preferred the pink and frilly room after all.

'I'm sorry I missed you tonight,' Lana said, suddenly quiet.

'Me too.'

'I'm not that ill. Just a bit of a snuffle really.'

'I realize.'

'She didn't want to go.'

'I thought as much.'

'You don't mind?'

'Mind? Not a lot . . .' Kitty looked away and wondered why Lana had mentioned it. What was the point? And if she hadn't been ill, why had she not insisted on going to the concert herself?

Kitty's elation returned over the next couple of days. The review in the local paper had singled her out for special praise. Camilla had come round personally to say that a friend in the audience had been so impressed that he felt sure Kitty would be able to get a place in college to study singing. And, best of all, her father had taken her to one side to tell her that no matter what it cost, to college she should go.

They were writing Christmas cards on the kitchen table. Amy was making mince pies. That intangible excitement of Christmas, which they had all been convinced had passed them by this year, had finally arrived. Amy had poured them all a sherry which had made both girls quite giggly.

Mike had come home from work early. He stood in the kitchen door looking at the scene – all three of them laughing and happy together as it should always have been.

'You're early.' Amy looked up from the pastry board.

'You all right, Dad? You look all in,' Kitty asked anxiously.

'Cup of tea would go down a treat.'

'You go and sit by the fire, Dad. I'll get it.' Kitty jumped up to put the kettle on.

Ten minutes later she took it through to the sitting-room. Her father was sitting in his favourite chair, his head back. He looked grey.

'Dad, are you ill? You don't look at all well,' she asked, with mounting anxiety.

The doorbell rang. She turned to answer it.

'Who could that be?' she asked, for people rarely came to the house.

'Kitty, I love you, you know. More than you'll ever realize,' Mike said, grabbing at her hand.

'That's nice, Dad. I love you too.'

The bell chimed again.

'You going to answer that or what, Kitty?' she heard her mother call from the kitchen.

'I'm going,' she called.

Two men stood on the doorstep.

'Mr Lawrence. Mr Mike Lawrence, is he in?'

'Why, yes. Come in.' She closed the door and ushered them towards the sitting-room.

'Dad,' she said, 'two gentlemen to see you. Would you like some tea?' she asked politely.

'That won't be necessary, miss,' the taller of the two replied.

'Who was it?' Amy asked as Kitty returned to the kitchen.

'Two blokes for Dad.'

'What they want?'

'I don't know, they didn't say.'

'Didn't you ask?'

'No, I didn't like to.'

'Big help you are,' said Amy, as she put another batch of mince pies into the oven.

For twenty minutes they continued writing their cards

and Amy did her baking. They could hear the rumble of the men's voices from the other room and frequent long silences. Finally the door opened and Mike appeared. He crossed to the kitchen while the two men stood in the hall.

'Look, girls, I've got to go out,' he said, faltering over the words.

'Go out? Where to?' Amy said sharply.

'I'll get it sorted.'

'Get what sorted?'

'Amy, please,' Mike said. 'Just let me go.'

The way he spoke frightened Amy.

'Who are you?' she said to the men in the hall, her anxiety making her voice shrill.

'We're police officers, ma'am.'

'Police officers? Here? Why?' Amy sat down with a thump on the kitchen chair.

'Officer, could I? Just five minutes,' Mike said in a pleading voice.

'All right, sir. But no longer.'

Mike closed the door and advanced towards the table, three pairs of eyes watching him anxiously.

'It's like this. I've been found out. They've come to arrest me.'

'Arrest you? What for? I don't understand,' Amy said, waving her hand in front of her eyes as if there were cobwebs to be brushed aside.

'For embezzlement.'

'Oh, Dad.' Kitty was on her feet, her hand held out to him, but he seemed not to be aware it was there.

'I did it for all of you. It would have been all right, I know it would have, but with Christmas coming I got careless and they did a spot-check audit at the shop last week. That's why.' He stood, his shoulders sagging, and Kitty saw her father age before her eyes.

'You mean you've been nicking from the Co-op?' Amy said nastily.

'Yes.'

'How much? How long?'

'For too long.'

'Can we pay it back?'

Mike laughed hastily. 'No. There's been too much.'

'But what for, for Christ's sake?' Amy demanded.

'What for? You mean you don't realize? For everything. For all your schemes, your new furniture, for the girls.' Mike too was shouting and shaking as if something in him had snapped.

'My fees?' Lana spoke for the first time.

'Yes, your fees. How else could I have afforded it all?'

'You mean I can't go back to school?' Lana's voice was rising dangerously.

'No, Lana. I'm sorry,' Mike said dejectedly.

'I hate you,' Lana shouted. 'How could you? You bloody old fool!'

'How could you allow yourself to get caught? You were never any good for anything.' His wife looked at him with loathing as she put her arms round her younger daughter's heaving shoulders.

The door opened.

'Time's up, mate,' one of the policemen said apologetically.

'Yes, officer, thanks.' He looked about his kitchen and at his family, bewilderment in his eyes.

'Oh, Daddy. Not my daddy!' Kitty sprang to his side and clung to him. One of the men gently prised her away. 'Oh, Dad. I love you. I love you,' she called. Blinded by tears, she could barely make out his figure as the two officers led him away. As the front door slammed shut, Kitty broke down.

'Oh, look what the stupid bastard's made me do! I've burned my mince pies.'

Kitty looked at her mother with disbelief and raced for the safety of her room.

INTERMISSION

Some nights Kitty had a dream. Always the same dream, and it frightened her. Why did it keep occurring? What was its significance?

She was standing in a large black void. If she looked up, to left and right of her, there were great swags of ruched red velvet which she feared were about to suffocate her. A great noise began and she felt it hit her with physical force, making her step back. A noise like the sea makes on a shingle beach but louder, much louder. And then Mike appeared beside her and handed her a bunch of dahlias, but as she looked at them the flowers shrivelled and blackened in her hands. She glanced anxiously up at her father, knowing he would explain. But when she looked it was his face there, it was still him, except that it was black and distorted, eyes bulging.

Then she would scream.

Then she would wake up, sweating and shaking and full of foreboding.

ACT TWO

1965–1970

1

Kitty did not enjoy visiting her father in prison, but for two years now, whenever she could get away, she had forced herself to take the bus to Maidstone. Despite not wanting to go, she missed Mike and needed to see him. The old buildings, with their echoing corridors and clanging doors, stank of humanity. No amount of disinfectant could remove it, only adding yet another unpleasant layer on top of the cooking smells which reached into the furthest corners of the prison. Father and daughter would sit opposite each other at a small wooden table in a large bare room with barred windows, surrounded by the noise of a hundred others, and would make polite small-talk as if nothing was more normal than to be meeting like this. Yet Kitty only had to look into Mike's eyes to see the pain his incarceration caused him, to note the nervous way he moved his head, glancing over his shoulder, to realize the fear he lived under.

She longed to be able to ask him to tell her everything, to unburden himself, to say that she could and would share his pain and humiliation. Instead, they talked of his dahlias which Kitty now tended as best she could and which were a sorry sight compared with the way they had once looked. But she lied and said they were a picture. She told him about the new kitchen sink and her job in the local department store – but never spoke of Amy nor of her own lost dreams.

The visits so depressed her that after one of them she had got off the bus at the zoo, just outside Maidstone, thinking that to break her journey with something interesting might help. As she walked up the long tree-lined approach to the zoo gates she could feel her spirits lifting. But once inside and standing looking at the caged animals, she saw in their eyes the same expression of degradation she had seen in her father's. She turned on her heel and ran from the place, and never went back.

She knew she should want to visit Mike as often as the authorities allowed, but secretly she was relieved she could not – it was a great excuse not being able to get time off work as frequently as her father would wish. As it was, those Wednesdays she did go had needed long and hard negotiation with the head of her department to let her off an hour early to catch the bus. Wednesday was early closing; if they moved his visiting day – as she knew they could at a moment's notice – then she wouldn't be able to go at all, and she was deeply ashamed at how she longed for that to happen. Kitty felt confused that she could think like this, and yet need to see him. But she had to go, no one else did.

After her father's trial the changes at home had been many and rapid.

Kitty had left school with no regrets – she could not have faced the taunts of the other girls that her father was not only a thief but a jailbird as well. She had gone to see Mr Davenport who owned the local department store that bore his family's name. She knew that he had known and liked her father, and hoping that that liking was sufficient for him to trust Mike's daughter, she asked him for a job. A kindly man, he took her on. He could not save her from the whispering and sly taunts of the other assistants, all of whom had followed the trial avidly in the local paper, but she did not know them like her school-fellows, and so could pretend to herself that what they thought of her did not matter.

She was sent to haberdashery, which was the least popular department, but she did not mind. The endless counting of buttons and measuring of elastic and ribbon, the constant tidying which a well-stocked department required was soothing in the way it kept her busy. She knew that had she been sent to fashion or furnishings there might have been long stretches of the day when she would have had time to think or daydream, neither of which she wanted or could afford to do.

Kitty knew that if she allowed herself to dwell on what might have been then she could become bitter, and she didn't want that to happen to her. To keep her mind occupied after work she had joined an evening class and was learning Italian, the better to enjoy the small collection of opera recordings – predominantly those by Maria Callas – she was slowly buying.

Camilla had suggested to her several times that she audition for the local operatic society, but each time Kitty had refused.

'But to have such a voice and not *use* it,' Camilla had fretted.

'It wouldn't be enough,' Kitty had said simply. If she couldn't sing with the best she didn't want to, she had decided one day. She did not know where such a notion had come from and she laughed at its arrogance, especially coming from one who had sung in public just once, but that was how it was. She had not given up hope – she wasn't like that – she had simply filed the idea of being a singer away in her mind until there was some point in thinking about it again.

Amy had gone back to hairdressing, working in a small salon further up the High Street from Davenport's. Not that Kitty saw much of her mother, only on Friday, pay day, when she went to Liptons with her to help carry the shopping home. Oddly enough she got on better with her mother than before, for Amy was different now. Kitty had to admit her mother was happier without her husband. She whined and nagged less, she wasn't so house-proud, surprisingly she wasn't even bitter. In a strange way it was as if she had erased Mike's existence from her life. She never mentioned him, never asked Kitty how he was after one of her visits. Even his photographs had been removed, all except the one in Kitty's room, but since Amy never went in there Kitty supposed that one did not count.

Lana had recovered quickly from her initial anger and disappointment at not returning to her school. Portman wrote to her regularly and she replied occasionally. At first she missed him and longed for him, but with new interests and a boy of her own age she had met, it soon passed. It was not in Lana's nature to be downhearted for long.

Lana did not work at a regular job as her mother and sister did, but she had managed to get a fair amount of photographic modelling work, mainly for knitting patterns. She had had two jobs demonstrating – one a new lemon-squeezer in Davenport's kitchen department, but she had been so hamfisted that the manager had asked the manufacturer to replace her. She had had more success at the Ideal Home Exhibition with a hand-cream promotion, but her dream was to be called for the Earl's Court Motor Show. She had been in the chorus of the local pantomime at the Empire and Amy had spent all her wages going to see her girl every evening.

Lana was still taking lessons, paid for somehow by Amy, at Miss de Souza's. One thing about Amy had not changed – her ambitions for her younger daughter.

Kitty had a friend now – a best friend, that elusive creature whom she had missed having at school. Jenny Sale was the same age as her – eighteen. She worked in the shoe department at Davenport's. She was plump, untidy and fun, with a loud, outgoing personality in total contrast to Kitty's quiet privateness. They complemented each other well.

Jenny wanted to go to London to work and was constantly trying to persuade Kitty to go with her. For all her
confidence, she did not have quite enough courage to take
such a step on her own. Kitty would have loved to agree to
go but she could not, it would make visiting her father even
more difficult. She tried to explain her reluctance without
actually using the words, for she hated to say 'prison' or
'prisoner' to anyone. Jenny did not understand – she must
have been the only employee in Davenport's who did not
know about Kitty's father.

'I can't go, Jenny, even though I'd love to.'

'But why not? You told me you don't give a fig for your
mum.'

'It's not that. It's something else.'

'What then? A feller?'

'Don't be silly . . . It's my father, he's away, you see,
and I have to visit him.'

'What, in a hospital?'

'No . . . in . . . in a . . . prison.' She looked away from
her friend's big brown trusting eyes.

'Oh, why didn't you tell me? You poor love. How awful
for you.' And as Jenny hugged her close to her ample breast
Kitty knew that she had found a true friend.

The biggest change of all had occurred eighteen months
into Mike's sentence with the arrival of Cyril Robinson in
their lives. Amy had taken to going out on a Saturday with
Molly, her friend from work, and met Cyril at a dance at
the Pavilion, off the High Street.

For a month Cyril had wined and dined Amy in a way
she was not used to but to which she soon became addicted.
He had a large mauve American car with an eight-track
stereo system and quadrophonic speakers which was so
new that no one of Amy's acquaintance had seen or heard
its like before. He sported American suits and ties; his

greatest disappointment was that he hadn't been born American.

After that first month of intense courting he had moved into Number Fourteen. He drove up with the spacious boot and back seat of his car piled high with matching yellow and black tartan luggage – from the States, naturally. He blasted his horn – more klaxon than hooter – and Amy rushed out of the house, made-up and in high heels at ten in the morning, and flung herself into his arms. He lifted her up and twirled her around and Kitty, watching from her upstairs window, saw for the first time how pretty her mother had once been, and could be again.

Along the Avenue pristine curtains twitched as many pairs of eyes registered what was happening. Great was the gossip behind panelled front doors and over suppers that night. Kitty felt mortified, Lana thought it a great excitement, and Amy declared she didn't give a damn what the neighbours said. She'd shocked them enough already with a jailbird for a husband, so no doubt this latest event would come as no surprise, she'd said with a hard laugh.

It was strange to have a man in the house again, and room had to be made on the bathroom shelf for his shaving paraphernalia and his after-shaves and deodorants – something else new to wonder at. Kitty had no idea such products for men existed, but Lana was more knowledgeable and told her how Portman had used French ones.

It was also awkward to have a man in the house again. With just the three women it didn't matter if one of them went to the bathroom half-naked, but it did now, at least for Kitty who always made sure her dressing-gown was tightly buttoned and belted. Lana felt no need to make such concessions.

Kitty did not take to Cyril. Both Amy and Lana found him handsome but Kitty could not see what they saw in him. He was too thin for his six-foot height and his skin was pockmarked from adolescent acne. She supposed he had nice eyes, and certainly any girl would love to have such long lashes. He had a generous mouth but his teeth were discoloured. He was growing his dullish blond hair to shoulder length and Kitty felt it might have looked better for more frequent washing. He was six years Amy's junior, though with Amy looking young for her years it would have been difficult to tell. He was pleasant enough, always in a good humour, and he made Amy laugh. He evidently helped out financially, for roast beef appeared again on Sundays, there were chocolate biscuits in the barrel, and a bowl of fruit stood on the sideboard. And Amy always had a bottle of Drambuie for a night-time tipple.

Kitty analysed her feelings and concluded she resented him for taking her father's place. It wasn't Cyril as a person she disliked but his position in the household. She hated the noises that came from her mother's bedroom at night. She covered her head with her pillow to try to shut out the rhythmic banging of the bed, the sighing and the moaning that seemed to go on for ever. She felt herself consumed with jealousy but she knew it was her father's jealousy she was feeling.

Cyril bought them presents by the score, pretty scarves, pieces of jewellery, scent. Kitty always accepted them, not quite having the courage to refuse, but she put them away in a drawer and never used them, for to do so would have been a betrayal of Mike. When she went to visit her father she never told him about Cyril.

2

Cyril had so many contacts, and a finger in so many pies, that he always had trouble saying what it was he did. He sold second-hand cars, he dabbled in government surplus, he owned a house he had turned into bedsits.

'Call me an entrepreneur,' he said.

'He's a handy guy to know,' Amy would say to her friends, unaware that she had began to pick up the slight American accent that Cyril had taken care to cultivate. 'Anything you want, my Cyril can get you.'

Once Amy had confided her hopes and dreams for Lana to him, it was no time before he was making many telephone calls on her behalf – he'd had a line put into Number Fourteen, much to Amy's pride. The telephone calls worked, for Cyril knew a bloke who knew a bloke – he always did.

'Fancy singing at a hotel, doll?' he asked Lana over supper one night.

'You bet. When? Where?'

'Just outside town – Saturday. I've got you a spot singing with the band – two songs first, see how you go.'

'With a band?' Lana's face glowed.

'Just one thing, doll. Say you're eighteen, there's my angel.'

'I'll say anything. Do anything. Oh, Cyril, bless you.' She leaped up from the table, ran round to his chair and flung her arms about him, hugging him tight.

'Hang on there. Don't want to make your mum jealous, do we?' He carefully rearranged his hair which Lana had ruffled in her enthusiasm.

'You do say some things, Cyril.' Amy grinned across at him. 'But thank you, my darling. I won't forget this in a hurry.'

'No trouble. My pleasure.'

'What shall I wear?' Amy asked.

'Quite honestly, Amy, I don't think it's a good idea if you come,' Cyril said seriously.

'Oh no? Why not? Kitty and I should be there to support our Lana. What you say, Kitty?'

Kitty managed to say nothing, mumbling a response which could be taken either way. She was certain her mother could not care less if she went or not. She was right, for the mumble was not queried.

'At Lana's first real professional spot she doesn't need the worry of family and friends out front. She'll be better on her own – I'll be there to keep an eye on her.'

'But I'm always there, no matter what it is she does . . . she needs me . . .' Amy whined, for the first time since Cyril's arrival. 'What do you say, Lana? You'll want your mum there now, won't you?'

'I think Cyril's right, Mum. You'd be so nervous for me and it might get at me – you know. This won't be like de Souza's shows – this'll be real.' Lana smiled her most brilliant smile at her mother, which for once didn't work.

'I think it's bloody mean. After all I've done for you,' Amy said sulkily.

'Please, Mum, don't make it difficult for me. I have to listen to Cyril's advice.'

'Tell you what, doll. I'll record it for you. It'll be an historic night, we should have it on tape.'

'We haven't got a tape-recorder.'

'Haven't we?' Cyril winked at Lana. 'You just wait there.' He left the room, they heard the front door open, and then he returned carrying a large, heavy box. 'Got no tape-recorder? What's this, then?' he said as he slit open the box.

'Oh, Cyril. How marvellous.' Amy was clapping her hands with excitement as Cyril set up the huge tape-recorder, putting the large wheel of tape on one side and threading it through to the other. 'Can we try it out?' She had apparently forgotten her original disappointment.

Cyril put the microphone in its socket and then plugged the machine in. Amy and Lana leaned forward eagerly.

'Testing, testing. Mary had a little lamb,' Cyril said self-importantly. Dials flickered as the large spool of tape slowly wound. He rewound it and they heard him. 'Testing, testing . . .'

'Isn't that marvellous? Is it difficult to use, Cyril? I mean, could I manage it?' Amy asked.

''Course you could – easy as pie, it is. Just make sure the tape is threaded correctly and that you've plugged it into the electricity.' They all laughed. 'Come on then, Lana. Give us a song.'

'I couldn't,' Lana said, suddenly blushing, which surprised Kitty who had never seen her blush before.

'You're going to have to be better than this on Saturday otherwise they'll want their money back damn fast.'

'They're going to pay me?' Lana said with genuine surprise.

''Course they are, doll. You don't do nothing for nothing in this life, that's for sure.'

'How much?'

'Less expenses there should be a fiver in it for you.'

'Five pounds!' Lana squealed with excitement.

'And if I'm right there'll be plenty more dosh where that came from.'

'Oh, Cyril, what a wonder you are – we've been trying for years to get somewhere, haven't we, Lana?'

'I always wanted to be an actress more.'

'You stick to singing, my girl – there's a lot more money to be made from that lark, I can tell you. Look at that Cilla girl . . .'

'But I don't know what to sing.'

'Give us a tune, anything.'

'Well, switch it on, Cyril,' Amy ordered.

'It is on, doll.' Cyril grinned.

'Oh Lor', no! You mean that thing's been taking down what we've been saying?'

'Word for word.'

'Gracious.' And for some reason Amy patted her hair and sat up straight in her chair.

'I'll sing "Too Young".'

'All right, then. Just trill a bit – let's get the levels right.'

Lana sang in her clear pretty voice; it was a good choice of song for it suited her blonde, blue-eyed, innocent-expressioned youthfulness. Cyril thought she would go down a wow with the rather jaded clients of The Laughing River Roadhouse – well, certainly with the male clients. He did not want Amy to know where they were going and so had lied and said it was an hotel – more respectable-sounding.

'Rewind it, Cyril. Let's hear it.'

Cyril rewound the tape to the very beginning and Amy screamed when she heard herself.

'That's not me!' she shrieked.

'It damn well is.' Cyril laughed at her discomfort.

Finally they reached Lana's singing.

Amy wiped a tear from her eye.

'Lana, you're wonderful,' she sighed when it had finished.

'It's not too bad, is it? I've heard myself before, of course – Portman's got a recorder but it's smaller than this, his is Japanese.'

'This is for real professionals. Better repro,' Cyril said, a shade huffily, Kitty thought.

'What about you, Kitty? Your mum tells me you sing too.'

'Oh, I don't know . . .' Kitty said modestly but she was longing to try. How wonderful it would be to hear how she sounded.

'We don't want her caterwauling – horrible noise it is.' Amy laughed.

'That's not very kind, Amy. What a thing to say to your own daughter.'

'It's true, though. Kitty doesn't mind me saying so, do you, Kitty? She's used to her mum. You either like the stuff she sings or hate it. Me? I'm the latter.'

'Don't take any notice of your old sourpuss of a mum, Kitty. Give us a warble.' Cyril pushed Amy in a gentle, familiar way which made her laugh and not mind being called names.

'I don't think so,' Kitty said quietly, all longing to sing having passed.

'Suit yourself.' Cyril shrugged and turned his attention back to Lana. 'Now, girl. What shall we do for your second song? And you should have something in reserve for an encore.'

'How about "I Remember You"?'

'Right on. Anything sloppy will go down a bomb, I can guarantee.'

Kitty left the three of them planning Lana's Saturday night performance. Frequently now she felt in the way, as if the three of them were a unit and had no need of her.

When the Saturday came Lana was sick with nervous excitement. She could not stop being sick; by late afternoon she looked wan.

'I can't do it,' she said to her mother, her face beaded with sweat from the last vomiting attack.

'Yes, you can. You're always like this, don't you remember Miss de Souza's concerts? You'd heave all day before one of those. Now, sit still, let me finish brushing this hair out.'

Lana called Portman long-distance, something she hadn't thought of doing since the telephone was put in.

The line was bad and she had to shout, which was unfortunate since she didn't want Cyril or her mother to overhear. She managed to make Portman understand what she was doing.

'Lana, I'm disappointed . . .' she heard him say clearly and then the line crackled and she thought she heard him say, '. . . you were born to act . . .' but she couldn't be sure. And when she replaced the receiver she wasn't sure if talking to him had made her feel better or not.

Then came the excitement of putting on the new dress her mother had bought her – short, red and shiny. It was so short that in the car she felt vulnerable because she couldn't cover her knees.

'Don't worry about that, doll. With pins like yours, flash 'em.' Cyril laughed and placed his hand on her knee. He took a long time removing it.

The Roadhouse had seen better days, and Cyril had not wanted Amy to come because it had a somewhat unsavoury reputation. The grounds, once its pride and joy, were a tangle of overgrown shrubs and undercut grass. The lake for which it had been famous for boating parties and midnight swims was weed-choked. The building was wooden, in need of paint, the garishly coloured light bulbs slung in line with the eaves were chipped, and there were gaps where bulbs had broken.

Inside wasn't much better, with the worn carpet and musty, under-aired smell of stale tobacco smoke and beer. It was sufficiently far out of town for the police to ignore it, especially since the day in the 1950s when a policeman had been shot in the grounds. Lancelot Friend, the proprietor, had a nonchalant attitude towards licensing laws and soliciting. Most of his clients drove down from London – less than an hour away – since it was well known that The Laughing River had bedrooms available and women to go with them. And it was a handy place to plan villainy away from prying eyes.

Lancelot eyed Lana up and down appreciatively.

'Right little corker, your niece, Cyril.' He winked at Lana who, not sure what to say, decided to say nothing and certainly not that she wasn't Cyril's niece.

'Do you want her to do a run-through?' Cyril asked.

'I don't think that'll be necessary, looking like that it won't matter if she sings as flat as a pancake.' Lancelot smiled but it emerged more as a leer.

Lana began to wish her mother was with her. But then, looking about her, she was glad she wasn't. Cyril had said she was to sing at an hotel, this was a horrible place, she knew her mother would be as disappointed as she was at the reality.

'It's a start, doll,' Cyril said as if reading her mind and, taking her hand, led her to the dressing-room.

'At least there's a star on the door.' She smiled.

'Atta girl . . . You powder your nose. I'll come and collect you in good time for your stint. Hello, fellows,' Cyril said to the band, who were emerging from the dressing-room next door, 'I've sheet-music if you need it for my little canary here.'

Lana was pretty certain that the band – a drummer, saxophonist, pianist and acoustic guitarist – were drunk, the drummer worst of all. They leered at her too, which made her feel apprehensive about the ordeal to follow, and said they knew her songs by heart and not to bother with the music.

The floor-show would not start until ten. Lana was to be on first, followed by a comedian, and then the act the clients had come to see, a stripper, Fifi La Marr.

Fifi joined Lana in the dressing-room. She was dressed in jeans and a sweater, her hair in a pony-tail. She wore no make-up and looked dowdy and all of her forty years.

She heaved a large make-up case on to the dressing-table.

'You look a bit pale, love.'

'I've been sick all day.'

'First gig?'

'Yes.'

'Then have a swig of this.' She handed Lana a bottle of brandy. Tentatively Lana took a sip. 'Tip it back, sweet-heart, you'll need more than that to settle your tum.' Efficiently she began to unpack her make-up on to the dressing-table, having first wiped it down with a damp cloth.

'I've told Lancelot I don't know how many times to clean this place up, he never listens.' From the bottom of the capacious bag she took a bunch of artificial flowers in a small vase, which she plonked down. 'There, that cheers the dump up a bit, don't it? How old are you, love?' she said suddenly, swinging round to face Lana.

'Eighteen.' Lana stuttered as she lied.

'Oh yes?' Fifi cocked a cynical eyebrow.

'Honest.' Lana blushed.

'Don't bother about me, love. I won't tell a soul. What are you, fifteen?'

'Sixteen,' Lana whispered, fearing they might be overheard.

'Well, take my advice. Don't let Lancelot persuade you to do anything but sing.'

'Like what?'

'Like sleep with the blokes.'

'You're joking!'

'Wish I was. This joint's one step from a knocking-shop. You shouldn't be here. Have you got an agent?'

'No. Just Cyril – he's my mother's boyfriend.'

Fifi dived back into her bag and brought out a card. 'An amateur? Never works. Take this. Give him a ring, Des-mond Frances – he's straight, which is rare in this racket, and he'll get you better bookings than this with your looks.'

'Why, thanks.' Lana slipped the card into her own handbag.

'Feeling better?' Fifi patted her stomach.

'Much, thanks.'

Lana then spent a fascinating half-hour as she watched Fifi apply her make-up, don her wig, and change from a dowdy, nearly middle-aged woman into one who, at a reasonably short distance, could pass for glamorous.

'You ready, doll?' It was Cyril who, without knocking, had put his head round the door. He nodded and smiled at Fifi who did not return the smile but looked him up and down coldly.

'Good luck, kid.' She beamed at Lana.

The stage of The Laughing River Roadhouse was small but reasonably well lit. In front of it was a minute maplewood dance-floor over which hung a large revolving mirrored sphere that sent shards of light like silver confetti down on the dancers. The music was coming to an end. Lancelot leaped on to the stage.

'Ladies and gentlemen, you're in for a treat tonight. It's not many can say they were there when a star was born.' There was no reaction to this spiel for the clients were talking amongst themselves as they made their way back to their tables which were arranged, each with a small, redshaded light, around the rest of the room. They continued to talk as Lancelot called out, 'Lana Lawrence!' and the drummer gave a roll. There was a scattering of applause as Lana stepped into the spotlight and up to the microphone. The band, despite their condition, went into the intro competently enough, as if playing on autopilot. As Lana began to sing, a clatter of knives and forks was added to the talking as the audience tucked into their steak sandwiches and chicken in a basket.

Lana looked about her as her sweet, clear tones rang out, but no one appeared to be listening to her. She turned to look at the band but they didn't seem to be listening either. She felt the sickness returning, she feared she was about to retch. She stopped singing. The band, at first unaware that she had, continued blithely. Then one musician noticed and stopped, then another, until even the drummer, tapping away in a world of his own, realized he was playing alone.

Cyril was standing next to Lancelot at the bar at the back of the room. His heart sank, the glass of rum and Coke in his hand shook.

'God save me from amateurs,' Lancelot said with feeling, rolling his eyes heavenward. 'Double Scotch, beer-chaser, Sue,' he said to the tired and overworked barmaid who was also his girlfriend – when he remembered.

Lana stared at the audience who had finally realized there was silence from the stage. 'Thank you,' she said, smiling brilliantly, turning from left to right so that everyone was included in the smile. 'I was just thinking, if I can bother to come out here to this dump to sing, I wonder if you could bother to listen to me?' Again the smile flashed, beautiful, all-encompassing.

The audience sat stunned for a second.

'Cheeky cow!' a man at the back shouted.

'Give her a break!' shouted another.

Then several clapped and some laughed and one or two cheered her. But finally they settled down and dutifully sat silent.

'Well, let's hear you then!' called two men in unison.

'Bugger me!' Lancelot said, wiping the sweat from his brow with a red spotted handkerchief.

'I told you she was something else,' Cyril said, feeling his knees weak but smiling with a confidence which had been sadly lacking a minute before.

Twenty minutes later the place was in uproar as Lana took her bow. It wasn't what she sang, or that her voice was beautiful – it wasn't. They applauded and stamped for more because she had given it everything she had got. She had belted out her numbers – gone was the sweet, tinkling voice to be replaced by one with a raucous edge but far more emotion. Still they shouted for more but Lana had left the stage.

'Bugger me,' it was Cyril's turn to say. He turned to Lancelot. 'See.' He grinned and held out his hand.

'Let her give 'em one more.'

'Not likely, leave them panting for more, that's my motto.'

'How much did we say? Ten?' Lancelot was fishing in his breast-pocket for his wallet.

'Sod off. Fifteen we agreed and twenty if you take her back next Saturday.'

'You're on.'

'But not for twenty, Lancelot my old friend, we're not turning out for less than thirty.'

'Don't be greedy, Cyril. It don't suit you.'

'Me greedy? That'll be the day.' Cyril laughed. 'No, it's for the little girl.'

'Humph.' Lancelot did not sound convinced. He looked at his for once happy audience. 'Agreed, but a full thirty minutes and one encore,' he said, as the comedian bounded on to the stage to a wall of boos and catcalls.

Backstage Lana was shaking. It was not with cold, nor fear.

'That's elation, love. You did really well. You could have knocked me over when that big voice came out of a little thing like you. That's a good gimmick. I hope your mother's boyfriend realizes,' Fifi said.

'Thanks,' Lana said, gratefully accepting the bottle of brandy as the door burst open and Cyril rushed in, lifted her up and swung her round at great risk to everything in the small, cluttered dressing-room.

'You were a star, doll!' he shouted triumphantly. 'You didn't tell me you could sing like that. Christ, I was sideswiped.'

'I only do that for my friends. Mum likes me to sound like Julie Andrews.' Lana laughed.

'Then don't listen to your mum, for Christ's sake.' Cyril was laughing with excitement.

'She needs careful management,' Fifi said, looking at Cyril long and hard as if trying to remember if she knew him from somewhere.

'She's got that – in spades. Nothing beats family. Come on, doll.'

'But I wanted to watch Fifi.'

'No. We've got to get on home.'

'Did you tape it?'

'Yes. It's all in the bag.'

'Bye, Fifi, see you again I hope.' Lana waved goodbye.

'Yeah, see you around I expect,' Fifi said, but as the door closed, she was shaking her head with concern – she'd seen it all before.

Outside in the car-park they climbed into Cyril's car.

'Me purple passion wagon,' he said, still laughing.

'Why couldn't I have watched Fifi?' Lana asked, settling back into the soft leather upholstery.

'Lana, her act's disgusting, that's why. And you're too young to see the likes of it. By the way – here you are. Your earnings.' He handed a note to Lana.

'Five quid for less than half an hour – I can't believe it.'

'And the same again next week, doll. I tell you, you're going to be in the money. There's just one thing, honey. Best not tell your mum we were here – I don't think she'd approve. Best say we were at The Clarence – keep her sweet.' Lana happily agreed – she liked secrets, especially from her mother, it made her feel quite grown up. He put the car into gear and they pulled out into the road.

Ten minutes later Cyril swung the car off the road and up a dirt-track into a wood.

'Where we going?' Lana asked.

'You'll see,' Cyril said as he gently eased the big car along the track and into a clearing. 'I just thought you might like to say a proper thank-you to Uncle Cyril.' He grinned at her.

'What can you mean?' Lana said archly but with a sinking heart. She knew exactly what he meant.

'Something like this.' His hand was on her thigh and sliding up beneath the short, short skirt. 'Now you know what I mean.' His fingers were under her panties and he was kneading her gently.

She felt nothing, but she knew how to pretend and it was better if she did, he'd been good to her, she didn't want to hurt his feelings. She wanted to sing again.

'Well, here's a wet little pussy.'

'Is it?'

'Let's get it wetter, shall we?'

3

Cyril was no fool. He was aware that he was out of his depth with Lana. When he had first heard her sing he had thought her sweet voice was more suited to church halls and village concerts. But, given her looks, he felt he might be able to get her the odd job in the various roadhouses and nightclubs he knew where, invariably, the proprietors owed him favours. With luck he might make a little money from her.

Instead, what had happened? She had another voice he had not known about. She had belted out those songs in a way he wouldn't have thought possible from one so small and slight. But that voice made anything possible. She could become a pop star, be on TV, travel the world, make a fortune. The public were hungry for new faces, new voices. But how to handle the situation to his best advantage?

He drove to London and looked up an old mate, Ken, who had been in ENSA during the war, but had not managed to succeed on the peace-time stage and had gone back to the security of plumbing. Ken was happy to call his old agent Ted Richardson and arrange a meeting for Cyril. It took time since Ted had moved offices several times since Ken's performing days, but after various calls to other old friends he was tracked down and Cyril had an appointment for that afternoon.

Ken himself would have been surprised by the change in Ted Richardson. When Ted had acted as an agent for Ken he had worked from a small cluttered room over a strip joint off Wardour Street. He drove a Ford Prefect and while he was a natty dresser it was always in a conservative way. He was podgy, with the beginnings of a beer gut, wore horn-rimmed spectacles which aged him, and lived in Hendon with his sweet wife who loved to keep house.

Cyril found himself in a large suite of offices. The entrance hall was furnished with sleek black leather and steel furniture – 'Bet it's from Heals,' thought Cyril. A large tub of potted plants like a small garden stood in one corner. A girl with long blonde hair was sitting at a large black desk; her blue eyes were thickly outlined in black eyeliner, her pale pink lips had a pretty pout, and when she stood up, the length of her white leather-booted legs beneath her mini-skirt would have made any man part with a year's wages to spend just one night with her.

Cyril had to wait to see Ted, but in such surroundings, with such a woman to look at, he did not mind in the least. He picked up a magazine and pretended to be reading it while he took surreptitious looks at the dolly bird, resolving that when Lana was a star he'd have a secretary just like that one – maybe even her.

When the intercom buzzed and she stood up again and indicated to him to follow her he had an instant hard-on at the sight of her pert buttocks undulating under the tiny skirt. He was glad he was still carrying the magazine as he was shown into a spacious office.

Ted Richardson the agent had metamorphosed into Tristan Riviera the manager. His initials were about all he had kept from his previous existence. He was now slim, heavily tanned, fashionably dressed in flared trousers and open-necked shirt. Around his neck hung not one but three heavy gold medallions. The spectacles had been replaced by contact lenses, his hair had been restyled, lightly permed and tinted. The Ford had been changed for a Rolls Royce and the little woman in Hendon for a six-foot black model with whom he lived in a penthouse off Park Lane. In five years of the pop music phenomenon he had grafted hard, been smart and had made himself a millionaire. Cyril felt he was in the presence of a god as he shook hands.

'Cyril, good to meet you. A friend of old Ken's is automatically a friend of mine.' He gestured expansively for Cyril to sit opposite his enormous rosewood desk in a chair of white suede which made Cyril feel he was sitting on a cloud.

'Nice set-up you've got here,' Cyril said admiringly, knowing that when a favour was needed, compliments were in order.

'Not bad, is it? Though I sometimes feel a bit cramped,' Tristan said, picking up one of three phones as it rang. Cyril looked about him at the framed posters of famous groups which evidently this man handled – he couldn't have come to a better cove, he thought to himself.

'Well, where were we . . .?' Tristan started, again to be interrupted by the middle phone. He shrugged an apology to Cyril and took the call. When he replaced the receiver he dialled the receptionist. 'Hold all calls, Cleo, I'm in conference,' he said, which made Cyril sit up straight and feel as proud as punch. 'Now, what can I do for you?'

'It's not for me exactly. It's for a friend of mine. I promised him I'd get some info about the pop industry,' Cyril said cunningly.

'Oh, yes? Is that so?' Tristan said in such a tired, worldly sort of way that Cyril feared he might have been rumbled.

'Yes. A friend,' he said firmly. 'It's his little girl – cracker of a looker – tiny, like a bird. Blonde, blue-eyed, sexy. And she's got this voice – great big voice – all bluesy, like. It comes as a bit of a shock coming out of such a small frame.'

'You want me to hear her?'

'No. Nothing as presumptuous as that. You must be up to here with hopefuls,' Cyril said hurriedly, patting the underside of his chin. 'He wants to know how to promote her, how to get her started.'

'What experience?'

'Not much. Odd clubs, so far.'

'Good grounding. If she can survive the small clubs she must have something.'

'Oh, yes, I agree. But she's hungry for more, you see. She wants the big time.'

'It's a hard road. Not many make it. She needs strong, experienced management for a start. You've got to build, you see, not too fast and not too slow. Throw a novice into a gig like the Marathon Club with three thousand screaming punters and they can freeze. And you don't get a second chance in this game. You've got to aim for the Marathon or the Zipper – down the road – dangle them like a carrot. But give her six months on the lesser venues first – that's what I've always done, and with success.'

'Yes, I can see that. I was at the Marathon myself one night and one group, to be honest, just dried up – the place was in an uproar. I felt really sorry for the poor sods – they were rigid with fear.'

'Exactly, and who was out there witnessing it? DJs, record company scouts – bad management that, Cyril.' Tristan was being expansive because Cyril reminded him of himself when he'd first started, hungry for success and money – asking for a friend, my arse, he thought. He's got a little canary and he doesn't want anyone else in management to hear her. He was also being expansive because he doubted if Cyril would crack it – so few did – and when that happened, why, he'd be around to pick up the pieces. He'd picked up several acts just by being patient.

'First thing is to get her a promo tape. Here . . .' He opened a drawer, took a card from a stack and scribbled a message on the back. 'Give this to Ginger, one of the best recording non-company studios around. And I've written a note to ask him to look after your friend.'

'Thanks, Tristan, that's very kind of you.'

'It's nothing,' Tristan said, smiling expansively. He could afford to – he owned the recording studios in partnership with Ginger. With so many kids trying to break into the industry it was making money hand over fist, with the added advantage that Ginger reported back sharpish when he heard any group or singer that he felt might be any good.

'That done, take it to the record companies – don't send it, it'll disappear with all the thousands of other tapes sent in every month. Approach the booking agencies with demo and pics. And work out an image for her – she's got to have an image of her own. What's her name?'

'Betty Saunders.' Cyril lied rather ineffectually because he wasn't expecting the question and he stuttered over the name.

'No good, a name like that. Got to have an instant recognition factor.'

'What about Lana? I've always liked the name.'

'Yes.' Tristan smiled thoughtfully. 'Unusual, short. I like

it. But Lana what? Lana Locket? No. Lana Lawn – no. What about Lana on its own?'

'Like Lulu?'

'Well, yes, why not?'

'Don't you think it's too close, like we – she'd – be copying?'

'Maybe.'

'I wondered about Lana Lea.'

'Yeah, yeah, you could. Or rather, your friend could.'

'I'll tell him.'

'She'd be best off with a professional agent. It costs, but in the long run she'd make more.'

'No, my friend doesn't want to do that. She's only sixteen, you see. He wants to look after her himself.'

Cyril liked Tristan and he liked him even more when he realized, as he left, that he had given him a good three-quarters of an hour of his time. Even as Cyril crossed the offices to the door the telephone began ringing again.

Cyril did not go straight home. He called Amy and said he was staying over. He window-shopped for the rest of the afternoon and then returned to his friend Ken's. They sat up most of the night over a bottle of Courvoisier planning what Cyril's best line of action was – he felt he could be straight with Ken who was now safely out of the business.

Cyril did not return to Amy and Number Fourteen. Cy Best returned. Cyril to Cy, Robinson to Best – in wide, flared cream trousers, a black jacket, a red shirt, a hand-painted kipper tie with his hair dyed really blonde and skilfully layer-cut. It had cost him a fortune but just seeing Amy's reaction proved it was worth it.

'Just look at you, Cyril. You look wonderful, and years younger.' Amy hugged him tight.

'It's for Lana.'

'My Lana, how?'

'She's going to be a star, Amy – I just know it. If I'm to manage her – as I hope you'll agree I should – then I've got to look the part. There's no arsing about in this business.'

'Of course you should manage her. You don't think I'd trust her with anyone else, do you? And bless you, my darling. I've always said she'll be a star and now you're saying it too. And now it'll happen. I just know it will.' She hugged herself with excitement.

'There is a problem, Amy. It's going to cost. I've got a bit set by but not much.'

'I've got some. I've been salting it away for years, without Mike knowing, just for such a time as this. What do we need it for specifically?'

'Making her over. To us she's perfect but she can be even more perfect. We need professional advice – clothes, make-up, hair —'

'I can do her hair.'

'Amy darling, you're a wonder, but for this I think Lana needs to go to London.'

'Oh, I see.' She looked down-in-the-mouth at this information.

'Don't be hurt, lover. Nothing personal. But you know, I walked about town yesterday really looking at people. London's different to here, the folks have got style. That's how I want our Lana to look.'

'I see that.'

'And her name. We've got to change her name, something snappy.'

'Not Lana. You can't change that, Cyril. I chose that name for when she was a star.'

'No, honey. Lana's perfect. But I wondered about Lea?'

'Lana Lea,' Amy said, and then repeated it several times. 'Oh, yes, I like that. I'm sure she will too.'

'And me. I'm changing too, to Cy Best – what do you think of that?'

'I like it. All young and trendy, isn't it?' Amy giggled.

Cy did not hang around. Using Amy's savings – he saw no reason to use his own quite considerable nest egg, after all Lana wasn't his daughter – he had taken a lease on an office in London.

'Got to be at the centre of things, doll. No one will take us seriously if we're based out here in the suburbs. I can get there and back easy enough, it's barely an hour by train,' he explained to a doubtful Amy.

The office was on the small side but big enough for the important-looking desk he bought, with a black leather swivel-chair. Amy had been a bit put out by the cost of these.

'Image, doll. It's the name of the game,' Cy told her as she signed the cheque.

He had a telephone – a nice red one, he liked the colour red. He bought a large potted plant, a couple of posters and another black leather chair for guests. A filing cabinet and a typewriter completed it.

There was an outer office, where one day a gorgeous secretary would sit. Even he hadn't quite had the nerve to suggest to Amy that she pay a secretary's wages. But he'd bought a desk and chair and another poster so it didn't look too bare.

And then he set to work.

Pink, he had decided, was to be Lana's colour – it was her favourite, after all. Not the soft baby pink of her youth, though, but searing pinks, scorching pinks. They began to shop for her daytime clothes. Cy hired a dressmaker who specialized in stage clothes and soon Lana had two sensational outfits on order – one a mini-skirted dress in cerise chiffon and the other a pink, pearl-encrusted trouser-suit with a matching trilby. Amy winced at the cost.

'You'll get it all back in spades, honey, don't worry.' Cy rubbed his hand over her rump in reassurance.

Even the stationery was pink with *Lana Lea* in red italics on the top. Cy's first preference had been for a pink telephone but the GPO didn't run to one.

He did suggest that Lana's hair be dyed pink too but Amy put her foot down at that idea. Unknown to her, however, he'd got a rather expensive pink wig on order. 'Image, image' was like a mantra running about his skull these days.

As for himself, he thought that since Lana was to be all pink, he'd dress only in red, as a foil. He ordered a scarlet suit from his tailor, who was quite put out by the order but forced himself to make it all the same. With this Cy wore pink shirts, red ties and red suede shoes.

On Ken's advice he began to take Lana out on the town so that she would be seen, begin to become a fixture, be noticed. And he had to admit that the two of them – she in pink, he in red and both with hair so blond it was almost white – made quite a stir wherever they turned up.

It cost him – he had decided he could hardly ask Amy to pay for nights out up West, as she might have wanted to come too and that would have ruined the impression he was trying to create. Slowly he inched the two of them towards the right crowd – the hot groups, their managers, agents, record producers. He had imagined that within weeks they would have made instant friends by the score with these people who had, for the most part, also come from nowhere and in many cases disappeared back there after a short stint in the lighted shaft of fame. It wasn't like that, though. He and Lana seemed to be perpetually standing on the outside of this exotic group, looking in but never invited to belong.

Ken came to the rescue with a list of small-time clubs

and the pubs that had begun to put music on the board. It seemed he still lived in hopes of putting the soldering-iron away one of these days and so kept a close watch on who was employing what. One look at pretty Lana in her pink outfits and they were not only willing to offer her spots but happy to have her back again and again.

Within six months there wasn't a week when Lana did not have work of some sort. But Cy realized she was becoming bored and restless with the back-rooms of pubs and the makeshift clubs, usually in basements, which had sprung up in an attempt to emulate the Cavern. She was desperate for a break.

And then the call they had prayed for came. A scout from Simple Records had heard Lana sing in one of the clubs she was beginning to despise. The company asked for her demo tape. They waited for one nervous week before the call came that they wanted to see and hear her in the flesh.

4

Lana, as usual, was sick all morning before her audition with the record company.

'At least it's keeping me slim,' she joked to Cy as they sped along in his American car, now resprayed red, though Lana would have preferred it to be pink. Cy had balked at that, it was his car after all.

At the recording studios she gave it all she had. It was not easy, stuck alone in the large, windowless room, which was bare of furniture and pictures, with only instruments scattered about and overflowing ashtrays and empty cardboard coffee-mugs littering the floor. The room was sound-

proofed to silence so that when a disembodied voice
emerged from the speakers, it made her jump and giggle,
which annoyed her for she felt such a reaction was not cool.
She looked nervously at the huge microphone looming over
her, but, as the voice had ordered, she put on the earphones. She had never used these before and they felt
awkward stuck on her head. Standing on a slightly raised
dais, she could barely see the company's technicians
through the plate-glass window that separated her from the
brightly lit control-room. Someone appeared with a tall
stool for her to perch on and then she could see them, and
wondered if it had been better when she couldn't, for their
faces were totally expressionless. Only Cy, at the back,
grinning broadly and willing her to succeed, gave her the
courage to launch herself into a song, uncomfortably
accompanied by the sound of a pre-recorded backing group
coming through the earphones. She hated every minute of
it.

When the record producer said he liked her voice but
not her material she had to race out of the studio, find a
lavatory, and be sick again.

In the car, in the car-park, Cy was dabbing somewhat
ineffectually at her face with his handkerchief, mopping up
her tears.

'What did he mean?' she sobbed.

'Something I should have thought of. It's no good
singing other people's songs, doll. That way we'll always
be stuck on the club circuit. You've got to find your own
material or write it yourself.'

'I can't do that, I don't even read music, I could never be
bothered to learn.'

'Do you write lyrics?'

'I never tried.'

'Maybe you could. Maybe you've got another talent
hidden away there that you don't know about,' he said

encouragingly. 'Kitty reads music . . . she can play the piano, how about her?'

'She might. I don't know, she's never said she could compose.'

'We'll ask her – can't do any harm. And if I know your mum she'll tell her she's got to.' He laughed as he put the big car in gear. He was beginning to reverse out of the parking bay when a young man raced up and banged on the window.

'Loved your voice, Lana,' he said, completely ignoring Cy.

'Thanks. Not that it got me anywhere.'

'That's just it. I've got some stuff I've written . . . well, I thought maybe we could run through them, see if there's anything you like?'

'Honest? I'd love to.' Lana was smiling now.

'They really liked you in there but it's no good just churning out Beatles songs – you've got to have your own sound.'

'Hang on a minute, son.' Cy had turned the engine off. 'Just who are you?'

'I'm a session musician – piano, guitar, saxophone – I play them all. Toby Evans.'

He held out his hand and Lana shook it. 'I was just hanging around waiting for the Wall Nuts to arrive. They're recording this evening.'

'You know the Wall Nuts?' Lana was wide-eyed with excitement. 'I'd love to meet them.'

'That can easily be arranged.' Toby smiled at her and Lana suddenly felt excited, the lovely glow that zipped through her body when certain men looked at her in a particular way. Watching them, Cy felt a surge of what he recognized as jealousy. Toby was a good ten years younger than him, he guessed. And he was pretty sure that Toby's hair was naturally blond. Worst of all, Toby in jeans and a tight black silk polo neck jumper, with just a simple blue and silver waistcoat over it, suddenly made him feel over-dressed and, he hated even to think it, a mite ridiculous.

'We've got to be getting along,' he said abruptly, switching the ignition on.

'When can we meet?' Toby shouted over the row of the engine.

'Give me a call,' Cy yelled back as he pressed down on the throttle a little too hard and the huge car leaped forward.

'Why did you do that? He might have helped me,' Lana asked with an angry expression.

'And he might not have helped but hindered.'

'What do you mean?'

'The music world is full of hustlers like him. Writes music, my arse.' He snorted. 'It was you he was after, more like.'

'You don't know that. How dare you decide everything?' she said, furious now.

'No, but at least I'm sure he won't be screwing you.'

'But the songs – I need songs.' She banged one hand into the other in a gesture of frustration.

'I'll find you songs, doll. Don't you worry.'

Instead of driving home Cy took them to the office first. He'd had a fridge installed now and in it he had a couple of bottles of champagne – bought on expenses.

'To make up for your disappointment,' he said as he opened one.

'Cy, you are so sweet to me. Thanks.' She smiled up at him, her anger completely gone.

'And I've got this, see.' He began to pull down the seat of the put-u-up delivered only yesterday. 'Better than the back of the car.'

'You think of everything, Cy.'

'That's what a manager's for,' he said, leaning forward

and grabbing hold of her through her flimsy pink shirt. He pulled her towards the bed.

'That hurts,' she complained.

'Go on, you like it.' He tugged harder.

'Maybe I do.' She laughed, even though she didn't.

'Then you'll like this even more.' He tore at her clothes, pushed her face down on the bed and slapped her hard across the backside.

'No, Cy,' she said, with hardly a hint of complaint. 'No.'

'Who's been a naughty girl then?'

'Me.'

'What did you do?'

'I looked at Toby's crotch.'

'I didn't like that.' He hit her again, enjoying the sound of his hand on her bare flesh.

'I'm sorry.'

He struck her again. 'You won't do it again?'

'No, Cy. Never.'

He turned her over. Quickly he unzipped his trousers and released his huge penis.

'Which do you prefer, then?' he demanded.

'Oh, yours, Cy. No one's got a cock as big as yours.' She put her hands up to caress it.

'Apologize to it,' he demanded.

Lana scrambled on to her knees.

'I'm sorry,' she said, giggling as she took the large member into her pale pink lipsticked mouth, and thinking how silly men were.

'Please, Kitty,' Lana was imploring.

'Look, it's not that simple. I don't write music – I just play it. I'll help you that way, if you want. But I can't just conjure up songs out of the air, that's a special talent.' She returned to her bowl of cornflakes.

'I think you're being difficult, Kitty,' Amy said. 'It's not often we ask you to do anything.'

'Mother, I've just explained.' She laid down her spoon. 'If I could I would. Unfortunately I can't.'

'Then I'll never be a star,' Lana wailed.

'Of course you will, doll. This is just a little bit of a hiccough. I'll find you a songwriter and that's a promise.'

'You were both late last night,' Amy said suddenly.

'These sessions take for ever,' Cy said easily. 'You wait around for hours, nothing seems to be happening, and then zap, it all comes together and then there's all the haggling.'

'What haggling? They said they didn't want her.'

'It wasn't as simple as that, Amy. Oh dear me no. There was hours of debate and argument. Your little girl almost made it, didn't you, Lana?'

'Yes,' Lana said obediently.

'Next time, if there is a next time, I think I'd like to go,' Amy announced.

'Oh, I shouldn't bother, Mum. It's ever so boring,' Lana said with a big grin which she directed straight at Cy before leaving the table and the room.

'Why did Lana look at you like that?' Amy asked, buttering another piece of toast as Kitty picked up her bowl and also left the room.

'I don't know. Perhaps she's got the hump?'

'Not Lana, she's never grumpy in the morning. No, it was odd.'

'You'll get fat if you put any more butter on that toast,' he said to change the subject, for he was beginning to feel a little uncomfortable.

'What a thing to say.' She laughed at him. Thin as she was, she knew she would never be fat, so she had no need to feel insulted.

'Doll, tell me honest, do you think I look a berk in my

red suit?' He looked at her carefully, wanting to catch any change in her expression.

'You? You look lovely.'

'Honest?'

'Yes. Trendy, that's what you are. I like a trendy man.' And she put her hand under the table and began to feel for his scrotum. Cy groaned inwardly – he was knackered, he'd screwed Lana witless last night, he doubted if he could oblige her mother this morning.

As she waited to see her father, Kitty wondered how anyone could live for twenty-four hours in this smell. Maybe they got used to it and didn't notice after a while; she hoped, for her father's sake, that this was the case.

'Hello, Kitty.'

She swung round to see Mike. One of the kinder warders was on duty today and so they were able to hug each other. Kitty found this difficult for her father's clothes also smelt of vegetables, tobacco smoke and urine. She tried to keep her distaste from registering on her face.

'How's my darling, then?'

'I'm fine. Got a raise this week. I'm even allowed to cash the till up at the end of the day.' She laughed.

'That's trusting of them in the circumstances,' Mike said.

'Oh, Dad, I didn't mean—'

'It was supposed to be a joke, only I seem to have got out of the habit. And Lana?'

'She's doing really well. You'd be so proud of her, Dad. She can manage to make a living from singing – not much, but each month she seems to get more work. And last month she nearly got a recording contract. It's only a matter of time for her.'

'And you? What about your singing?'

'I practise,' she lied. She didn't, she couldn't find the

heart to do it. 'I was thinking of joining the local operatic society.'

'That's a good idea.'

'I thought about it – just as well it was only a thought – they're full. It seems the last thing they need is another soprano – if I'd been a tenor . . .' She laughed and shrugged her shoulders.

'I've been thinking a lot about you, Kitty. It's so unfair what's happened – you stuck in that bloody shop when you should be learning. Have you thought of moving to London? I was talking to the chaplain about you, there's lots of choirs in London you could join. Get yourself a voice coach . . . if it was just one lesson a month it would be better than this.'

'I couldn't go to London, Dad.'

'Why not? What's to keep you? Me?'

Kitty looked away since she could not answer him. She felt his hand search for hers.

'You've not gone because it would be more difficult to visit me, that's it, isn't it?'

'No.' She shook her head.

'It is. Oh, Kitty, I love you for that. But you've got to learn to think of yourself. You go. I'll be all right. I don't want you making sacrifices for me, do you understand? It's too much to deal with.'

'Oh, Dad.' She looked at his eyes blurred with tears.

'Can't this Cyril help you?'

Kitty choked on the tea she was sipping. 'I beg your pardon?' she spluttered.

'It's all right, Kitty. I know.'

'But how?'

'I got a letter.' From his pocket he withdrew a letter which, judging from its state, had obviously been read many times. 'It's from your mother. She wants a divorce, says she wants to marry this Cyril bloke.'

'Oh, how could she?'

'I don't blame her. She's an attractive woman and still young, even if a slip of a thing like you at nineteen regards forty-four as over the hill. Why should she waste her life? She doesn't come to see me, so why should I even hope she would wait for me?'

'I'm sorry, Dad.'

'What's he like?'

'He's quite nice really, I suppose. I didn't like him much at first – I think I was jealous for you. But he's very kind and generous and he works ever so hard for Lana's career. He's a bit flash-looking – dyed hair and an awful red suit – but I suppose he needs to look like that in the pop business.'

'How long has this been going on, Kitty?'

She looked everywhere but at him.

'Kitty?'

'Must be nearly a year.'

'You should have told me.'

'I couldn't. I'm sorry, but I just couldn't do it to you.'

'That was kind but misplaced. I think it was harder finding out this way.' He tapped the letter. 'Where's he live?'

Kitty felt trapped. Her mind raced, trying to find a lie to give him but she couldn't find the words.

'He's living with you all, isn't he?' Her father's voice was bleak with despair.

Kitty looked down at the table and saw her father's hands, clenched into tight balls so that the knuckles were white, like bleached bones, she thought with a shudder.

'Isn't he?'

'Yes, Dad.'

Mike slumped on the hard wooden chair. He looked a strange yellowish-grey like that day when the police came for him.

'Dad, are you all right? You've gone a funny sort of colour.'

'Does he make her happy? I mean, really happy?'

'Please, Dad, don't.'

'I have to know, Kitty.' He looked at her imploringly.

'Well, yes, I think he does.'

'And he doesn't play around – like, he's faithful to her?'

'As far as I know. Why, yes, I'm sure he is. If he's not with Mum then he spends all his time with Lana.'

Mike sat silent, deep in thought, and then he shook himself almost imperceptibly as if making a decision.

'Tell your mum it's all right, will you?'

'Are you sure? Just that?'

'Yes. And Kitty – I need to be alone now. But remember, I love you.'

'I love you too, Dad, you know that.'

'Yes. That's about the only bloody thing I do know, now.'

5

Fortunately Cy had had a telephone extension put in his and Amy's bedroom and so it was he who answered it when it rang at just past seven in the morning.

'Cy Best,' he said with effort at such an hour. But within a second he was awake and sitting bolt upright in bed, disturbing Amy who grumbled into her pillow.

'I'm her father,' Cy said.

Amy sat up too, looking at him with a puzzled expression. He hadn't told her he had a child. She began to speak but Cy held up his hand for silence. He listened intently for several minutes, saying the occasional 'Yes'.

'Who was it?' Amy demanded as he replaced the

receiver. 'You never told me you had a family. You married?' she asked suspiciously.

'I said I was *your* father because they would hardly have talked to me if I'd said you were my bit of stuff, would they?'

'Who wouldn't have talked to you?'

'The prison.'

'The prison?' she repeated inanely. 'What the hell are they calling at this time in the morning for?'

'It's Mike.'

'What's he done?'

'Topped himself.'

'He's what?'

'Sorry, doll, there was no other way to tell you. In the night, they said.'

'What on earth made him do a stupid thing like that?' Amy asked indignantly.

'They didn't say.'

'Bloody fool.' Amy slipped her legs over the side of the bed and fumbled for her dressing-gown, which had fallen on the floor. 'Who's going to tell the girls? Did he think of that? Selfish sod.'

'Aren't you upset?' Cy asked, watching her with fascinated curiosity.

'No. Why should I be? He gave up any rights to my sympathy when he went to clink – I can't tell you how ashamed I felt, and poor Lana having to leave school.'

Cy shivered. 'Well, I hope you'll be a little more sorry if I curl up my toes.'

Amy swung round from the dressing-table where she was brushing the tangles out of her hair. 'Of course I will, silly.' She smiled at him. 'You're different.'

'In what way?' he asked diffidently.

'You wouldn't allow yourself to be caught.' She laughed. 'And you know how to make a girl happy.'

'He tried.'

'Wrong department.' She laughed again and this time wriggled her hips suggestively at him, which shocked him even more.

The telephone had also woken Kitty. It was almost time to get up anyway, she thought, so with resignation she climbed out of bed.

Washed and dressed, she ran downstairs to put the kettle on and was surprised to find her mother and Cy still in their nightclothes, sitting at the kitchen table, sipping tea.

'Morning. You're up early. Any tea left in that pot?' Kitty asked.

'Kitty, I think you had best sit down,' Cy began.

Kitty looked at them questioningly as she sat down on one of the kitchen chairs. Her mother was sitting unnaturally upright, ramrod stiff. She did not move, only her hands kept plucking and pleating folds of her dressing-gown.

'Yes?'

'It's your dad, he's dead,' Amy said baldly.

'Amy . . .' Cy said, shocked.

'Don't be silly, Mum. I saw him yesterday.' Kitty laughed a small nervous laugh.

'It's true.' Amy's face was expressionless, like a mask.

'No. I can't believe that. Please don't say that.' She put up her hands as if to ward off the words.

'You've got to be told,' Amy said practically.

'Is it true?' Kitty looked at Cy, her eyes full of fear. Cy put out a hand and took hold of hers.

'Sorry, doll . . . but yes . . .'

'How? He wasn't ill. Was it his heart? What was it?' The questions tumbled out of her, the words jumbling in her haste to know.

'He killed himself.' Amy's voice was hard and cold.

Kitty looked at her mother with disbelief. Her hand shot to her mouth as if she was about to be sick. 'Oh no, oh no . . .' she began and then she screamed, a shrill, agonized wail. 'Daddy,' she cried.

'What the hell's going on?' A bleary-eyed Lana stood in the doorway. 'Kitty, what's the matter?'

She stepped quickly towards her sister who was sitting erect at the table, rocking back and forth, crying, 'No, no.'

'No, what?' Lana looked at Amy who sat opposite, lips pursed.

'It's your dad —'

'Amy, careful —' Cy tried to stop her.

'He's dead.' Amy put her hands on the table and appeared to be studying them. 'So that's that.'

'Oh, God, no. Oh, Kitty . . .' Lana put a trembling hand on Kitty's shoulder. 'Oh, Kitty,' she cried, and Kitty stood up and put out her arms like a robot and they held each other, both crying, both calling for their father.

'I don't see why you're taking on so, Lana. He let you down badly,' Amy said crossly, beginning to rub her hands together as if she was washing them.

'We let him down,' Lana sobbed. 'I never went to see him.'

'That was your choice,' Amy snapped.

'No, it wasn't. You didn't want me to. You told me you said you hated him and anyone who befriended him was against you.'

'I said no such thing.'

'You did, the day he was sentenced. I listened to you, and now look what's happened.'

'You think he'd still be alive if you had condescended to see him? Well I never, what conceit.'

'What do you mean?' Lana looked wildly about her. 'What does she mean, he might still be alive?'

'Dad killed himself, Lana,' Kitty said wearily. All

emotion suddenly drained from her, she felt exhausted and longed to sleep, but feared that sleep might be a long time coming.

It was Lana's turn to cry out, to try to assimilate news which it was impossible to comprehend.

'I can't believe that,' she sobbed. 'Not our Daddy.'

During all this Cy had sat facing them, feeling awkward in the presence of so much raw emotion, patting a hand here and another there. But he was also shocked to the core by the coldness and hardness he saw in Amy. After all, he reasoned to himself, even if she no longer loved Mike, he was still the father of her children. There should have been something left, surely. He shuddered as he thought of the loneliness and sadness that Mike must have suffered to do such a thing as to string himself up with a sheet from the window bars. He hadn't met the man, but living in his house, sharing his family, so to speak, he had begun to feel he knew him.

'I wish now I'd looked after his dahlia patch for him,' he said suddenly.

'What on earth for? I never liked dahlias,' Amy replied.

'Stop it! You bitch, you evil bitch – don't take his dahlias away from him too. He grew them for you.' Kitty was on her feet, white-faced and shaking. 'Don't talk like this,' she shouted.

'Don't you speak to me like that, miss. Bloody cheek.'

'Oh, go to hell!' Kitty shrieked, and ran from the room.

'How could you, Mum? How could you be so cruel?' Lana said before slamming the door and racing after Kitty.

'God, what a fuss about nothing.' Amy stood and emptied the tea-leaves into the sink strainer and refilled the kettle. 'So what do I do now? Do the authorities cope or do I?'

'Do you want me to make the arrangements for you?'

'Would you, Cy? I'd appreciate that. I feel I just don't want to be involved, you know?'

'I'll do it, but by God, Amy, you've shaken me today. I never thought to see someone as cool and uninvolved as you are.' Cy shook his head.

'I stopped being involved the day I met you. You wouldn't want it any other way, surely?'

'But you've got the girls to think about.'

'They'll get over it.' She shrugged.

'What made him do it? I wonder if we'll ever know.'

'Oh, it was probably my fault. I wrote to him asking for a divorce.'

'You did what? Christ, the poor old bugger.'

'I told him I didn't want to wait another five years – reasonable enough in the circumstances.'

'It wasn't just that, was it? You told him about me, didn't you?'

Amy had turned her back and was spooning tea into the pot. She did not answer.

'What did you write him about me?' Cy said, his voice hard, a sound she was not used to.

'I told him the truth. That I loved you and I wanted to marry you.' She had turned away and was leaning against the sink, clutching the teapot to her for comfort, like a hot water bottle. There, she thought, she had said it, what she wanted and had never dared hint at before.

'Well, I'm damned.' Cy laughed. Amy relaxed and smiled. 'Sorry, doll, you've another think coming. I'm not marrying anyone and that's a fact.' He stood up. 'And if I did do such a bloody stupid thing it would be to someone younger than me.' This made Amy suck in her breath sharply. 'I'd best get on to the prison, find out what's got to be done,' he said, as if unaware of the hurt he was causing.

He left the kitchen and a stunned Amy, still holding the teapot.

'Oh, yes, yes, you bloody will,' she yelled at the closed door and hurled the teapot at it. She sat down abruptly at the cluttered kitchen table, her body slumped as if defeated.

'Oh, Mike, you stupid bugger,' she said aloud. 'Why?'

She stayed like this for some time, gazing into space, thinking, remembering. Suddenly she began to cry silently, the tears rolling down her cheeks. She was not crying for Mike as he was now, not even for the Mike of ten years ago. She wept for the tall and handsome soldier he had been, who had swept her off her feet. She grieved for that time of happiness they had enjoyed – too short to last a lifetime.

'Silly bugger,' she repeated. He'd been a good provider. He'd given her everything she'd wanted and even things she hadn't. He'd been kind and considerate, faithful – all the things a husband should be. She knew no man would ever love her as Mike had done, certainly not Cy. But it had never been enough, that was their tragedy.

'Stupid sod.' She wiped her tears away almost angrily. 'What a thing to go and do!'

She stood up, got a bucket from under the sink and began to clear up the mess she had made with the shattered teapot.

6

It was hot in the limousine going to the crematorium. All Kitty could think of was that her father had missed this sudden bout of good weather, that this was a spring he would never see. But even as she thought it, she could not really believe it was so.

She sat in the back of the car with Cy between herself

and Lana, holding their hands. No one spoke, and she almost wished they would, that Cy would tell them a joke or something. It was wrong of her mother not to be here, she hadn't even wanted to send flowers until Lana had bullied her into doing so. She would never be able to understand Amy's hatred of her husband. He had been misguided, weak and stupid, Kitty could recognize that, but this did not detract from his motives. He had paid an unbelievably heavy price for his love for them all. Kitty wondered if she would ever be able to forgive Amy's intransigence.

They had to wait in the car until the people attending the previous funeral dispersed. This took some time as they lingered reading the cards on the many wreaths. It had been a large funeral and the chapel must have been packed, with standing room only. Crematorium officials were trying to move everyone along as sympathetically and unobtrusively as possible but without much success, judging by the angry and affronted expressions which greeted them.

The funeral after theirs wouldn't have a long wait, that was for sure, Kitty thought. She doubted if there would be any other mourners.

The log-jam of people finally moved on. Lana in a black mini-skirted suit and large black hat and Kitty, in a black coat which was too heavy for the warm weather, followed the coffin into the chapel. Canned music was playing and Kitty felt no sense of God's presence.

She remembered nothing of the service as afterwards she thanked the vicar who had conducted the proceedings, a vicar she did not know. Since her father had never attended church she doubted if he had known her father either, even though he had probably come out with fine words about the man – she realized she had heard none of them.

'Are you Kitty?' he asked, to her surprise.

'Yes.'

'Might I have a word with you outside when I've spoken to the other mourners?'

'Yes,' she said, and it was only then that she was aware that other people had been present. She found herself thanking an ex-manager of the Co-op – the one her father had taken over from – who had nothing but kind words to say, as did her own boss, Mr Davenport. Camilla was there, in tears, which was odd as she hardly knew the man, but it was what one would expect from Camilla, Kitty thought, as she kissed her and thanked her. There were several men from the British Legion, a couple of prison warders who had taken the trouble to come to pay their respects, and their next-door neighbours from both sides were also present. Seeing them there, realizing that none of them was standing in judgment, knowing that they had liked and respected her father, made Kitty cry and wonder why none of them had visited him in prison when he was alive.

The priest appeared at her side. 'Shall we walk a little?' he asked, taking her by the arm. 'We won't be a minute,' he said to Lana and Cy in unmistakable dismissal.

'My dear, your father spoke to me about you often. He told me of your talent and his fear that you would not pursue it.'

'I'm sorry?' she said questioningly, unsure who he was.

'Of course, you don't know me. I'm the prison chaplain. I got to know your father well over the last three years. A good man despite having strayed. Never a bad man but one who had been misguidedly led into dishonesty. A tragedy.'

'Yes, it was.' Kitty felt gratitude towards him.

'I have an address here. It's the vicar of St Swithin's in London – he has contacts with a large choir and knows many people in the world of opera. I promised your father that I would find it for him, but here I am, in these sad circumstances, giving it to you instead.'

'Thank you.' She took the paper and put it into her pocket without reading it, she could not think of her future and choirs on such a day.

'Why did he do it?' she asked.

'Maybe this will explain it to you.' He handed her a letter. 'I'm afraid it had to be opened by the prison governor – routine, you understand.'

'Have you read it?'

'Yes. The governor asked me to.'

'And does it make things clearer?'

'Yes, I think it does, even if I doubt it will help you at this time.'

'I can't read it now.'

'No, perhaps better not. When you're calmer, when you're alone.'

Kitty stood on the gravel path beside a bed of rose bushes, each with a name attached to it, not sure what else was expected of her.

'Well, thank you. You've been very kind,' she said, suddenly aware that her state of mourning gave her pre-cedence over his age and the cloth he wore, and she held out her hand to end the interview.

'My pleasure. And do try to go to London as your father wished and look up Peter Hawkins at St Swithin's.'

'I might. I'm not sure of anything at the moment.'

She thanked him again and then looked for the car. She walked quickly across the grass towards it, approaching from the rear. She was about to open the door when through the glass she saw Lana kissing Cy and Cy's hand burrowing high up her skirt.

Shaken, Kitty got into the front of the car and sat rigid with shock beside the driver. She knew from the sly and amused look he gave her that he too was aware of what had been going on in the back. She was sure she could hear them sniggering.

She sat looking straight ahead, clutching her father's letter and the chaplain's note.

Amy was waiting for them.

'It's traditional,' she said, pointing to the ham tea she had laid out. 'See, I do know how things should be done.'

'I'm sorry, Mum, I couldn't eat a thing.'

'First you complain I don't care enough. Now, when I do something right, you don't want to know. I don't understand you, Kitty.'

'I said I was sorry,' Kitty said, close to tears.

'I could eat a horse,' Cy said, but she could not look at him.

'And anything else put in front of you, no doubt.' Lana laughed. Kitty turned away in disgust and raced to her room, slamming the door shut behind her. As she sat on her bed she wondered how many times she had done that in this house – rushed to the sanctuary of her room. She wondered how long it was to continue and knew it could not be for long, not now. It took her some time to calm down and even longer to get the courage to open the letter. It was two pages long, and precise. Mike wrote of his love for her and Lana but also of his love for Amy. He told her that he could not face a life where someone else had taken his place at Number Fourteen – his house. It was bad enough in prison, knowing that Cyril was there, in his bed, with his wife. On the outside it would be a living hell, and he feared he could never keep away – and then what? He asked Kitty to explain all this to Amy, to whom he found he could not write, at least not with any sense of dignity, and after all that was all he had left. He begged Kitty's forgiveness and understanding. He implored her to go to London and to try to learn to sing. He told her she was to look up an old friend of his, a Corporal Fred Turner, who had a souvenir of him for her. He gave the address across town, and that was it.

It was a letter that made Kitty want to cry at the waste and a letter which made her angry that her father could think only of himself and leave her. She read it a second time and decided she would not tell her mother she had received it, let alone reveal the contents. Amy would be cruel about it, she knew. Kitty could not be sure what her reaction would be if her mother denigrated her father's last wishes. She locked the letter away in a small box she kept in the child's school desk Mike had made her and which she now used as a dressing-table. She selected a record – Mozart – from her small collection and put it on the turntable.

She looked up as there was a knock on the door, but ignored it. The knock was repeated and, when again Kitty did not answer, the door was opened gingerly and Lana's head appeared round it.

'Can I come in?'

'I'd rather you didn't,' Kitty said shortly.

'Look, I've brought you this. You must have something.' Lana held out a bowl of trifle in one hand and a glass of sherry in the other. The sight of the trifle made her feel sick but she took the sherry.

'You saw, didn't you?' Lana asked, edging into the room.

'Unfortunately, yes.'

'You won't tell?'

'Mum? What would be the point? No doubt she'll find out for herself sooner or later – she's no fool, you know.'

'I don't want to hurt her. I think she really loves Cy.'

'And you don't?'

'Don't be daft. He's too old.'

'How can you let him do things like that to you if you don't love him?'

'It's nothing to me.' She shrugged. 'It's him, it's what he wants and in any case he's earned it, he's done wonders for my career.'

'You sleep with him, then?'

'Yes.' Lana shook her head defiantly. 'Not that there's much sleeping.' She began to laugh but could not sustain it and tears began to form in her eyes. Kitty sat on her bed, the sherry glass in her hand. She did not comfort her sister, she still felt too angry, but it was an anger mixed with a new sadness.

'It shouldn't be like this, Lana,' she said, concerned. 'It should be a beautiful thing to do with someone you love.'

'You reckon?' Lana said with a downcast expression. 'You've done it, have you?'

'No, not yet. I couldn't just *do* it. I'd have to be in love first . . .'

'Wouldn't we all? But it doesn't always work out that way. Oh, heck, it isn't that big a deal. It's the men, they want it more than I do. Don't be cross with me, Kitty, please.'

'I just don't get it. You were so upset at Dad's dying and then you behave like that, today of all days, and at the bloody crematorium with the driver watching and Cy smirking all over his face. God, I felt so ashamed for you.'

'I *am* upset. I loved him too, you know. I'll always regret saying I hated him that night they arrested him. I didn't hate him – I just said it, just in the moment.'

'You've a fine way of showing you're upset.'

'I know, I'm sorry. I can't explain it. It just sort of happened. Cy said people often feel randy at funerals – you know, "Life must go on", I suppose.'

'I don't understand you.' Kitty turned away, not wanting to pursue this conversation further.

'I don't understand myself.' Lana laughed. 'Just forgive me, Kitty. I don't want to fall out with you – ever. But in any case . . .' She paused. 'There's lots you don't know.'

'What?' Kitty looked up.

'I can't tell you, honest, I would if I could,' she said, remembering her promise to Portman and wishing she had never made it.

Kitty looked at her pretty sister, saw her sad expression and wondered what she could not tell. Something bad had happened to her.

'If you ever want to talk, I'm always here.'

'I know, Kitty. Perhaps I will one day . . .' She shrugged her shoulders, knowing even as she said it that she never would. What had happened with Portman and Portia was something that made her feel uncomfortable with herself when she thought about it now. She doubted if she would ever confess it to anyone.

'I won't say anything, promise,' Kitty said finally, but wishing there was such a thing as a mental rubber that could erase such scenes from the memory.

'There, I told Cy you wouldn't. Come on down. Cy's got some red wine.'

'No, I don't think so, thanks.' Kitty pointedly turned up the volume on her record-player and Lana left her.

It was hearing the noise of loud laughter coming up from the sitting-room that made Kitty change out of her black skirt and blouse and into jeans and a T-shirt. How could they? How could anyone laugh and be happy today? Silently she let herself out of the house and walked across town to the address her father had given to her.

Corporal Turner was expecting her. He had served with Mike in the war, he told her, and they had kept in touch over the years through the British Legion. Only a bad cold had prevented him from being at the funeral.

'I've had this since a week before they arrested your dad. He must have known the game was up, I suppose. I hoped he'd get a message to you.' He handed Kitty a tin box. She did not want to open it in front of him, in front of anybody, she did not want any witnesses to her reaction to its contents. She thanked him and, refusing tea, walked back the way she had come. She turned into the park and sat down under the old magnolia tree which was in full, majestic bloom. There she undid the box. Inside, in a paper bag, was a pile of banknotes. With them was another letter from her father, dated December 1963 – nearly two and a half years ago.

Kitty darling,
I had to get this to you in this roundabout way in case the police find out about it and take the money back. Yes, it's Co-op money as I'm sure you've guessed. This is all that's left.

I'm pretty certain I've been rumbled and I expect the police any day now. Fred Turner will look after this box for me until I get out. I planned to use it to start anew with Amy. But then I got to thinking, what if something happened to me while in the nick, what then? Well, something has happened to me, as you know. So I want you to have the lot.

Use it. Use it for that voice of yours, that's what I took it for. There's £1000 which should keep you going for a bit until fame and fortune find you – as I know they will.

Don't tell a living soul about this. And don't bank it – they might be keeping an eye on your account. And don't get any silly notions about returning it, will you? What would be the point now? Let me do something for you.

They'll probably check with you what the souvenir was, so here's my dad's old half-hunter watch.

My love,
Dad.

Kitty sat there for a long time, a puzzled expression on her face, holding the tin box and wondering what to do. She knew what she should do. But she also knew she wasn't going to give the money back. This knowledge shocked her. But in a funny way she felt she owed it to her father to keep it and to use it, even if it was stolen. She took out the watch, stuffed it into her pocket, and slipped the bag of money into her waistband. She threw the tin box into the shrubbery.

Back home, it sounded as if a party was in full swing in the sitting-room.

Kitty crossed the hall to the telephone and dialled.

'Jenny? Is that you? It's Kitty. You still on for London?'

'If you go it's for good, and that's flat.' Amy was at the kitchen sink, her shoulders rigid, her mouth set in a thin and angry line.

'Mum, I don't want to leave like this.' Kitty stood in the doorway, her small case on the floor beside her.

'Then don't go.'

'It's not that simple, is it? I've arranged with Jenny.'

'You could unarrange it. You don't have to go anywhere. This is your home. What's it look like, you pissing off and me just a widow?'

'Oh, come on, Mum. You don't give a damn that you're a widow – you'd grown to loathe Dad.'

'Didn't he give me cause?'

Kitty looked down at her feet and said nothing. What was the point? They'd been over this subject time and again. They'd never agree on Mike's motives, nor on who was to blame for them.

'And now you're scarpering. How do you think I feel?'

'Relieved, probably.'

Amy swung round with a look of such loathing on her face that Kitty took an involuntary step backwards.

'And what does that mean?'

'Be honest, Mum. When have we ever got on? We've nothing in common—'

'And whose fault is that?'

'You've got Lana.'

'Do you want the truth?' Amy stepped forward menacingly. 'Do you?'

Kitty shrugged, but she was shaking.

'I wish to God I'd only ever had Lana. She appreciates all I've done for her, the sacrifices I've made – not like you. I never wanted you. Never! I felt dreadful from the moment you were on the way. I did everything I could to get rid of you – drank gin till it was pouring out of my ears, hot baths, the lot. I knew, you see, deep down inside me, as soon as you were there in my womb, I knew how it was going to turn out. I knew I'd never like you.'

Kitty felt as if her mother had attacked her physically. She felt her face tauten as if it had been struck. She bent down and picked up her case.

'Then there's really no point in my staying, is there?'

She turned and walked out of the room with as much dignity as she could muster, along the hall and out of the house – for ever, she vowed.

7

After only one week in London Kitty regretted she had not been able to move there sooner. In that short time she and Jenny had done so much, had such fun, that if anything was needed to show Kitty the dull monotony of her life at home, it was this seven days.

The minute they arrived they had booked into the YWCA, so they felt safe. They had window-shopped in Oxford Street until they were sure their feet would drop off. They had sat on a bus, on the top deck, to see the sights and had chatted with the conductor who had let them stay on it for the next round trip, for free. They had been to the cinema twice and were shocked at the price compared with home. They had sat in the gods in the theatre from where the lighted stage was a tiny rectangle far below them. They had had their first curry, their first Chinese meal. They had learned how to make two cups of coffee last a whole evening in a coffee bar off the Tottenham Court Road, which had live music.

They were tired, not just from all the activity but because they had fallen into the habit of sitting up talking half the night in their shared room. Jenny had been a friend for two years now but not at this level of intimacy, for as the rumble of London's traffic faded far below them as the night ticked on, they talked about everything. Jenny was the only person Kitty had told of her jealousy of Lana, of the agony she had suffered at losing her father, who she realized was the only person who had loved her. Kitty told Jenny of the pain her mother had inflicted upon her, and it was Jenny alone who heard of Kitty's secret dreams. Kitty found that sharing these things with her friend relieved her of a lot of the guilt she felt.

Confiding was not new to Jenny, so that everything she told Kitty in turn had in all probability already been told to someone else. But Kitty did not know that, and clutched Jenny's secrets to her with gratitude.

One thing they were both agreed on – they would find a flat to share and search for boyfriends.

'Here we are, in London, in the mid-sixties. Everyone's making love like crazed weasels and we're still virgins,' Jenny complained one night.

'You realize we're probably a rarity in this city?'

'Too right. And it's got to change – I'll drink to that. To the loss of our virginity,' Jenny said solemnly.

They had toasted this promise with the sweet sherry Jenny loved. Drink in bedrooms was not allowed at the YWCA, but she had smuggled in a bottle.

On the Saturday they had gone to the Lyceum ballroom and danced themselves silly, and had drunk Bacardi and Cokes which had made them sillier. There they had met two young men, Clive and Martin, who had walked them back to the YWCA and arranged to take them out the following day.

Back in their room, Jenny had produced another bottle of sherry from the bottom of her bag, and they had spent the next hour getting slowly drunker and arguing who was to go out with which boy. The decision was finally reached that Martin, at six foot, would be best for Kitty, while Jenny, who was shorter, would settle for five-foot-eight Clive.

'It'll look neater all round,' Jenny said sagely.

'Oh, undoubtedly,' Kitty managed to say with difficulty, 'we've got to have everything tidy.' But she was secretly pleased, she thought Martin by far the more interesting of the two.

'Indubitably,' Jenny replied, going one better.

The following day Jenny was banging on the lavatory door. 'Come on, Kitty, we'll be late. What on earth are you doing in there? We can't expect them to wait.'

'Just a minute,' Kitty shouted from her perch on the lavatory lid, where she was standing trying to prise the cistern open. It made a grating noise as it finally moved. She paused – had Jenny heard?

'You all right? What was that odd noise?' Jenny demanded.

'I'm fine. I dropped the loo roll holder,' Kitty lied, as she gently slid her precious bundle of notes, wrapped tightly in a plastic bag, into the cistern. She eased the lid back on, making a mental note not to use this one again. She had decided it was too dangerous to carry her money with her, and that if thieves struck here, they would target the bedrooms rather than a lavatory used by dozens of people.

'About time too,' Jenny said as Kitty emerged. 'You

spend ages in the loo every day. You got a bad tum? I told you you shouldn't have had that hot dog last night.' Jenny fussed about her as Kitty washed her hands.

'No, I'm fine.'

'Something up? You can tell me.' Jenny put her arm about Kitty's shoulder.

'If I do, you might regret it,' Kitty said enigmatically, which only seemed to whet Jenny's appetite.

'Tell me, please . . . Don't be a meany,' she kept repeating as they walked along the sunny streets, semi-deserted since it was Sunday.

Kitty wanted to tell her, longed to unburden herself, to gauge Jenny's reactions. Would it be shock and horror that Kitty, at second hand, was a thief too? If it was, then she'd have to return the money. She could do it anonymously after all, just pop it in the post and her conscience would be clear for ever.

'It's a bundle of money my father stole from the Co-op,' she said abruptly, stopping in the middle of the pavement as they approached the Embankment, where they had arranged to meet Clive and Martin.

'What?' Jenny looked shocked. Kitty's heart sank.

'You heard. Awful, isn't it?'

'How much?'

'£1000.'

'Bloody hell!' Jenny whistled. 'Lucky old you,' she added.

'You mean that?' Kitty asked anxiously.

'Of course I do. Wish my dad would do something like that for me.'

'I've been worrying about it—'

'Kitty, you're not thinking of sending it back, are you? Hell! You are. Don't. Don't be so bloody daft. What good would it do?'

'It would make it right.'

'Would it? I bet your father wanted you to use that for

singing lessons, didn't he? No doubt the Co-op got the insurance money, it's all so long ago – their accountants probably wouldn't know what column of figures to put it in. You'd make trouble for loads of people.'

'Oh, Jenny, I love you. You're so immoral.'

'Quite,' Jenny said with mock dignity. 'Have you been stuffing it in the cistern or something?'

'Yes. I change the toilet – a different one every day.'

'It should be in the bank.'

'I daren't. What if they're allowed to check my account?'

'I'll take it and put it in my account. If anyone asks I'll say it's a present from my dad. He'd lie for us.'

'Would you?' Kitty asked, but she felt doubtful. It was a lot of money and how well did she know Jenny? She wouldn't have a leg to stand on if Jenny decided to spend the lot. But the worry of finding a different hiding-place every day was beginning to tell. 'That's so kind of you, Jenny.' She had finally decided.

'We'll bank it tomorrow before we go for our job interviews. Then, as and when you want some, just let me know and I'll withdraw it for you. Look, look, there they are! You never know if the creeps are going to turn up, do you?' She laughed as she waved and both girls began to run towards the young men who were standing beside the ticket office of one of the Thames pleasure-boats.

'Hampton Court do you both?' Clive asked them.

'Wonderful!' said Jenny, linking her arm in his and marching confidently ahead.

'Looks as though everything's been decided,' Martin said with a shrug, holding his arm up for Kitty.

'Jenny thought we'd look better together because I'm taller than her,' she said gauchely. She had never been on a serious date before, for the simple reason she had never met a boy she was interested in. But Martin was different. For a start he was so much older – at least twenty-five, she reckoned. And he was better-looking than anyone else she knew. He had longish black hair which for some strange reason she wanted to ruffle – she'd thought that last night too. He had brown eyes with lashes far longer than hers and thick, dark eyebrows, one of which he could cock at will, which gave him a wonderfully sophisticated air. He had full lips above a finely chiselled chin and high, almost Slavonic cheekbones. There was a confidence about him which she liked but which also made her feel nervous.

'I'd rather hoped it was because you liked the look of me.' He smiled at her in the funny, crooked-lipped way she found instantly attractive without exactly knowing why.

'Oh, I do . . . I do . . .' she said, and immediately knew she had spoken too quickly.

'That's settled, then.' They walked on to join the others who had already bought the tickets.

The day was warm, so they opted for seats on the open deck.

'Who's for some wine?' Martin asked once they were settled.

'No, thank you,' Kitty said with a shudder. 'Last night I drank too much. I've got a bit of a headache,' she explained.

'Then you must have a drink – hair of the dog.' Martin smiled at her. 'Clive, get some wine.'

'But Martin . . .' Clive frowned at Martin and pointedly shoved a hand into his trouser-pocket.

'Don't worry, my man, I shall pay,' Martin said grandly, flicking open his wallet and producing a note. 'Come on, Clive, don't hang about. White, I think. And check it's properly chilled,' he called after Clive's departing back.

'I think I'll go with him.' Jenny jumped up and slithered through the crowd after him.

'Does he always do what you tell him?' Kitty asked, aware that Martin was very much in control.

'Always.' He sat down beside her.

'Anything?'

'Anything.'

'Silly him.'

'Why? He loves me.'

'Don't be silly. He's a man.'

'So? Can't a man love a man? Don't you love Jenny?'

'No, of course not. She's my friend.'

'How sad,' Martin said, and he studied her face carefully. So intense was the stare from his deep brown eyes that Kitty had to look away. 'So, who do you love?'

When Kitty didn't reply, she felt Martin's hand beneath her chin forcing her to look at him. 'Who do you love?' he repeated.

'I loved my father but he's dead.'

'No mother?'

'Yes.'

'Ah, I see, but you don't love her?'

'No.'

'How perfectly sensible of you, mothers should never be loved, it gives them something to moan about – have a good martyrdom.'

'Then you don't love your mother?'

'I don't know. I never met her.'

'Then how do you know?'

'I listen to my friends talk about their mothers, and when I do I'm glad I haven't got one – they all sound like grief to me.'

'You're an orphan, then?'

'Yes, abandoned at birth, in a Selfridges carrier bag, on the steps of St Martin's-in-the-Fields.'

'How romantic.'

'I'm glad you said that, I think so too. It's where my name comes from – Martin Field, see? It's why I'm an actor too – that church is where lots of actors have their memorial services, so I reckon my mother was a desperate out of work actress and that's why she left me there.'

'I've an interview for a job at Selfridges tomorrow.'

'Honestly? How extraordinary. Then that is the link – we

were destined to meet.' He laughed at the notion. 'Dear old Selfridges – salute the grand shop.'

'I think it's wonderful you can joke about it,' Kitty said, full of admiration.

'Why not? The whole of life is one big fucking joke if you ask me.'

Kitty tried not to show that she was shocked by his language, she didn't want him to think her too unsophisticated, she sensed he wouldn't like that.

'Did you say you were an actor?' she asked quickly, to cover her confusion.

'RADA-trained, my dear. Doesn't it show?'

'I wouldn't know, I've never met an actor before.'

'Well, there's an excitement for you – we're an unusual breed.'

As the day progressed, this proved to be true. Kitty had never known two people with such confidence and such an irreverent attitude to life in general. Everything seemed a joke and nothing was to be taken seriously. She did not always find the way they pranced about amusing, though, particularly when they attracted the attention of strangers. It was all a bit like showing off, and artificial too, as if they were both intent on being noticed, and not only by her and Jenny.

'You don't understand the soul of the performer, that's your trouble. You think it's just for effect?' Martin said with such perceptiveness that Kitty could not look him in the eye. 'Aha! I'm right.'

'Kitty does understand. She's going to be a performer too – you should hear her sing.'

'Really?' said Clive with interest. 'Pop?'

'No, opera. She's got this fantastic voice, she's come to London to learn, haven't you, Kitty?'

'If I can. I've been given the name of one contact, I'll see to it when Jenny and I are settled.'

'We'll help you, won't we, Martin? We know masses of

singers. A friend of mine—' But Clive did not finish for Martin was on his feet.

'Come on. Time's winged chariot, and all that crap. We've got to catch the tube . . .'

When they returned to central London they had a curry, washed down with beer, and Kitty was loath for the evening to end. They were invited back to Clive's flat but both somewhat prudishly refused, although they accepted a good 'snog', as Jenny called it, in a dark mews before they said goodnight.

The next day they banked the money and were both offered jobs in Selfridges. That evening they went to the cinema with Martin and Clive but again returned to the YWCA. Kitty was in a state of excitement she had never experienced before. All she could think of was Martin.

'That's love,' Jenny teased her.

'You sure?'

'Positive. Does your tummy go squidgy when you think of him?'

'It does.'

'Would you mind washing his socks?'

'No, I'd love to.'

'Then it definitely is.' Jenny laughed. 'Lucky you, Clive doesn't affect me like that at all.'

A week later, after a walk in a park, they returned to Clive's flat. Or rather, they returned to Clive's room in a flat shared with six others – all, they learned, actors and all, like Clive and Martin, out of work. Martin was sleeping on the floor since he had no place of his own.

'Clive, my man, go and get us fish'n'chips and a bottle of plonk,' Martin ordered.

'No can do, mate. Sorry.'

'Why not?' Martin looked up, a cross expression on his face.

'Because it's Sunday, that's why not.'

'Then take Jenny with you down to the pub. And come back in two hours,' Martin ordered.

'Whose room is this?' Jenny demanded.

'Mine,' Clive said.

'Then why let him boss you about like that?'

'Because he likes it, don't you, Clive, old darling?'

'I don't mind,' Clive said, getting to his feet from his position on the floor – Martin was sprawled on the bed, Kitty was sitting with her back to it, and Jenny was on the chair.

'Of course he doesn't mind – he knows what true friendship is. Now, go – there's good folk.'

Kitty began to get to her feet.

'Oh, not you, sweet bird of youth,' Martin whispered in her ear. Kitty sat down again. She felt mesmerized, knowing she should go, not wanting to, yet also longing to be away from there.

'What are you doing, Kitty?' Jenny asked.

'I think I'll stay,' she heard her voice answer, almost as if it was someone else's.

'You sure?' Jenny asked.

'Don't fret, Jenny. Frowning mars your pretty face.' Martin smiled at her, the same slightly crooked smile that so charmed Kitty. But it did not have the same effect on Jenny.

'Cocky bastard, aren't you?' she stated rather than asked as she made for the door.

'If that's how you perceive me, Jenny, my love,' Martin drawled in reply. 'I thought they were never going, didn't you?' he said, when Clive had finally closed the door.

'I should have gone with them.'

'Nonsense. Destiny decided we were to meet and destiny must be obeyed.' He patted the bed beside him. Slowly she moved from the floor and sat primly on the side of the bed.

She knew why she was there, what was about to happen. Again she had that strange dichotomy of wanting and not wanting. Of knowing what she should do, and finding she couldn't.

'I love you, Kitty,' she heard him say.

'Don't say things you don't mean,' she answered, not looking at him.

'But I *do* mean it. I saw you, wanted you. I've loved and longed for you all day. I've resented the strangers with their prying eyes. I love you, girl. It's that simple and that complicated.' He pulled her down so that her head was resting on the pillow beside him. He was caressing her face with the gentlest of touches, as if memorizing her features, like a blind man.

'I long to be loved.' She sighed.

'And so you are. So very, very much.'

He kissed her, and the kiss, his tongue parting her lips, exploring the inside of her mouth, was like no other kiss she had ever experienced. She felt waves of pleasure ripple down her body to nestle between her legs. Slowly he felt her breasts, undoing her brassière so smoothly that she wasn't even aware that it was loose until she felt his fingers teasing her nipples, and the waves of pleasure changed to jolts of joy. And she was moaning as he took one breast into his mouth, his hand playing with the other, while his hand crept stealthily – oh, so stealthily – down her body until he was caressing her where no man had ever touched her, and her moaning became louder.

She had no recollection of either of them undressing, but soon their flesh was touching the whole length of their bodies, and she felt his penis hard against her. She manoeuvred her body, longing for him to enter her, wanting only that.

But he made her wait long, agonizing minutes as he licked her, nibbled at her, sucked at her.

'Please, soon . . .' she sighed in desperation.

'Just a little longer,' he teased her.

She thought she would claw him to death before he finally mounted her and she could feel his huge, hard flesh begin to enter her. She tensed, waiting for the pain, as gently he slid into her, and then he paused and then he was pushing harder, then harder, as he penetrated her hymen. And she raised her body to his and the pain became pleasure, and he was in her and Kitty knew she had never experienced such feelings as this as he rode deeper into her – back and forth, up and down. Then she felt the strongest feeling, like no other, and she arched her back as if afraid of it, as if it would take her away. And she heard herself cry out with joy. He was riding her, calling her name, until with a great groan he too arched his body before collapsing on top of her.

She lay quietly, listening to his breathing return to normal, enjoying the feel of him as the hardness disappeared, enjoying the sensations of his sweaty body on hers. She held him tight to her at this happiest moment in her life.

'Martin, I love you too,' she whispered.

He looked down at her. 'You might have warned me you were a fucking virgin!'

8

Three weeks later, at Selfridges in her coffee-break, Kitty searched Jenny out in the shoe department and caught up with her as she made her way from a customer to the stock-room.

'Can you get away for coffee?'

'I'm due to go now. Give me five minutes,' Jenny said. 'I don't think this old trout intends to buy anything anyway.'

'I'll get yours, then.'

'Yes, and a Penguin, I'm starving.'

'I thought you were going on a diet.' Kitty smiled.

'Monday. I'll start one on Monday,' Jenny replied as usual.

In the large staff canteen Kitty found a table away from the main crowd and waited for Jenny.

'I was wrong, the old trout bought three identical pairs of shoes. I ask you, at nearly ten pounds a pair. Why do all the wrong people have money? She was so bloody miserable, too.' Jenny flopped down on the seat opposite. 'God, I'm knackered, aren't you?'

'Yes. It's harder work than Davenport's ever was and I used to think that was hard,' Kitty replied, as she edged one shoe off with the other and wriggled her toes for relief.

'What's lingerie like?'

'Not too bad. At least I don't have to measure the women – some of them smell – BO.' Kitty wrinkled her nose. 'The stock is interesting, not like buttons and elastic. Some of that underwear, though – God, I could die for it.'

'One day, my friend. One day you'll have all the super lingerie a woman could want. But it won't just materialize unless you do something about it. Have you called the St Swithin's bloke yet about the choir?'

'No, I haven't had time, but I will.'

'I've heard that before.' Jenny sank her teeth into the Penguin biscuit. 'Oh, that's better.'

'I will call him soon, I promise. It's just that at the moment so much is happening in my life that I don't think I could cope with any more new experiences,' she explained. 'Jenny, I need some of my money.'

'No problem. I'll meet you at lunchtime – the bank's just across the road. What do you want it for?'

Kitty's first reaction was to tell Jenny to mind her own business, but then, Jenny was an accessory after the fact, so to speak, in banking stolen money. Kitty supposed she had some sort of right to know.

'I need the deposit on a flat.'

'You've found one?' Jenny sat up, her face alive with excitement. 'Thank heaven, no more YWCA.'

'Yes, but . . . well, I didn't find it, Martin did.'

Jenny slumped back into her chair. 'I see,' she said in a tight, controlled little voice.

'No, Jenny, I'm sure you don't understand at all. I know how you feel. But Martin's tired of sleeping on other people's floors. He wants a home – he wants it with me. I know we planned to share, but this one's come up and it's only got two bedrooms.'

'And of course darling Clive must have that one.'

'Well . . . yes. There's a sitting-room too but it wouldn't work if you had that, now, would it? Not with the hours they keep.'

'I wouldn't share with Martin Field if you paid me.'

'I know, that's why I thought you wouldn't mind too much.'

'Of course I mind, what do you take me for? I'm supposed to stand back and watch my friend ruin her life over a shit like that —'

'He isn't a shit.'

'He is, and you know damn well he is. Mark my words, Kitty, you'll end up paying all the bills and feeding them – well, maybe not Clive, he's got some honour left, at least.'

'What's Martin ever done to you?'

'Stopped my best friend doing what she should be doing – organizing voice teachers, that's what.'

'He doesn't stop me.'

'Doesn't he? Didn't Clive arrange for you to meet some-one in the chorus at Covent Garden and Martin stopped you?'

'I had to help him with his lines . . . he had an important audition the following day. He'd have done that for me if the tables had been turned.'

'If you think that, then you must think everything is possible – pigs no doubt fly in your neck of the woods.'

'Oh, Jenny, don't. I love him. I'm crazy about him. Don't you understand, the bloody singing means nothing now?'

'Well, it should. OK, you're in love, though why beats me – he's an egotistical creep, if you ask me.'

'I'm not asking you.'

'Love him, sleep with him, obviously from what you've told me he's volcanic in bed. But don't go off your rocker and *live* with him. I know your virginity had to go one day – Christ, I spend my time trying to find someone who'll oblige me by taking mine, only I've had no offers so far . . . *and* I'm twenty next week.'

'Jenny!' Kitty couldn't help laughing.

'But oh, my dear Kitty! Sweet, innocent Kitty – why him? Why? Why? Why?' Jenny banged her fist on the table so that the coffee-cups rattled.

'I don't know, Jenny.' Kitty reached out to touch her friend. 'He's not the easiest person to get on with, I'm the first to admit. But he makes me feel alive and important to him. And, of course, he loves me.' As she spoke, her voice was a mixture of pride and almost surprise that it should be she in this position.

'How much do you want me to draw?'

'Two hundred pounds.'

'Two hundred! What on earth are you renting? Buckingham Palace?'

'It needs one or two things. I can pay some back into my singing fund with overtime in the run-up to Christmas.'

She had not seen the flat, only heard of it from Martin who had found it in a house off the Earl's Court Road. When she did, it was with a disappointment which she wasn't quick enough to hide.

'I knew you wouldn't like it,' Martin said sulkily.

'Of course I do, don't be silly. Once I've cleaned it out and we've painted it, and I've made some curtains, it'll be lovely.' She forced her voice to sound optimistic, which was difficult given the seediness of the flat. The mustiness of dirty, second-hand furniture was everywhere. The threadbare linoleum floors could not have been swept in months and the antiquated cooker in the inadequate kitchen was thick with grease.

'I told Clive we're having the big bedroom,' Martin announced.

She'd have to buy a bed, she thought, as they inspected their bedroom, there was no way she was going to sleep on such an unwholesome-looking object. She peered out of the window down into the backyard of the converted house, which was full of rubbish from overspilled dust-bins.

'So what do you think?' Martin asked. 'Do we take it?'

'There's nothing else?' she asked hopefully. He shook his head. 'It's fine,' she said, for it was what he wanted to hear.

'Great, let's christen it then with some sex!'

'Not on that bed.' She looked away from him.

'No, no. On the floor – I can fuck you just as well on the floor.'

She wished, as he grabbed at her, that he did not speak of making love to her in such a way – it degraded something wonderful.

Working hard at the store, sorting out the flat, frequently being woken up by Martin in the small hours as he stumbled into the flat, invariably drunk, never saying where he had been, was beginning to take its toll on Kitty. Several times she had fallen asleep sitting at the table in her coffee-break, which had not gone unobserved. Shadows began to appear beneath her eyes and she was losing weight at an alarming rate.

'Don't you eat?' an anxious Jenny asked.

'Yes, of course I do,' Kitty lied in response. The truth was that she was cutting lunch to save money and at night she had given up cooking supper since Martin was so rarely in to eat it. She usually had a slice of bread and jam – cheaper than cheese.

Living with Martin was not easy. Kitty was not happy, but there seemed to be little she could do to alter the situation. She loved him, she couldn't change that. She had known he could be difficult before they had moved in together. She had not fallen into the trap of thinking she could change him. She was aware that what fascinated her most about him was his unpredictability. He could walk through the door in a thunderous mood and not speak to her all evening. Or he could bound in with a bunch of flowers, a bottle of wine or a box of chocolates and fuss over her, make her laugh and make her feel important. Since the two moods were in fairly equal proportions, she found the dark days easier to take, knowing sunnier ones would quickly follow.

Then he got a job. A real part, an important part in a play, and everything changed.

9

It seemed to Kitty as if shutters had been opened on their life together, and the sunshine allowed in. Even the little flat looked different, less drab, more inviting.

Until now Kitty had paid for most things – she had not minded, she was the only one earning and so it was fair that she should pay. But now Martin had money, only rehearsal wages at first, but he gave half of it to Kitty.

He was up early instead of late. Often he was out of the flat before she had left for work to run round the local park, to get fit, he said. He was at rehearsals for most of the day, she presumed. And when he returned he was ravenously hungry and she cooked for them both. He was drinking very little so that his head was clear in the mornings. Kitty had never dreamed such contentment could exist. Then Clive got a job as a spear-carrier at Stratford and moved out, and they were alone, and Kitty wondered what she had done to deserve such happiness.

When the play opened – in the suburbs, but everyone was confident it would move to the West End for a long run – Kitty sat in the audience feeling sick with apprehension for Martin. She need not have worried. The man was wonderful, everyone around her agreed, and she knew that the cheers at the end were mainly for him.

At the first-night party afterwards, in an Italian restaurant, Martin was almost incandescent with pride and success.

'You know you're living with a genius, don't you?' said a gruff voice behind her.

'Oh, yes, I do.' She swung round to find Olive Hardy, the play's producer and director. Olive was a short, stocky, chain-smoking woman of uncertain temperament who had started her theatre group on a shoe-string. She had the talent to coax and bully from actors performances even they did not think they were capable of. Her touch for choosing the right play was becoming legendary.

'What do you do, my dear?'

'I work at Selfridges – selling knickers.' Kitty smiled. Martin had taught her to say that, he said it was funnier and lingerie was a pretentious word.

'Are you resting?'

'Oh, no, that's all I've ever done.'

'Not enough. You won't keep him when he takes off if all you're doing is selling knickers.'

'I'm sorry?' Kitty looked puzzled, unsure if she had heard right.

'He will be bored by you, my dear. Bored out of his skull. I thought I'd best warn you.'

'Thank you,' said Kitty, wanting to hit Olive hard across her complacent face.

'If you take my advice you'll find something else to do that he can be proud of. Go to university, get a degree. You look intelligent enough. But a shop girl!' Olive chuckled, a wheezing smoker's laugh.

'Thank you for your advice, Miss Hardy. As it happens, I think he's quite proud of me since I've managed to support both of us until the pittance you pay him came along.'

Olive put out her rough, calloused hand and took hold of Kitty's. She tried to pull away but Olive only held on harder.

'I didn't mean to insult you, that was very rude of me. I apologize. I'm trying to help you. I've watched you looking at Martin all evening. You're besotted by him. He'll go to the top, that one, and I'm only trying to warn you so that you'll be there with him.'

'It's not that easy. What happens when this play's over?'

'This one will run and run, I can promise you. After? After they will be queueing up to book Martin Field.'

But the evening was ruined for Kitty. She could not get Olive's words out of her head.

And Olive was wrong. The play lasted three weeks. No West End impresario took it up. No producers were clamouring for Martin. Olive herself had flown to Australia for a six-month season in Sydney.

Kitty was at her wits' end not knowing what to do for Martin. His disappointment was dreadful to witness. He lay in bed all day and drank all night. And whatever she said to him irritated him out of all proportion.

'Jenny, I need another fifty quid,' she said, almost as an aside, as they rode down in the shop lift together to their different departments.

'No can do,' Jenny said airily.

'I beg your pardon?'

'You heard me loud and clear.'

'But I've got an electricity bill to pay, and Martin needs new shoes and a winter coat, and I promised him.'

'I'm sorry.' Jenny stepped out on her floor.

'What have you done with my money?' Kitty was right behind her.

'I've done nothing. It's safely in the bank and there it stays until you start to use it for the reason it was given to you.'

'But it's my money.'

'Agreed. But I'm looking after it. You've got £645 left. The rest you've frittered away on that no-hoper. Well, enough's enough. You'll thank me one day.'

'£645?' Kitty looked at Jenny aghast.

'That's what I said.'

'I didn't realize . . .'

'I know.'

'But how the hell am I supposed to find the time for singing lessons? I'm rushed off my feet all day.'

'Make time – that's how most people start, I should imagine.'

It was Christmas Eve. Kitty and Martin had been together for five months. A strange five months, she thought, as she carried the shopping the three flights up to the flat off the Earl's Court Road. Still, Martin seemed excited at the prospect of Christmas.

'It'll be the first Christmas I've ever spent in my own home,' he had told her, bringing tears to her eyes.

By volunteering for every shift possible Kitty had made sure they had enough money for it to be a bumper one. There was no point in the expense of a turkey for just the two of them, so she'd bought a chicken instead. But she'd stuff it, just as she had seen her mother do. She had bought a Christmas pudding since she had not thought to make one in time to mature. They had wine, a bottle of port, nuts and a baby stilton in a pot. She'd bought Martin a new jumper and a pair of shoes. She did not expect anything in return, for she knew he had no money – one day, she told herself.

She opened the flat door.

'You can't come in, not yet,' he called from the sitting-room.

In the kitchen she unpacked her groceries and waited. He appeared in the doorway. She looked up at him and smiled.

'You know, I think I love you more every day,' she said. He looked so handsome standing in the doorway, his thick, black, shoulder-length hair flopping forward, so that his fine, high cheekbones were accentuated even more. His dark brown eyes looked at her, she knew, with love. And he smiled his crooked smile. 'You really are the best-looking man I've ever seen.' She laughed.

'Why, thank you.' He bowed.

'I do hope our children take after you and not me.'

He looked away and for a moment she wondered if she should have said that.

'Come and see what I've done,' he said, holding out his hand, laughing at her. She relaxed. 'But close your eyes.'

He led her in to the sitting-room.

'All right. You can open them now.'

She saw, in the corner of the room, a small Christmas

tree lit with candles and decorated with balls he had made from silver paper.

'Oh, Martin – it's perfect.' She clapped her hands together excitedly.

'And see.' From the base of the tree he took a gaily wrapped parcel. 'For you.'

'Martin, you shouldn't . . . what am I saying? Of course you should. I love presents.' And she flung her arms round him and hugged him tightly to her.

She looked at her watch. It was already eight and she had the chicken to stuff and mince pies to make.

'I've work to do,' she said, making for the kitchen.

'I'm just off down to the pub. I promised a friend of mine I'd meet him for a quick jar.'

'Fine. See you later.' She stood on tiptoe to kiss him.

He didn't come back.

10

When, after the Christmas break, Kitty did not turn up for work for two days, Jenny decided to go and find out if she was ill, even though they were not officially speaking to each other. It was a very bedraggled Kitty who eventually opened the flat door to her. Her eyes were puffy from weeping, her hair was unkempt, and she looked as if she had been sleeping in the same clothes for days.

'What the hell's going on?' Jenny demanded, once Kitty had welcomed her with open arms.

'Martin's gone and I don't know where or why. He popped out for a drink on Christmas Eve.'

'And you haven't seen him since?' Kitty nodded. 'And you spent Christmas all alone?' Again Kitty nodded.

'The shit. The out-and-out shit!' Jenny exploded.

'Don't say that. He might be ill. He might be lying in a hospital somewhere.'

'No such luck!' Jenny snorted. 'Have you tried telephoning the hospitals?'

'I tried the local ones – he's not there. Then I ran out of money for the box. I haven't got any left . . .'

'So you haven't eaten?'

'No. I didn't want to. I had a feast here and couldn't face it. I gave the chicken to the cats that congregate round the dustbins – they enjoyed it.' She managed a weak smile.

'Did you make mince pies?'

'Yes. But I'd have had to force them down.'

'Got any left? I'm starving.'

'You're not on a diet, then?'

'No, Monday . . .'

At that Kitty laughed.

'Thank God for that laugh – it's obviously not terminal,' Jenny said as she accepted the plate of mince pies and began to tuck in.

'Did you go home?' Kitty asked.

'Yes. We had a wonderful Christmas – all five of my brothers and sisters made it this year. But we always have a great time, my mum's a genius at making sure we do.'

'Mine wasn't. By the time we sat down to eat we were all apologizing to her that she'd had to work so hard.' Kitty could smile at the memory now. 'But I don't think I'll ever enjoy it – my father was arrested at Christmas, and now this.' The miserable expression returned.

'I saw your mum in the High Street,' Jenny said, not allowing Kitty to return to the subject of Martin again.

'Really? How is she?'

'She looked blooming, though, to be honest, I think

she's a bit long in the tooth for a mini. Of course she had a moan about you never going home. I said you were so busy with work.'

'She said she never wanted to see me again – what's her problem? You didn't tell her about Martin?'

'What on earth do you take me for? Don't be daft, of course I didn't.'

'Did she mention Lana?'

'Mention her? She never stopped talking about her. Apparently she's doing really well now. She's got a recording contract in the offing.'

'That's good news, she deserves it.'

'But who's this Cy bloke? I thought she was living with someone called Cyril.'

'She is. He changed his name – thought it trendier.'

'He was right there. Cyril? I ask you. Sounds like a grand-dad, doesn't it? Well, this Cy bloke's doing well. He's handling a couple of groups now and Lana's singing with one of them.'

'That's great. They probably write their own material, that's why she's up for another contract. But I think she really wanted to be a solo artist.'

'Do you mind if I eat this last pie?'

'No. You carry on.' Kitty watched her friend enthusiastically biting into the mince pie, thinking that she shouldn't, for she could be pretty if she shed a couple of stone. 'I'm glad you came, Jenny.'

'So am I – but only for the food.' She grinned. 'Tell you what though, Kitty. Let's make a pact – don't let's ever fall out over a fellow, ever again.' Jenny leaned forward, serious now.

'No. They're not worth it, are they?' Kitty's smile was wider now. 'You still at the Y? You don't fancy moving in here, do you?'

'You mean that? I'd love to. But what if his nibs shows up?'

'There's Clive's room – he's with the RSC now. He's even had one line to say.'

'Martin wouldn't mind?'

'What's there to mind about? It's you who doesn't like him, not the other way around. And in any case he probably won't come back. It'll help me if you move in – the rent and everything.'

By the following evening Jenny had booked out of the YWCA and was cosily installed in Clive's room. She was one of those lucky people who with a swatch of cloth here, a well-chosen cushion there, a collection of shells and a picture or two, could transform a room into a home in a trice.

Jenny had lied to the personnel officer at Selfridges, saying that, worried by Kitty's non-appearance, she had gone round to her flat to find her alone, suffering from the flu and unable to telephone. So Kitty was able to return to her job, and since she looked so terrible no one questioned Jenny's tale.

After work one day a month later, Jenny told Kitty she was taking her out for the evening.

'Where?'

'Never you mind, it's a surprise,' Jenny said, as they boarded a bus. Twelve stops later they got off, walked up a leafy suburban road and stopped outside a church.

'St Swithin's! Jenny, you're impossible.'

'No. Concerned for you. Come on. I telephoned the vicar, he's expecting you. You're to audition for the choir he's involved with.'

'Don't be silly, I've no music with me. I've not prepared anything – I haven't sung for months.'

'You've got a voice, haven't you? Well then, just sing,' Jenny ordered as she rang the vicarage bell.

As they had both expected someone old and doddering, they were surprised to discover that the vicar, Peter Hawkins, was a youngish man in his thirties. Somehow, Kitty found, his youth made it easier to explain how she felt about singing, that she had no idea if she could sing, that in any case her voice was rusty from lack of use, and she wasn't even sure if she wanted to join a choir.

'Well, let's find out, shall we?' Peter smiled and went over to the grand piano which took up a large amount of space in his book-cluttered study. He handed her a pile of sheet-music. 'Choose what you like.'

Aware that her hands were shaking, Kitty leafed through the music with rising panic – there was nothing she knew. Until she saw 'Cherry Ripe'.

'I know this one from school.' She handed him the music.

'Do you want to stand here so that you can see the music and words?'

'No, thanks, I remember them.'

She stood opposite him while Jenny quietly, for her, sat in an armchair beside the coal fire.

Peter began to play. Kitty took a deep breath, opened her mouth and nothing happened.

'I'm so sorry,' she said, obviously distressed.

'It's all right, Miss Lawrence, or may I call you Kitty? Relax, it's only me and your friend here, we're not going to hang you if you sound like a fog-horn.'

'Yes, silly of me.' She smiled, coughed, nodded to him and they began again. She stood with her eyes closed, and this time she sang, at first a little uncertainly and then more strongly until her voice was filling the room with sound. The music faded away. Tentatively Kitty opened her eyes. Jenny was sitting as if transfixed, but seeing Kitty looking at her anxiously she winked and raised a thumb encouragingly. Peter sat silent, looking at his hands still lying on the keyboard.

'How old are you, Kitty?' he asked.

'Twenty next birthday.'

'That's fine.' He looked down at his hands again.

'So what do you think?' Jenny stood up. 'Go on, say something, do, if it's only goodbye.' She gave a laugh but it emerged as a rather strangled sound; she was nervous for her friend.

Peter seemed to shake himself. 'I'm sorry. It's just that I'm not sure what to say.' He half-turned on the piano stool so that he was facing them. 'For a start, that song is not the best choice you could have made, Kitty, especially when you haven't sung for so long – it's quite demanding.' He smiled again and Jenny thought she would burst with impatience. 'You see, I don't like to raise hopes unduly. I'm not a professional musician, only an enthusiastic amateur. But I think – and you must realize it's only my non-professional opinion – well, I think you could, with training, have a remarkable voice. I think you're right to doubt if you want to join a choir – it's a big voice, a soloist's voice.'

Jenny squealed, rushed across the carpet, tripped on a frayed piece and virtually fell on to the vicar, unceremoniously planting a kiss on his startled face.

'She hasn't left it too late, then? I've been nagging her for ages to do something about it.'

'No, a voice like hers won't reach its full maturity for some time. Had she trained earlier, before her voice was formed, it could have ruined it for ever. You'd be surprised by the number of proud mothers who do that.'

'Thank God for Lana then, vicar.' Jenny blurted out. Kitty frowned at her.

'And who's Lana?'

'The younger sister. Her mum thinks she's the one with the talent and so she ignored Kitty.'

'Lana has got a lot of talent,' Kitty said loyally.

'Yes, but different to yours. Not as important,' Jenny said with equal loyalty.

'Then thanks be for Lana. Kitty, let me tell you what I

suggest. If you could come here for several evenings, you and I could work at a little repertoire for you.'

'Yes, I could do that.'

'Can I come too?' Jenny asked.

'If Kitty doesn't mind.'

'Of course I don't. Then what?'

'I want you to sing for a friend of mine – a professional. Do you have any money?'

'A little – not much.'

'£645,' Jenny blurted out.

'Voice lessons are expensive. If I'm right, he'll suggest music college for a few years. Hopefully you'll get a scholarship, but it will still be expensive.'

'I could get work, I could work in the evenings – a waitress, a barmaid.'

'Still, we're jumping the gun a bit here. Let's do as I suggest and then I'll arrange for you to sing for Ben in a couple of weeks.'

When they finally left, Kitty hugged Jenny out on the pavement.

'Thanks. I'd never have done it without you bullying me.'

'I suppose that's a compliment. But why not? You must have known you could sing beautifully.'

'No, I didn't. Once at a concert I sang in I thought . . . maybe. But then, when my dad went to prison, I didn't feel like singing. Maybe I wanted to be a success for him. And then my confidence sapped away. And finally I wasn't sure if I could any more.'

'You know, I think I hate your mum.'

'Oh, don't say that, Jenny. She can't help herself – how could she judge me when it's a kind of music that's alien to her?' Kitty explained.

Jenny smiled at her. 'We'll show her, though, won't we? We'll show her which daughter is the star.'

Felix Masters was attending to his toilette with his usual studied care. Looking after himself to ensure he always looked his best gave him inordinate pleasure. Hair, skin, teeth, nails, all perfect – he smiled with satisfaction at his reflection.

Felix could easily pass for mid-thirties; he did not look the forty-five he was. He was proud that he could still fit into the clothes he wore when he was twenty. He had had the good fortune to be born to moderately successful and beautiful parents; he had never wanted for anything and had been handsome from birth.

His father's untimely death in a railway accident, when Felix was eighteen, had given him sufficient funds to use as a bedrock for the fortune he had always intended to make. He was blessed with a quick brain, and a shrewd grasp of figures and the ability to work when others were dropping with fatigue had ensured that his ambition was realized – Felix played the markets like a maestro.

He devoted nearly as much energy to remaining handsome. He swam every day of the year, and played energetic tennis in summer and violent squash in winter. While loving food and good wine he watched his diet carefully, balancing a rich meal with a frugal one, and so had kept his body slim and taut.

He made a final check of his appearance in his mirror, idly wondering what he had been invited to Benjamin Cooper's for this evening. He knew why he had been.

Felix couldn't help but admire Ben's nerve. He hadn't heard from the man in months, and then, with only two days' notice, he had been invited – though perhaps summoned might be a better description – to dinner that evening. Felix supposed a lot of people he knew would have taken offence and refused. But he wasn't like that, he was sufficiently assured of his own importance not to be too easily slighted. And he liked the old rascal, his dinners were good, and this evening was free in his diary, so why not? Even though he knew it would cost him.

Money – that was why he'd been invited, that's why most people were invited to Ben's. He was like a spider in a web, seducing the rich with his table, his contacts, putting words into the right ears for those in search of honours. When he thought he could get no more he dropped them as if the spider had spat them out. It puzzled several people, it amused Felix. Ben was a good barometer of the state of the fortunes of many in the City who boasted of their wealth. When they no longer sat at Ben's table, this was a sign that they were in financial difficulties, and awareness of this had often helped Felix in his buying and selling.

He'd heard rumours recently that Ben was on the prowl again. Although it wasn't long since the last fund-raising, this was not surprising. Ben could get through a government grant, intended for a year, in a matter of weeks.

What would it be tonight? A new, expensive, latest-technology lighting system – the best. Ben always wanted the best, and why not? Felix was the same. Perhaps he was looking for the fat fee he needed to fund his latest masterclass – Ben had been innovative with these, and with good results. New costumes? New instruments? He'd pretend to be dense, play Ben along, tease him. But no doubt he'd write the cheque, he usually did.

To the world Felix was a cold fish – he'd heard this said of him when people thought he was out of earshot. He did not mind what they said, though, for he knew it wasn't true. He had passion for those things that were important to him.

Felix had three great and expensive passions. Himself. His collection of Victorian prints. And opera.

He had decided long ago that he did not need a wife, it would make life too complicated and untidy. Even as a younger man he had not needed sex often and he was certain it would be irksome to feel duty-bound to perform just to keep a wife from becoming a shrew. He was sure in himself that when he sat in an opera house and listened to a great singer, the joy he felt, the physical pleasure it gave him, lasted longer than would any quick matrimonial fumbling.

It was this love of opera as much as his liking for Ben that would ensure the outcome of the evening. Ben Cooper was not only the Principal of the Hampstead Conservatoire, he also owned his own small opera touring company – taking music to the masses, he said, not that Felix had ever heard of the company being swamped by peasants desperate for culture. But it was a nice idea, a good nurturing ground for new talent, and Felix was happy to help.

Tonight, he knew, the food would be excellent, the wines sublime, and the talk and gossip would be about the musical world Felix loved and wished he had the talent to be a true part of. He called to Mrs Moffat, his housekeeper, that he was about to leave and not to bolt the door, please – something she did with irritating regularity.

Felix's cab pulled up in front of the large detached Victorian house in Blackheath where Ben had lived from birth. Must be worth a pretty penny by now, Felix thought, as he sprinted up the steps and rang the bell.

Frieda Cooper opened the door. Her face lit up with a beautiful smile when she saw Felix, and she kissed him on both cheeks in welcome. She was a stunning-looking woman, full-breasted, tall, dark-haired and with an intelligent expression – Felix loathed women with vacuous faces. He sometimes wondered whether if he'd met Frieda first he wouldn't be married after all. It was a mystery to all their friends why she had chosen Ben, who was twenty years older, small, dark, fat, untidy, forgetful and ugly to boot. But they shared one great passion – music – and a second – food. It was because of Frieda that Felix knew the dinner would be wonderful.

'What is your grasping husband wanting money for tonight?' Felix grinned as she helped him off with his coat.

'It's such a relief that you know why you're here, Felix, and I don't have to pretend with you.' Frieda chuckled, a lovely deep sound – Felix hated women with high-pitched voices. He was aware, though, that she had neatly side-stepped his question.

He walked behind her as she led the way to the large drawing-room. He watched her graceful movements under the long-skirted dress and wondered if he should have an affair with her, but instantly gave up the idea. Too complicated, too messy, and in any case he was too fond of Ben.

'Ben! How are you, you old rascal?' They greeted each other enthusiastically, and a maid, hired for the evening, brought Felix a glass of champagne.

He was surprised to find only one other guest in the room. Normally Ben invited a good ten or a dozen people. Quickly he glanced at his watch to see if he had made a mistake and arrived early.

'No, you're not early. Just you, Peter and me tonight, Felix,' Ben said, having seen Felix's quick check of the time.

'Peter, lovely to see you. How's St Swithin's? How's the choir – the Bach Ensemble, isn't it?'

'Why, yes. Well, thank you – going from strength to strength, in fact. But St Swithin's roof's in a mess.' Peter smiled warmly, pleased that Felix had remembered so much about him. His memory for people and facts was one of Felix's biggest assets.

The four of them dined splendidly on turbot, rack of lamb and an apple and apricot tart of Frieda's making, the pastry of which was sublime. It was during the cheese, a stilton at peak perfection, that the doorbell chimed and Frieda excused herself and did not return.

'I've laid on a little treat for you, Felix. For you alone.' Ben tapped the side of his nose with one long musician's finger. 'Shall we go?'

Carrying large brandies, they entered Ben's music-room, which Felix had always admired for its space and beautiful parquet flooring but most of all for the acoustics which Ben, with help from a sound engineer, had made as ideal as humanly possible.

It was a large room which ran the width of the back of the house. It had french windows which in summer opened on to Frieda's beautiful garden but on winter evenings were screened by full, heavily lined curtains of rust-coloured wild silk.

Frieda was at the far end, by the grand piano, talking to a young woman who could have been her twin but for the ten years' difference in their ages.

'Good heavens, I didn't know Frieda had a sister,' Felix said with surprise and interest.

'She doesn't. It's a remarkable likeness, though, isn't it?' Ben smiled a very private smile. He knew very well how much Felix admired Frieda – his was the first name to spring to mind when he had first met the girl. 'No. This is Kitty Lawrence, who has kindly agreed to give us a small concert to make the evening perfect, haven't you, my dear?'

Kitty smiled shyly as she shook hands with Felix. He was far too handsome, she thought – Martin had left her with a deep suspicion of handsome men. And his blue eyes were cold as he looked closely at her, as if approving her in a way which made her feel very uncomfortable. She wasn't sure she liked this man at all.

'How very kind of you. And what are you going to perform?' Felix asked, using all the charm for which he was famous, and totally unaware that it was falling on barren ground where Kitty was concerned.

'The vicar and I thought we'd start with some Rossini.'

'Excellent.' Felix smiled warmly at her, hoping her sing-ing voice was as charming as her speaking one.

'And this is Kitty's friend Jenny.' Felix shook hands, noting Jenny's plumpness, of which he disapproved, and her pleasant, honest face, of which he did approve.

'Enchanted.' He bowed slightly and Jenny giggled at his formality, which quite put him out. Peter sat down at the piano and Frieda dimmed the lights as they took their places in the comfortable armchairs which were set in a row with small tables for glasses between them.

A single bright spotlight shone down on Kitty who stood tall and straight in front of the rust curtains. She wore a full-length, royal blue, empire-line dress of complete sim-plicity, which she had bought for this occasion. Her hair was loose and held back from her face by a matching Alice band. Oddly, she carried a long red chiffon scarf in her hand that did not contrast happily with the strident blue of the dress.

Dreadful colour, thought Felix, and worse cut. But in a better dress, with a little skilful make-up and her hair decently cut, she could easily look as stunning as Frieda, he mused as the pianist began.

Kitty closed her eyes and began to sing. For three-quarters of an hour she entertained them. At the end she felt exhausted and empty as she bowed gracefully to the clapping which sounded silly from four pairs of hands, she thought, but then total silence would have been worse.

'Delightful, Kitty, and thank you,' Ben said, standing up and taking her hand.

'Delightful,' Felix repeated. It had been, but it was also puzzling. The girl had a voice, for sure, but a raw voice, totally untrained. He shook her hand.

'I'll get you a taxi,' Ben said.

'We came on the bus . . . we don't mind going back on one, do we?' Kitty looked over to the corner of the room where Jenny was sitting grinning from ear to ear with pride like a fat Cheshire cat.

'I think a cab would be more suitable,' Jenny said firmly.

'Jenny's right, my dear. It's late now,' Ben said, fussing about her, helping her with a tweed coat that looked dreadful with the dress. And he and Frieda showed both girls out.

Felix was left with his brandy and a silent vicar who sat looking worried and studying his hands as if surprised to find them at the ends of his arms. Felix did not try to make conversation; the man had played well, and he knew enough about musicians to realize that some took time to unlock themselves from the magic of performing.

'Well then, Felix. What did you think?' Ben asked as he bustled noisily back into the room, moving swiftly for one so corpulent.

'Charming, Ben. Totally charming – but I hated the dress.' Felix smiled.

'More brandy?' Ben poured them all another generous glass. 'Remarkable voice, didn't you think?'

'A strong voice, yes. But very rough in places, Ben, wouldn't you say?'

'Of course, her breathing's all wrong, she doesn't even know how to. But the middle register, didn't you hear it – the resonance, the depth? An excellent middle. Of course the top and bottom aren't there yet, but she's not twenty, it'll come . . . And when it does, Felix, I'd lay money on that slip of a thing being one of the voices of the century.'

'Really?' Felix was unsure, but then he would be the first to admit he did not have Ben's ear.

'Oh, yes. It's one of those voices that won't even be at its best until she's thirty. I'm excited. God, Felix, what an opportunity, what an honour to be in at the very beginning.'

'She's obviously had no tuition.' Felix was finding it difficult to get quite as carried away as Ben.

'Peter coached her for this evening and that's it. She was even thrown out of the school choir for singing too loud. She's perfect, untainted material.' By now Ben was marching up and down the music-room, not actually tearing his hair out with elation but looking as if he was.

'She must obviously be trained, then, if you think she has such potential,' Felix said mildly.

'She *must*.' Ben shouted the word. 'That's the problem, though. No money.'

'But you could award her a scholarship, Ben. One of the many you've managed to arrange.' Felix smiled slyly at him.

'And I shall, I shall. But you know and I know and Peter here knows the bursaries are never enough. Everyone else gets help from their parents. This girl has no father and her mother won't help. She works as a shop girl – so no money. Just a few hundred set by.'

'A shop girl?' Felix sounded amazed.

'She's had no chances, Felix. None whatsoever. I want to help. I have to help.' Ben was jumping up and down again, looking wilder by the minute.

'Of course you must,' Felix said calmly. 'That was a wonderful dinner, Frieda.' He stood up as if to go.

'But Felix, you don't seem to understand what I'm trying to say.'

'But I do, my dear Ben. You want me to support this young woman through college and after, I suppose, until she's established. Am I right?'

'Well, yes – just through college, I thought, but —'

'Your tart was better than anything I ever ate in France, Frieda.' Felix grinned, enjoying himself enormously.

'But Felix —' Ben was almost wailing as Felix began to cross the room.

'One thing, Frieda, could you do me a favour?'

'I'll try, Felix.'

'Could you take that girl out and buy her a half-way decent dress and send the bill to me?'

'With pleasure, Felix. How kind of you.'

'You mean . . .?' Ben was nearly exploding.

'Of course, Ben. When have I ever refused you?' Felix was laughing now. 'Not that I can hear what you're hearing, but then you're the expert and who am I, a mere businessman, to disagree?' He shrugged his elegantly jacketed shoulders.

'You'll be doing mankind a service,' Ben gushed.

'Oh, come, Ben, that's a bit of an exaggeration. But it suddenly struck me, it might be rather amusing to sponsor an artist in this way. I'll call you tomorrow and we'll talk figures, Ben.'

'Thank you, Felix. I'll make you proud of her.'

'There's just one thing. I don't want her to know. Pretend it's another bursary or something, will you?'

Felix decided to walk part of the way before hailing a taxi – a good walk, on such a cold February night, would not be a bad idea after such a meal. As he walked he thought about what he had heard. What if Ben was right? What if tonight he had heard the first performance of a great diva? What if she succeeded, and because of him and his help? It was an exciting prospect. She would be his soprano, created because of him. It was an extraordinary thought.

Then he thought of the girl. With professional guidance she could look lovely. There had been something very sweet and vulnerable about her tonight. A wariness, as if she had been bruised.

12

In the taxi, travelling back to their flat, Kitty barely spoke; she could not, she felt in a daze. Jenny, sensing this, remained silent too. But once home, Kitty changed and began pacing the tiny room, plumping cushions, rearranging the perfectly aligned ornaments on the mantelshelf and then putting them back in their original positions. And now she could not stop talking.

'Everything felt so right. The voice, my body – everything!' she said excitedly.

'You sounded right, too,' Jenny said, rooting in a drawer where she was convinced she had hidden a half-eaten Mars bar from herself.

'It's an odd feeling. The vicar told me about it. You can be singing and there's a moment, very special, when you're all at one. I wasn't quite sure what he meant but it happened tonight, I'm sure it happened – it was half-way through the song from *Carmen* and . . .' She hit her forehead with the flat of her palm. 'Heavens, it's so difficult to explain. But it was as if the music and I had melted into each other.' She looked at Jenny, who had given up her fruitless search for the chocolate bar.

'Interesting,' Jenny said in a flat-toned voice.

'But also – and he didn't tell me this – also, just for a split second, it felt as though everyone in the room had joined me.'

'Sounds what everyone says an orgasm's like.' Jenny grinned.

'But I was thinking in the taxi,' Kitty continued as if she hadn't heard, 'if it could be like that with so few people, I've been wondering – *if* one sang in front of a huge audience and *if* the moment came, would the effect be even stronger if it was shared with thousands?'

'Like a multiple orgasm at an orgy?' Jenny suggested, and Kitty laughed and threw a cushion at her.

'You're so prosaic, Jenny.'

'It's as well we're not all artistic, someone's got to keep their feet on the ground.'

'I'm sorry to go on so.'

'Don't apologize, it's interesting, but don't expect me to understand half of what you're talking about.'

'It's odd, when I sing, I sometimes feel almost as if there's someone else inside me doing it.'

'Sounds uncomfortable.' Jenny smiled.

'Tonight, I really thought we – this other person and me, I mean – might be able to do it – become a real singer.'

'Of course you will, I don't doubt it. Fancy some hot chocolate?'

They drank their chocolate and then the remains of one of Jenny's bottles of sweet sherry. The combination made them both feel sick.

'Look here, I know you're excited, but I've got to get some shut-eye, and now I feel sick I want to get to sleep before I am,' Jenny said after an hour of listening to Kitty, who still seemed unable to stop talking or moving about.

Reluctantly Kitty went to bed too, but she lay awake in the dark, staring at the ceiling, her mind in turmoil as she allowed herself to dream impossible dreams.

During the following week, Kitty found it difficult to concentrate on brassières, nightdresses and knickers. Several times the supervisor had had to speak sharply to her when, away in a world of her own, she had inadvertently ignored customers. The assistants she worked most closely with became exasperated with her, and finally one told her that if she didn't pull her finger out and add her weight, she for one wasn't going to speak to her. Kitty was finally given the task of checking and tidying the stock-room so that calm could be restored on the shop-floor.

She hadn't known what to expect, that was her problem. Peter Hawkins, while kind and helpful, had merely hinted that perhaps Professor Cooper might be able to help her. And when she had sung for him the first time, one afternoon when she had sneaked off from work, he had said nothing except that she had a lot to learn. Then the invitation had come to sing to his guests after his dinner-party and still nothing had been said, even when he had shown them to the door, so that she was unsure why she had been invited.

For the first four days following the party Kitty was convinced that she would hear something, even though she did not know what. The post came after they had left for work so each evening it was with a pounding heart and butterflies in her stomach that she checked her mail. But for a week and a half she had been disappointed. She decided that she had imagined that her recital had been a success, imagined there had been that special moment of rapport with her audience, imagined she had a voice worth bothering about.

'Why not give the vicar a call from the phone box?' Jenny suggested one evening when again there was nothing in the post.

'I couldn't do that.'

'Why not?'

'I just couldn't. I mean, it would be so pushy.'

'Well, you've got to find out, otherwise you'll go bonkers.'

'But if I did and they hadn't liked me, then I'd have to hear him say it, wouldn't I?'

'I've never heard anything so wet. I'll telephone him for you.'

'No, you won't!' Kitty swung round to face her. 'Don't you dare, Jenny. Do you understand?'

'OK. OK. Keep your hair on.' Jenny shrugged her shoulders and left Kitty fretting while she went into the kitchen to open a tin of spaghetti hoops for their supper. She didn't think it was her imagination, but from odd things Kitty had said she wondered if, come the end, she wasn't going to be blamed for everything – for arranging to meet the vicar and for Kitty having had her hopes raised. She'd only acted with the best intentions, she told herself as she opened the biscuit tin in the hope that there might be a chocolate digestive lurking there. But there wasn't.

Consequently, when after a fortnight they returned from work to find a letter with the Hampstead Conservatoire logo in the top left-hand corner, Jenny was as excited as Kitty and probably more relieved.

'You open it, I can't.' Kitty thrust the letter at her and Jenny could see her hand was shaking.

'Gosh, you are pathetic at times,' Jenny said, but in her teasing way. 'Give it here.' She scanned the letter quickly and then re-read it to make sure she had made no mistake.

'Well? What does it say?' Kitty was virtually hopping from one leg to the other.

'It says, my girl . . . it says . . .' Jenny was smiling broadly, enjoying the excitement, enjoying building up the tension. 'You've been awarded a scholarship to commence immediately.'

'A scholarship? Me?' Kitty said with disbelief.

'Well, they haven't awarded it to me, that's for sure.'

'Let me see, let me see!' Kitty grabbed the letter back and read it and then clutched it to her. 'Imagine that! They liked me – they must have. I wonder who Catherine Willow was? The Catherine Willow Memorial Scholarship. Doesn't it sound grand?'

'Very,' Jenny agreed.

'It should be enough money to see me through, that's if you stay on living here. Oh, would you? Oh, do, please say you will.'

'Where else would I go? And, more to the point, why should I want to go?'

'But how do I get time off to see Professor Cooper on Thursday?'

'You take it off, that's what. You've got to tell them anyway that you're leaving, haven't you? Just explain what's happened.'

'That's true. Oh, Jenny, I think I could die of happiness.'

'Fat lot of use that would be. Tell you what, we've got to celebrate. Let's go out and have a Wimpy.'

'Yes, let's. And finish up at the pub and have a couple of Bacardis.'

'Why not?'

'I tell you one good thing, Jenny. Since we went to St Swithin's and all this started I've hardly given Martin a thought.'

'Honestly?' said Jenny, apparently all innocence. But she was laughing inside.

Max Leitman was not happy. He liked things to be orderly, he always had done – his Teutonic ancestry at work, he was convinced. So he had not been happy when Cooper called him into his office to announce that a new pupil was starting, not at the beginning of a scholastic year, not even at the beginning of a term, but in the middle of one. It was not usual, nor was it right. It put schedules out and irritated Max inordinately. Nor had he been any too happy to be told that this particular pupil was to receive the maximum attention possible, to the extent that once they had removed the rough edges, once Max had done his job, which was to teach her how to sing correctly, Ben Cooper was talking of asking Madame Gina Cellini to give her extra tuition. Cellini cost a fortune and only took the *crème de la crème*, and that normally after years of study. To make matters worse, in Max's opinion, she was not half as good a teacher as he was. Ben Cooper must be screwing the girl, Max finally concluded as, on the Thursday, he awaited the arrival of Kitty, who was to be assessed by him. His temper rose to dangerous heights when the telephone on his desk rang and it was Ben to say that Cellini had graciously agreed to sit in on the session.

Max slammed the receiver down angrily and strode to the window where he stood looking at the early March sunshine on the lovely display of daffodils in the garden. But his anger blinded him to their beauty.

He fingered his light brown, neatly trimmed beard. His spectacles slipped slightly and he pushed them back on to the bridge of his nose with an irritated gesture. He wondered, not for the first time, if he wouldn't be better off handing in his notice at the end of this scholastic year and looking for a position elsewhere.

He would have no difficulty finding somewhere else. Max was good at his job, loved it and lived for it. Music was his life. Like everyone in the world of music, he had once dreamed of a great career as a professional. But, unlike most, Max was able to look at himself and his abilities with a ruthless honesty and realize he would always be second-rate. If employed by the great companies he would only be able to look forward to the smaller roles. To be a lead singer he would end up in second-rate touring companies, and he didn't want that. He had worked on the stage long enough for it to be a wrench to leave. He knew he would miss the companionship, the excitement – everything. But Max was a perfectionist and he wanted to be the best. He had turned to teaching and had discovered that he was first-rate at that.

Being the best at the Hampstead Conservatoire had been, and was, an uphill task. Not that the talent wasn't there, it was. Not that the facilities weren't here, they were. It was Ben who made things difficult. He spent money like water, and he had fancies. And when a fancy beset him he would throw money at it which might have been better spent elsewhere.

This young girl, Kitty, or whatever her name was, was a typical case. Without consulting anyone, including Max – the one person who should have been consulted, should have heard her – Ben had doled out a non-existent scholarship to her. The Catherine Willow Scholarship? 'Bah!' Max said aloud. He'd never heard of it, manufactured by Ben for the occasion no doubt. It certainly wasn't one of their real scholarships, all those were awarded in the spring for the following autumn – why, in a month's time he would be in the thick of auditioning young hopefuls for them. He had never even heard of a Catherine Willow until Ben had dropped this annoying bombshell. Ben was a maverick who treated this school as if it was his own to do with as he wished.

She was probably no good anyway, Max thought, as he turned his back on the window.

Kitty was flustered. She had been in such a state that she had caught the wrong bus. She had been on it for some time before she came to her senses and realized she was heading for Islington.

The Conservatoire was several hundred yards from the bus stop and she had had to ask the way a couple of times, before, out of breath, she pushed through the gate. She looked at her watch. Despite everything she was half an hour early. What should she do? Walk in? No, she dared not do that. She decided to wander around the garden for a while.

Kitty had never been near a music college before and had not known what to expect. Certainly not this large, elegant mansion set in such beautiful grounds. She did not know that the founder, Lady Ashington, who had founded the school, to specialize in singing, in the last century, had specifically chosen this position because it was away from the fog and grime of central London. The clearest air was essential for her pupils' voices, in that generous and enlightened lady's view. In another era Flora Ashington, possessor of a fine contralto, would herself have been a famous singer. Sadly for her, encased in the strictures of Victorian etiquette and society, she could only perform for her own enjoyment and that of her friends. To compensate, from the vast fortunes left her first by her steel magnate father and then by her wealthy, aristocratic husband, she had founded this establishment for the talented under-classes who were free to sing on the stage. Intended for singers only, the school had expanded over the years and now taught instrumentalists, conductors and composers. It had grown to be a full-blown conservatoire.

The Conservatoire was smaller than similar establish-ments elsewhere, but what it lacked in size it made up for in prestige. After a hundred years its reputation for excel-lence was world-wide. Alicia Belle, born Alice Brown, world-famous soprano, Arturo Costa, born Henry Clerk, world-famous tenor, Anna Weisbaden, born Ann Smithers, greatest Wagnerian singer of them all, had all trained here during the past fifty years. There were others, good, honest, reliable singers, to augment those three legends. Competition to get in here was fierce in the extreme and Kitty had no idea of just how incredibly lucky she was.

With still fifteen minutes to go until her appointment Kitty climbed the wide steps to the porticoed terrace and rang the bell. When no one answered she pushed the door open and stepped into a large circular hall with white marble pillars and a black and white chequered floor. A staircase with intricate brass banisters and handrail, gleam-ing in the sunlight from a cupola above, soared to an elegantly curved landing. Tall, shiny mahogany doors, all closed, stood sentinel around the hall. The place was a haven of calm and peace. There were no chairs to sit on and no signs to tell Kitty where to go. She stood forlornly and wondered what to do now.

'Are you lost?'

Kitty looked up to where the voice had come from. Hanging over the landing rail was a young man with a large head, a mane of frizzy hair and owl-like spectacles, wearing a huge red and green striped scarf twined round his neck.

'Yes. I've an appointment with Professor Cooper at three.'

'You've come to the wrong entrance.' The young man loped down the stairs on legs which looked too skinny to support his weight. 'Come with me.'

He led Kitty along a carpeted passageway whose red walls were covered in etchings of composers and musicians. At the end was a simple white door beyond which was a scruffy corridor with chipped paintwork and scuffed rush matting on the floor. 'Welcome to the real world.' He grinned. 'What are you here for, a job?'

'No. A sort of audition, I suppose.'

Kitty's guide stopped so sharply that she almost cannoned into him.

'You sure?' He turned, a puzzled expression on his face. 'Auditions start next month – it's hell here then, white-faced, nail-biting would-be students throwing up in the bogs. Hell!'

'I've already been offered a place – the Catherine Willow Memorial Scholarship.' She realized she was boasting but could not help herself.

'Odd. Never heard of it. Then you start in September?'

'No, immediately.'

'Even odder.' He stopped, knocked on a door, walked in and beckoned Kitty to follow. 'Mrs Jackson, I've a young woman here who thinks she's starting mid-term. Can't be, can it?'

'Miss Lawrence? You're early,' the fat, grey-haired woman said accusingly. 'The professor is delayed. Show Miss Lawrence round the school for fifteen minutes, Paul, then take her to Max in Studio One, would you? I don't know what else to do with her.'

'Sure.' Paul shrugged and he and Kitty trooped out again. 'Don't take any notice of her, she's a menopausal old bag.' He walked quickly, explaining the different parts of the building as they moved through a confusing number of corridors and up and down innumerable flights of steps.

'This is the Prof's dream come true – put up five years ago.' Paul opened a small door and Kitty found herself in the balcony of a good-sized theatre, decorated in white and midnight blue. A stark but beautiful modern steel chandelier hung over the main auditorium.

'This is where we hold concerts, recitals – operas, even. Before this was built they had to hire theatres, you see. But the Prof's a whizz at screwing bread out of people. He wants to build new practice rooms next, about time too. I'll show you.'

Kitty's tour took in two large cavernous rehearsal rooms, classrooms and private teaching studios, all of which were in use, so she could only peer through the windows.

'These are the practice rooms,' Paul said, opening the door on an upper floor which led to a narrow corridor on each side of which were small bare cubicles with sound-proofed tile walls. But from each one the muffled sounds of instruments emerged. A soprano was trilling in one.

'As you can hear, the sound-proofing is almost useless. Hopeless as they are, it's still a fight to get the use of one. Best thing is to get in early in the morning and to bag it.'

'Are you a singer?' she asked.

'God, no – I'm relieved to say. I'm a pianist. The singers think they're an élite. What are you, a harpist?'

'No, a soprano, actually.'

'Really?' he said unabashed. 'I'd have sworn you were a harpist. Let me show you the library.'

But she reminded him of the time and he guided her back to the front hall.

'My, you are important, aren't you? Studio One, no less,' he said, as they stopped in front of one of the tall doors. Kitty smiled nervously for the tone of his voice was mildly sarcastic. 'You wait in there. I'll find Max for you.'

The studio had evidently once been a drawing-room. The ceiling was finely moulded and a starkly beautiful mantelpiece was still in place, even if no fire burned in the grate. The floor was of fine parquet on which the sun, pouring through the french windows, shone. There were two grand pianos, side by side. A gilded harp – what *had* Paul meant? A bust of Beethoven on a plinth, one sofa and four armchairs. The rest of the room was bare.

Left alone, Kitty found that her nerves, which had subsided a little, returned with gusto. The room seemed suddenly airless, and she searched in her handbag for a tissue to wipe her hands, aware that they had become too damp to shake hands.

The door opened and a young man walked in.

'Hi!' he said breezily. 'You've got your music?'

'Yes.' She fumbled with her old music-case, the one she had had since school. 'Here.' She handed him the sheet-music that she and Peter Hawkins had agonized over.

'What do you want to start with?'

'I thought the Rossini, what do you think?'

'It's all the same to me.' He shrugged, opening the piano lid as he did so.

Max Leitman entered and introduced himself, but did not shake Kitty's hand. He sat in one of the chairs and stared at her so intently that she had to look away. He was staring at her because she wasn't what he had anticipated. Ben Cooper had had several affairs with students in the past but he always chose blonde, smallish and giggly ones, in total contrast to his stunning wife. If this was a girlfriend of Ben's she was different. For a start, she looked like Frieda Cooper. Max was staring because he hadn't expected some-one so tall and dark, with such a serious and intelligent expression. If she hadn't been so frightened she would have looked quite beautiful in his eyes.

He coughed loudly, as if to stop such thoughts, and Kitty jumped and giggled, saying she was sorry even though she was not sure what she was apologizing for. The spell was broken and just then the door opened and Ben swept in accompanied by Cellini – once known as La Gloriosa by the opera aficionados in Milan, but now large and bloated. Kitty recognized her from her photograph on record-sleeves and wished she was the fainting kind, she had not expected this.

Again the door opened. With relief that showed in the depth of her smile, Kitty saw Peter Hawkins enter with a blond and handsome man whom she felt she knew, although she was in too much of a state to remember from where. The small group chattered among themselves, shaking hands and kissing Cellini, and ignored Kitty as they finally decided who was to sit where.

'Right, Miss Lawrence. Let us begin.'

The accompanist began the introduction. Kitty took a deep breath and closed her eyes. She was quite expecting no sound to emerge and was amazed when it did. She was barely a third of the way into the song when Ben Cooper clapped his hands.

'Next, Miss Lawrence.'

Kitty felt quite affronted at being stopped in full flow – had it been that bad? she wondered in mounting misery.

'Is it possible for you to sing with your eyes open?' Cellini demanded.

'I'm sorry,' Kitty said quietly.

'What did she say?'

'She said sorry, Gina,' Ben explained.

Kitty began again, and to stop herself closing her eyes, sang to the bust of Beethoven instead. Again she was stopped before she had finished.

'But this voice is totally untrained. What on earth am I

doing here, Ben? You can't expect me to teach such a novice.' Cellini appeared to double in size with indignation.

'Gina, my darling, would I expect you to? Just listen. Max will sort her out, won't you, Max? He'll do basic groundwork and then, when she's ready, we'll send her to you. I just wanted you to hear what we have found. My dear?' He smiled at Kitty who now felt only stark terror; she wished she had the courage to tell them all to go to hell.

'"*Si, mi chiamano Mimi*",' she almost whispered instead. Cellini shuddered visibly, but whether at her accent or her choice, Kitty could not be sure.

This time she forgot and closed her eyes. Convinced it had all been a disaster, she decided to sing for herself. As Puccini's music worked its magic she forgot where she was, she sang because she loved the music, she sang for herself, she had nothing to lose. And this time, they allowed her to finish the aria.

The music faded and Kitty, aware once again where she was, stood there miserably, forcing herself to look at her judges who were now huddled together. Only the handsome blond man, who sat slightly apart, said nothing but smiled encouragingly at her. Diffidently, she smiled back.

If the others thought they were speaking in whispers they were wrong. To her mortification, Kitty could hear everything they said.

'Well?' said the Professor.

'She can't breathe,' Max said. He walked across to Kitty. He breathed deeply, his slim figure suddenly marred by the barrelling of his chest and gut. 'Feel that,' he ordered.

Kitty reached tentatively out to touch him, his stomach was taut and as hard as a rock.

'Muscle,' Max said proudly. 'You'll discover muscles you never knew you had. We sing from here.' He pointed to the bulge. 'Forget this.' He made a slicing motion of his throat.

'She walks like a camel.' Cellini finally spoke. Kitty did not know where to look but blushed at the woman's rudeness in speaking of her as if she was not there.

'That's no problem. We'll get her the best deportment specialists, she can learn to move, stage-work. You know she can, Gina, my sweet angel.'

'True. Certainly she's got a fine resonant middle. I think the higher register will be achieved, but the lower?' Cellini looked across at Max.

'I'd have thought there was little problem,' Max said calmly, while inwardly he was seething with excitement. But he was puzzled, too. No matter how good this girl was, he had planned to say she wasn't, to refuse to teach her – and here he was doing the exact opposite.

'And together, Gina, you and me – what can't we achieve?'

'Oh, Max, such a flirt.' Cellini laughed. She stood up, and with surprising grace for one so large walked across to the piano. Nodding at the young accompanist, she began to sing the same aria. Kitty stood transfixed at the beautiful sound, her senses felt bombarded, assaulted, absorbed by beauty – and this was someone retired, someone past their best, she thought despondently.

'There, my dear, that's what we shall do for you. You have something, Ben is right. When Max has taught you how to breathe, how to sing, then I, Cellini, will coax the greatness out of you.' Cellini smiled at her, and Kitty found she could forgive her anything just to hear that voice – even hearing that she moved like a camel.

It was early evening before Kitty was free to go home. It was strange to be returning from a different direction. She was looking forward to seeing Jenny. At least tonight they would have something different to talk about. Both of them, some time ago, had acknowledged how boring their lives had become – working in the shop and then coming home and talking about the shop. Some days they felt as if they never left the place.

'Jenny, it's me. I've so much to tell you,' Kitty called out as she entered the flat.

Jenny appeared in the doorway to the sitting-room. She stood with her hands on her hips, legs apart, defiance in her stance and an angry expression on her face.

'What's the matter, Jenny?' Kitty asked, puzzled, as she hung up her coat on the peg in the hall.

'Have I got a surprise for you!' She stepped back to let Kitty pass.

'Martin!' she exclaimed at the sight of the familiar figure. She had often dreamed of this moment. She had spent hours planning what she would say. She knew she would enjoy telling him exactly what she thought of him and his treatment of her and where he could go. She took a step further into the room. She held out her arms. 'Oh, Martin,' she cried, and fell sobbing with relief into his arms.

13

Lana was having fun and was sure she was about to have more. She was doing what she had longed for – performing in front of a live audience. This was the start of her second week on the road, performing in one town for one night and then on to the next. The consensus was that Cy had never been out of London and the Home Counties for he'd sent them zig-zagging all over the country. From London they'd gone to Bedford, then cut across to Worcester and down to Bristol, which had not been too bad. However, the drive from Bristol to Moffat in the Borders had been hair-raising in their clapped-out converted ambulance. After Moffat they had gone to Selkirk, on to Newcastle, down to Pontefract and now they were heading for Cambridge. It was tiring, but Lana had found the constant movement suited her, although admittedly until Moffat she'd been travelling with Cy in his big American car. On Thursday, however, she'd joined the others in their transport.

She sat in the back of the ambulance, bouncing about as it rattled along. The outside of the vehicle was painted a wild psychedelic pattern in reds, blues and gold which went well with the group's name, the Mantras. Lana and the Mantras – she'd liked the sound of it the minute Cy had introduced her to the band.

As they sped along Lana thought about everything that had happened in the past few weeks. She'd got on well with the boys from the start. Two of them were plasterers, another was a carpenter and the fourth a mechanic, which was just as well in view of the number of times the ambulance broke down. Once called John, Fred, Peter and David, they were now Spit, Flick, Mush and Fun to the fans even if, in private, they kept to their old names.

She hadn't liked the sound they made very much, though, nor the music they wrote. The lyrics of their songs never made any sense to her, and musically it was as if they longed to be a rock band but didn't quite have the courage to go all the way, clinging instead to a pop sound which did not sit happily with the raucousness that lurked just below the surface. Consequently they were neither one thing nor the other and Lana was never sure which way they wanted her to sing, so she just belted out everything and hoped for the best. Cy insisted they were good and were going places and would take her with them, but Lana doubted it.

Cy was confident these days, strutting about in his red flares, weighed down by a huge gold medallion, almost childlike in his excitement and pride. Lana hadn't the heart to point out to him that until he'd met her what he knew about music could have been written on a pin-head. Why, she'd even heard him listening to Doris Day! She'd promised, laughing, not to tell the band about that – provided she got a nice present, she'd joked. To her surprise Cy took her seriously and gave her a crazy pair of gold hoop earrings, big enough to sit a parrot on, she'd said. Cy had wangled a night in a hotel for them both which he seemed to regard as an even bigger present, although she didn't.

Despite her misgivings about the Mantras' music, she'd gone along with Cy's plans for this tour. She had no choice if she wanted to get out of the small crummy clubs and the pubs. At least they wrote their own stuff and she had five songs they'd written for her. And one, 'Wham! Wham! Wham!', had been good enough to give them a recording contract with Jupiter Records, a new and admittedly small company but with a go-ahead marketing team and a hunger for new talent.

'It couldn't be better, doll,' Cy had said as they left the studio. 'Think of the investment these bods have had to make – the premises, the equipment. Must be in hundreds of thousands. Makes the mind boggle. They've got to succeed, babe, they go up and you and the lads go with them.'

'Don't I have to sign any papers?'

'No, doll. Nothing for you to worry about.'

'Who does them, Mum?'

'She asked me to do it. I'm your legal representative since you're under age.'

'Not for everything.' She laughed, giving him a shove.

'Thanks be to God.' He rolled his eyes heavenward.

'Sounds a grand title, legal representative. What's it mean?'

'It means you needn't bother yourself about anything to do with boring old paperwork – just get on with the singing.'

'It's taking so long though, Cy. I always dreamed of it happening overnight, and here we are, it's over a year now and we seem no further on.'

'You what?' Cy stopped dead in his tracks. 'You've just got a recording contract. They've arranged for you to share the bill with the Wall Nuts on their next nationwide tour. I'd already arranged a week's tour for you and the Mantras and you say you're no further on. Bollocks!'

'Yeah, you're right. I'm a real ungrateful bitch, aren't I?'

'You can say that again.' Cy laughed and slapped her across her rump. Lana frowned. She wished he'd stop doing that and sometimes she wished he'd find someone else. He made it so obvious to everyone that they were a pair that she never had a chance to meet anyone else. She'd have liked to have a boyfriend her own age for a change. It didn't cross her mind to get rid of Cy herself, though, she didn't want to hurt his feelings, not when he'd been so good to her.

On Thursday the routine had changed for Lana when Cy had had a call from London. One of the members of the other group he was managing, the Space Men, had died – everyone presumed from an overdose of something. And a replacement had to be found quickly.

'Will you be all right without Uncle Cy to look after you?' he'd asked Lana as she watched him packing.

'Of course I will, don't be silly. It's only for a few days and we'll meet you in Cambridge.'

'Right on, babe. But no funny business now, no drugs or booze or hanky-panky, you understand?'

'Who with?'

'Those randy muckers out there.' He nodded towards the room next door where they could hear the four boys laughing and joking and jamming away.

'Them? You have to be joking!' Lana scoffed at the idea. 'They're too busy with their groupies.'

Cy's motor car could not have gone ten miles beyond

Moffat when Lana answered a knock on her door. It was Fred.

'Fancy a party now the old boy's gone?' He grinned.

'Groovy!' she said excitedly, for Cy did not like her to party with the others. 'I'll just get changed.'

The party was not at all what she had expected. There were no other girls there for a start, no nice food.

'Where is everyone?' she asked.

'They'll be here soon. Have a drink.' Dave held a glass out to her.

'What is it?' she asked suspiciously, looking at the tumbler of amber-coloured liquid.

'It's a Harvey Wallbanger, orange juice mainly.'

She sipped at it. 'That's nice. Funny name,' she said as she sat down on the sofa and crossed her legs, flashing her thighs. She giggled as she saw the spark of interest in the young men's eyes. 'Now, behave yourselves.' She laughed, wagging her finger at them, and recrossed her legs, allowing them a tantalizing peep at her white-knickered crotch.

The drink slid down so easily that she was soon holding her glass up for another and then another. She was having great fun, she decided, as the four boys flirted outrageously with her, something they had never done with Cy around. It was nice to be having a good time for once.

The noise level in the hotel room increased in proportion to the alcohol consumed. Then someone put on a record and they began to dance, taking it in turns to partner Lana who could not seem to stop – she felt as though she was floating. As the men tired she danced alone for the sheer joy of it; she found herself caught up with the rhythm of the music pounding into the room and gyrated her body with abandon.

She was not sure what happened next nor how, for by then she was too fuddled by drink to remember anything. She must have passed out for she awoke several hours later with an appalling headache to find herself sprawled naked on the double bed with the Mantras stretched out around her, also naked.

She lay there for a second, wide-eyed with shock. Then she slid as gently as possible from the bed so as not to wake them. She found her scattered clothes and hurriedly opened the adjoining door to her own room.

She took a shower, scrubbing herself clean and then starting all over again, soaping her entire body – she washed herself again and again.

What had happened? She closed her eyes with anguish at the thought that they might all have laid her. She looked at herself in the long bathroom mirror and shuddered as she saw a dozen bruises beginning to form. The bastards, she thought, as she lay wearily on her own bed and covered herself with a blanket. Why her?

'Hi, Lana,' they all greeted her with a smile later that evening as they prepared for the night's gig. 'All right then, girl?'

'Yes, thank you,' she replied as she climbed into the ambulance. She had meant to ask them what had happened but when it came to it she found she couldn't. She felt shy with them and afraid of what the answer might be. Maybe it had been her fault, maybe she'd led them on as her mother would say. Perhaps she wouldn't mention it, cooler not to, she told herself. And if she didn't talk about it maybe she could make it all go away and forget it.

'Come on, Dave, let's get this show on the road,' she said instead, all bright smiles and a swish of blonde hair.

Now here she was rattling down the A1 from Pontefract en route for Cambridge to link up with the Wall Nuts for the start of their tour. Until the incident in Moffat the week had been fun, even if most of the gigs Cy had arranged were pretty dismal halls and clubs. Still, they were all in a good mood, for they were beginning to make money at last. Dave had worked out that at this rate in six months they would be able to pay Cy back the money he'd lent them for the ambulance and their stage clothes. And once they were on the road with a group as famous as the Wall Nuts, things could only improve.

Lana had to acknowledge she was tired now, as she tried to make herself comfortable on the lumpy seat in the back of the ambulance. The nightly performances and the mad dashes to get from one gig to another were draining her of energy. The boys were convinced that Cy didn't own a road-map and had no idea that to get from Bristol on the Wednesday to play in Moffat on the Thursday, in this creaking vehicle, had been a nail-biting, suicidal experience.

'I wouldn't put it past him to have us play in Thurso one night and Penzance the next,' Fred complained.

'He'll kill some poor buggers one of these days,' John added.

'If only someone else but me could drive,' David pointed out.

It wouldn't be like this for much longer though, Lana thought, as they bumped along – they had been driving through the night to get to Cambridge in time to rehearse. Deep down inside her, she felt a total conviction that the big time would come soon. There were still days when she couldn't see how, but they tended to be few and far between. Mostly she was optimistic, it wasn't in her nature to be depressed for long.

'Can't you sleep, Lana?' John was leaning over her.

'Nah . . . and you can forget whatever you're thinking,' she replied rather waspishly. She thought it safer to talk to them sharply, she had no intention of a repeat performance of the other night.

'As a matter of fact I wondered if you'd like one of these – help you sleep.'

Lana lifted herself on her elbow to see what he was holding in the palm of his hand. 'What are they?' she asked suspiciously.

'Sleeping pills – barbies. Do you good.'

'How many do I need?'

'Just take two. Best not to overload the system.'

'Ta,' Lana said, swallowing them down with a swig from the bottle of brandy she always carried with her these days. She settled back and quickly drifted into sleep.

'Shit, just look at that!' Dave exclaimed.

'Bugger me!'

'Lucky sods!'

Lana woke and sat up groggily. Her head was splitting. She scrabbled around in her handbag for a mirror and studied herself carefully – she looked dreadful. Her mouth felt like the bottom of a birdcage and her head was pounding. She flopped back on the seat. 'What's going on?' she croaked.

'Just look out the window,' Dave said over his shoulder through the sliding panel which separated the main part of the ambulance from the driver.

Lana hauled herself up and tweaked back the curtain. They were parked in a courtyard behind a large wooden gate which two policemen were closing.

'Glory be!' she exclaimed. Outside stood a huge, shiny black pantechnicon, with 'The Wall Nuts' in large gold lettering on the side. Up and down the ramp a team of roadies were busily unloading a sound system and equipment that the Mantras could only dream about. But what had caused the exclamations was the equally black and shiny luxury coach parked beside it – the air-conditioned, portable-televisioned, best sound-systemed, double-bedded luxury of the Wall Nuts' personalized transport.

'That'll be the day, Lana, when we have one like that. Pink, of course.' John smiled at her. 'Crikey, you look rough.'

'I feel it. I think I'm going down with something.'

''Course you're not – you can't, not now. Here, take

these.' John rooted in his bag and produced an envelope out of which he shook some yellow capsules. 'These'll help.' He gave them to her.

'What are they?'

'Uppers. That's what you need to pull you back from the downers last night.'

Lana looked at them suspiciously. She hadn't been in the business long but long enough to have learned a thing or two about drugs and what they could do to people.

'I don't do drugs,' she said primly.

'You can't call this doing drugs.' John laughed. 'Just a couple, help you through the day – it's going to be a long one, chick.'

'Just this once, then. If the Wall Nuts see me looking like this they'll never let me on with them.' She swallowed two of the pills but they stuck in her throat. Frantically she felt for the brandy bottle. Taking a long draught she managed to get them down.

The other boys took pity on Lana when they saw her and suggested she take a taxi to the bed and breakfast Cy had arranged for them across town in Chesterton. There she could have a bath and a nap, and be back by two when the lighting and sound systems would be up and tested in the giant marquee.

Lana was grateful. She always felt useless at this stage of the proceedings. Not that the Mantras had much equipment to set up – and she wasn't strong enough to be useful, except for sitting in the middle of the hall to tell them if the sound levels were acceptable or, more usually, audible.

She walked into the market square and picked up a cab from the rank. She regretted paying the cabbie off when, after five minutes of banging on the door of their digs, she still hadn't managed to get anyone to answer. She made one last effort, banging the door knocker hard, for she had realized that the bell didn't work. And this time she yelled through the letter-box as well.

'Who's that?' a woman's voice asked suspiciously from behind the panelled door.

'Lana Lea – I'm with the Mantras group. Cy Best booked us in.'

There were the sounds of bolts being drawn and chains unhooked and the door swung open to reveal a bleary-eyed woman in a long kaftan with no shoes on her grubby feet.

'Sorry, I thought you might be the landlord – or worse.' She grinned. 'Come in.'

'I know I'm early but we've been on the road all night and I'm desperate for a bath.'

'Fancy a cuppa first?'

'That would be smashing.'

The woman, who introduced herself as Paula, led the way to the kitchen at the back of the house. The room was in chaos with dirty crockery and saucepans, an overflowing rubbish bin and an unmistakable smell of cats. She put the kettle on the gas hob.

'Toast?'

'Lovely.'

While Paula prepared their breakfast Lana looked out of the window on to a garden which was surprisingly neat, given the state of the kitchen.

'Nice garden.'

'I like gardening – hate housework, as you can see. I'd like to live in the country one day, grow my own veg and live the pure life,' Paula said dreamily, as she opened a tin of tobacco and from it took a small bag containing a knob of hash. With deliberation she laid out a Rizla cigarette paper, measured the tobacco, scraped the hash on to it with a small silver knife and neatly rolled a cigarette.

'Pretty little knife,' Lana commented. Some pure life, she thought with an inward smile.

'Nice, isn't it? That was a present from Cy – only he was Cyril then. I think I prefer Cy.'

'You know him?'

'We go back a long way.' She laughed a husky sort of laugh. 'We were married.'

'Honestly?' Lana sat down beside her, interested now.

'Still are – on paper. We never seemed to get round to a divorce. Only makes the lawyers rich – no one else.'

'He never said – sly old bugger.'

'He wouldn't. Likes to keep things close to his chest.'

'My mum would kill him.'

'Your mum, why?'

'She's in love with him.'

'But I thought it was you he was screwing, that's what he said on the phone.'

'Did he?' Lana asked and looked away so that Paula should not see the hurt expression she knew was on her face. How could Cy talk about her like that to someone else? She might sleep with him out of a warped sense of duty, but all the same, it was something private and precious, certainly not something to be blabbed about.

'Blast! Look, I've burned the toast.'

'Doesn't matter. I don't mind it scraped,' Lana said, recovering her composure quickly. There was no point in alienating Paula, not if she was to find out as much as possible about Cy.

Over what passed for breakfast she learned a lot of interesting things. That Cy had started his career as an encyclopaedia salesman, that he'd done a spell as a Borstal boy, that he'd made a small fortune dealing in drugs but had felt the police were breathing a little too close and had got out, leaving his friends to take the rap. Paula told Lana all this with obvious pride in Cy and a great deal of amusement – it was an interesting breakfast.

Lana lowered herself into the warm bath. She'd had to scour the tub first, the rim around it was black. She didn't particularly like the look of the towel either, so she'd put that on the filthy floor to stand on. She'd just sit and dry naturally, she decided, it was a warm day.

She lay back in the water, expecting to relax and also certain she would have to fight sleep, but the opposite happened. Her mind was racing with a torrent of thoughts and ideas. Her heart was pumping fast. Instead of the long leisurely bath she had planned she found herself soaping herself quickly and then leaping out.

She sat on the edge of the bath to dry but discovered she could not sit still. She found a ragged cloth under the basin and washed the floor over. Using some of her tissues, she wiped the window and mirror clean. As soon as she was dressed she ran downstairs to find Paula. She saw her in the garden weeding, so she put on a pinny she found behind the back door, and began to clean the kitchen as a surprise for her.

It was quite extraordinary, the extra energy she found she had. It was unlike her to clean anything in a house, or even want to, yet here she was enjoying herself immensely. She liked this sensation, the alertness, feeling alive. She would ask John to get her some more of these pills.

'Who are you?' Slim Fletcher, lead singer and guitarist of the Wall Nuts, was leaning indolently in the doorway of their bus watching the passing scene; two large muscular security men stood at the bottom of the steps.

'I'm Lana Lea, singer with the Mantras,' Lana said somewhat breathlessly, as she looked up at Slim standing on the steps above her. He was dressed from head to toe in softest black leather, his long black curly hair glinted in the June sunshine, his thick, full red lips were smiling at her. She felt she should pinch herself in case this was all a dream. Slim was one of her heroes and here he was chatting her up – at least Lana was pretty sure that's what he was doing.

'The what?'

'The Mantras.'

'Never heard of them.'

'You will,' she said with spirit.

'Fair enough.' Slim grinned. 'Fancy a glass of champagne?'

'Lovely.' Lana smiled back. As she climbed into the bus she swished her long blonde hair over her shoulders, knowing full well the effect this invariably had on men.

The outside of the bus was striking, the interior was fabulous. The windows were tinted so that no one could look in but those inside could look out. They were made to slide open wide should the Wall Nuts decide to wave to their fans. The carpet was white with a thick pile, and the ceiling and walls were covered in black suede. In the sitting area white leather easy-chairs alternated with black. There was a large hi-fi system and at the press of a button a panel shot open to reveal a refrigerated bar.

'It's fab!' Lana said, looking about her, memorizing every detail to tell the others. From this room a small corridor led the length of the bus, she presumed to the bedrooms, finding the thought scaringly thrilling.

She watched as Slim expertly opened the bottle of chilled Roederer Cristal. She couldn't believe she was here – after the Beatles and the Stones, the Wall Nuts were the most popular band of all. Not as neat as the Beatles had once been, nor as untidy as the Stones, they had not fallen into the psychedelic silk and satin style of dressing either. They wore black and white – invariably leather. They were all tall, all black-haired. Their music could be raucous rock, yet Slim could sing a sentimental and lyrical ballad which would go straight to people's hearts and then into the charts. They were genuine musicians and respected by everyone in the business.

'You're a singer, then?'

'Yes, I am. Thank you.' She accepted the glass of champagne, unaware that the glass was Baccarat.

'Been on the road long?'

'Just the last week – it's my first time.'

'Enjoy it?'

'Yes, it's been a lot of fun, you could say.' She smiled at him over the rim of her glass, aware that she was signalling with her eyes that she knew why she was here and it was all right by her. After her experience the other night she'd vowed she wouldn't sleep with anyone again, but this was different, Slim was something else. She'd had a crush on him for years but now, seeing him in the flesh, she was pretty certain that for the first time in her life, she was falling in love. She'd never felt this excitement, this almost breathless anticipation, with anyone else – it could be the effect of John's pills, of course, but she didn't think so.

'Is this your first May Ball?'

'Is it a ball? I didn't know – I just go where I'm told.' She suppressed a giggle. She wanted to impress Slim, make him realize she was different from the groupies, that she could be special to him, given a chance.

'They're famous . . . very grand affairs.'

'Really? Things are looking up, then.' She crossed one small neat leg over the other, exposing an expanse of thigh beneath her short pink shirt, and then immediately uncrossed it, thinking that perhaps she should not be too forward, that she must not behave like a scrubber.

Slim crossed to the hi-fi, slipped an LP from its sleeve and placed it on the turntable. To Lana's surprise classical music filled the bus.

'You like Vivaldi?' Slim asked.

'Goes down a treat,' she replied, presuming he was referring to the champagne. 'You like this sort of music, then.' She nodded her head towards the hi-fi.

'Of course.'

'My sister plays this stuff all the time. She's training to be an opera singer,' she said with pride, never having thought a time would come when what Kitty was doing could be of any interest, or use, to her.

'Honestly? Where?'

'Somewhere in Hampstead, I think. I haven't seen her in months. Last time she was home I was away for the night.'

'Then she's good, only the best get into the Hampstead Conservatoire.'

'Yeah, that's it, that's where she is. Is that so – what you said about the best? Gosh, our Kitty.' She shook her head. 'All I can remember was she had this blooming big voice that drowned everyone else out.'

'You don't sing opera then?'

'Me? Don't be daft. There wouldn't be enough money in it for me.' She sipped her champagne.

'If you get to the top you can make a killing as an opera singer – they command fortunes.'

'Really? I didn't know that.' Lana looked around her again, wondering when he was going to make a move towards her. She didn't want to waste time talking about Kitty.

But he didn't seduce her. Her reaction confused her, part of her was disappointed and yet another part was pleased he hadn't leapt on her, that he seemed sufficiently interested in her to sit and talk.

For over an hour they chatted about gigs and music, how they felt about it, and how the Wall Nuts had got started. She enjoyed talking with Slim but she took even more pleasure in watching him. By the time he looked at his watch and said he was sorry, but he had to go to the marquee to check all was fine, she had decided he was the most beautiful man she'd ever met.

'I'll come with you.' Lana jumped eagerly to her feet. She was beaming as she entered the marquee, her arm slipped nonchalantly through Slim's – not that he had taken hold of her, she had just planted it there, but who was to know?

The marquee was huge and people were bustling about. Florists were fussing over elaborate arrangements. A bar was being set up, and Lana had never seen so many bottles of champagne in one place before.

'They look after themselves, these university types, don't they?' she said.

'The tickets cost an arm and a leg.'

'They'd have to, with you playing.' She laughed at him.

The Wall Nuts' roadies were hauling the heavy sound equipment into place. Once it was in position they had to move it all again when the road manager shouted at them for being senseless berks. The May Ball committee were in heated argument with the Wall Nuts' lighting engineers who wanted their strobes placed in a way that the committee felt would mar the general ambience. Judging by the language, the Wall Nuts were likely to win. The air was heavy with the smell of fresh male sweat as the roadies hauled and swore, their muscular bodies damp, their skimpy T-shirts sticking to their skin. It was only three and yet the excitement in the air was electric and Lana could feel it beginning to affect her.

There was a huddle of worried-looking people on the stage.

'What's the problem?' Lana asked.

'It'll be the sound levels, it's always a problem in a marquee. It's the fabric and canvas walls, they deaden the sound – it's a right bummer. I'd best go and see if I can offer my advice,' Slim said, letting go of her arm. 'See yer . . .'

'Yeah, see yer later, alligator.' Lana giggled and then regretted it, wishing she had said something less obvious.

The rest of the Mantras were sprawled somewhat incongruously on spindly gilt chairs which by evening would be placed around tables covered with gold cloths to match the gold and white striped lining of the marquee.

'Did you get the message from Cy, Lana?' Dave called out above the off-key screeching of an electronic guitar emanating from the large, slate-black speakers.

'No.'

'He's gone to Hamburg to audition.'

'He gets around.' Lana shrugged her shoulders but was inwardly pleased that she could now concentrate on Slim.

'See you're getting friendly with the Wall Nuts,' John said slyly.

'Getting?' Lana laughed. 'Gracious, Slim and I go back a long way,' she lied, not quite sure why.

Dave said something but she could not hear, no one could, for the Wall Nuts had started to rehearse. Sitting so close to the stage, the noise blasting out was deafening. The whole place vibrated with sound which seeped into Lana until she felt her entire body rocking to the distinctive Wall Nuts' beat. This was what she wanted – music like this, singing with a group like this, the fame it would bring her. She'd had the Mantras. She was disappointed when after only one number, apparently satisfied with the set-up, the Wall Nuts laid down their instruments.

'Your turn,' the Wall Nuts' road manager called out to the Mantras. 'But don't move nothing. Understand?'

Beside the Wall Nuts' equipment – the best that money could buy – the Mantras looked very much the poor cousins as they set up in their turn. They ran through their introduction number, 'Mantra Man', and then it was Lana's turn. Knowing Slim was listening, she launched herself with far more enthusiasm than usual into 'Wham! Wham! Wham!' This was her chance. Lana always used the microphone provocatively, bending the stand down towards her, caressing it, and she tried to make her act outrageous, winding her legs round the stand, writhing against it – this was what the audiences wanted, she had learned.

She could have burst with pride when, at the end, she heard applause – no one applauded at rehearsals. It must be Slim, she told herself.

But it wasn't. A tall man moved out from the shadows at the side of the marquee.

'Portman!' Lana jumped off the stage and hurtled across the dance-floor and into his arms. 'Portman, what a lovely surprise!'

'I didn't expect to hear you sound like that,' he said, touching her cheek gently. 'Nor looking like this.'

'Nor did anyone, Portman. But it's making me a success . . . a real success.'

'That's nice,' he said noncommittally.

'Come and meet the boys.' She took his hand and dragged him towards the group who were beginning to clatter off the small stage. Slim strolled up to join them.

'Well, isn't this nice.' Lana smiled as she looked at them – Portman, her past, the Mantras, her present and Slim? Slim, her future – oh, she did hope so.

14

'Now it's your turn – tell me everything, I can't wait to hear!' Lana flashed her most brilliant smile at Portman, sitting opposite her at the small table in the Copper Kettle on King's Parade, where they were drinking coffee and eating sticky buns. It was a large, broad smile and she spoke effusively, for she had suddenly realized that, to her shame, they had had two coffees and so far she had been doing all the talking. 'The school, tell me all about the school.'

'Why did you stop writing and calling me?' he asked.

Lana bit her lip. 'Oh, you know me, Portman – I never liked writing.'

'There's always the telephone,' he said reasonably.

'I know, but at home my mother forbade me to use the phone because of the expense. And I never seem to have

any money when I want to use a call-box,' she lied effortlessly, rewarding him with another of her smiles. She
should have called him, she thought, she had been wrong
to drop Portman and Portia the way she had.

'We were both very hurt, Lana. We had felt we were
more important to you than we obviously were.'

'*You* stopped calling and writing to *me*,' she said
defensively.

'We both felt, when you didn't respond, that you didn't
wish to have further contact with us. We were not going to
push ourselves where we were not wanted, and in the
circumstances we were in no position to make a fuss.'

'What circumstances?'

'You know damn well – your age, us *in loco parentis* – all
that.'

'Portman, don't be an old meany, don't be cross with
me.' She pouted. 'I didn't realize I was that important to
you. I thought when I left you'd just transfer to one of the
others.' She was being sly but she was curious to know
what had happened after she left the school.

'You'll always be special. There was no one to take your
place.' He put out his hand and touched hers gently. Lana
looked away quickly. She liked Portman, she always would,
but she didn't want to go back to him, not now, since Slim
had come into her life. 'I saw a poster, that's how I knew
you were playing at King's – it's my old college, you know,'
Portman continued. 'We did think of coming to the May
Ball. But then we decided we were too old.'

'Don't be silly – you're not that old!' Lana immediately
giggled, trying to turn something she shouldn't have said
into a joke. 'Oh, sorry, that sounds awful. I didn't mean
. . . you're not old at all, really, are you?' She floundered,
realizing she was making matters worse. 'Oh, Lor' . . .'

'Don't worry, Lana. I realize I am old in your eyes even
if I don't feel I am.' He laughed good-naturedly. 'By the
way, we closed the school.'

'Oh, no, why? It was such a marvellous school.'

'It was never the success we hoped for – too isolated, I suppose, and we could never get the numbers up. We were under-funded, too.'

'How's poor Portia? It must have broken her heart.'

'She's fine. In a way, although it was sad to lose the school before we had really had time to prove our theories, it's nice to have the place all to ourselves again. And Portia is very busy these days; she was asked to choreograph a new ballet by Tim Shotter. You've heard of him?'

'Nope, 'fraid not.'

'He's a master. It was a great artistic success, if not a monetary one. Now she's concentrating on that and, of course, she'll help me with my music.' He paused and sipped his coffee, watching Lana intently over the rim of the cup. She did not react.

'I've come into quite a bit of money,' he continued.

'That's nice for you.'

'So I can go ahead . . .' Again he sipped the coffee.

'With what?' she eventually asked.

'My musical.'

'You don't mean that after all this time you've done it? Our musical? The one you promised me? How wonderful!' She was very animated now, leaning across the table. 'Tell me all about it, you must be so excited.'

He bent down and produced a bound script from his briefcase. 'I had thought you might like to look at it, but now —'

'You bet I would!' She grabbed the red binder from his hand and noisily riffled through the pages, searching for the lead part. 'Portman! It's set in a nunnery – wow! Kinky! I love it.' She returned to scanning the pages. 'And I'm Sister Cecilia – I must be – she's got the biggest part. How many songs does she get? How much dancing is there?' The questions tumbled out of her in her excitement.

'Lana, my dear, it won't work. Look, I wrote it for you, you know I did. And you would have been Cecilia, but—'

'*Would have been* Cecilia? What do you mean?'

'It's your voice, Lana. It's changed, it's totally wrong for the part now. You had such a sweet, clear voice. I mean, the voice you have now . . . well, it's fine for what you do but not for a musical set in the cloisters.'

'I can still sing like that if I want. I can sing any way you want me to.' She leaned across the table, her face creased with anxiety.

'Can you? I doubt it. And there's your image – the way you look, your dress, your make-up, it's all wrong. I need someone with the bloom of innocence on them – as you once had.'

'Till you took it,' Lana said bitterly as the realization of what he was saying sank in.

'Don't be angry with me, Lana. You're doing well in your chosen field – everyone I've spoken to says so.'

'Then use me. It'll be good publicity.' She leaned forward, hopeful again.

'Maybe if you were very famous. But you're not, are you? Using you is too big a risk for me to take. You're a rock singer—'

'Yes, I am, because times have changed. People want my sort of image, my style of music, not soppy stuff,' she said with spirit. 'Will you get backers for something so much against the trend?'

'I can finance it myself if necessary, but as it is I've several backers interested.'

Lana looked out of the window at the passing crowds but, blinded with disappointment, she did not see them. Portman watched her with a satisfied expression which she was unaware of.

'I've approached Avril Kepple – you remember Avril, don't you? She's been doing very well on the West End stage – small supporting parts as yet, but she might be ripe for this lead.'

'Avril? Before you'd heard me?'

'She kept in touch with us, you didn't. She's very talented.'

'My eye! She can't sing – she trills, she's got no rhythm,' Lana said, bitter disappointment making her ignore the admiration she had once felt for Avril.

'Lana, you know that's not true. You took different paths, that's all. If you'd kept in touch with me, let me know what you were doing, I would have advised against the career move you have taken.'

'I did call you, when I first started singing in the clubs. I called and asked you what you thought.'

'You telephoned me once and I told you straight I thought it was a bad idea. Now I've heard you I know I was right.'

'Well, I'll bloody well show you. I'm on the up now – I'll be such a star, you'll be proud you once knew me and furious you didn't use me.' Lana stumbled to her feet, her head lowered so that he could not see the tears in her eyes. She fumbled for her handbag and left without saying goodbye, weaving her way out through the tables in the crowded café. Portman watched her and felt immeasurably better – that would teach the little bitch, dropping them the way she had. It was a small revenge for the pain she had caused both him and Portia.

Lana ran along King's Parade, not sure where she was going. She hurtled into St Edward's Passage and cannoned into Slim, out for a walk with his bodyguard Ferdie. She did not recognize him at first in his disguise of dark glasses and black fedora hat pulled low over his brow.

'Hang on, hang on. What on earth's the matter?' he asked as Lana burst into floods of tears in his arms.

'Oh, Slim! Life's such a bitch!'

'I think you need a calming drink and a bit of a chat.'

He took her arm, linked it with his, and they walked back into King's Parade. On the other side of the road the main college gate was already besieged by a crowd of screaming Wall Nuts fans. Heads down, Ferdie at their side, they almost ran along the road, crossed to St Catherine's College and walked briskly to the rear. Showing their passes, they were allowed through the gate and into the back court of King's where the Wall Nuts' bus was parked safely away from souvenir and autograph hunters. It was guarded by a bored-looking policeman and several of the Nuts' own security men. Of the Mantras' ambulance there was no sign, they had been moved elsewhere apparently – such treatment was for the stars alone.

Inside the luxurious coach Slim poured the large brandy Lana had asked for. From the sleeping quarters they heard a rhythmic banging and a woman sobbing and groaning.

Lana looked down at her drink, feeling very embarrassed and wishing the primeval noises would stop, for they were impossible to ignore.

'That's Pitch – randy sod. That's his third today that I know of.'

'And you?' she asked, admiring his thin expressive face, his large dark eyes – so dark they appeared black – and his mass of long, black, curly hair. There was something almost satanic about his appearance.

'Me?' He laughed. 'I'm the good boy, didn't you know?' And to her disappointment he sat opposite rather than beside her. 'Now, what was all that about?'

'Well . . .' she began, continuing with difficulty since the noise carried on and she found the rhythmic sounds and what they implied were arousing her. 'Well . . .' She tried again but was too flustered to continue. 'Would you mind shutting that door?' She nodded towards the one leading through to Pitch's sleeping space.

'Bit off-putting, isn't it?' He stood up quickly, crossed the room and slammed the door shut. 'Now, where were we?'

When she had finished explaining, managing not to cry – she felt instinctively that Slim was not a man who would be moved by tears – he sat for what seemed an age, stroking his cheek with his long fingers as if summing up what to say to her.

'I know it's hard, Lana. But in this game you've got to decide what you want and go for it – not get side-tracked. There are too many out there waiting to take your place.'

'It's all right for you to talk. You're rich and famous. You're a wonderful musician – it's been easy for you.'

'You reckon?' He snorted. 'I tell you, it's been a bloody hard fight and graft. We started just like you and your group . . . grotty gigs for peanuts. A crooked manager, contracts promised that never appeared, turning up at venues only to find we'd been cancelled, or worse, arriving and finding no punters. Nothing that's happened to you hasn't happened to us. And I had to fight even to begin. I was at the Royal College, I was supposed to become a classical violinist – I threw it up for this. My father disowned me, hasn't spoken to me once since, and I broke my mother's heart – so she says!' He laughed. 'So don't tell me I had it easy.'

'But don't you see, I want both. I want this world and I want to be on the stage too.'

'Perhaps you will – one day.'

'But I want to *now*. That musical was written for *me*, not Avril! Portman promised me. It's all so unfair.'

'It was written for you as you were then . . . not you as you are now. You must see that.'

'But I could change back.'

'Could you? Why? Aren't you happy with what you're doing? I can tell you this, Lana, if you're not you won't succeed. You've got to love it, feel you can't and won't do

anything else. Know you can't live without the buzz,
without the adrenalin. When I'm on stage I feel like . . . oh,
like it's one giant orgasm . . .' He leaned forward as he
spoke, his face alight with enthusiasm. She longed to touch
him, to smooth back his hair, to outline his full and
sensuous lips with her fingertip, but something told her
she must not.

'I do. I really love it,' she said, puzzled by his passion.
Although she thought she was doing what she wanted, she
felt none of this. But she was not willing to admit it.

He moved closer and took hold of her hand. She felt her
heart jolt.

'Lana, my sweet—' he began just as the door burst open
and a naked Pitch strolled into the room.

'Hello,' he said. 'And what have we here? A little pink
chick. Fancy a threesome, bird?' he asked, waggling his
penis at her.

'No, thank you,' she said with dignity, but found herself
blushing. She felt mortified. What was it about her that
made men think they could treat her any way they wanted?
Still, if she was honest, if she hadn't met Slim, if she didn't
feel the way she did, would she have been upset? Wasn't
someone famous like Pitch exactly who she had longed to
enter her life? Not any more, she found herself thinking.

'Lay off, Pitch,' she heard Slim say, and she could have
kissed him out of gratitude. She looked up to see him
standing holding his hand out to her.

'Time you were going, I think.' Reluctantly she allowed
herself to be pulled up from the sofa. His arm about her
shoulders, Slim led her to the door.

'You know, this Portman bloke might have a point. Have
you thought that perhaps this is all wrong for you – the
way you sing, the image? You've got a wonderfully inno-
cent-looking face, like a little girl's – quite a turn-on.'

'Oh, Slim.' She smiled, hope rising again.

'Tell you what. When this tour is over, come to my

place. I've got a studio there – we could play about, find out what you can do. How about it?'

'Thanks, Slim, I'd love to.' And she virtually jumped down the steps.

Lana had left the bag containing the sweater she wanted for her performance that night in the Mantras' ambulance. She had to ask the bored policeman where the vehicle had been parked. It had been moved out of the college and was on a side road since there were no fans to besiege it. She entered the ambulance and found three girls in identical jeans, their heads covered with scarves, their breasts bare, sitting on one of the bunks. Dave and John were giggling as they massaged them and measured the circumference of the breasts and the length of the erect nipples.

'What on earth are you doing?' Lana asked.

'It's a tit competition. Want to join in?'

'No, thanks.' She took her bag from under the seat. 'Oh, by the way, John, you haven't got any more of those little helpers, have you?'

'Sure, gal.' He slipped a packet into her hand. The three girls were giggling stupidly.

'You know what, you lot?' Lana said. 'I think you're being totally juvenile.'

'Oh, my! And who's lost her sense of humour?' Dave shouted at her as she let herself out of the scruffy and, she noticed, smelly ambulance.

Lana returned to her digs. She had some idea of resting before the performance but she could not relax. She felt tired but her body was still demanding movement. She swallowed two more of John's pills, washing them down with brandy. Almost immediately she felt as if a clock inside her had wound itself up – she was ready to go. Of Cy there was no sign.

*

Lana paced up and down the room assigned to the Mantras, off the great court where the giant marquee was. She felt she was on a high wire, alive with an excitement she had never known before. During the last minutes before she went on for their first set she took two large draughts of brandy and stood ready and waiting, as hyped-up as she had ever been.

'Lana, love, you look bloody marvellous!' The door had burst open and there was Cy.

'I thought you'd gone to Hamburg,' she said coldly.

'Cancelled.' He shrugged.

'Well, get out of my light, you two-timing turd,' she said as she swept past him.

15

The public bar of the Firkin and Whistle was crowded as usual on a Friday night. From the large back-room came the thump, thump of a not very good band and the wailing of an even worse singer. The air was thick with cigarette smoke and the sour smell of stale beer spilt in the crush.

From one end of the long mahogany bar Jenny sema-phored to Kitty at the other end. Kitty looked at her watch and held up her hand, showing four fingers and her thumb. She'd be lucky if she did get away in five minutes, more like ten, she thought as she pulled another pint. She rang the money up on the till and swung round with the change, smiling brightly as she did so, even though her feet were killing her.

Jenny was waiting for her in the coffee bar next door. They always met there, the coffee being cheaper than the only drink they really liked, Bacardi and Coke – Jenny had given up on her sweet sherry. Also Jim who managed the bar liked them and allowed them to share a coffee between them.

Kitty slumped down on to the blue plastic seat that did not look the least like the leather it was supposed to fake. Jenny slid the coffee-cup over to her. She took a sip.

'You look awful, you know.'

'Why, thanks, that's all I need.' Kitty laughed, pushing her hair back wearily from her face. 'Ugh, this coffee's tepid.'

'And I was thinking tonight, when I was standing at the bar, you shouldn't be working in that smoky atmosphere. It can't be doing your voice much good, now can it?'

'But what else can I do, Jenny? You know I'm desperate for the money.'

'You could kick that no-good bastard out for a start –'

'Oh, Jenny, not now, please,' Kitty said with exasperation. 'Jim, could we have two more coffees?' she called out to the proprietor.

'You won't listen to reason, that's your problem. He's nothing but a parasite. When did he last contribute anything, tell me that?'

'He does what he can. There's not much work around at the moment.'

'Not much work! The theatres up West are booming. He's no good, more like.'

'Jenny, please, I don't want to argue with you. We made a pact, remember? We'd never fall out again over men . . . drop it.' She looked about her at the white painted coffee bar with its badly painted murals of Sorrento, the Chianti bottles in their straw baskets hanging from the ceiling, the juke-box playing in the corner.

'What's that music?' she asked. 'It's very powerful.'

'That's the latest from the Wall Nuts. It's Number One – "Come Get It Baby".'

'Ghastly title but it's a strong melody. I never hear any music like that normally – only if I come in here.'

'You're changing the subject,' Jenny said accusingly.

'Look, Jenny, I love Martin and I'm happy with him, and that's all there is to be said on the subject. And, incidentally, he's a very fine actor –'

'Who can't get work. Oh, yes, I see. He's back, then?'

'Yes.' Kitty fiddled with the ashtray on the table.

'How long did he go walkabout this time? A month?'

'No, three weeks.'

'And you sit waiting for him like a dumb chick. I don't understand you.'

'No, I know you don't. But maybe you will one day when you eventually find a fellow,' Kitty said sharply.

'Ouch!' Jenny said, grinning broadly – her inability to find a boyfriend was no longer bothering her as it had once done.

'You're pushing the boat out tonight, Kitty,' Jim said as he placed the two foaming cappuccinos on to the plastic, imitation marble table.

'I'm fed up, Jim, that's why.' She smiled up at him. If only she'd do something with her hair and make-up, he thought for the umpteenth time, she could be beautiful if she tried. 'Fancy working here?' he said suddenly.

'Honest? Jim, I'd love to.'

'I don't pay much, can't afford to . . . but the tips are good and I don't want no messing about with National Insurance and all that crap.'

'Neither do I.' She laughed.

'Right, when can you start?'

'Tomorrow?'

'Great. I promised to take the wife out tomorrow evening. I can trust you – not many buggers you can.'

'But Jim, I won't know how to run this on my own.'

'Of course you will – nothing to it. Fancy a piece of cake? On the house?'

'Thanks,' Kitty and Jenny replied in unison.

'You can't work Saturday afternoon as well, Kitty. That's madness,' Jenny said.

'I can, easily. I'll get up earlier to study. I have one singing lesson at ten – I can do it, no problem.'

'I just meant it's too much for you . . . you're working too hard. Why can't *he* get a job in a pub?'

'Dear Jenny, you're such a mate.' Kitty blew her a kiss. 'He'll pay me back one day when he's rich and famous – you'll see.'

Kitty felt she could drop with fatigue as she let herself into the flat. But before she opened the door she could hear the noise of a party in progress. Oh, no, she thought, not again.

She did not mind Martin inviting his friends back to the flat – it was company for him when she was out at work. But she did resent these big parties. She knew what would happen, no sooner had she got in than they would want food – food she could not afford to give them. She resented the money Martin would have spent on drink, even if the others had chipped in. And what annoyed her more than anything was that too often after evenings like this people did not leave. She was just as likely to get up in the morning to find strangers asleep on the floor – if she was lucky they left, but too often one or two stayed for weeks at a time until Martin tired of their company and they eventually went.

She closed the door quietly, holding her breath as she did so, as if by not breathing she could prevent the Yale lock from clicking too loudly. She inched down the passageway on tiptoe and opened her bedroom door, hoping there would be no one in there – that had happened before now, much to her embarrassment, although the couple she had walked in on were oblivious to her.

The room was empty. She listened and then switched on the light. She kicked off her shoes and sat on the edge of the bed massaging her aching feet. She longed for a cup of tea but the chance of the kitchen being empty too was remote.

She sank back on the pillows with relief. She lay looking at the ceiling and the shape made by the large white paper lantern she had bought. If she blew she could make it sway and the patterns change.

She had lied to Jenny. She wasn't happy with Martin, how could she be? She was being used by him and she knew it but did not know how to stop it. If she tried to reason with him he became icily indifferent to her, and she hated that.

When, over six months ago, Jenny had left the flat, unable to put up with Martin's moods and unable to keep quiet for her friend's sake, Kitty had had a long, serious talk with him. She showed him the bills and her bank statement and explained how, without Jenny's contribution coming in, she would need money from him. He was reason itself, told her not to worry and that of course he would help. He popped out for a drink and she did not see him again for ten days. That was when she had been forced into looking for her part-time job. She had to keep the flat.

He appeared again as if nothing had happened; when she asked him where he had been he told her Scotland, how in the bar he had met a friend who had told him of a touring company there looking for someone just like him. But as he poured himself a drink she noticed that his hand was shaking. He might have been to Scotland but she was sure it had also been a stupendous bender.

When she had first started at the Conservatoire she had been desperate to discuss her day with Martin. The school was not a friendly place. To become a professional musician, preferably a soloist, was everyone's goal here, and so everyone was a rival. Normal friendships were impossible in such an atmosphere. Everyone worked hard, for the threat of expulsion if pupils did not achieve satisfactory end-of-term assessments was not an idle one – there were too many outside waiting to take their place – so there were no clubs or teams to join, where perhaps friends could have been made. Even Paul, Kitty's guide on the first day, had distanced himself; students getting preferential treatment, as Kitty was, were immediately regarded with suspicion and ostracized.

She needed to talk to someone, especially at the beginning when she was worried and puzzled by the regime. She learned French and Italian, she studied music theory and composition. She had piano lessons but she did not sing. The work was hard for, unlike the others, she had no musical training apart from her piano lessons. She wanted to sing, her scholarship was for singing – so why didn't they let her? She would have liked to talk this over with Martin since she was far too afraid of everyone at school to ask the reason.

For six months her lessons with Max Leitman were more like lessons in gymnastics or physiotherapy than singing. Max was teaching her to breathe.

'You wouldn't contemplate running a marathon having done no exercise for twenty years, would you?' he asked her one day when she had sighed audibly at the regime he set her. 'It would kill you. So, if you sing an opera in your present condition you'll shorten your voice's life. Do as I say and your career will last at least ten, maybe fifteen years longer.'

She felt happier once he had explained it to her. So she exercised, building up the muscles supporting the diaphragm, making a solid wall around it, to give it room to expand to the maximum. Like an underwater swimmer, she learned to inhale and hold her breath and then to exhale slowly. And each week she could do it for longer as her chest cavity grew stronger and her knowledge of her body, and which muscles were where and for 'what, increased.

And then, at last, her singing lessons proper had started and she had weathered the insults from Max that she was useless, hopeless, a nothing, as he pushed her harder and higher and harder and lower, carving out of her depth and resonance and range. And now she fully understood what Max had done for her. Her breathing and her control of it across her vocal cords was, he had explained, comparable to a bow across the strings of a violin. The long cavities in her mouth, throat and nose – her resonators – were comparable to the violin's wooden body. She could hear the difference in her voice herself as, using Max's techniques, she converted breath into resonating sound. When she got it right there was nothing to compare with the elation she felt; when it was wrong she had never known such despondency. But Max would have nothing to do with this emotion and would bully her into trying again and again until she had it right, and then again and again until she had it effortlessly right.

The learning was an exciting process and Kitty would have liked to share that with Martin too. Even more, she would have liked him to understand her excitement when, at last, Ben Cooper and Max had decided she was good enough for her first lesson with Gina Cellini.

Kitty had approached the lesson with trepidation. Cellini never went to the Conservatoire to teach, one went to Cellini. She lived in a large detached house not far from the school. Kitty was shown into her studio, a big room with wide windows overlooking a wonderful garden. Left alone, she looked about her. The room was furnished as if from another era, with great vases of madonna lilies on several tables, a velvet buttoned chaise longue, and knick-knacks everywhere. There was a large pearl-handled fan on the wall signed by Nellie Melba, and a pair of her shoes in a glass case. Beside it in another glass case was a faded corsage of orchids once worn by Jenny Lind, with a small pair of opera glasses which had once been hers too. There was a signed photograph of Mary Gordon and on the walls were framed posters of some of the operas in which Cellini had sung the principal roles.

'Ah, I see you're admiring my little collection.' Madame Cellini bustled in, surprisingly light-footed and graceful for one so large. 'See this.' She handed Kitty a letter, but it was in German. 'From Lotte Lehmann, to me.' She smiled and translated the note, which praised Cellini's voice, for Kitty.

'Now, to work. Let's see what Max has managed to achieve with your disastrous breathing.' She crossed to the grand piano in the centre of the room and indicated where Kitty was to stand. Remembering Cellini's aside that she moved like a camel, Kitty concentrated on gliding across to the piano with head held high, and stood, feet slightly apart and one hand resting in the palm of the other, as the deportment teacher had taught her.

'A scale, maybe?' Cellini smiled across at her as she stood with sticky palms and a churning stomach, wishing she had stayed in Selfridges, with no need to put herself through this sort of agony. Calm down, she told herself, and took a deep breath. Cellini gave her a note on the piano, Kitty sang the scale and then another.

'Right. Warmed up, are we? What would you like to sing for me?'

'"*Sempre libera*",' she said in a whisper.

'Well, I hope you can sing louder than you speak.' Cellini laughed a trilling, singer's laugh. 'But at least you're moving better.'

Kitty surreptitiously wiped her hands down the folds of her skirt. She had been practising the aria from *La Traviata* night and day for weeks. She could do it, she would do it. She nodded her head to show she was ready. The accompaniment began.

As she finished and her voice echoed away, her shoulders slumped with relief. It was over.

'You're screeching your top notes, you know. Why? Have they not taught you *piano*? Sing this.' A stubby finger plonked on to the white key and Kitty sang the note as softly as she could, and the next and the next. She looked at the keyboard and saw that she had sung top E. She had never thought that possible.

'There, you see. It's possible. Anything's possible.' Cellini was chuckling. 'You've worked hard this past year, haven't you? And it shows. I doubted these notes would come quite as sure and pure and, thanks to me, *piano*. I congratulate you. I was wrong.' Kitty smiled in response. 'But now we know they are there we shall conserve them for later. We shall concentrate, my dear, on building a strong base with the lower and middle range – that way we ensure that the top notes will be strong and long-lasting. I always liken it to building a house on rock or sand. We shall build your top register on rock.'

'Thank you.'

'You've a good voice, I hear a golden quality there. If you work with me and do as I say, then one day, maybe, you will have a great voice.'

'Yes, Madame Cellini,' said Kitty, close to tears of happiness at such praise from one so celebrated.

'And please, try to learn to sing with your eyes open!' Cellini admonished, but with a smile.

Kitty had raced home that evening full of what Madame had told her, what she had learned, the belief she now had that perhaps the impossible was possible and she could be an opera singer. As she changed for work in the pub she had excitedly told Martin about her day. But his bored expression showed only too clearly that he was not interested.

She resented it; for she herself had sat for long hours

listening to his theories on acting. The few times he had parts, she had spent hours helping him learn his lines. It had to be a two-way thing, surely? She noticed how he would invariably change the subject when one of his friends inquired how her studies were progressing, and she had begun to wonder if Martin resented the career she wanted to make for herself.

She sighed, swung her legs off the bed and felt with her feet for her shoes. She had better join him for an hour, not to do so would be wrong. She checked her face in the mirror. The truth was, she told her reflection, that although she was lonely living with Martin, she was lonelier without him. And she was not sure that she could cope with loneliness.

16

It was over six months before Lana could take Slim up on his offer to visit his private studio. Slim had omitted to tell her that after their successful tour of Britain the Wall Nuts were off to Europe on an extended one. But the Mantras were not to accompany them; another, better, support group had been signed up for that.

During the British tour, Lana had tried several times to be alone with Slim again but had never succeeded – there were always too many people around or, in the rare spare time they had, Slim would go off on his own, driving his black Porsche into the country.

'He writes poetry out there,' Pitch had explained to her one day when she asked to see him. 'Don't stop him. Where do you think our lyrics come from? The music's the easy bit.' And he'd put his arm around her and had come on to her, but she'd pushed him away. She didn't want anyone but Slim.

After the tour Lana was exhausted, but Cy had arranged only three days' rest for her at home before they were off again touring the clubs, though with no big group to support this time. At first Lana had been resentful, she felt she needed three weeks of rest, not three days, but after twenty-four hours of her mother's fussing she was desperate to leave.

'Don't you think you're drinking too much, Lana?' Amy asked.

'Nope,' she'd replied monosyllabically, and had wandered out into her father's weed-infested garden where she sat on top of the Anderson shelter and missed him. But most of all she missed Slim.

Cy could not understand what was wrong with her. He tried to get her into bed several times when her mother was at work but the thought of him made her feel sick now.

'Come on, doll. You used to enjoy it.'

'I don't fancy you, I never did, if you must know. I don't like liars. I don't like two-timers. And if you don't take your hand off my crotch I'll tell my mum, so help me, I will.'

She cut her first record, 'Wham! Wham! Wham!', and on the flip side 'Tomboy Girl'. It sank without trace. After it was released Lana listened to Radio One all day and never heard it played once.

'What happened with all that talk of promotion they gave us?' she asked her mother.

'Leave it to Cy. He'll give them a bollocking,' Amy replied.

If he did, it made no difference – it still wasn't played and was so far down the listings it might just as well not have been released at all. When Lana nagged Cy into asking about sales, she wished she hadn't – they were abysmal.

'I thought they got people to buy hundreds of records

throughout the country to make sure it was pushed up the best-selling lists,' she complained.

'Oh, you mustn't listen to all you hear out on the road, doll,' was Cy's explanation. 'There's a lot of bullshit about.'

After a month she knew the reason. Jupiter Records had found a new female singer, Dee Dee Dane – at sixteen, nearly four years younger than Lana. But, as Lana argued, it wasn't her fault the record company had taken so long to release the record that she was almost over the hill.

She plodded round the circuit with the Mantras who now thought her boring and no fun at all. If it wasn't for her brandy and the uppers Lana didn't know what she would do with herself. Then John stopped giving her any more pills.

'You're getting too expensive for me, Lana. Get your own.'

So she did, but she'd had to have a tantrum with Cy first – the five pounds in wages he had first given her had gone up to ten for each gig, but she needed more. She managed to get him to increase it to fifteen pounds and found a friendly roadie and relied on no one else.

If she was boring to the Mantras they were even more boring to her. They had discovered heroin, and it sickened her so much to see them shooting the stuff into their own veins that she had to look away. And when high they were distant from her in a world of their own, as if the real world and she in it no longer existed. They were like zombies, their only motivation was planning how they were to get the next fix. She wanted out, she was getting nowhere.

'Let me go solo, Cy. I can do it.'

'You're not ready for it.'

'I am. And the Mantras have had it. They're dope-heads, you know they are. They're no-hopers and I don't want to be associated with them.'

'Oh, my! There's grand talk. You'll do as I say, madam. You'll stick with the lads, they're OK.'

When things changed, however, they changed in a hurry.

Lana had a letter from Slim, posted in Italy, giving his private telephone number so that she could call him when he returned – the only way she'd get through to him past his army of minders. She was ecstatic. Despite all the groupies hurling themselves at the Wall Nuts, he had remembered her from all those months ago. She was different. She was pleased now that she hadn't had sex with him, for that would have made her like all the others.

Cy had a new band, the Balloons, he was excited about and it looked as though, unlike the Mantras, they might make it. They were a cross between the early Beatles and the Tremeloes. Cy had high hopes of them, especially when their first disc went into the charts at 115. At least with this new band to occupy him he'd given up trying to persuade Lana to go to bed with him.

She was due to play a venue with the Mantras in Sheffield and then the following night at Camborne. For the first time in her career, however, she had to cancel. She had tonsillitis and there was no way that she could sing, nor would Amy let her go, so one of the others had to take her place.

She was tucked up in bed at Number Fourteen, full of antibiotics and asleep, when at three in the morning, racing down the motorway, David went to sleep at the wheel. The ambulance crossed the central reservation, crashed into an oncoming articulated lorry and then burst into flames so intense that identification of the group could only be made from their dental records.

Lana's reaction, when she was told the news, was one of hysterical disbelief. She began to shake and could not stop, and when the tears started it was as if they would never cease. Amy called the doctor who gave her a sedative which calmed her down and enabled her to sleep. But the sleep only delayed facing the reality.

Lana was in shock on two levels. There was her grief for the group. She might have begun to feel trapped by them and to think they were no-hopers, but she had liked them as individuals once. In her sadness she forgot the bad things and only remembered the good. And she was shocked at how close to death she herself had been, and it frightened her.

However, within a few days and with the resilience of youth, she had shaken off the fear. She was free of them now and the future beckoned. She attended their funeral at Mortlake Crematorium dressed in pink from head to toe because she thought that was what they would have liked. The press was there and her photograph was in every paper the following morning.

Unlike most pop stars who welcomed the press into their homes at any time for the sake of publicity, Slim never allowed them near his. So Lana had never seen photographs of the house in the papers and magazines and was not prepared for it to be so huge or so beautiful.

Slim had sent a car to meet her at the local station. As they approached a pair of large wrought-iron gates, the chauffeur turned round in his seat.

'I'd get down if I were you, miss,' he advised.

By the gate was a cluster of young girls who, upon seeing the car, streaked towards it, screaming loudly. They started banging on the roof, clawing at the windows, peering inside. When they saw Lana they became shriller, shrieking abuse at her and spitting so that saliva like snails' trails slid down the windows.

Lana had no intention of getting down. She was enjoying the attention and waved regally at the fans, beaming. This enraged them. As the car passed through the gates, they hurled stones at it.

'You shouldn't do that, miss. That lot's capable of lynching you if they get at you.'

Lana laughed. 'Silly bitches,' she said, twisting round in her seat and doing the V-sign out of the back windows at the mob who were now clinging impotently to the gates.

The snaking drive, surrounded by woodland, eventually opened out into a small park. Slim's house nestled in a valley through which a river flowed. It was part Elizabethan, with a Victorian wing which masqueraded as Elizabethan too.

Lana had not known what to expect to find inside the house, but certainly not the perfection that was there. It was furnished in period with fine pieces of furniture which glowed from being lovingly polished, and great vases of flowers were everywhere. Log fires burned in all the rooms. Slim, who had no wife or mistress to her knowledge, was evidently house-proud.

'Slim, it's fab,' she said with genuine admiration. 'Real smartsville.'

'I'm glad you like it. It's been a gas finding the right things for it. Drink?'

'Brandy, please.'

'I was sorry about the Mantras,' he said as he poured her a tumbler of Napoleon brandy. Lana was getting to know her brandies and was impressed.

She shrugged her shoulders. 'These things happen. David always said it would. That one day Cy would expect them to get from Land's End to John O'Groats in a night and they'd all be killed.'

'Poor sods.'

'The police said they wouldn't have known anything, they were all asleep – including the driver,' she joked weakly.

'Bet it made you feel a bit creepy.'

'You can say that again. It freaked me for days. Did you see my picture in the papers?'

'Sorry, can't say I did.'

'Here, look. I've got a cutting.' She delved into her handbag.

'It's a good one of you,' Slim said kindly, handing it back to her. 'What about you now? What will you do?'

'Cy's got another band, the Balloons – they've got a singer, though she's no good,' Lana said on principle, though she'd never heard her. 'I asked if I could audition for them but Cy won't hear of it – probably screwing her, most like.'

'I've heard he's your stepfather. Is he?'

'Nah. He's been living with my mum for the past five years. I reckon he'll be moving on soon.'

'And you?'

'I wish I could. I hate being at home – you know mothers – she fusses the whole bloody time. I've no privacy.'

'Then move out.'

'I can't. I've no money.'

'The Mantras can't have done that badly – they were always on the go. Haven't you got some put by?'

'I don't know. Cy sees to all that side of things for me.'

'Then I should ask him if I were you.'

'Yeah, you're right. I'll do that.'

'Right. Bring your brandy, and let's go and have a dekko at my studio. I'm a bit chuffed with it.'

He had every right to be – it was marvellous and, though small, was fully equipped to professional standards. It was custom-built in the grounds but joined to the house by a corridor which was decorated with posters of the Wall Nuts' gigs, gold discs and photos of the group. One wall of insulated glass in the sitting area gave on to a walled Japanese garden. Double doors led to the sound-proofed studio proper with its slightly elevated stage. 'I need to be on a stage, even if it's only a foot high,' Slim explained. He took Lana into his control-room, showed her the mixer unit, and explained how it worked. Then he played her a tape of experimental music he was working on.

'It's so pretty,' she said, as the tinkling sounding music died away. 'How do you do it?'

'I record sounds – anything that takes my fancy. Birds, the wind, sea, the Kenwood chef, the boys fishing.' He laughed. 'Then I cut and splice and edit them into something hopefully like music.'

'Then you achieved it,' she said, genuinely impressed.

'Not quite. There's a long way to go yet. But one day, when the Wall Nuts are no more, why, then I'll release this sort of thing.'

'You are clever, Slim.'

He bowed. 'Now, what are we going to do about you? Do you know "Greensleeves"?'

'Yes. Well, I don't know the words, but it's the sort of song you know and you can't remember when you learned it, isn't it?'

'Exactly. So, here are the words. I've got a backing tape here – like to go out there and sing it for me?'

'Me? "Greensleeves"? You're joking?'

'No. I'm serious. Try it.'

She let herself out of the control-room, walked self-consciously over to the microphone and put on the large earphones hanging there. Slim raised his hand to her and flicked a switch and an orchestral accompaniment to 'Greensleeves' came through the earphones. Lana sang. She had difficulty with some of the high notes, which surprised her; there would have been a time when she could have hit them easily. She looked across at Slim and grinned, and he raised his thumb. She took off the earphones and joined him.

'Not bad,' he said. 'Listen.'

She covered her ears as she heard herself.

'Shit! What a screech!'

'No, but listen. It's there, can't you hear it – a really pretty sound. It'll come back, I'm sure. If you rest your voice for a few weeks, give it plenty of honey – I swear by honey – I think we can get it back. And I'll take you to see my throat specialist in Harley Street. He'll examine you and see if you've any nodules on your vocal cords – probably not.'

'But why, Slim?' she asked, bewildered by his interest and concern but excited too.

'Look, Lana, you're a stunning-looking girl but you're done up all wrong. You've got another voice there – that's the one you should be nurturing. The way you sing now, all raunchy blues, that's forced, I can hear it. It's not how you were meant to sing.'

'So?' she said, telling herself she must not feel affronted but must listen to his advice.

'There are loads of girl singers doing what you're doing at the moment. You should be different – all sweet, inno-cent. The forbidden girl-child – that sort of thing. It would be different. That way I think you would succeed.'

'But why, Slim?'

'Because I like you.'

She felt her heart lurch. 'If you think it would work for me . . .'

'I'm sure it would.'

'What will Cy say?'

'What can he say? You've no Mantra group any more. With that voice you don't need a group. With what I hear' – he tapped his ear – 'you could go solo.'

'I've always wanted to do that.'

'And so you shall.'

'Or maybe I could still get that part in my friend's musical I told you about?'

'And why not? Tell you what, move in here. I'm not doing anything for a good three months – I like a big break after a tour. Let's do some work together.'

'Oh, Slim,' she said, a dreamy expression of happiness on her face.

Lana did not look forward to telling Cy that she wanted what amounted to time off. She had taken ages getting ready, outlining her eyes in heavy black eyeliner and sticking on two pairs of false eyelashes, because that was how he liked her to look.

She climbed the stairs to his crummy little office in Soho knowing that the thigh-high, white leather boots she was wearing would turn him on faster than anything. She had decided this morning that if necessary she would let him make love to her again if it meant she would get what she wanted.

Pushing the door open, she was surprised to find a receptionist sitting at the desk in the outer office. Until now it had always been empty.

'Hello. I'm Lana, come to see Cy.'

'You got an appointment?' the girl asked, flicking open a large desk diary to check.

'No. I don't need one.'

'Everyone has to have an appointment to see Mr Best, he's a very busy man,' the girl replied frostily.

'Oh, don't be so bloody wet, he'll see me.' She turned, slipping off her short pink fun fur as she did so.

'But he's with a client,' the by now anguished secretary said.

'Piss off, there's a love,' said Lana, pushing open the door. 'Cy, I need to talk to you —' Lana stopped dead in her tracks as a young woman rose to her feet.

'Hallo, Lana, what a lovely surprise, long time no see!'

'Avril! What are you doing here?'

'I'm sorry, Mr Best, she pushed right past me,' the girl was saying, pleading with her eyes.

'That's all right, Caroline, don't fret. This here's my step-

daughter.' Cy patted the girl on the rear. 'Make us some
coffee, there's a doll. Well, Lana, nice to see you. You know
Avril, then?'

'Yes, I was just on the point of telling you, we were at
school together, weren't we, Lana? Great days.' Avril
smiled up at Lana. If anything, Lana thought with annoyance, Avril was even more attractive now, and she was
sure her legs were longer. Lana sat down on the second
leather chair – that was new too, she thought, there had
only been one chair before and no secretary-cum-
receptionist.

'Yeah, great fun. So, what you doing these days?' Lana
asked, as if she had no interest whatsoever, although she
was burning with curiosity inside.

'I needed an agent. I'd never bothered before, but this
time, well, it looks as if it could be a long run and if we
transfer to Broadway . . .' Avril crossed her fingers and
tapped Cy's desk for luck.

'What have you landed?'

'The lead, actually.' Avril giggled nervously as if not
quite used to saying these words yet. 'In a musical. We go
into rehearsal after Christmas. Portman said I should come
and see Cy —'

'Portman? So he pulled it off?' Lana's voice was bleak at
this news.

'Yes. He said agents were such sharks but that since Cy
was almost your father he'd look after me, see I wasn't
cheated.'

'And I will, Avril, doll. You've landed on your feet
coming to Best Artistes.' Cy smirked at her and Lana would
have loved to hit him across the face. Portman had sent
Avril here on purpose, she was sure, just to rub her nose
in it. He must have known loads of other agents . . .

'This show – it's the one about nuns?' Lana managed to
ask with difficulty, snatching at the possibility that Portman
might have written another musical.

'Yes, I'm to play the Abbess.' Avril giggled again.

'Won't she make a wonderful nun – right turn-on, with that lovely blonde hair and all.' Cy was grinning this time.

'You won't see her hair, it'll be covered with a wimple, or whatever they call it,' Lana snapped crossly.

'Oh, no, there's a wonderful scene in the chapel, late at night, me in a shift, my hair tumbling down my back, and I have to sing this wonderful Ave Maria he's composed.'

'Ah!' said Cy.

'Sounds puke-making,' Lana muttered.

'Still. I mustn't keep you, Cy. A busy man like you. I'll get along. You'll draw up the papers for me to sign? Right. Well, Lana, lovely seeing you. Come and see me, I've a super flat in Chelsea – Daddy bought it for me.'

'Oh, super,' Lana echoed.

'Here's my card. Give me a bell. Bye,' and picking up her *real* fox fur from the floor, and in a flurry of expensive-smelling perfume and clanking of gold bracelets, Avril was gone.

'She makes me sick,' Lana said, opening her purse and taking out her hip-flask.

'I think she's lovely. She'll be a star, that's for sure.'

'You know that was meant to be my part she's playing? She's only second-best.'

'Then why aren't you?'

'How could I? I was under contract to the Mantras – I didn't know they were going to fry themselves on the M1, did I?'

'Lana, what a thing to say! Poor lads. They haunt me, you know.'

'Good,' said Lana, snapping her purse shut. 'Then I'm glad I'm not the only one.'

'So, doll. What are we going to do with you now? I've a nice little group I might be signing up—'

'You're really going places aren't you, Cy? How many is it now?'

'I've six groups and you, of course, doll.'

'And sweet Avril now.'

'Yeah, sweet Avril – you said it.'

'Who's she?' Lana nodded to the door.

'Caroline – my receptionist, secretary, you name it. Dad's a lord, imagine that!' He laughed. 'I'm going to train her to be a booker, aren't I, doll?' Cy said as Caroline appeared with the coffee.

'Sorry I took so long but we were out of milk. I had to pop out.'

'Better late than never,' Cy said, aiming another pat at the pert rump. Caroline giggled as she left the room.

'You screwing her?'

'You've a lovely turn of phrase, Lana. 'Course I'm not.'

'Um!'

'True. I'm as straight as a die these days, you ask your mum. I only ever cheated on her with you.'

'That'll be the day! Anyway, Cy, I know you're not going to like it, but I want six months off.'

'Six months!' Cy whistled through his teeth.

'Yeah. I'm knackered – and the boys buying it, that really upset me, I need time to get over it.' She could make this her excuse and sound convincing, for she doubted if she would ever recover totally from the boys' death, even if sometimes she chose to sound flip about it – her defence to the cruel reality.

'I can understand that, doll. But six months is a long time to be out of the business, you know that.'

This was wonderful news, Cy was thinking. With the Mantras dead, what to do with Lana had been on his mind. She wouldn't fit with any of the other groups he was handling, and she wasn't good enough to go solo – women singers like her were ten a penny. Six months was a long time, she could get bored with the whole business, and by then he would really be heading for the big time – new office, new artists.

'I'm willing to take the risk. I want to use the time to get my voice in shape and write some of my own material.'

'Really?' Cy said with real interest now. It was expensive having to use or buy other people's music, if Lana pulled it off they could save a fortune in shared royalties. And if she was finished, he could use the stuff for his other groups, and still save. 'That's a good idea, Lana. An artist should be creative.'

'Slim's invited me to go and stay with him and work in his studio,' she finally said proudly. Cy was taking this so well that she decided to be straight with him.

'Has he now?' This was getting even better. With her at Slim's he could visit, wheedle his way in, meet people, make contacts with those up there on the giddy heights.

'There's just one thing. I need more than the fifteen quid you're giving me.'

'Yes?' he asked suspiciously.

'I want twenty-five pounds a week.'

'Christ, what on earth for?'

'I've things I need to get. And it's ridiculous me having only fifteen. We must have earned enough for me to have that.'

'And spent it. Don't forget the expenses incurred – the boys never finished paying for the ambulance, you know.'

'What about the insurance money?' Lana said sharply.

'Not paid up yet, something about the brakes . . . how about twenty pounds a week?'

'Twenty-five.'

'You never paid me back for all those lovely clothes I had made for you – you still owe me.'

'I can't manage on twenty! Not being away from home.'

'Tell you what I'll do, doll. I'll give you £500 in a lump sum, to last you the six months. What do you think of that?'

'Oh, Cy. Thanks a million.' She jumped up and kissed him – maths had never been Lana's strong subject.

On the train home Lana felt elated. She felt grown-up for the very first time. She had a huge sum of money in her purse, she had Slim waiting for her, and she was leaving home at last.

'How could you do this to me!' Amy stood in the kitchen, clutching a tea-towel to her, tears pouring down her face.

'Mum, I'm nearly twenty. It's time I left,' Lana said wearily. They had been arguing for what seemed hours. 'I've decided, Mum, and that's that. I thought you would be pleased – this is my big chance.'

'The sacrifices I've made!' Amy whined, as if she had not heard a word Lana had said.

'Oh, for Christ's sake, Mum, shut up!' Lana said with exasperation. She stopped for a moment and looked away with a surprised expression at the vehemence with which she had spoken to her mother. It wasn't like her to lose her temper like this.

'After all I've done for you —'

Lana swung round angrily. 'You did what you did for me because you wanted to. You got a kick out of it. You've been living through me for bloody years.'

'Stop it! Stop it! Don't say such things.'

'You never did anything you didn't want to in your life, Mum. I'm grateful for what you've given me but don't expect me to spend the rest of my life thanking you, because I'm not going to. Is that understood?' And she slammed out of the kitchen and raced up to her room where she began to pack.

Amy sat at her kitchen table for some time, her petite frame slumped despondently. She had never expected to

hear Lana speak to her like that, not after all she had done
for her. Two daughters, both ungrateful. She sucked in her
cheeks and pursed her lips with disapproval.

'She'll be back,' she said aloud. 'She'll always need me,
no doubt about that.' She stood up and put the kettle on.
'Kids,' she muttered as she lit the gas.

17

Kitty was enjoying what she had begun to think of as a lull
in her relationship with Martin. He had a job. There was
no disappearing for days on end, no drinking, the play
came first. He gave her money, brought her presents, made
love to her regularly and she was happy.

She was enjoying working at the coffee bar. It could be
busy, but when it was slack Jim never minded if she popped
out to the shops, sat having a coffee with Jenny, or studied
her books and scores.

'Just think, when you're famous and singing at Covent
Garden, this place will be inundated with fans making a
pilgrimage to your roots,' he said one day, as he polished
the chrome on the espresso machine.

'I think you've a long wait.' Kitty laughed, looking up
from the score of *The Marriage of Figaro* which was to be the
Conservatoire's production this year. She had the part of
the Countess, an honour which was filling her with terror
but also with a determination not to fail, to do justice to
such wonderful music.

'Jenny says you've a wonderful voice and will go straight
to the top.'

'Jenny's a born optimist and she loves me. It's harder

than that. Do you know, I heard of one touring company which held nearly four hundred auditions for a soprano – and they pay peanuts.'

'You wouldn't think there was that number of singers in the world.'

'Exactly. And of that four hundred I bet there's not one who'll make it to La Scala or the Paris Opéra, where it counts to have sung.'

'Why do you do it, then?'

'God knows, I don't. I suppose because once I'd found that I could sing it was the only thing I wanted to do. I couldn't stop now, even if I end up working in the wardrobe department and never set foot on the stage. I'd have to be close to the music.'

'It must be a wonderful feeling, though, to open your mouth and have a gorgeous sound come out. Me? I sound like a frog.'

'It depends, there are days I'm sure I do too.' She laughed. 'There are times when the voice behaves and I think, yes, this is easy. And others when I can't get it to do anything I want and then I almost hate it.'

'That's odd. You referred to your voice as if it was someone in its own right.'

'Did I? How strange.' She smiled, but it did not seem so odd to her, she had become used to this entity living inside her which was part of her and yet not part. Days when she was certain her voice had a will and a life of its own.

She was still always tired. Her studies and the evening work plus looking after the flat were taking their toll.

'Kitty, you look too tired, why?' Madame Cellini demanded one day at a lesson.

'I have a little job in the evenings, last night we didn't close until two.'

'This is preposterous. You must not do it. I insist, you sing, only you sing.'

'But I need the money, Madame. My scholarship doesn't cover everything.'

'Then you are playing at singing and will never succeed.'

'I'm not.' Kitty felt sufficiently angry to argue with the great woman.

'You listen, young lady, and you listen hard to me.' Cellini bore down on Kitty, backing her into a chair and looming over her with her great bulk. 'There is only one thing in your life now, if you wish to succeed – music and your voice, your God-given voice. You don't have time for stupid little jobs. You need a good diet – just look at you, you lose weight every week. Fine, now it would not be good for you to be overweight – audiences, stupid people, demand slim, elegant sopranos, to the detriment of the voice, in my opinion. But you are turning into rag and bone, and there's never been a good voice to emerge from a poor vessel. You need sleep – plenty of sleep. You are like an athlete. Unless you are fit and healthy you cannot sing, and you are wasting your time and I most certainly am wasting mine.'

'Please, Madame. Please, you don't understand.'

'No. I, Cellini, have spoken. I don't wish to teach you any more . . . not until you take things seriously.'

'But singing's my life.'

'Is it? You have a man, yes?'

'Yes.'

'Ah, I thought so – and he has no money?'

'No, he doesn't, he's an actor.'

'If you want a lover you find a rich lover and one who loves music. A singer cannot afford to support others. Don't you understand? You concentrate your energies on yourself. No financial worries, no poverty-stricken lovers, no children. The voice. THE VOICE!' Cellini had whipped herself into a fine spate of emotion and was shouting at Kitty, gesticulating violently. Kitty looked at her in horror as she felt her world collapsing about her, and ran from the studio, fighting back her tears.

The following day she was summoned to Ben Cooper's office. Max Leitman was already there.

'I gather you had a slight contretemps with Madame Cellini yesterday, Kitty,' Ben began, his face stern. 'Have you any idea how fortunate you are that Cellini, of all people, has agreed to teach you?'

'Of course I have. But it wasn't me, it was her – she went for me. She accused me of not being serious about my work, and I am, Professor, I am. Ask Max here.'

'Well, it's not what she says. She says you are up until all hours, you don't eat and you'd rather spend time with your lover than study.' The Professor did not consult Max.

'Then she's lying if she said that. I've got a job because I need one, my money – for which I'm grateful – still isn't enough to live on in London —'

'And support a lover —'

'I don't. Sometimes he's out of work and I chip in. He'd do the same for me,' she said loyally. 'Please, Professor, believe me. I live for my singing, I can't work harder than I do.'

'Very well, Kitty, I believe you. But I suggest you go out and buy some flowers. Here,' he dug into his pocket and produced a couple of notes, 'use this. Buy flowers, go round to Cellini and apologize. Crawl if necessary.'

'Yes, Professor,' Kitty said, even though she was thinking she'd like to smack Cellini rather than apologize, as she closed the door.

'What do you think, Max?' Ben turned to the teacher unaware that Max was upset by the conversation he had just witnessed; he did not like to think of Kitty with a lover.

'I think she's too good, that's our problem. Cellini knows it and can't deal with it. Maybe Kitty has the potential to be even better than her. It's jealousy, pure and simple.'

'God, these women!'

'But what voices!' Max smiled.

'Do you think she'll take her back?'

'Oh, yes. She'll enjoy the reflected adulation when Kitty's a star and she can claim all the credit for teaching her. No doubt, one day, she'll be saying she discovered her,' Max said with a cynical expression. 'They'll be kissing each other within the hour.'

'Right. Well, I suppose I'd better try and find some money to increase her allowance – it'll be hard, mind.'

And unfair on the others, Max thought, but he said nothing.

After Max had left him, Ben telephoned Felix Masters. He gave a glowing report of Kitty's progress and the hopes they had for her before asking for more money. Felix had been wondering how long it would take Ben to get round to the subject of money. He agreed to contribute another three hundred a year.

Max, at home that night, felt depressed. He hadn't known Kitty lived with a man, he'd somehow got the idea she shared a flat with a shop girl. It bothered him sufficiently for him to get very drunk. Over the past eighteen months he had grown very fond of Kitty, too fond perhaps. He had said nothing to her – he had felt it would be wrong. Unlike Ben, Max did not indulge in relationships with those he taught. Now, he supposed, he would never tell her how he felt. He gloomily poured himself another whisky – a large one.

Kitty and Cellini had made friends again after their scene, and if anything, Kitty felt that their relationship had deepened, that Cellini was working even harder on her voice. She accepted the extra money from Ben with heartfelt thanks and promised to give up her evening job, with every intention of doing so. But her increased grant arrived at the same time that the rent on her flat went up, and Martin needed a new suit to go for an important audition. So Kitty lied to Max and Cellini and carried on working, although she did manage to eat more regularly and to put on a little weight.

When, three months later, the breakthrough came for Martin, it was so sudden that neither of them could believe it had happened. Martin had got into films. He signed a five-year contract for an annual salary that until now they had both only dreamed of.

'The first thing we do is get out of this grotty flat,' Martin told Kitty as they celebrated over a bottle of champagne.

'I'll be sorry in a way – it's been our first home.' She looked about the shabby sitting-room and remembered the happy times they had had there – she had taught herself to forget the bad times.

'Only the best for you now, my girl. The big time looms.' He laughed.

'Cellini said I should only have rich lovers.' She was laughing too.

'Wise woman, your Cellini.'

'Oh, Martin, I'm so happy I'm almost afraid of it.'

'Don't be a goose. I love you.'

'Really?' She looked at him, her eyes brimming with tears of happiness. 'You haven't said that to me for so long.'

'How remiss. I love you, Kitty, I love you.' He sprang up, crossed the room and opened the windows that overlooked the dustbins and caterwauling cats. He stuck his head out and shouted, 'Hear this, London, I love Kitty Lawrence. I love her, really I do.'

'Oh, Martin, you fool.'

'That do you? Come on then, let's fuck.'

At his words Kitty felt the magic moment recede.

*

There was no new flat, Martin had bought the lease on a house in Fulham. Kitty could not believe it when he took her to see it and ceremoniously carried her over the threshold.

'It's enormous,' she said, once they had explored all four floors. 'What shall we do with all this space?'

'We'll find a use for it, never you fret. You can have a studio, me a study. We can have a bedroom each, if you like.' He smiled slyly at her.

'I don't like,' she replied, nuzzling his neck.

'We'll fuck like crazed weasels here in the biggest bed that Heal's sell.'

'Martin, there's just one thing. I've never said before . . . but could you stop talking about you know, that word? We make love, you and me, don't we?'

'After all this time.' He laughed. 'What a funny thing you are. Sorry, girl, I screw and I fuck, you can make love, I don't mind.' She never mentioned it to him again.

Their weekends were spent exploring junk shops and street markets for things for their house. They had both agreed they did not want it to look instantly furnished. They wanted it to appear as if it had evolved over the years.

Surprisingly, Kitty found she missed her evening job. Martin was frequently out in the evening and then she would slip round to Jim's, often meeting Jenny there. Jenny refused to visit the house for fear of bumping into Martin.

Martin was working hard on his film. He said he could not get time off to see Kitty sing in *The Marriage of Figaro*, he had an evening shoot. She did not mind, knowing he was working, and it meant that Jenny could come in his place.

After the performance Kitty was approached by an agent, who gave her his card for when she left college; she felt delirious with success. And the handsome blond man who had been at her audition and, she had noticed, always attended the concerts, finally introduced himself as Felix

Masters, going out of his way to congratulate her. Kitty was not sure if she liked him, though. He had a smooth sophistication and a look of wealth about him that made her feel uncomfortably gauche when talking to him. And it was not until much later that she realized he had also been there the evening when she had sung for the Professor's dinner guests. She wondered why he had not mentioned it.

After two months of filming Martin began to grow restless and edgy and, unusually for him when working, he started to drink, moderately at first and then increasingly heavily.

'I thought you were so happy,' Kitty said one evening, in an attempt to find out what was going wrong.

'That's when I thought it was going to be a good film, but it's going to be a bummer.'

'You don't know that. Surely no one can tell until it's finished?'

'The director's crap, the cameraman's crap, the script is crap and so are the other actors.'

'And you're not?' She laughed, trying to tease him into a better humour.

'No, I'm not.' He swung round to face her. 'I'm a bloody fine actor, the best. And this trash I'm involved in will be of no use to me at all.'

'But perhaps the next film will be better,' Kitty said encouragingly.

'I doubt it. I knew I shouldn't have signed that contract. I knew I should have stayed where I belong, on the legitimate stage.'

'But you couldn't get work there,' she said reasonably.

'I would have, you stupid cow!' he shouted, moving towards her with such an enraged expression that she stepped back, frightened he was about to strike her. 'And why did I sign? Because of you and your endless nagging and whining. It's your fault and I hate you for it.'

He disappeared for only one day, while Kitty lied to the producer's secretary that he'd eaten something that disagreed with him, and prayed he would not be gone long.

He returned with a sheepish expression and a bunch of flowers.

'You didn't mean it, did you? That you signed because of me? I wouldn't do anything to hurt you, you have to know that,' she said to him as they lay in bed, having cemented his return by spending the whole evening there.

'Of course. I was angry – with everything except you. But you were there and I took it out on you. I'm sorry, I won't say anything like that again and that's a promise.'

She smiled at him, she could not remember him ever apologizing before.

'Just one thing, Kitty. Never lie for me to cover up for me. I do what I want, do you understand? I don't make excuses to anyone.'

She promised, even though she did not understand why.

The film finally ended and there was to be a post-production party which the star, Heini Walters, was hosting at a fashionable Italian restaurant. Kitty had never been to anything so glamorous, there would be film stars and actors and actresses. She wanted to look her best.

What to wear was no problem. There was to be a concert at the school soon and Frieda Cooper had insisted on taking Kitty shopping to buy something suitable. They had chosen a midnight-blue, stiff taffeta dress with a low-cut tight bodice, a huge stand-up collar that framed her face, and a full, short skirt. The minute she put it on she felt a million dollars.

'You look a million dollars,' Frieda said.

'That was exactly what I was thinking!' Kitty laughed, twirling around in front of the mirror in the exclusive dress shop. 'But, Mrs Cooper, I could never afford this dress and you've bought me several others.'

'It's paid for out of school funds,' Frieda lied, still following Felix Masters' instructions that Kitty was not to know.

So for the party she could wear the dress, with the matching suede stiletto-heeled shoes that Mrs Cooper had also insisted on buying. But what about her hair, her face? She had discussed this too with Frieda, who had advised her to put her long hair up in a French pleat. A kindly assistant on the Elizabeth Arden counter in Selfridges, whom Kitty knew from the days when she had worked there, advised on make-up.

So the Kitty who arrived at the restaurant looked older, more sophisticated and more beautiful than she had thought possible. When she had finished dressing and seen her image in the mirror in her bedroom she had giggled nervously, almost surprised that it was her.

Now she sat in the small bar area waiting for the party to arrive. She had arranged to meet Martin here. She was early by five minutes, but an hour later she felt acutely embarrassed. She had stupidly brought only enough money for her taxi, and could not even order a drink. She knew it was not her imagination that people were staring at her.

The rest of the party were an hour and a half late.

'Good God, is that you?' Martin said, peering at her as she nervously stood up and dropped her handbag. 'Why are you dressed up like a dog's dinner?'

'I thought . . .' she said, blushing to the roots of her scraped-back hair, and looking about her saw that all the men were dressed in jeans and sweatshirts, and the girls in flares and blouses, or skirts and sweaters. 'I just presumed . . .'

'Well, I think your friend looks stunning, Martin.' Heini Walters stepped forward and kissed Kitty on the cheek.

'May I?' he said. Putting his arm up for her to take, he led her over to the long table to which the hovering waiter ushered them.

Martin sat scowling further down the table while Kitty sat with Heini on one side and Peter Potts, the producer, on the other, and the long and very boozy meal began.

'Excuse me, did I hear someone say your name was Kitty Lawrence?'

'Yes,' she replied to the handsome young man who sat opposite her.

'And Lana Lea is your sister?'

'Yes, that's right.'

'I've been working with her. My name's Toby Evans – I write music.'

'Really? Have you? I'm afraid we've rather lost touch.'

'So she said. You're an opera singer, she tells me.'

'Oh, no, not yet. I'm still at the Conservatoire. One day, maybe. But Lana, how is she?'

'She's just fine. She's got over the crash.'

'Crash?' Kitty said, feeling stupid she did not know and embarrassed that she should have to admit to not knowing what her sister was doing.

'The group she sang with—'

'The Mantras?' Kitty said with relief – she'd heard all about them from Amy on one of her rare trips home.

'They were killed – luckily Lana wasn't with them.'

'How dreadful. I didn't know.'

'It was in all the papers.'

'I never read them. That's just terrible,' she said, suddenly full of anxiety for the sister she thought she cared nothing for. 'How do you know her?'

'Oh, I work a lot for the Wall Nuts. I've been doing some stuff for their next LP. Lana's working with Slim . . . she's changing her style. She's good.'

'Yes, she always was,' Kitty said with a sudden spurt of pride, but unaware of the importance of Slim. 'I suppose it seems odd, my not knowing about her,' she said, still feeling acutely embarrassed.

'Good God, no. Families drift, don't they? I've four brothers and I couldn't tell you what one of them is doing now.' She smiled at him gratefully.

It was two in the morning before the party broke up. In all that time Martin had not spoken to Kitty. Nor did he in the studio car that drove them home – not until they were in the drawing-room they had so carefully and lovingly furnished.

'Why did you treat me like that?' Kitty demanded as Martin angrily swung open the drinks cupboard. He took out a bottle of bourbon and filled a tumbler. 'Don't you think you've had enough?' she said, and immediately regretted it.

'Mind your own fucking business. If I want to get legless I will, without your permission. And while we're on the subject of treatment, who the hell do you think you are, humiliating me like that?' He glared angrily at her, waving the bottle of bourbon in the air.

'Humiliating you? What the hell do you mean? I was the one who was humiliated.'

'You let that slimy toad Heini goggle at you, paw you—'

'I did no such thing,' she said indignantly.

'Dressed up like a high-class tart. Just look at you.'

'How dare you, you pig?'

'They were all ogling you – that creep Toby, even my producer, *my* producer. You thoughtless cow.'

'I was talking to them, making polite conversation – not that an animal like you would know anything about that. What else was I to do? You were ignoring me and too busy pawing those women sitting either side of you.'

'We mortals sat below the salt,' he intoned. 'Christ, Kitty, do you have any idea what a bore you are? A pompous, unmitigated bore.'

'Martin, what's got into you? Stop it, please.'

'You started it, not me, not this time. Now you can take the consequences. You bore me to tears, you have done right from the very beginning.'

'Then why did you stay with me?' she said with spirit.

'Because it suited me to. That's why. But not any more. I'm up to here with you, Kitty, and your endless nagging and complaining. "Don't you think you've had enough?"' He mimicked her expertly. 'Living with you is like being married to you – it's dull and it's predictable.'

'Martin, you don't mean this.' She took a step towards him, her hand outstretched, wanting to touch him, to stop him.

'I do. I mean every fucking word I'm saying. You even bore me in bed – and that's the truth. And for Christ's sake don't cry, I can't stand it when you snivel.'

'I'm not going to cry, I've done all my crying over you, you ungrateful creep—'

'Aha!' He held his hand up triumphantly. 'I knew it was only a matter of minutes and that would be said. It wouldn't surprise me if you haven't got a little book somewhere with every penny you've ever spent written down in it – you're mean enough.'

'Mean!' she screamed. 'Mean! How dare you, you pig, you filthy pig!' And she sprang across the room and hurled herself at him and began to pummel his chest with her fists. He laughed. His laughter made her dizzy, made a mist fill her eyes, and she lunged at him, kicking and clawing. She brought her knee up and aimed between his legs with all her strength. He screamed in agony, grabbed at his scrotum and lurched across the room holding himself, howling.

'You four-ace cow.' He lunged across the room and seized her. He slapped her hard across her face, banging her head from side to side. And then his hands were round her throat.

'No, Martin, no. My voice —' she cried, before he began to squeeze.

'Oh, your fucking boring voice. Mustn't hurt your bloody voice, must we? Me, ruin me, but not your flaming . . .' The pressure of his hands increased, she felt herself fighting for breath, saw the room go red as she kicked and clawed at him. Then she went limp and closed her eyes and prayed as she'd never prayed before. It worked. His fingers released her neck, he threw her down and, for good measure, kicked her as he blundered from the room.

Kitty lay on the carpet, still fighting for breath. She gulped down air in great rasping gulps. The pain in her throat was intense. She sat up and slumped against the sofa, fighting the panic, forcing herself to calm down. She touched her throat gingerly and stood up slowly, pausing, waiting for the dizziness to pass. She turned to look in the mirror over the fireplace – they'd bought it in a shop in the Portobello Road and had been so happy to find it, she thought inconsequentially, and marvelled that she did.

She looked in the mirror. She could already see red marks on either side of her neck where his hands had tried to squeeze the life out of her.

'Not my voice,' she said, hoarsely, to her reflection in the mirror. 'No one does that to my voice,' she repeated. She opened her mouth, drawing air painfully down into her lungs. She tried to sing and no sound came.

18

'You've been very fortunate, Miss Lawrence,' the Ear, Nose and Throat specialist finally said after a long and nerve-racking examination the following day. 'There's internal as well as external bruising and your vocal cords appear to be swollen, but they are undamaged. I'm afraid it may be some time before you can even contemplate singing without doing damage. Certainly I wouldn't want you to try until you've seen me again. Say two weeks from today?'

'Thank you, doctor.'

'And perhaps a change of address?' He smiled kindly.

'I have already – this morning, in fact. I'm staying at the YWCA until a friend and I can find a flat to share.'

'A female friend, I trust?'

'Oh, yes, doctor. I think I'll give boyfriends a rest for a while, like my throat.' She still spoke in a whisper even though by now it was late afternoon, but she smiled.

It had been a long and difficult day. First she had packed quietly so as not to wake Martin and have him attack her again. She felt dreadful, as if she had drunk the bottle of bourbon, not him. Her throat and her whole body ached and she felt completely drained.

She had arrived at the YWCA before Jenny had left for work. They had stowed her cases in Jenny's room and for once Jenny did not lecture her. She could not eat, but drank endless glasses of ice-cold water as she pondered what she should do.

'Look, Kitty, I think you should go to the Conservatoire and explain what's happened.'

'How the hell can I? I'd be too ashamed. Maybe they'd ask me to leave . . .'

'Don't be silly, of course they won't. You could have been attacked in the street, you don't have to tell them it was Martin.'

'How many people do you know who have been strangled in the street? They'd guess.' She held her throat when she spoke, as if supporting it, but this did not help, it still ached abominably.

'Well, you've got to see a doctor and one who knows what he's talking about . . . do you know one?'

'No.' Kitty shrugged miserably.

'I'll skive off work and come with you, if you like.'

'Jenny!' Kitty said with relief.

On the bus to the Conservatoire Kitty decided that the best person to speak to would be Max Leitman. She liked him enormously, and he was younger than most of the teachers and might understand better.

In Max's studio Kitty was relieved when Jenny did most of the talking. After quickly assessing Max and deciding that she liked him and that he was to be trusted, Jenny told him far more than Kitty really wanted him to know. She watched him as the sorry tale unfolded, saw his jaw stiffen, watched him ball his hands so that the knuckles showed white.

'If you want, Kitty, I've a spare room in my house,' he offered. 'It's not very grand but it's convenient – Golders Green. You're welcome to stay as long as you like until Jenny can find somewhere else for you to live.'

'Mr Leitman, you're so kind. But I'm not sure . . .'

'I'd accept, Kitty. Anything's better than the Y,' Jenny said. 'I'll soon find a flat.'

Kitty looked doubtful but it wasn't because she didn't trust Max. It was just that she felt safer when she was with Jenny.

'The next thing is to see a specialist – see what damage has been done. The bastard, going for your voice, that must have been deliberate.' Max crossed the room to the telephone and made a call to the throat specialist the school always used. 'I'm free at four when he can see you. I'll come too.'

So when Kitty emerged from the doctor's surgery Max and Jenny were sitting anxiously waiting for her, to hear what the doctor had said.

Max owned a battered lime-green VW Beetle and he drove them to pick up Kitty's cases. The VW had not been built to take so much, and when the small boot was full and the back seat covered with cases, there was no room for Jenny.

'I'll look after her, don't worry. And come over when-ever you feel like seeing her,' Max said to the still fretting Jenny.

'Well, I really should get myself sorted out and go to work tomorrow, or I'll get the chop.'

'Bye, Jenny, thanks.' Kitty's voice was barely audible.

'Don't talk – do as the doctor told you. I'll talk for both of us.' Max patted her hand. Kitty settled back into her seat and felt strangely safe, and smiled her thanks to him.

Max was an easy person to live with, she found. Although the sitting-room, where he spent most of his time, was an untidy clutter of books, scores, librettos and a dozen different instruments scattered about, it was also a cosy room with well-worn but comfortable armchairs, a coal fire and a mass of Victoriana inherited from his grandmother. It was a room that one never had to worry about making a mess in. It was a companionable room.

The kitchen, in contrast, was as neat as a pin, and she learned, with gratitude, that Max loved to cook, especially if he was to share the result with someone. So delicious were the suppers he concocted that she feared she would put on weight and become the fat soprano of cartoons.

The bedroom she was given was delightful, large and airy and at the back of the house, overlooking the garden. It belonged to Max's sister Sheila, who was a doctor working in Africa. She had left her possessions behind and, looking at the pictures on the walls and leafing through the books on the shelves, Kitty felt that she would like Sheila if and when she ever met her.

Max had decided that it would be better if Kitty did not return to the college before her next appointment with the doctor. He reassured her that he could teach her in the evenings and at the weekends so that she would not fall behind with her work. He felt she needed some peace and quiet, not just for her throat, but for her spirit. For Max could see that Kitty was mentally exhausted, even though she didn't realize it herself.

They quickly settled into a routine. Max would leave for work, letting Kitty sleep on. When she awoke it was to find a note from him wishing her well, or telling her something funny he had heard or seen, and with a shopping list for that evening's supper. She would quickly dust and hoover and after a bath would walk to the local shops. In the afternoon she listened to music on Max's wonderful hi-fi system, the best she had ever come across, with the widest selection of records she had seen outside a shop. She would study but would have the kettle on in time for Max's return.

As he prepared the supper she would sip a glass of wine and he would gossip about his day. While their supper was cooking they would have a lesson, with Max at the piano, and phrase by phrase they would work on whatever Cellini had set Kitty to study. Max would sing and Kitty was surprised by his fine tenor voice, for he had not told her of his own thwarted ambitions. As he illustrated how it should be done, she would listen, frustrated at being unable to join in. While they ate they talked of music, little else. Together they would wash up and then, over a whisky, the conversation would ramble on until the small hours, interspersed with music as Max would leap up and place a record on the turntable to prove a point.

Kitty had never enjoyed such companionship. She had not known the pleasure of sharing an interest with someone who felt even more passionately about it than she did. She was convinced that during these evenings she learned more than she had in the previous eighteen months.

She would sit curled up on the sofa as Max talked of his life, and his acceptance that he could never be the success he had once longed to be. She told him she was sure that was to be her lot too, but he would not hear of such a thing. She would be a diva – he knew it. She would smile gently at him, thinking that he was just being kind.

As the first week slipped into the second there were times when Kitty longed for Max to say something personal to her, to touch her. She would watch him when he wasn't aware, studying his face, finding it pleasing. He was younger than his beard made him look. Behind his spectacles his brown eyes were kind and intelligent. She loved his hands, with their long, elegant tapering fingers, and she often wished for them to caress her. She was surprised by this reaction for, after Martin, she had told herself that she never wanted to be involved with a man again. But Max was different – he was gentle and sweet and considerate. Her feelings for him were not the passionate excitement she had felt for Martin, but she counselled herself that maybe a calmer, less sexual, more mutually respectful relationship would be better for her, and more lasting. Sometimes during the day she would plan that she would tell Max that evening how much she liked him, and hope that speaking up might lead to something more. She even practised aloud what she would say. But when the evening came, she had lost courage and remained silent.

Max was finding the situation hard. He had been right, Kitty was an ideal companion, and his feelings were deepening as each day passed. But he was afraid to say anything to her. She made no move, nothing she said or did could be interpreted as an equal interest on her part. Had it been anyone else he would have spoken up, but after the dreadful experience she had just been through he hesitated, for he was sure that the last thing she would want was an involvement with another man. But there was another problem too; to Max, Kitty's voice came first, it always would. The voice was more important than his emotions. The voice stood between them, for already, in his eyes, Kitty was different. What on earth made him think he had the right to presume that a romantic relationship could develop between them when she was destined for great things? So he said nothing.

He was horrified to learn that she had never seen a full-scale opera. Because of his contacts in the operatic world, he went two or three times a month. He needed the contacts, and the tickets, which were quite unaffordable on his salary, were given to him free.

He waved them at her excitedly. 'See! Two tickets for Sylvana Gotli singing Mimi at Covent Garden!'

She backed away from him. 'Oh, it's kind of you, but take someone else, please.'

'What on earth for? You've never been to an opera, I want to take you.'

'But I don't want to go.'

He sat down. 'Tell me, tell me why not, what frightens you about it?'

'What do you mean, frightens?' She tried to laugh.

'There must be something. All my other students take any opportunity. They spend hours queuing for the gallery. You should too, it's fun, apart from being an essential part of your education.'

'I couldn't, could I? I had to work in the evenings, there was never any time.'

'Never? Please, Kitty, tell me, let me help you.' He put out his hand and took hers. 'Sometimes if you talk things over, it helps. Problems disappear.'

She looked at him anxiously. Was she being stupid? Would he understand?

'You're right. I am frightened. I am sure that if I see a great singer perform I'll know I couldn't do it, could never be as good, that I'm totally wasting my time.'

'But you listen to records all the time.'

'They're different, they have to be, I'm sure. A recording is one thing, a performance . . . that will be something else. And if it isn't – I don't want the let-down.'

'You're right about recordings. Nothing on earth can beat a live performance, the magic, the excitement, the great voices swirling about you.'

'Exactly,' she said.

It took Max a whole evening, but he won. The next day Kitty accompanied him to Covent Garden, to hear *La Bohème*.

This was a building she had dreamed about. She had seen pictures of it but now she was here. They joined the throng milling about the entrance and Kitty found herself catching the excitement of the others. They checked in their coats. She had worn her midnight-blue taffeta dress and feared that with no jewellery she would look very underdressed, but not everyone was smartly turned out. Some people were wearing ordinary clothes, others long dresses and jewellery.

'They sit in the boxes,' Max whispered in her ear as if reading her thoughts. He took her arm and moving slowly with the throng they inched their way through into the auditorium and to their seats in the stalls, red and gold and opulent.

'Oh, it's so wonderful, far better than any picture of it,' she said, gazing about her. He handed her a pair of opera glasses.

'Now you can spy on the rich in their boxes.'

'Oh, I couldn't.' She giggled.

'Don't disappoint them, they like it.' He grinned.

The orchestra was tuning up, the audience was rustling with anticipation. There was a great burst of applause as the conductor took the rostrum and raised his baton, and it was as if everyone was holding their breath as they waited for the music to begin.

The heavy maroon and gold curtains swung slowly back and within minutes Kitty felt she was in the Parisian garret with Rodolfo. She clutched at her throat as, off-stage, they heard the first golden notes sung by Gotli. With the arrival of the great diva the opera lifted on to another plane of pleasure.

Sylvana Gotli was a large woman, and somewhat middle-aged to be playing the young Parisian Mimi, and she looked in far too robust health to be about to die. She was famed neither for her acting ability nor for any swift or light movement on stage. But when she sang, so sensitive was her voice, so golden the sound, so brimming with emotion, that these defects paled into insignificance.

Kitty resented the intervals when they left their seats and sat on the red carpet of the great staircase. She did not want to talk, she wanted to hold the music within her, safe from all interference. How could people bother with food and drink when the sound of that voice was like champagne itself?

At the end she stood with everyone and clapped until her hands ached. She would have liked to cheer with the rest, but had to remain silent as the audience called the singer back time and again, showering her with flowers. Tears were cascading down Kitty's cheeks unnoticed, unchecked. She felt drained, as if it had been she who had played Mimi.

Outside the theatre they walked for a while in silence, neither wishing to break the spell. In Trafalgar Square Max led her to a wooden seat. He took her hand.

'Well?'

'Could I, Max? Would I? Will I ever be able to sing like that?'

'You will, my sweet. I promise.'

'I don't want anything else in my life but that, Max. Even if it's just once to have that sound, to hold a large audience as she did tonight.'

'You'll do it more than once, I'm sure.'

'Yes, I will. I've got to. If I fail there'd be no point to anything,' she said with a strange, determined but almost frightened expression as she seemed to gaze into the future.

It was a look that made Max want to hold her tight, support her, keep her safe from all the trials ahead of her. But he looked away, too shy by far.

'But you know,' Kitty said, as if coming out of a trance, her expression changed completely, 'I did feel that her *tessitura* was a little bland, didn't you? And Mimi is not exactly a taxing role, is it? And honestly, I think the day of the static soprano is gone – we need drama, great acting like Callas. I'd want to *act* the part, not merely sing it.'

Max laughed. 'If I needed any persuading that you were destined for great things, that little speech proves it. Who else but a budding diva would presume to criticize the divine Gotli?'

And this time he hugged her but, she registered, it was a very brotherly hug.

19

Lana's planned six months living at Slim's had slid almost imperceptibly into nine. He never questioned her living there and she never asked if he minded. She had her own room, spacious and beautifully furnished even down to a record-player.

She was not the only guest. There must have been a good dozen and a half others, but as they came and went with their various women, it was difficult to be more exact about the number. Most were musicians of some sort and all, evidently, helped in some way by Slim. His voice and drama coaches, his guitar teacher, his recording engineer, his agent, his manager, his music publisher, his doctor – all, at one time or another, were enlisted to help further the career of one of his protégés. And all of them, dependent on their large incomes from Slim's mega-earnings, were happy to oblige.

Added to all these was Slim's staff of cook, driver, minder, three gardeners and his housekeeper, Sam, a faded blonde beauty who had been a model until heroin had wrecked her career. Reformed now, but with her looks ruined for all time, she had been taken in by Slim to run his huge household, which she did efficiently.

There was never any need to be alone, for every night was like a party. Anything went.

Since everyone congregated in the den, a cavernous room at the back of the house that had once been the servants' hall, the rest of the house was rarely used. The fires burned without warming anyone, the flowers went unadmired, and a monastic hush reigned.

Except in the morning, when no one was up, the den, on the other hand, was always noisily busy. Lana thought it would have been more accurate to call it a play-room. There was a pool table, a vast collection of board-games from all over the world, the largest TV set obtainable and the best hi-fi system. There were also a Hammond organ and a 1950s' juke-box. Leading off the room was a comfortable small cinema furnished with blue leather armchairs. Even with so much to amuse them there were, inevitably, rows, when one person wanted to watch television and another to play the organ.

Any drink was available – but there was more. Every evening Sam appeared with bowls of hash, bowls containing pills of various colours – uppers and downers – and glass sheets with cocaine in ruler-straight lines. These she put on a coffee table as another hostess would lay out the nuts and Twiglets. The use of heroin was banned and anyone who broke that rule was asked to leave. One of the original members of the Wall Nuts had died of an overdose of heroin and Slim had had nothing to do with the stuff since then. No one but Sam knew where the drugs were

kept and only she had the key, so that, should there be a
police raid, she could quickly stash everything away in a
special hiding-place. There had not been a raid but Slim
wasn't taking any chances.

The point was that no one was ever censorious of others'
needs. If Lana became legless from alcohol – which was
often – there were plenty of people to put her to bed and
there were no lectures the next day. And those who
preferred to spend their days in a drug-induced haze were
permitted to go their own way.

There was uninhibited sex for those still interested and
it was only a week into her visit, with Slim away, that Lana
watched her first orgy begin. It was one of the few nights
she went to bed early and sober – she had not liked what
she saw, it made her feel uncomfortable, and reminded her
of how it had once been with the Philberts, an episode in
her life that she now wished had never happened. For Lana
was in love – with Slim. How she wished she could erase
the past, how often she dreamed she was still a virgin,
saved just for him.

Everyone adored Slim, he could do no wrong in anyone's eyes. Here in this house, with all these dependants
about him, he was an emperor. Lana, to her disappointment, only saw him when they were working. He rarely
joined the others in the evenings. He might look in but
never stayed. She had seen him drink but never drunk,
and she noticed he never touched drugs. And sometimes
he went for days without even joining the others for meals.

One wing of the house was Slim's quarters and no one
was allowed there without an invitation, something which
was not often extended. Lana watched the other women
like a hawk, to try to work out which of them Slim was
sleeping with. She had the deepest suspicion it might be
Sam, even if, to Lana at twenty, she looked old and ugly at
thirty.

There was much rivalry as to who Slim was favouring

the most. And if one person was lucky and was summoned by Slim, or he spent time talking to an individual for any length of time, then the downside was a lot of petty jealousy from the others. Lana, who spent time in the studio with Slim, was consequently very unpopular. But then she, more than most, had a great deal to be grateful for. She had listened intently to his views on her career. He advised her to stop the loud and raucous singing, telling her she must retrieve the sweetness of tone that went with her strange air of innocence.

Throwing out the pink outfits, the PVC and thigh-high boots and changing into flower-sprigged cotton and lawn clothes was easy enough. Changing the heavy make-up and false eyelashes to make-up that was so subtle it did not seem as if she wore any was done in a trice by a skilled make-up artist. Lana felt odd in this new garb and wondered how easy it would be to behave in a way to suit the new image. But the voice was the main problem.

She had damaged it. Nearly five years of singing in smoke-filled clubs and bars, belting out the music over people talking and then having to strain to be heard over the Mantras with their poor equipment had taken their toll. The pretty, high soprano voice had gone for ever. And worse, she had found there were nodules on her vocal cords.

It was Slim who had paid for the expensive operation by the best man money could buy. It was a risky operation, one that could leave her with no voice at all if she were unlucky. But luck and the surgeon's skill were on her side. She emerged from surgery forbidden to talk for two weeks and to sing for two months. When she did – nervously and, at her own insistence, alone in the room – it was to find that her voice was lower but with a slight huskiness she thought might be attractive, and which the others raved about.

Toby Evans had written the music of two songs for her,

and Slim the lyrics. Both were pleasant ballads, well suited to her, everyone agreed. Her favourite was 'Trying Again', a bitter-sweet song of lost love recaptured.

After her operation Lana worked hard honing and perfecting her sound, working at her new stage image. Without at first realizing it, she found that she was drinking less, maybe half a bottle of brandy instead of the whole one she had worked herself up to. She occasionally took some speed, and even more occasionally barbiturates; she did not need them any more. She had a goal now and a perfect teacher in Slim.

Slim promised Lana she would be on the bill when the Wall Nuts had their next tour, scheduled for late the following year. He would arrange a recording contract for her with the band's recording company and her record would be released to coincide with the tour. She would be a star, it was inevitable.

Now she could read in the newspapers of the great success of Portman's musical, the rave reviews, with interest and pride for him. She could not help feeling a twinge of jealousy for Avril's success, and when the awards began to go her way she did allow herself to dream of what might have been. But then there was the other side. If she had been able to perform for Portman, she would not have been here now with Slim.

Lana felt she had never known such happiness. There was just one cloud – Slim himself. He liked her, that was obvious, why else would he take so much trouble over an unknown girl? Why, then, did he never touch her? Why didn't he ever attempt to seduce her? She had become celibate, even when she thought she would crawl up the wall with frustration. But she did not want Slim thinking she was anybody's.

And then the invitation to his quarters finally came. Lana was shaking with excitement as she bathed and dressed. Ten o'clock she was to be there – ten at night! It could only mean one thing. She sprayed herself all over with perfume, took ages choosing a dress and decided against underwear except for a frilly suspender belt holding up her white stockings – men, she knew, loved that. She studied herself in the mirror. She looked perfect, she decided, the child-woman Slim was always going on about. She allowed herself a large glass of brandy and sprayed her mouth out so he would not smell it.

When she entered Slim's sitting-room she was disappointed to see a large man there, heavily bronzed and fashionably dressed.

'Lana, I'd like you to meet my manager, Tristan Riviera,' Slim said, getting to his feet as she entered the room. He was the only man she knew who stood up for her, and she loved him for it.

'Hi!' Tristan waved a heavily jewelled hand at her.

'How do you do, Mr Riviera,' she said almost breathlessly. Her initial disappointment that Slim was not alone was tempered, for here she was in the presence of the most famous manager–agent of them all, a legend in the pop world. The number of successful groups he managed were legion. If Tristan Riviera took an interest in you, your future was assured.

'Tristan, please. All my *friends* call me Tristan.' He smiled, showing a mouthful of perfect white teeth, too perfect to have been born with. 'Slim and I have been talking about you, Lana. I've listened to your tapes, and I'm impressed.'

'Why, thank you, Tristan.' She accepted the large glass of brandy Slim handed her.

'Seeing you, I'm even more impressed.'

Lana hung her head modestly which, she thought, fitted her new image well, and wondered if it wouldn't have been smarter to reject the brandy and ask for orange juice. Oh, fuck it, she thought, and sipped at it.

'You've an agent, I hear?'

'Yes, Cy Best.'

'I know Cy. In fact I've a pretty shrewd idea he came to see me three or four years ago to pick my brains over what to do about you. In fact I suggested your name to him if memory serves me right.'

'Then I'm grateful, Tristan. It's a nice name,' she simpered.

'How do you feel about Cy representing you?' Tristan asked.

Lana's mind raced. This, if she wasn't mistaken, was her big chance. 'Well, he's hardly representing me at the moment.'

'Really?'

'Yes. After the Mantras were wiped out he seemed to lose interest in me. He's been here several times but I think it was more in the hopes of worming his way in with Slim. I used to see him when I went home to my mum's – he lives with her – but he never mentioned work and I never asked 'cause I was happy here.' She looked at Slim when she said this, injecting all her longing for him into the look.

'You've got a mum – that's good. I see you living with her, stay-at-home girl, no boyfriends and a pretty pink and white room, all frills and organdie with shelves full of cuddly toys. That would be novel in this day and age, wouldn't it?' He slapped his thigh with enthusiasm at his own marketing strategy.

'I'm not going back to live with her,' Lana said shortly, forgetting her new sweet-little-girl image for the moment and accepting a refill.

'Just for publicity, my dear. Nothing else. The problem is, before I can represent you we have to get you out of any contract you have with Cy. The record company is no problem – I can close Jubilee Records with a snap of my fingers, if I care to. But if Mr Best gets wind of my interest in you, he's not going to let you go.'

'I see that – Cy's no fool,' Lana agreed, realizing she was

having to concentrate very hard on what Tristan was saying since she felt rather woozy.

'Exactly. So, Slim and I have been talking, and the best plan of action, we think, is for you to approach him and ask him to release you from the contract – get it in writing.'

'What do I say?'

'That's up to you, my dear. You know him better than most. Another drink?'

Lana looked up and it was only then that she realized Slim had left the room without her noticing, and she vaguely remembered hearing a telephone ring in an adjacent room. She was alone with Tristan. He poured her nearly a tumblerful of brandy.

'Oh, you'll get me squiffy.' She giggled.

'And why not? It might be fun,' Tristan said softly, sitting on the sofa beside her, and before she knew what was happening one of his beringed hands was sliding up her leg, under her skirt, plucking at her suspenders. 'Nice,' he said.

Lana felt her body go rigid and her mind was in a fuddled turmoil. She didn't want this man, she didn't want anyone but Slim. Why was it that men always came on to her like this? All they ever wanted from her was sex, she thought miserably.

'Relax, little kitten,' Tristan said huskily into her ear, his fingers beginning to delve higher. 'No panties, naughty!' he chuckled.

'But Tristan—' she began.

'I thought you were a reasonable little bird. I thought you wanted to succeed more than anything.'

'I do, Tristan.'

'Well, then. Don't you think it would be nice if you and I got really friendly? I'm good to my birds, you know.'

'But Slim—' she said nervously.

'Now who's going to tell him?'

Lana closed her eyes as she felt his fingers begin to enter

her, massaging her roughly. His full mouth found hers, he stank of cigar smoke. He held her tightly with his other arm and she felt trapped and physically overwhelmed by him. And mentally she was afraid of him and the power he could exert upon her career.

'Oh, Tristan,' she said, pretending to sigh, opening her legs wide for him, totally unaware that Tristan told his most important client, Slim, everything.

Lana, having thrown her old clothes away, had to borrow a leather mini-skirt and boots from a girlfriend of one of the other musicians. She had to revert to her old style of dressing for if Cy saw her in her sprigged cotton or muslin he might become suspicious that something was afoot.

She had arranged to meet him at home at Number Fourteen. She had decided to confide in her mother. She was certain that to make her a star her mother would agree to anything, and that with Amy on her side she stood a better chance of Cy agreeing. And if her mother proved awkward she knew what to do, she'd spill the beans on Cy's sexual interests.

Two days later she was sitting at home with Amy, sharing a bottle of wine and waiting for Cy to arrive from London.

'It's lovely to see you again, Lana. I don't see nearly enough of you,' Amy said, the familiar whine in her voice.

'I'm sorry, Mum. But you know what it's like.'

'No, I don't. But then I would if I saw you more,' Amy said sharply.

'I can't leave London, Mum. I've got to be at the centre of things – hear the gossip, know what's going on.'

'That's what Cy says. If I see him once a week, I'm lucky.'

'But he's getting successful, isn't he?'

'Oh, yes. I've no complaints there. I've had all my money

back and a load on top – do you like the new three-piece and carpet?'

'It's lovely, Mum. Heard from Kitty?'

'Kitty!' Her mother shrugged her shoulders. 'She comes back every couple of months, but I don't know what for, I think she's as bored with me as I am with her. She turned up one day and said not speaking was silly – so it is, but she was the one who left, not me, as I pointed out to her. Doesn't bother me if she comes or not. She's off to Paris in September.'

'Paris? Why?' Lana asked, not taken in at all by her mother's declaration. Even if she didn't want Kitty at home she'd want to know what she was up to.

'Another school, or something. Says she's got more to learn – seems odd to me, if you can sing you can sing, can't you? You haven't got to go to Paris.'

'Slightly different singing, Mum.' Lana laughed.

'Bloody awful row, if you ask me. She brought some tapes here and I had to listen out of politeness, but when you think people pay good money to listen to that – it beats me. "Why couldn't you stick to Gilbert and Sullivan?" I asked her – now they have a nice tune here and there. She laughed, said she understood how I felt, but I think she was lying.'

'How can she afford it?' Lana asked curiously.

'Some scholarship she's won. I will say that about Kitty, she's never been a drain on me, she's always been independent.'

'I'd like to see her again. You got her address?'

'Yes, somewhere – I'll give it to you before you leave. She's sharing a flat with that friend of hers, Jenny. You know, the fat girl who works in Selfridges.'

'Maybe it's Kitty who'll be the star and not me,' Lana said, all innocence as she saw an opening in the conversation.

'Don't talk so silly. It's always been you. I knew it from the day you were born.'

'That's what I want to talk to you about, Mum. I'm worried. I'm not getting anywhere with Cy – he's lost interest.'

'Has he now?'

'You've heard of the Wall Nuts, haven't you? Well, Slim – their lead singer and guitarist – well, he wants to look after me now, and with him, Mum, the sky's the limit.'

'Why should he want to do that?' Amy asked suspiciously.

'Because he loves me. I think he's going to ask me to marry him. He's a wonderful man, Mum. I must arrange for you to meet him one day soon. But his manager – one of the biggest in the business – he wants to manage me. Oh, Mum, this is it. I can do it with them. World tours, Number Ones – the lot.' She was leaning forward, her face glowing with excitement.

'Then what's stopping you?' Amy asked, already caught up in her daughter's excitement.

'Cy. We signed a contract with him – or rather, you did.'

'Me? I signed no contract.'

'But he said you'd made him my legal representative. So, I presumed . . .'

'No, he never asked me to sign anything. The only signing done was when I kept having to loan him money to get him started and I demanded it be drawn up, all legal like.'

'Mum, you're a genius!' Lana jumped up and kissed her mother warmly.

'We all know that.' Amy laughed, but stopped as they heard Cy's key in the door. 'Who's going to tell him?'

'Not me.' Lana pulled a face.

'Oh, well. In a way I shall enjoy it, I think the bastard's two-timing with that fat spotty secretary he's got.'

Lana almost sighed with relief that her mother had not been difficult.

Ten minutes later Cy's face was red with anger as he confronted the two women.

'Haven't you heard of honour?' he was shouting. 'I had no contract, it wasn't necessary, I thought – we were family.'

'But you're doing nothing for the girl. She needs to get on. Others are interested in her and she has to go with them.'

'Who?'

'I'd rather not say,' Lana said quickly, to forestall her mother proudly spilling the beans. Contract or no, Lana was not sure, without advice, if Cy had any claim upon her.

'I don't believe this is happening. Our little girl. Oh, Amy, how could she do this to me?' he appealed. 'God, I don't want to go to law with our little girl. Amy, talk some sense into her.'

'There's a matter of money to discuss too, Cy,' Lana said coldly. She hated it when men whined.

'What money?' He swung round to face her.

'The money I earned, and you kept. Remember, you only gave me a fiver to begin with and then fifteen, and only in the past year did I get twenty. I want the rest.'

'Now, hold on a minute. There's the money on the ambulance – still not paid back – and with the boys dead I consider that your responsibility. There's all your clothes and expenses. If you want the truth, there's bugger all left,' he said slyly.

'Cy, there must be something, they were doing quite well.'

'Not well enough, Amy – that's the trouble.'

'I want the money from the first contract you signed with the venue operators. I'm not talking about the second contract, Cy.' Lana was smiling sweetly as she spoke.

'First contract, second? What the hell are you going on about? Sure I signed your contracts for you, took my 20 per cent and that's that.'

'But it isn't, Cy, is it? There was always one contract with the venue and then there was the contract between you and us – and the difference in the sums involved is what interests me.' She was not smiling now but staring coldly at him. Cy looked uncomfortable. She had not been sure if he had cheated her and the Mantras in this way but she'd heard from other groups how common the practice was. She had hit the nail on the head, Cy's discomfort told her that.

'Lana, explain this to me. What contracts? What's been going on?'

'One of the oldest tricks in the book, Mum. Cy here would book us into a gig. He would arrange a fee with the operator, say £75 – they would draw up a contract which he would sign as our manager. Then he'd draw up a second contract with us, for say £40 less his 20 per cent. So the Mantras and I would share £32 and he would grab £43 – simple. And he did that every time, I reckon, and no doubt he's still doing it with his new groups. I bet they would be interested to know what little games he plays with their money.'

'You're lying,' Cy said aggressively.

'No, I'm not. It's one of the reasons you can't keep anyone – in the end they know you're shafting them. I'm pretty sure the Mantras were thinking of leaving you and, contract or no, there's nothing you could have done, especially if they had gone to the police. You've lost two other groups already who'll make it big – and that's why. You're a greedy little fart, Cy. You'll never be anything if you keep screwing the groups.'

'Cy, tell me this isn't true.' Amy looked at him anxiously.

'It's true, Mum. Just look at his face. The Mantras would have had it out with him before he killed them – expecting the impossible of them and their vehicle.'

'That's slanderous!' Cy yelled.

'Yes, unprovable, I agree. But the truth all the same. How do you sleep at nights, Cy, with that on your conscience?' She clicked open her handbag and took out the letter that Tristan had given her. 'Sign this and I won't breathe a word.'

Reluctantly Cy picked up a pen and signed. 'You're a cold, ungrateful little cow, Lana, do you realize?'

'And you're a nobody, Cy, and you'll stay one.'

'Cy, Lana, don't. We were all such friends.' Amy was wringing her hands.

'Exactly, Amy. What's it matter who had what money? We were a little family, I was working for our little doll here . . .'

Lana looked at him cringing, saw the ridiculous blond hair, the clothes which were designed for a younger man, and wondered how she could ever have let him touch her. She thought of all the hours she and the Mantras had spent on the road, in dim and run-down halls, in seedy digs, and she knew she hated him and wanted to finish with him once and for all.

'Don't give me that crap, Cy,' she said coldly, and turned to face her mother. 'It might interest you to know, Mum, he's married – got a wife in Cambridge he never got around to divorcing.'

'Lana, how can you say such things? Cy's been good to you.'

'Oh, yes, Mum, better than you realize. It wasn't just his secretary he was screwing, it was me too!' Lana said finally with satisfaction, picked up her coat and stalked out of the room.

Amy stood on the hearthrug, her face twisted in astonishment which quickly turned to anger.

'You bastard. Is this true?'

'I couldn't help myself, Amy. The kid came on to me so

heavy. I'm only a man.' He backed away from the furious woman. Like so many men he was afraid of female anger.

'You bastard. She's right, you are a creep. And if she won't tell on you, I will. If that money from those there crooked contracts isn't in my bank account by Monday I'll go to the police. I'll shop you!'

'To be honest with you, Amy, I'm well shot of the lot of you. I've only kept in with you in case the doll pulled herself together and did something,' he said from the safety of the doorway.

'What you mean by that?' Amy yelled.

'Your sweet little Lana drinks like a fish and is shacked up with Slim of the Wall Nuts, and he's an alcoholic and a drug-taker, just for starters – if you must know,' was Cy's parting shot as he quickly escaped from Number Fourteen for ever.

20

'But Mum, I can't interfere in Lana's life. You know we're not that close,' Kitty said into the telephone. She stood patiently listening to her mother's shrill voice the other end. 'I'll do my best. Bye . . .' She replaced the receiver and straightened the telephone on the small table. She and Jenny had been sharing this flat for five months now and Kitty, who was obsessively tidy, was constantly straightening things since Jenny was the complete opposite.

'Trouble?' Jenny asked from the sofa where she was engrossed in *True Romances* and a box of Maltesers.

'Looks like. Mother's got it into her head that Lana's a drug addict, living in sin with a bloke called Slim, who,

she reckons, is an evil influence. And whom she might
marry.'

'Not Slim Fletcher of the Wall Nuts? He's as famous as
God. Lucky old Lana,' Jenny said excitedly. 'She wouldn't
be taking drugs, would she?'

'I don't know. I don't know her well enough to tell.'

'You're a peculiar family. What an odd thing to say about
your own sister – "I don't know her well enough". Hell,
how old is she, nineteen, twenty?'

'Twenty.'

'How long does it take you to know someone?' Jenny
snorted.

'It's all right for you. You're part of a family. I'm not. We
never were a close unit. But I've got to check it out, I
suppose. I don't even know where this Slim bloke lives.'

'I do. He's got a bloody great mansion in Oxfordshire.
Everyone knows where he hangs out.'

On Saturday, with no classes to attend, Kitty caught the
Green Line bus for Oxford. Jenny had wanted to come with
her, in the hope of meeting Slim, but Kitty had resisted. If
Lana was in a mess, as her mother said, then Kitty, out of
loyalty, wanted as few people as possible to see it.

She had no difficulty finding Slim's house. Evidently
everyone except her knew where he lived. She took a taxi
from Oxford and after three miles the driver stopped
outside a pair of large wrought-iron gates which were firmly
shut.

'Here you are, miss. Slim's Pad we call it hereabouts.
Might be difficult getting in, you know. Do you want me to
wait, make sure you do?'

'No, thank you, that won't be necessary,' said Kitty,
conscious of the cost, as she alighted. It was raining hard
and a dozen fans stood miserably in the rain in the hopes
of seeing their hero, the reason they had for living – Slim
Fletcher.

Kitty walked up to the gate and rang the bell in the stone pillar. She peered through the wrought iron at a red-brick lodge house with creeper covering most of the brick. No door opened so she rang again.

'No one'll come, you know. They never do,' said one bedraggled fan who looked about thirteen, with damp hair streaking her face and not a vestige of make-up left on. 'They have to be expecting you. Then the man in the lodge pops out.'

'Can I phone? Is the number in the book?'

'Nah. He's ex-directory and even then they keep changing the number 'cause we always find out.' The fans laughed proudly at their own cleverness.

Soon Kitty was as soaked as the others and frightened she would catch cold and that it would go to her throat. She couldn't afford a cold, not now, not when she was due in Paris in three weeks' time. She wished she had not let the taxi go.

A small Mini swooshed up to the gate, the wheels spraying water as they hit the puddles. Everyone ducked to see who was inside.

'Toby,' they called. 'Toby, want to see my knickers?'

Kitty feared for the Mini as the fans swarmed about it, banging on the roof, crawling on the tiny bonnet. The tight-lipped young man beeped the horn. The door of the lodge opened and a disgruntled man appeared, wearing a large, shapeless oilskin.

Kitty suddenly recognized the driver of the Mini as the musician she had met at the wrap-up party for Martin's film. She leaned forward and tapped on the window. 'Excuse me,' she mouthed.

Toby looked at the young woman. There was something about her, something familiar. Gingerly he wound down his window an inch – it was a dangerous thing to do, the kids had been known to push a window wide open.

'Yes? Quick,' he said.

'Lana Lawrence, I need to see her – I'm her sister,' Kitty said anxiously.

'Slip through the gate as I drive through.' He wound the window shut as the first fan noticed he'd opened it. The gate swung open wide enough for the small car and Kitty. Two other men had appeared and with the gatekeeper manhandled back the fans off the car.

'It's Kitty, isn't it?' Toby said, opening the car door for her.

'Thank goodness you came along. I'm afraid I didn't realize it would be so difficult to get in. Perhaps I should have written to Lana first.'

Toby called to the gatekeeper to ring the house and let Lana know her sister was coming.

'Is it always like this?' She nodded back at the fans who were hanging on to the gate like large monkeys.

'It's a good day today, the rain keeps most of them away. On a bad day, and if Slim's been on the box or done a gig, those days we sometimes have to call the police,' Toby said as he drove the car at speed up the tree-lined drive.

'Good God! What a way to live.'

'I know. It's not for me. Slim's got everything a man could want here – pool, gym, cinema, recording studio, even an organ. But he hasn't got his freedom, has he? Look, see the alarms and the cameras.' He pointed to the trees.

'And my sister chooses to live here? She must be mad.'

'She doesn't go out much, few of them do. I prefer my own pad. It's too much like school here. Communal eating, communal everything!' He laughed, and Kitty wondered what exactly he meant. 'And there are the same jealousies and rivalries and crushes on the head boy – Slim. Not my cup of tea at all.' With a flourish he swung the car around the gravelled half-circle in front of the large, imposing house.

The front door swung open. Lana appeared, rushed down the steps and flung her arms round a surprised Kitty, proceeding to smother her with kisses. Smelling brandy, Kitty could only presume she was drunk.

'Kitty! I'm so pleased you're here. Slim's been longing to meet you.'

'Me? What on earth for?'

'He loves opera . . . come in . . . come, let me show you my room.'

It was a lovely, spacious room, with the biggest bed Kitty had ever seen, and wonderful paintings on the walls which she was sure were Pre-Raphaelites. The windows gave a stunning view of the immaculate gardens with parkland beyond.

'He lives like a millionaire,' Kitty said, turning from inspecting the view.

'He *is* a millionaire, silly.' Lana giggled.

'Mum says you're going to get married.'

'Nonsense. I just said that to keep her quiet. You know what a worrier she is about us.'

'About you.' Kitty smiled.

'Marriage is old-fashioned. You've got to be free to love, haven't you?'

'Have you? I don't know much about love, I'm afraid. My career comes first. I don't have time for men.'

'I'm the same,' Lana said seriously. Then you've changed, Kitty thought, and looking at her sister she could see that there had been changes. She looked young again, and pretty. And the long, empire-line dress in a blue and white print, with a white crochet shawl flung over her shoulders, suited her well.

'You look good,' Kitty said.

'Thanks. It's all Slim's idea – all part of my new image.'

The telephone on the bedside table rang. Lana dived for it.

'Yes, Slim, yes . . . of course . . . yes, I'll be proud to.'

She replaced the receiver. 'Guess what? He's joining us for lunch, he rarely does, you know. He wants to meet you. Gracious, I'm so excited. Do I look all right?' Lana asked anxiously.

'Wonderful. But could I do something to my hair? It's drenched.'

When Kitty had dried and combed out her hair, and hung her soaking mackintosh over a radiator, she followed Lana down to the dining-room. It was a huge room, panelled in dark oak, the windows set high in the walls over the panelling so no one could look in or out. There was a long refectory table laid for twenty or so and across it at the top, and on a stepped dais, stood another, forming a T-shape. This top table was set for three.

As they entered the room the noise level dropped dramatically and Kitty was aware of being stared at, of envious glances and whispered comments. Lana, holding her sister's hand, strode triumphantly to the top table.

'You sit here. Slim will sit in the middle.'

No sooner were they settled than a tall, thin man with a mass of curly black hair, which reminded Kitty of a portrait of a Stuart she'd seen in the National Portrait Gallery, joined them. He did not shake hands but nodded in greeting to Kitty. She saw that he had a long, fine-boned and very sensitive face with penetrating dark eyes. To her surprise, Kitty found him very attractive but in an uncomfortable way, as if, for no reason, she felt she should be afraid of him. But then she shook her head at such an idea; it was his dark, almost piratical looks which were causing such silly thoughts.

'Lana tells me you sing. Would you sing for me?'

'I've no music with me,' she blustered – she hated to be asked to sing when she was unprepared.

'I've plenty.' His dark, steady gaze was focused entirely on her and for a moment she had a strange feeling that they were alone in the noisy room.

'I'd love to,' she heard herself say.

As the meal progressed – delicious food, beautifully served – she began to understand what Toby had meant. But she thought it was more like a royal court might have been than the school Toby had described it as – and she was sitting beside the king.

She had feared Slim might want her to sing in front of everyone, but this was far from the case. When the meal was over, he stood up abruptly, took hold of her hand and led her from the room, Lana scurrying along behind them.

His studio was wonderful. He proudly showed her his collection of antique instruments, from sackbuts to a pianola. Kitty's favourite was a beautiful mother-of-pearl-encrusted harpsichord.

'They're difficult to play, aren't they?'

'Not that hard.' He sat down and began to play Scarlatti. Here, Kitty realized, was a very talented musician.

'Your turn.' Slim smiled at her when he had finished and acknowledged their applause. When he smiled his face changed completely and Kitty chided herself for thinking he looked like a pirate. And here in his studio, surrounded by his instruments and talking about music, his personality had changed too. He was relaxed, amenable, charming. Kitty found herself wondering if in the dining-room, with so many people present, he had been shy.

'What do you want to sing? I have the orchestral scores of lots of operas. Don't laugh at me, will you, but sometimes I like to sing to them. Can you do Mimi? Would you mind if I taped you?'

She laughed at the number of questions being fired at her. 'I don't mind if you tape me and yes, I'm studying *La Bohème* at the moment, though my teacher says I'm abominable.' She pulled a face and laughed, she was used to Cellini and her remarks now. 'I heard Gotli – then I had to learn it.'

'You were there? So was I. A wonderful, magical evening, wasn't it?'

'Yes,' she said simply, somewhat nonplussed at this star of rock and pop sounding so passionate about her music.

'What's Gotli?' Lana asked somewhat sulkily from the corner of the giant sofa where she had curled up to look like a little girl.

'A goddess, that's what Gotli is,' Slim informed her as he wound the tapes with swift and expert fingers on the huge turntable, listening, with the sound down, through large earphones. 'Got it,' he said. 'When you're ready.'

Kitty stood in the centre of the room and closed her eyes for a moment, breathing deeply. She opened her eyes and nodded to him, and Puccini's music poured from the hidden speakers.

She sang for two hours, fulfilling request after request.

'No more,' she said laughing gaily. 'I can't. I'm tired.' She patted her throat.

'Oh, please,' Slim begged.

'I'm sorry, I mustn't. Six months ago I damaged my throat, and I'm still restricted. I shouldn't really have sung so long for you but I did no practice this morning.'

'Kitty, I can't tell you what this has meant to me. It was a truly moving experience. My own opera singer, singing just for me.'

'A student opera singer, let me correct you.'

'But what a voice you have! It can only get better.'

'Oh, look, poor Lana, she's gone to sleep. Amazing, with me making all that noise,' she said quickly to cover her confusion at his compliments – praise always embarrassed her.

'You'd like some tea?'

'I'd love some,' she said, thinking what a strange place this was. Her mother had asked her to investigate if Lana was all right in a den of drug-drenched iniquity. Instead she had spent a very cultural afternoon and was now about to have tea.

Somehow the tea turned into drinks and the drinks into supper. Lana had woken up as Slim poured the drinks.

'How long have I been asleep?' She yawned.

'Two or three hours,' Slim said. 'You missed a wonderful performance.'

'I heard most of it. I was listening with my eyes closed.'

Slim winked at Kitty.

'What do you think of my sister's voice then, Slim darling?'

'There aren't any words to describe how I feel,' he said, staring at Kitty so hard that she found she had to look away.

During dinner, Lana found it increasingly difficult to disguise her boredom. She hid several yawns behind her napkin, there was little she could do about her eyes glazing over, and there was one dreadful moment when she actually dropped off to sleep, although she was fairly sure the others hadn't noticed. They wouldn't, she thought bitterly, as she watched them deeply engrossed in their endless music talk.

Kitty looked at her watch. 'Good heavens, look at the time. My flatmate will be worried sick. Could you call me a taxi, Slim, to get to the bus station?'

'You've missed the last train, let alone a bus,' Lana said peevishly. Now Kitty would stay the night and this interminable conversation would continue.

'I'll run you home,' Slim offered, much to Lana's surprise – he so rarely went anywhere.

'I hate to put you out.'

'It's no problem.'

'I'll come, company for you on the way back,' Lana volunteered.

'No, there won't be room. I'll take the Porsche.'

'But is that safe . . . your bodyguard?' Lana was saying, flapping her hands ineffectually.

'I often go out alone at night in my Porsche,' Slim said a shade sharply.

'Do you?' Lana asked, disappointed that she hadn't known this about him – she wanted to know all there was to know.

On the drive back to London they talked yet more and Slim, at Kitty's insistence but very reluctantly, put one of his group's tapes into the music system. He had been amused when she had confessed she did not know his music. She listened intently and, to both their surprise, announced that she liked the rhythm, the baseness, as she put it, of the music. But best of all, she said, she liked Slim's voice and the lyrics.

When they arrived at her flat she explained she could not invite him in for fear of waking her flatmate who was a light sleeper – not strictly true, but after the opulence of his place she was shy of allowing him to see their rather shabby flat. He kissed her chastely on the cheek, pressed a pile of his group's cassettes into her hand, and even as she thanked him, gunned the powerful car and roared away as if he in turn was embarrassed by her praise.

21

Kitty had never been courted in her life. She was not prepared for what was to happen.

During that afternoon with Slim she had mentioned in passing that the following day she was to sing in St Swithin's church. She often did, she told him, as a favour to the vicar, and to thank him for getting her started on her career.

She told herself she had not expected to see him there. But then, was she pretending to herself? Had she told him on purpose in the hope he would show up? In his black velvet clothes and flared trousers, he looked incongruous amongst the congregation in its Sunday best. He was waiting for her when the service was over and took hold of her hand as soon as she appeared, which seemed a natural thing for him to do and something she liked.

As they left the church two photographers jumped out from behind a couple of gravestones and snapped away at them, flash bulbs popping. Shielding Kitty's face with a large fedora he'd been wearing, Slim raced with her through the churchyard to his car – a chauffeur-driven white Rolls Royce today – with the journalists in hot pursuit. Once in the car, behind the tinted windows through which no one could see, they collapsed into the seats laughing.

'I wouldn't swap places with you, it must be ghastly being chased like that.'

'When that stops happening it'll be time for me to worry, for then I'm finished. You have to resign yourself to it and be grateful. Don't forget there was a time when I longed to be chased by photographers.'

'And the fans at the gate, don't you mind them? I mean, watching for your every move.'

'Yes, they're a problem. There's a small group who camp there, you know – silly little bitches. They're barely out of nappies. We look after them as best we can. My house-keeper takes soup and sandwiches out, that sort of thing. And if any of them get ill I get my doctor to see them – there's not much else I can do, they won't go away. And it wouldn't look good if I sued them for trespass, would it?'

'You couldn't invite them in, could you? The house seems full already.'

'What? My entourage?' He laughed. 'Sometimes I wish they'd all go and leave me alone.'

'Why don't you ask them to? It's your house.'

'I don't like being lonely. I like to know they're there if I want to talk to someone,' he said thoughtfully. 'I spent a lot of time alone when I was a kid – I hated it.'

'They seem so obsequious, though, doesn't that give you the creeps?'

'Not really. I quite like it. Makes me feel important. I suppose I like the power I have over them.'

'Slim! That's a dreadful thing to say.'

'Is it? Don't we all want that? Aren't relationships like that – one person wanting power over the other?'

She thought of Martin and shuddered.

'I don't go in for relationships, so I go for this alternative, I suppose.' He shrugged his shoulders at her surprise at his honesty.

'No relationships? What about Lana?'

He looked at her and smiled quizzically. 'What's Lana been saying? There's nothing between us. I met a little girl with a lot of talent, singing the wrong stuff with the wrong band, with a lousy manager who didn't even know how good she really is. She was heading for drugs and booze with the speed of an express train. I decided to rescue her.'

'Quite the little Sir Galahad, aren't you?' Kitty said icily. She did not like to hear criticism of her sister from others. Slim looked at her, puzzled, as they drove up outside her flat.

A flustered Jenny was on the pavement arguing with two men with a black transit van with the Wall Nuts' logo on the side.

'Thank goodness, you're here – I said I thought there must be a mistake,' Jenny said, rushing up to Kitty as she got out of the car.

'What's up?'

'They've got a bloody harpsichord in there. They say it's

yours. I told them you were going to Paris and it couldn't possibly be yours.'

Kitty turned and looked at Slim.

'A present. You liked it,' he said bashfully.

'Don't be silly, Slim. I couldn't accept it. It's priceless. You love it. It's too much to give someone you hardly know.'

'I can find another,' he said, beginning to look shamefaced.

'Slim, it's a wonderful gesture but one I could never accept. I've nowhere to keep it for a start.'

'I'll look after it for when you return.'

'I can't play it.'

'I'll teach you,' he said eagerly.

'No, Slim. I refuse to accept it. It's too big a present. It would put me in a difficult position. You must take it back. Thank you for the lift.' And with Jenny beside her she walked swiftly up the steps to their front door, shut it quickly, and stood leaning against it listening for the sound of the car and van engines to tell her he had gone.

'My, I am impressed.' Jenny giggled.

'I'm not. I've never heard of anything so stupid – nor so vulgar.'

'He is dishy though, isn't he?' Jenny said dreamily.

Slim did not accept defeat. The following three nights when Kitty returned from college it was to find another present as well as a bouquet of flowers. But Slim had also decided to take her literally, and every present was small: a minute malachite elephant, a tiny crystal ladybird, a miniature silver harpsichord. She relented with this one and called him on the telephone number which was always attached to the gift.

'Small enough not to put you in an impossible position?' His voice on the telephone was full of laughter.

'They're all lovely and very precious to me.'

'Honestly? And you'll take them to Paris?'

'I will.'

'And can I see you?'

'When?'

'Now. This evening. I've got tickets for the opera,' he said, laughing at his own slyness.

The days that followed were among the most carefree and happy Kitty had known, yet also some of the most confusing. Every moment she was not at lessons Slim was with her. He sat in on her practice, he took her out to eat – breakfast, lunch, dinner. And they talked – how they talked!

She found it easy to tell him all about herself, her hopes and fears, the hurts from the past. He seemed to want to know every tiny detail about her. She could understand this for she wanted to hear everything about him.

He told her of his lonely childhood left in the care of an endless string of nannies as his ambitious banker father and his wife pursued their social ambitions. If a nanny became too fond of him, she was sacked. His talk of sadistic prep-school masters made Kitty want to weep for him, as did his stories of his time at public school where his lack of interest in sport and his love of music distanced him from his peers.

He was movingly articulate as he described how the realization that he wanted to create music and not just play someone else's had made him give up his place at college. His choice of a career had alienated him from his parents, and it hurt. He wanted them to be proud of him, he wanted them to see his house, ride in his cars, *approve* of him.

She laughed at his tales of life on the road playing clubs in dark and dirty basements which, judging by the size of the audiences, were impossible for most people to find. Of

the false hopes when contracts promised never materialized, of fees so low that he was at one time virtually
starving. Of how long it had taken for the individual
members of the band to find each other and to evolve the
sound that had eventually made them famous and rich.

They finally made love. Kitty had not meant to do so,
telling herself it was the last thing she wanted or needed.
But then she could not help herself, and falling into his
arms and into her bed was finally the most natural thing to
do.

Slim loved her. It was not her imagination, he constantly
told her so in words as well as actions. She had dreamed of
being loved, had longed for Martin to love her, to tell her
so. But now it was happening she found herself backing
away from it, discovering she was almost afraid of Slim, of
his love and the commitment it would mean. And yet she
was almost sure she was falling in love with him. *Almost
sure*, for everything was new. She had not felt like this with
Martin – there wasn't the same stomach-churning excitement he had induced in her. She did not feel she would die
if Slim left her, as she had with Martin. But with Slim she
felt a calmness, despite the excitement he generated, a
sense of security, which was odd, given who he was and
his lifestyle. And she felt a strange glow inside her that told
her all was well with her world.

All this could not have happened at a worse time.
Having previously poured all her energy and concentration
into her work, she now found it difficult to concentrate.
These last few lessons with Max and Cellini before her
departure to Paris were important as they filled her head
with vital musical do's and don'ts for her time there.

'Aren't you enjoying singing?' Cellini asked her one
morning.

'Not particularly,' Kitty replied apologetically.

'So it sounds,' Cellini said sharply. 'There's a man, I
presume.'

'Well, yes . . .' Kitty found herself blushing.

'Then drop him.'

'I beg your pardon?'

'Tell him to go. You have no choice. It is too soon. You have only energy enough for your own voice – nothing else.'

'But I think I love him.'

'Bah!' Cellini threw her hands up in mock despair. 'Love? What is love? It doesn't last, my dear, but your voice will, if you care for it.'

'You mean if I'm to sing then I càn't expect a normal life?'

'That's exactly what I'm saying. And if you must marry, then you can only contemplate it with someone involved in opera. Who else would understand the dedication you must expend? Who else would have the patience to deal with your schedule? One month a year at home, if you're lucky. The rest alone in strange cities and strange hotels, one week here, the next there, the telephone your only link with home. It is not exactly conducive to matrimonial bliss, now is it?'

'But a schedule like that is only for the stars.'

'And?' Cellini raised an eyebrow. 'I have taught you, it is sufficient, a diva you shall be! Now we waste time, I'd like to hear that final phrase again, it sounded harsh . . .'

After this lesson with Cellini, Kitty walked back to the school, turning over in her mind what she had said. Surely Cellini was being too sweeping in her statements? Kitty began to list in her mind all the married opera stars she could think of, and sure enough, with the exception of two, their partners were all in some way involved professionally in opera or the music world. The remaining two had rather sad-looking husbands who accompanied them everywhere, always photographed, it seemed, a few paces behind, who called themselves managers but whose tasks amounted to organizing the luggage and relaying their wives' many complaints to the theatre or hotel management.

She knew that she was afraid of Slim's protestations of love. She had assumed it was because she was scared of being hurt again, as Martin had hurt her. But was that it? Had she subconsciously known that her voice would get in the way, that it would end in her having to choose?

That night Slim had taken her to the theatre and to supper afterwards, and then, mysteriously, he drove her to a flat in a mansion block in Kensington.

'You can live here,' he said, having shown her round the spacious flat with its large, airy rooms.

'But I already have a flat.' She smiled at him.

'Not a patch on this one, though, is it?'

'No, but then I could never afford one like this.'

'I'm not asking for any rent. I'm just saying that you and Jenny can move in here.'

'It's very kind of you, Slim, but I couldn't possibly accept, it wouldn't be right.'

'I love you even more when you go all prim and proper on me.' He grinned. 'You'd be doing me a favour, Kitty. I never use it. It was my accountant who suggested I buy the damn thing. You and Jenny would be looking after it for me.'

'I don't know.' She sounded more doubtful now. Put like that, it made things different, and if she accepted she would still have a base in London. Nor would she have to worry how Jenny was going to cope without her.

'It would just be a stop-gap until we got married,' he said nonchalantly.

Kitty stood in the middle of the large and ornately furnished drawing-room and felt as if time had stood still. She was sure she had not imagined that the clock on the mantelpiece had been ticking and had now stopped.

'Don't look so scared, you're supposed to look pleased! Have I jumped the gun?'

'I've got to go to Paris,' she heard herself say.

'I know, but I can pop over at weekends and you can fly

back here – I'd pay,' he added, hurriedly forestalling her objections. 'I'd never stand in the way of your career, Kitty, you must know that. I'm so proud of you and what a success you're going to be.'

'But it wouldn't be right, Slim. I wouldn't be totally committed, and if I marry I have to be. I don't want a part-time marriage, I'd want kids, I'd want to stay at home. It's too soon, you see.' She looked at him anxiously, knowing she loved him, longing to say yes, wishing she could forget her voice, her dreams, but knowing also that if she did she would spend the rest of her life wondering what might have been.

'And you can have all that when you want it, when you feel the time is right for you.' Slim took her hand and led her over to the long white sofa. He put his hand up to her face and leaned forward to kiss her. She turned her head away.

'Don't, Slim, please,' she said, fully aware that if she allowed him to kiss her, the decision she knew she had to make would be impossible.

'I don't understand. We've been so happy these past few days. You are everything I've ever wanted, you're the woman I've dreamed about . . .'

'It can't be. It's not as if we move in the same worlds.'

'Oh, come on! In a way we do. We're both musicians.'

'I've got nothing but respect for your music, Slim, but you can hardly say it's the same.'

'It might be.' He looked at her long and hard. 'Look, Kitty, I've only told one other person this, so it's strict confidence time. I'm packing in the Wall Nuts.'

'Oh, no! Really? Why?'

'I've had enough. I've enjoyed it but I'm tired – tired of the tours, the music, the whole scene. All the birds and booze, it turns me off, these days. I've done it all now, I want to split and move on to something different. I want to be me, not part of something.'

'But what about the others? What will they do without you?'

'Find someone else to take my place or break up, I suppose. Most of them are fed up, if you get them drunk enough to admit what they really think. We've all got enough money to last us out and then plenty over. I'm twenty-eight, and that's old in this racket. I don't want to find myself doing the same thing at forty, even if that were possible, which I doubt. Can you imagine a forty-year-old rocker?'

'Not exactly.' She laughed.

'So what do old rock stars do?'

'I haven't a clue.'

'Promise not to tell anyone?'

'I promise.'

'I'm writing a rock opera. I'm writing all the music and Toby and I are doing the lyrics – no one else knows about it.'

'Slim, that's wonderful.'

'So you see, we would be in the same field. We could work together perhaps, I could write you in. Yes, that's what I'll do.' He was sitting upright now, excitement bubbling out of him. 'I can hear it now.' He tapped his head.

'Slim, don't. Look, I'm twenty-two, I can't even contemplate singing professionally until I'm twenty-five or six. Even then my voice won't have matured properly, I'll probably be nearer thirty before it does.'

'You sing wonderfully. What do you mean?'

'I couldn't sing in your opera, I'd probably be pushing myself too far too soon.'

'Bollocks.'

'It isn't. Speak to Cellini if you don't believe me.'

'Callas was singing on the stage when she was a teenager.'

'Yes, and look what happened – by her early thirties the

critics were out with their knives and destroying her confidence.'

'I've read it was because she lost weight – her voice changed. You're not fat, you won't have that problem.'

'It's not a risk I want to take. I intend to guard the voice and sing until I'm sixty,' she said defiantly, feeling almost angry that he could regard her future so lightly.

'So what you're saying is your voice and career are more important than me and your own happiness?'

'Yes.'

'You'll regret it.'

'Maybe, maybe not.'

'I won't give up. I'll keep on asking you.'

'And for years my answer will be the same. I have to do this, Slim, there's a great ache within me to succeed – I can't let anything stand in The Voice's way.'

'And I'm *anything*?'

'You know what I mean. You must understand, wasn't it like this for you?'

'No. I wanted to earn some bread – it became more serious later.'

'I'm not interested in the money, it's the fame I want, and to feel the joy my voice will give.'

'There's nothing wrong with money and earning it.'

'Some things are more important,' Kitty said firmly.

Slim watched her expression closely as she spoke. It changed, he noticed. In repose her face had a placid calmness to it, but now it was animated with emotion as she spoke, she looked alive, afire with ambition and love – but not, he sadly realized, for him, or at any rate not enough.

Still, he did not give up and they argued back and forth for another hour. Kitty had expected, given the way she felt about him, that she would waver, and had dreaded a confrontation such as this coming so early in her career. Instead the opposite happened; the more he countered her arguments the more entrenched she became in the view that she had no choice.

By the time she asked him to take her home The Voice had won. And it was only after he had left her that she realized that she had once again been talking about her voice as The Voice, as if it were apart from her, a being in its own right and she its custodian.

There was still another week before she had to be in Paris. She did not want a repeat of the previous evening's scene.

'Max, is there any chance you can arrange for me to go a week early?'

'Why?'

'Reasons.' She smiled at him, blushing slightly.

'I don't see why not. We can call your digs, see if they can take you; apart from that I know a good cheap hotel.'

'Bless you. Sorry to be a nuisance.'

'I'll miss you, Kitty,' Max said, suddenly serious, and his hand moved as if to touch her but then dropped down to his side.

'Me too, Max. Sometimes I feel sick with terror – a new school, new students, teachers, and my French is dreadful.'

'You'll be fine. And the French will come. Any problems, let us know. And eat properly, won't you?'

'Like a pig!' She laughed, her lovely, melodious singer's laugh.

'I could . . .' Max looked out of the window at nothing. 'I could come with you, if you like, see you settled in.'

'Oh, Max, you are a sweetie. How kind, but you mustn't trouble yourself, I'll manage.'

'It would be no trouble,' he said, turning his head away from her so that she did not hear what he said properly.

'Well, that's all, I suppose,' she said, standing up and wishing she had had the nerve to take him up on his offer. But she couldn't, of course, it had only been made out of

politeness. She wasn't sure what to do or say, she hated
goodbyes.

'Well, bye,' she said, feeling awkward.

'Bye, Kitty,' he replied, wishing he had the nerve to take
her in his arms and say goodbye as he really wished.

That afternoon Kitty had her last lesson with Cellini.

'This love affair you told me of.' Cellini looked at her
accusingly. 'It's not going well.'

'I . . . yes . . . but . . . how . . .' Kitty was flustered.

'It's in the voice, that reflects everything, hides no secrets
if you know how to listen – as I do. Your vocal cords are no
different from anyone else's, but the sound you can make
is a million times different. So why? Where does it come
from, this sound we make and others cannot? It comes
from within us, deep down in our minds. In our souls!'
Cellini waved her arms dramatically. 'So it reflects the state
of our mind, our soul. You are confused and sad, the voice
tells me.'

'I'm running away from him.'

'Aha! Is he poor?'

'No, very rich actually.'

'Then he doesn't understand opera?'

'He loves it.'

'A musician?'

'In a manner of speaking, yes.'

'Then he sounds ideal for you.'

'No. I think I might begin to love him too much. I think
he could become my life. It's too soon for that. Far too
soon,' she said sadly.

Cellini enveloped her in her arms and held her tightly.
'Ah, my little one, you have learned. It is hard but you are
wise.'

'I don't feel very wise.'

'But I tell you, you are. I resented Ben's insistence you

go to Paris – "Why," I asked. "I teach her like no other teacher. Kitty is my protégée." Now,' Cellini studied Kitty carefully, 'now I think it is better you go for a while. Distance yourself from this dangerous love. Find yourself another love but one you know you will always be able to turn your back on. And make doubly sure—'

'He's rich!' Kitty finished the sentence for her, laughing for the first time that day.

Kitty packed in a frenzy. By early evening she was at Victoria. Jenny was with her to see her on to the boat train.

'Promise, if Slim calls, you don't know where I am?'

'Promise.'

'He can be very persuasive.'

'Not with me he can't. I'm not giving your address to a living soul. Now get on this flaming train.' Jenny blew noisily into her hankie.

'I'll miss you so much, Jenny.'

'Shut up,' was the muffled reply.

'When I'm rich and famous you must come and work for me.'

'Can I have it in writing?' Jenny gave a lopsided grin.

'You and I don't need anything in writing, do we? God, Jenny, I'm so scared.'

'Don't be silly, go and sock it to 'em,' Jenny replied, tears streaming down her face.

Kitty climbed on to the train, her eyes blinded with her own tears. But as the train pulled through the suburbs she put her hankie away. She felt elated. She *knew* she had made the right decision, perhaps one of the most important of her career.

22

Lana was confused and troubled. For the last few weeks she had been sure that there was someone else in Slim's life. He was out most evenings, almost unheard of for him. The community had debated this endlessly and there was no one there who could remember a time when Slim had spent so much time away from his house and studio. No one, not even Toby, knew where he went and who he met. The group grew restless and then, as rumour followed rumour – Slim was in love, he was getting married, he was ill – they began to seethe with worry and fear. They felt threatened. Not knowing what was happening they feared the worst, that everything was about to change, that the comfortable, tidy niches that they had contrived for themselves were about to be taken away from them. The real world where money had to be earned and bread bought was feeling uncomfortably close, and the house was a far from happy place to be.

The only consolation Lana could find was that Slim always returned home early by their standards. He was invariably back by one, so whoever it was, he was not sleeping with her, otherwise why should he not stay the night? But her comfort was short lived when she tried this theory on the others and someone pointed out that perhaps he could not stay the night because the woman was married.

Since she had been living at Slim's, Lana had learned to control her drinking. Now, with Slim so little in evidence, and feeling as miserable as she did, she started again with the odd drink, and within a week the polite drinking had become a bottle of brandy a day, most of which she drank alone in her room. Since she could not sleep she was soon

searching out a supply of Mandrax to help her, and when
she awoke in the afternoon feeling too groggy to face what
was left of the day, she swallowed amphetamines washed
down by that day's fresh bottle of brandy.

Then Slim stopped going out, but Lana found herself
wishing he still did, for his moods were terrible. He barely
spoke to anyone and he kept away from them, shut up in
his private quarters. But his depression seemed to seep
through the walls of the house and to affect the others.
After one telephone call he went mad, hurling ornaments
and instruments through the windows, the sounds of
smashing echoing through the large house and making the
others almost cower with frightened incomprehension.
Then Slim, who only drank in moderation, began to drink
in terrifying earnest. He allowed no one into his quarters,
not even Toby. When the other Wall Nuts telephoned, they
found their calls refused. Slim's manager was reduced to
shouting impotently through a closed door that remained
firmly closed.

This state of affairs lasted a good month until one
evening, to everyone's surprise and envy, Lana was summoned to see Slim. Even in her drink- and drug-fuddled
state, she was shocked at what she found. His apartment
was wrecked, not an ornament had survived. The cushions
on the sofas and chairs had been ripped open dementedly.
Jam was smeared all over the keys of the Bechstein.
Cigarettes had burned holes in the carpets, the room stank
of stale smoke and brandy. The only things Slim had not
touched were the paintings on the walls, as if, despite his
fury, or whatever had engineered this frenzy, he could not
bring himself to destroy such beauty.

Just as the room had been wrecked, so Slim looked as if
he was busily destroying himself. He looked ashen with
fatigue; large dark circles ringed his once fine eyes which
now looked empty of emotion. His clothes were dirty and,

like the room, he smelt. As he poured himself yet another drink his hand shook and the bottle clattered against the fine crystal glass.

'I suddenly remembered,' he said to her. 'Of course, bloody fool that I am, I suddenly remembered, Lana would know.'

'Of course Lana knows,' she said to him in the soothing tones of a nanny to her charge. And since he did not look as if he was about to offer her a drink she crossed the room to the bottle and helped herself. She sat on the tapestried stool at his feet and smiled up at him, wishing that she hadn't been hitting the booze quite so hard herself and that she looked better. But then seeing the difficulty he had in focusing, she relaxed, it didn't matter what she looked like. She smiled again but this time to herself. It was she he had called to the inner sanctum, her patience had paid off, he needed her. 'So, Slim darling. What do I know?'

'Her address, she'd have told you,' he slurred.

'Whose address?'

'Your sister's, of course. She's pissed off to Paris and has left no address.'

'Kitty? What on earth do you want her address for?'

''Cause I bloody love her and want her to marry me, only she won't.' He spoke in a voice that wavered from a whining note to one of anger.

'Kitty!' Lana said, dumbfounded. 'Our Kitty?'

'Who else? Oh, Lana, for Christ's sake help me find her, I'm going mad here.'

'You and Kitty? I don't believe it. When? How? Why didn't you tell me?'

'I didn't want anyone to know. I wanted it to be a secret – our secret. She's something else, Lana. God, I love her.'

'Shut up!' Lana was on her feet now, glaring down at him. 'How could you? You've nothing in common. She's stuck up. She's cold. She's frigid.'

'Don't talk about her like that.'

'She's a sly cow. She comes here pretending it's to see me and then ends up pinching you. She must have planned it all along. She's a shit, an out and out shit!'

'I told you, shut up.' He was standing now, towering over her.

'She's so mealy-mouthed, butter wouldn't melt . . . sneaky bitch!'

Slim hit her then. She reeled from the blow. Tears spurted into her eyes.

'Slim, I'm sorry . . . it was such a shock.'

'Where is she? Her address, that's all I need.'

'I don't know. I hardly ever see her. My mother might know.'

'Then call her. Get it,' he ordered.

Lana burst into tears. 'Oh, for Christ's sake don't snivel. Get me the number,' he shouted.

'You don't understand, do you? I love you, Slim. I have from the first day we met. It's me you should be with, not her,' she sobbed out the words.

'You? You've got to be joking. You're just like the rest of them out there.' He nodded towards the door.

'I'm not. I'm here because I love you, not for what I can get out of you. Not like them.'

'In my book you're all the same, you're like parasites. You all think I don't know, but I do – you, none of you are here because of me the person, you've latched on to me for what I can do for you, what you can all con out of me.'

'Then why have us here?' she said with a little more spirit.

'Because you sometimes amuse me, the way you all scatter about like little ants.'

'That's cruel, Slim. Please don't talk like this. Please try and forget her. I'm here, I love you –'

'You instead of Kitty? Talk some sense. She's everything you're not. She's not a leech like you. She doesn't sleep around like you. You'll screw anyone to further your career, even old Tristan. You're a scrubber, Lana – nothing more, nothing less.'

'That's not true . . . I'm not . . . it was him . . . I hate you, you bastard.'

Slim laughed at that, his eyes suddenly full of expression again. It was the laugh that angered and hurt her more than anything else. She picked up the bottle of brandy and hurled it with all her might at the painting over the fireplace – his favourite. She turned to run to the door. As she opened it she swung round to face him. 'And if I knew where she was you're the last bloody creep I'd tell,' she screamed as she slammed the door shut.

She ran pell-mell down the long flight of stairs, opened the heavy oak door with difficulty and hurtled out into the freezing November night. In the forecourt stood three cars. All, she knew, would be open, all would have their keys in the ignition.

She chose the middle one, the Porsche in which he'd given Kitty a lift the night she had introduced them. She turned the key, the powerful engine roared into life. A cassette was sticking out of the player, she shoved it roughly in. The sound of the Wall Nuts' latest hit blared out into the night. She put the car into the 'Drive' position – she could not drive but had seen others do this. She pressed her foot on the accelerator and the car lurched forward through a bed of rose bushes, across the lawn. She laughed as she felt the branches of a tree scrape the immaculate paintwork, and pushed the pedal harder. She wrenched the wheel over to steer the car on to the drive-way. This was easy. She sang in time to the music. 'I'll show him,' she shouted to the night.

The car sped down the road. Ahead lay the wrought-iron gates with their large stone pillars. With difficulty she focused on the pillar on the left, pushed the pedal down into the floor of the car and drove straight for it.

The impact of crashing metal rent the silence of the night

as the beautiful car seemed to screech with agony. And then there was silence, the only voice that of Slim singing on the cassette:

> . . . and the diamonds of night cascade, down the lane of memory . . .
> Lane of memory . . . lane of memory . . .

INTERMISSION

The hospital corridor was empty as Kitty ran along it. She looked about her bewildered, confused by the plethora of signs. She was lost again.

'Please let me get there in time,' she muttered, as she tried another dimly lit corridor which stretched out as if into infinity.

'Can I help?' A woman had appeared from a side door, clutching her long navy cape to her against the night chill.

'Evelyn Blotter Ward, I think. But the line was bad . . . I was in Paris . . . that was early today . . . I couldn't get a flight . . . I don't know . . .'

'There, there. Calm down, my dear, or we'll be admitting you too,' the night sister said kindly. 'It's the Evelyn Blunt Ward and it's in the opposite direction. Come this way, just down here.'

'How is she, sister? Am I too late? My mother said . . .'

'Who have you come to see, my dear? That ward is the casualty ward, many come.'

'Lana, my sister. Lana Lawrence—'

'Ah, yes. You must prepare yourself for a shock. She's not too well and the bruising . . .'

Quietly the sister opened a swing-door. Instead of going into the main ward she opened another door and stepped back to allow Kitty to enter a side-room.

Compared with the gloom outside this room was brightly lit. A nurse was checking a bottle of saline which dangled on a stand. Kitty could hear the raucous, sucking noise of a machine that was clearing mucus from a tube which she could see inserted in Lana's neck. She dared to look at her sister, only it wasn't her any more. Her pretty face was swollen to twice its size and was a livid red and blue from bruising. A large scar ran across her cheek. Kitty's hand sped to her mouth.

'So you've come.'

Kitty swung round. She had been unaware of the figure sitting on the chair to one side while the nurses did their work.

'Mum.'

'I wish you hadn't. I wish you'd stayed where you were.'

'But Mum, you said . . .'

'I said I wanted you here. I did then. I don't now.'

The nurses looked at each other with embarrassment.

'I had to come.'

'Why? To gloat?'

'How can you say that?'

'What do you think I feel, seeing you standing there fit and well while my poor darling fights for her life? Look at that thing in her throat. Just look at it – her voice destroyed, while you, you . . .' Amy balled her fists.

Kitty said nothing but stepped back, stunned by her mother's vehemence.

'Why couldn't it be you? Why couldn't you die and let her live?' Amy hissed.

The nurses gasped almost imperceptibly.

Kitty looked at her mother, a long and pitying look. Then she turned and walked from the room, away from her mother, vowing never to return.

ACT THREE

1973–1980

1

The small room at the top of the simple *albergo* was hotter than an oven. Kitty lay on the narrow bed studying the cracks in the ceiling as she had done many times in the past days; she was convinced there were more than yesterday. The hotel, on a side road leading from the main square, was narrow, high and old. The window did not close because the frame was crooked, Kitty had to heave the door shut with her shoulder, and if she dropped anything on the floor it invariably rolled into the left-hand corner. She was sure that the whole place only stood up by being wedged tight between the equally tall buildings on either side. But what if they were in the same condition? What if there was an earth tremor? Then the whole lot could collapse in a pile of rubble. She was not sure if being on the sixth floor would save her or doom her. Hence her great interest in the cracks on the ceiling and their progress.

She sat up on the bed and lifted the one pillow, fluffed it up and turned it over, hopefully on to a cooler side. She lay back but could feel no difference.

God, it's hot, she thought. Surely it can't get any hotter? She was naked, and as she lay there, she could feel a pool of sweat forming between her breasts. She swung her legs over the side of the bed and sitting on the edge leaned across to the towel rail. The room was so small that there was little she could not reach from this one position. She wiped herself dry and from the bedside table took a tin of talcum powder and dusted herself. Perhaps she'd be better wearing something. Still sitting, she pulled open a drawer in the small chest of drawers and took out a clean cotton nightshirt which she put on.

Yes, she thought, that feels better, cooler.

Her long dark hair had slipped from the band holding it in place. She retied it, pulling it tight, rummaging in the drawer for clips to hold it high and away from her neck. In the drawer was a bottle of Calèche *eau de toilette*, she opened it and smelt it, breathing hungrily at the lingering sweet-flowered scent which was all that was left, for the bottle was empty – she had used the remains of it last week.

She looked intently at the bottle and stroked it. It was one of the many presents Henri had given her and the only one she had kept when she had made her dramatic break with him. Fool, she said to herself, she should have kept the jewellery, she could have sold it and then been in a half-way decent room, in a building that didn't threaten to collapse.

Henri. She smiled to herself and, positioning the pillow against the brass head-rest, leaned back on it and allowed herself to dream. Maybe she should have stayed with Henri, not been so proudly ambitious – a right fool she looked now . . .

Everything in Paris had started so well. Kitty had worked hard at the famous Conservatoire in Passy, one of the most prestigious in the world and cradle of many a great singer's career. Her tutors praised her. She realized now how much she needed their praise, for her confidence in herself was a fragile thing.

She had worked harder than any of the other students, often arriving early to do some study, some singing practice, before lessons proper started, and invariably staying late into the evening. Study, listening, practice, that had been her life and that was how she had wanted it to be.

She had neither the time nor the money for play, she told herself firmly, so she always refused invitations from her fellow students to go to the cinema, or to dance, or to while away the odd hour over a carafe of wine.

They soon stopped asking her, finding her dedication irksome and critical of them. She should have been honest with them, explained it was not just her work that kept her from them. But she felt shy, primarily because her French was not yet ready for easy conversation, but more importantly because she was working like a demon to drive out other demons – demons that, given half a chance, would slip in and take her down into the depths of misery like a high-speed elevator. So she filled her mind and soul with music. Slim . . . she missed him, longed for him and feared she might have made a mistake in spurning him. At night, though, she had no control and too often she dreamed of him.

If her fellow students had known all this, they would have understood her better. If that had been the case perhaps there would not have been so much jealousy when Kitty was singled out in lessons and later chosen to sing Rosina in the student production of Rossini's *The Barber of Seville*. Nor might there have been so much jubilation when she was a disaster in the role. 'Never,' said the review, 'has there been such a serious and dramatic Rosina, nor a clumsier one. Where was the comedy, the lightness of touch? Miss Lawrence, whose voice undoubtedly has potential, might be best advised sticking to the more dramatic roles – and certainly more static ones.'

She cried for hours over that review and dared not read the others for fear they were worse. She slumped into despondency and her lack of confidence, never buried deep, rose to the surface with a vengeance.

If only she had had the courage to say that her costume was impossibly ill-fitting and cumbersome to move in, that her stage shoes did not fit and hurt her. Or had Cellini been right all along, that she moved like a camel, and despite all the deportment and acting classes, she still did?

Had she not been so obsessed with her own performance she might have read the rest of the review with greater care and seen that she was not alone, that the orchestra, the student director, choreographer and conductor had all been equally lambasted, to the extent that there was a high-level conference of the tutors and Principal on what had gone wrong this year to make what was normally a prodigious showcase of talent into such a disaster.

It was at this time that Kitty met Henri. He lived in the apartment block next door and she had noticed him occasionally as he emerged from its entrance when she left her apartment in the morning. Their actual meeting was on the Métro when, her first bad review ringing in her head, she had, to her shame, begun to cry. Of the passengers who had looked at her with Gallic sympathy it had been Henri, using their being neighbours as an excuse, who had come to her rescue and insisted she join him for a drink.

He had nothing to do with music, he didn't even like opera, that was his attraction at that low point in her life. For she was so damaged by the review that she felt she wanted nothing more to do with singing. As a law student in his third year, Henri was a relief to her – a much-needed relief, for unwittingly she had become obsessed with music.

'What is it they say? Those who can, do, and those who can't, criticize,' he said sympathetically. His English was fluent.

'Yes, but had the review been good I would have thought the critic the most marvellous and intelligent man,' Kitty said logically, between sips of coffee.

'Maybe he never gives good reviews. Maybe his life is a disappointment to him and so he likes destroying people. Maybe he hates his wife and has no mistress because he's so old and ugly, and demented with sexual frustration.'

Kitty laughed.

'Ah, good! Then you can laugh at something.' He smiled at her.

'I'm sorry. I must be boring you,' she replied.

'I think that's unlikely.'

'Your English is wonderful, I wish my French was as good. Where did you learn?'

'In England. I was at school there for a few years,' he explained. 'My father felt it would be advantageous for me and I think he was probably right. Though now I don't get enough practice.'

She found she was disappointed as he flicked his fingers for the bill. She watched him as he settled it. He was not handsome in the accepted sense but had one of those slightly simian faces, peculiar to the French, which she found she liked more than conventional good looks. He wore his dark hair long, and used his elegant, tapered hands expressively. His black jeans, polo-necked sweater and jacket suited his slim body well, and he reminded her of Slim. He was slightly shorter than Kitty but she barely noticed this for she was used to being taller than most Parisians.

At the entrance to the *tabac* he paused. 'I don't feel like books tonight. Fancy a bite to eat? There's an excellent bistro round the corner from us – you probably know it?'

She didn't, and she accepted his invitation without hesitation. Kitty lived in a flat with a French family but could not afford full board. The idea, Ben Cooper's, had been that in this way she could learn French more easily. It hadn't worked out like that, however, for Madame Gilbert and her husband were unfriendly and saw no reason why, for the little Kitty paid for her small room, they should be required to throw in French lessons as well. To save money Kitty tended to eat bread, cheese, pâté and fruit. She did not mind, in Paris such a diet was hardly a penance. But the thought of a hot meal with good company was something she jumped at.

She went to bed with Henri that same night. In the morning she was embarrassed to face him. But even as she assured him it was not something she normally did, and it must have been the second bottle of wine which had made her lose her senses, she had no regrets. It had been a wonderful night and in Henri she had found a better, more expressive and certainly more sensitive lover than Martin, even if she did not feel as complete as she had with Slim. A week later she moved into Henri's apartment.

Henri's parents were rich and their son was spoilt. This two-bedroom apartment, finely and expensively furnished, carpeted, and curtained, had been his twenty-first birthday present. Judging by the quality of the food he bought, the number of meals they had out, the cascade of presents he showered on Kitty, his allowance must have been enormous. They rowed on her first day with him when he refused to allow her to contribute towards her keep.

'What do you take me for?' he said indignantly.

'More to the point, what do you take me for? I'm not a kept woman. I'm independent.'

'If you live with me then I care for you.'

'That's ridiculous and old-fashioned.'

'Then that's what I am.'

'Then I can't stay.'

'So be it.'

'Very well.'

She stood in the doorway, her one shabby case at her feet, and fumbled with the belt of her coat, her head bent so that he could not see the mixture of anger and sadness on her face as she faced the prospect of being alone again.

'Bye, then,' she said miserably.

'I love you,' he shouted suddenly.

'I need you,' she sobbed in reply.

'We're fools.'

'We are.'

'Over money.'

'Ridiculous.'

'And old-fashioned. Please stay, my darling.'

'Oh, please, may I?'

Honour was satisfied when they agreed that instead of her keep, Kitty should save an agreed sum and buy the occasional addition to Henri's collection of porcelain Napoleonic soldiers. They were expensive, so her contributions were spasmodic. She had little money left over but she was not to need it – Henri bought her make-up, clothes, shoes, jewellery and trinkets galore. She tried to stop him but this proved impossible, and it gave him such pleasure that even she realized it would have been churlish to refuse.

She met his parents, who liked her, and the fact that she was a budding opera singer especially pleased his mother for she was a fanatic opera buff. Kitty had always hated to be asked to sing in people's homes, which made her feel like a performing animal, she complained, but for Henri's mother, whom she had liked on sight, she made an exception. Henri's sister played the piano well and accompanied Kitty. It was perhaps one of the most critical performances she ever gave. At the end of her recital Henri's mother was in tears, her praise fulsome, her critique intelligent, and Kitty felt precious hope and confidence in her own ability wake from their damaged sleep.

A letter from Max commenting on her bad review had also helped. She had not realized that he and Ben read all the reviews from all over the world, even from the conservatoires and music schools, especially if one of their pupils was involved. 'He's a dyspeptic old goat . . . never known to make allowances. Mind you, we'd never have allowed such an out-and-out disaster here,' Max wrote snidely. And she knew it was true. Her present school might be regarded as the best, but Kitty didn't think so. She was building her voice, certainly, but only on the firm base already con-

structed by Max and Cellini. She'd have sung the role of
Rosina to acclaim in London, she could now confidently tell
herself.

She often heard news of Slim since Henri took several
English papers and the *International Herald Tribune*. A star
of Slim's magnitude was rarely out of the papers. So she
read that he had split from the Wall Nuts and was working
on a pop opera with Toby – just as he had said he would.
She could think of him now without pain, and the longing
for him, she told herself, had faded.

Kitty had often felt guilty, in that first year, that she had
not made any contact to see how her sister had fared after
the accident. After all, her disagreement had been with her
mother, not Lana. But she knew that an attempt to find out
anything would bring her into contact with her mother,
and the bitterness she felt towards her overrode any feelings of duty to her sister. Sometimes she wondered if Lana
had even survived, but something told her she had. Even
though she would never describe their relationship as close,
she felt she would have known if she had died, would have
sensed it.

Now the same papers that told her about Slim told her
about Lana. It was headline news around the world the
following June. Slim was married – and to Lana! There were
pictures of the wedding in every paper. Kitty studied them.
Lana was in a wheelchair, so thin she looked like a waif.
She was smiling broadly, however, like the Cheshire cat,
Kitty thought. But Slim looked serious and sad. Had he
married her out of pity or guilt? Kitty asked herself hopefully. Also smiling like a cat, but with the expression of one
who has eaten the cream, was Amy, standing proudly
holding one handle of the wheelchair, while Slim held the
other. She must be happy, Kitty thought, Lana had fame of
a sort after all. She found she was glad that Slim looked
miserable and then felt shocked at her own duplicity. She
had turned him down, so why shouldn't he marry someone

else? But she hated the thought and somehow it was worse because it was her own sister.

Slim's publicity manager had made sure that the suicidal crash had become an accident caused by faulty brakes. And the story of the little singer bravely fighting her way out of her wheelchair, the struggle of the surgeons to save her voice, held the nation enthralled for months and sold thousands of copies of newspapers.

And then one day the unfolding story took a different twist. The surgeons had declared themselves satisfied with their work, and Lana could sing again. This was big news, but even bigger was the information that she was to star in Slim and Toby's pop opera, now called *Musical Man*.

Kitty reacted angrily to this news. How could Slim do this to her – the role he had wanted her to play? And how dare Lana? Fine if she sang with groups, in clubs, but now she was muscling in on Kitty's world, in something called 'opera'. It wouldn't be, of course. No doubt it would be rubbish. But she frowned at that idea – no, she'd heard Slim's music. He was a fine musician, no doubt it would be good – a modern opera, no less. But Lana?

What was happening to her? Such stupid jealousy of her sister, which she hadn't felt in years. Kitty had the better voice, there was no doubt. So why should she feel like this? It was Slim, of course, she wanted him back. She resented her sister being not only his wife but his star – she was not even sure which hurt the most. She picked up the telephone to call him, tell him she had made a stupid mistake. But then she slammed it down again. What on earth was she doing? Why behave so stupidly? What did she care?

'Bully for her,' Kitty said, screwing up the newspapers and throwing them into the bin.

That night she had made Henri make love to her time and time again – she had to, she had not liked her reaction to the news that Slim was evidently happy with Lana. Until now she had told herself she loved Henri, and in a way she did, but not in the way she had loved Slim. Would she ever love like that again? And so she had to consider if she was using Henri, a thought which made her feel guilty and one she tried to bury from herself.

There was another ghost from her past. Martin Field was now an international film star, as famous for his roistering as his acting. He was still handsome – just. It would not be long before the drink-induced puffiness, already visible on his photographs, the dark circles around his eyes from lack of sleep, would catch up with him and cost him a starring role. He was about to marry a famous movie star. But Kitty found she could view this news with equanimity. At least one of her ghosts was laid.

Kitty's second year at the Conservatoire passed pleasantly. Henri had insisted he speak French with her so that now she was nearly fluent and could mix with the others easily. Once they had discovered she was not stuck up or difficult, her fellow students welcomed her into their group. Since Henri was a generous host there were many happy evenings at his apartment where her friends mixed with his.

Cellini came to Paris to give a masterclass. She declared herself more than pleased with Kitty's progress, and she approved of Henri. Kitty was amused at the recollection of Cellini's sly wink when she met him in his splendid apartment and assessed its value with a practised glance. 'I see you sometimes listen to the advice your old teacher gives you. Wise girl.' She smiled knowingly as she spoke
. . .

Kitty got up from the narrow bed in the hot hotel room and crossed to the small open window. She leaned out in futile search of a breeze. If she craned her head she could just see the lovely old main square of the town. She smiled as she watched a small child running after a ball, saw how the bright afternoon sun made the shadows so black that the child was like a silhouette as he ran into the square, followed quickly by an irate mother whose impassioned altercation with the boy clearly reached Kitty on the still air.

So what had gone wrong? Why was she here alone in this small Italian town with little money and fast-diminishing hope? Henri. Children. Italy. That was the order.

Why couldn't Henri have accepted their life as it was? Why had he wanted to change everything and, in so doing, her?

Marriage. He had proposed. He had done so beautifully. They had been celebrating her finishing her course at the Conservatoire. A wonderful meal, a wonderful concert, a wonderful walk on the banks of the Seine in the warmth of a summer evening. He had paused and had asked her to marry him, producing a priceless ring from his pocket.

Kitty had looked with horror at the ring as if it was a manacle and had backed away from him.

'You never discussed this with me,' she said accusingly.

'I didn't think it necessary. We live together. We love each other.' He shrugged his shoulders expressively.

'I told you, I explained at the very beginning . . . my career . . .'

'My darling, you can still have your career. I promise.'

'It's not possible. Not with you.'

'But why not? I understand. I like you to have a career. I'm not going to make you stay at home like some men would do. I'd be proud of you.'

'No, you wouldn't. How could you? You don't even like opera – you'd never understand.'

Silently they walked back to his car. Kitty sat beside him, her mind in turmoil. She didn't want this, she wanted to go on as they were. She wanted no changes, no risk-taking.

She spent half the night in tears as he begged and cajoled her, the ring on the bed between them.

'And what about children?' she asked suddenly.

'I realize you would not want them now. But there's plenty of time. You're only twenty-four, for goodness' sake.'

'I never want children.'

'Not now but later you will.'

'I won't. I can't. You see, I told you! I told you you would never understand – I was right.'

'What do you mean, you can't have children? You never said.'

'The Voice. I can't because of The Voice. It could ruin it, stretch my stomach muscles.'

'Oh, for Christ's sake, Kitty. There are some things more important than a bloody voice.'

'That's where you're wrong. There's nothing in my life that is.'

'Other opera singers have had children.'

'They risked it. Some were OK, some weren't. It's a risk I'm not prepared to take.'

'You're obsessed.'

'Yes. Didn't you realize?' she said sharply.

'I thought you loved me.'

'Don't you see? I'm trapped. This is more important than you or me.' She held her throat dramatically.

'Bullshit! Good God, I've never heard such conceit in all my life – you talk as if you're Melba or Callas. You're a singer, for heaven's sake. Maybe you'll make it, maybe you won't. And what then? What if you've thrown all personal happiness away and then fail? What then?'

He was kneeling on the bed looking angrily at her. She stood up and looked down at him.

'Well, one thing's clear. I'd never succeed married to you,' she said icily, walked to the spare room, took down her case from the top of the wardrobe and there and then,

in the middle of the night, she packed carefully, taking
with her only those things that belonged to her when she
had arrived . . .

And then Italy had entered the conundrum. In July she had
gone to Parma to take part in the Verdi Singing Competition, full of promise, full of confidence, full of hope. She
had entered the most prestigious international competition
for singers in the world. She would show him. She would
win. Her career as a professional would be assured.

She came nowhere.

She had gone to her hotel room and pulled the curtains,
and lying in the darkened room, had felt her life was over.
This competition should have been the next stage in her
career. Max had said so, Ben, Cellini, they had all spoken
as if her winning would be a matter of course. How could
she ever go home now? How could she ever face them after
all their care and attention, and see their disappointment?
She felt she had let everyone down, even Jenny who'd had
such faith in her. They had corresponded during her time
in Paris, but now Kitty could not write. She knew that if
she did Jenny would read between the lines. She could not
return a failure, she would only return a success.

Her disappointment had been slightly eased when, a
few days after the competition, she had been approached
by an agent, Jason Erikson. He was young, American,
charming, blondly handsome and talked knowledgeably
about her subject, and he wanted to represent her.

He had seduced her, it was almost as if it was inevitable,
she had thought. She was lonely, she needed love, her
voice needed love also. His love-making was not to her
liking, though. He was cold and brutal and she turned from
him and buried her head in the pillow and longed for Slim.
Always, when she was unhappy, Slim would creep back
into her soul.

Jason had done what he said he would – well, some of it. He had eventually arranged a series of concerts for her in half a dozen towns through Italy. He had found her an accompanist, Leila Vincenti, with whom she could work easily. And she had been content to sign a contract with him. The concerts began in the early spring and were not the raving successes she longed for, but they were fairly well attended, and if the applause was sometimes luke-warm, no one booed or threw anything at her. She did not blame them for the subdued reaction, there was something wrong with her voice. Oh, she could hit the right notes, no problem. She could remember every note. But it lacked feeling. It emerged from her automatically, it did not carry her with it, so how could she expect the audience to be carried with it also?

After the sixth concert there were no more bookings. She and Leila woke up in the small hotel in Naples to find that Jason had gone in the night with all their takings and Leila's few pieces of jewellery, leaving them with the bill to pay. Both of them felt too dispirited even to go to the police, but in a strange way Kitty felt relieved; she would never have to sleep with him again. That was why she was here, a year, almost to the day, since she had left Paris and Henri, in this small town in the back of beyond where there was a small opera house and a third-rate company. She had an audition for the chorus tomorrow, arranged by Leila who knew the first violin, or at least someone who did, Kitty could no longer remember.

She felt defeated, as she looked out on to the small town which, if she was lucky, would become her home. Lucky! She laughed at that. Where were all her grand dreams now? She felt like blushing as she thought of her ludicrous proud speeches to Henri and Slim. What right had she to think the way she had? It was always others who had fed her the dream, and she, like a fool, had believed them. She wasn't different. She was like a hundred others with a good voice. She had to come to terms with this knowledge and make the best of it.

She hoped Slim and Henri would never find out what had happened to her.

2

The Teatro della Repubblica was a pretty building built at a time when this small town had been enjoying better times. As its fortunes diminished so the fabric of the theatre began to crumble, as if in sympathy. The steps leading to the portico were uneven and caused many a fall. The pillars of the portico had been repaired often, and always with different shades of cement, so that they looked piebald. The gilt in the grand entrance hall was faded now, the plush threadbare, the carpet worn. The great chandelier had lost some of its crystal drops, and was dimmer than it once had been from the dust which was never removed. Inside the auditorium it was very much the same – the odd piece of gilt missing, lampshades on the sconces in the boxes, corridors were holed and lopsided and some seats were permanently in the down position. The once rich cherry-red curtains were maroon now, from years of accumulated dirt.

But despite all this, there was a charm to the place. It was often likened to a once great courtesan who had fallen on hard times but still tried to dress the part in clothes which had once been grand, and who wore paste instead of her diamonds which had been sold.

It was not a house for experimental, modern or lesser-known opera. *Bel canto* was what the townspeople wanted, and that was what they got. Visiting stars were a rarity; the management, unable to afford the fees demanded these days by anyone with a spark of star quality, relied mostly on their resident singers, none of whom would ever be invited to sing in an opera house of any consequence.

The sets were old, and even more worn than the rest of the building. As bits fell off, a local carpenter would be called in to tack on new pieces, and the stage manager, who had once thought he might like to study art, repainted them as best he could. A resident team of designers and craftsmen was out of the question.

The costumes were equally old and survived only because of the patient and loving care bestowed on them by Franca, a small, wizened woman who sat at her worktable in the wardrobe room as if rooted there. She had joined the company at fourteen and was about to celebrate her fiftieth anniversary with them.

It was an opera house which could only have survived in Italy where it was assured of a faithful following from the townspeople. From her first day in the chorus Kitty knew it was not going to be easy. Such a run-down company had never figured in her dreams. She told herself to be sensible, that it was a job, that at least she would not starve, and, like it or not, it was an opera house.

On her first day she had entered the busy communal dressing-room diffidently. She had greeted the others who had eyed her up and down; detecting her accent, those Italians among them turned their backs. Opera was Italian, and only Italians could sing, and only Italians had the warmth, the heart to perform. It was a refrain Kitty was to become used to over the months.

There was one free place on the bench in front of the mirror which stretched the length of one wall and was lit by bare bulbs. Kitty sat down and looked about her.

In the centre of the room were the racks of costumes for that night's performance of *Carmen* and the costumes for the following night's *La Bohème*. At the far end, Kitty could see a wardrobe assistant hanging up kimonos, so she realized that *Madam Butterfly* must be part of the season's programme. What a feast, she thought.

'What the hell are you doing in *my* place?' demanded the voice of one who could only be a contralto. Kitty swung round, flummoxed, and found herself facing an enormous woman – large in height as well as girth.

'I'm sorry. I didn't realize this place was taken, no one said.' She jumped up, flustered.

'Well, bloody realize in future. You sit down there with the other juniors.' The woman now spoke in English with a strong Australian accent.

The place Kitty had been allotted was a small table at the end of the room with a cracked mirror on it and no bulb. Aware that all eyes were upon her, she walked as if trying to make herself smaller towards the table and sat down again.

'Don't worry, I did exactly the same.' A girl sitting at the same table smiled at her. 'Dolores Torona.' She held out her hand.

'Kitty Lawrence.'

'That's not your stage name, surely? It doesn't sound like a stage name.'

'Yes, it is. Is Torona your name?'

'No. But I thought if Melba could call herself after Melbourne, I'd call myself after my home town – Toronto.'

'Ah, I see,' Kitty said, but she didn't. She had always thought it silly to try and sound Italian if one wasn't. 'Who's the gorgon?' She nodded in the direction of the Australian who was now in deep conversation with several of the others.

'Maria Alicia. She's from Alice Springs. Right cow, too.'

'Is she always so rude?'

'All the time I've been here. I'm glad you've joined, none of the others speaks to me. It's like being a new girl at school and she's the head girl. Maria can make or break you. You've got to learn that's her seat, her mirror. That first locker, the one with the toy koala bear on top, is hers. And when you make tea – which you will, we'll take it in turns – you have to remember she likes the first cup out of the pot and the Worcester cup and saucer is hers.' Dolores spoke quickly and earnestly.

'How grand.' Kitty grinned.

'But you must learn. You have to. She's so powerful, you see. She's the chorus master. If she doesn't like you she can place you right at the back of the stage, squashed against the flats, and the audience will never see you.'

'Doesn't the choreographer decide things like that?'

'They haven't got one, there's no need. They do the same operas over and over again with the same cast. They haven't got a *répétiteur* for the same reason.'

'I was always told that new productions were the life-blood of a company. I mean, don't they get bored doing the same stuff season after season, don't the audiences want something different?'

'Not here – I think the audiences would kill the management if they changed anything. They like it this way.'

'What are the chances of getting out of the chorus?'

'Minimal. I sussed that out pretty quickly. Fabiola and Lorenza, the two resident sopranos, would sing from a stretcher rather than give anyone else a chance.'

'Secondary roles?'

'That depends how your face fits with the Australian sow and whether you're willing . . .' But Dolores stopped and before she looked away, pretending to look for an eyeliner, Kitty saw she was blushing.

'Willing to do what?'

'You'll learn. I couldn't borrow your eyeliner, could I?'

Kitty had had her interview one day and was at work the next. For the next three days she was expected to sit through the performances and to learn the scores, but in fact she knew the operas by heart, being blessed with an exceptionally retentive memory, both for words and music.

They were surprisingly good. The sopranos were better than the tenors in voice, though all of them were past the age and size when they could easily be believed in as deadly, flirtatious Carmen, or lovesick Rodolfo. Yet the audience did not seem to mind the lumbering bodies nor the make-up larded on to hide the wrinkles.

Neither of the female stars spoke to Kitty and Dolores, but Kitty noticed that two of the tenors were more than a little friendly with two of the chorus. Amongst the chorus itself there were obvious liaisons but not as many as she had expected there would be.

Kitty was certain that there was a war going on between the orchestra and the singers. The conductor seemed to despise the singers as much as his instrumentalists and there were nights when the orchestra played at such a speed that Kitty felt it was a miracle the singers could keep up. On those nights, she later found, there was inevitably a football match on television.

She had entered the theatre thinking it was merely a way to earn enough to eat and that she would learn nothing. But she learned a lot.

Having upset Maria the first day, she had, as Dolores warned, been consigned to the back of the stage. Here she learned to use her height, to walk taller than she was, to exaggerate even further any gestures, any expressions she had to make – all to be noticed, and not just by the audience, for talent scouts and agents had been known to scour such companies looking for the right face, and hopefully the right voice.

She witnessed the tricks the principals got up to to annoy their partners, to grab attention. Bodies would be manoeuvred so that one masked another at an especially important moment in an aria, thus distracting the audience.

She heard high notes held just that little bit too long so that the other soloist was momentarily put off their stride. She saw how the conductor, when particularly annoyed for one reason or another, would alter the tempo, catching the soloists out in their breathing and so upsetting their phrasing. When such things occurred the tantrums backstage were volcanic.

It was guerrilla warfare that Kitty was witnessing, but to what end, apart from feeding inflated egos, or from boredom, she never found out. Miraculously, however, the operas still managed to cohere sufficiently to please the audiences.

Kitty learned to love the audiences. The house was rarely full but there was usually a respectable number. Unlike audiences in England, they sat eagerly in their seats, applauding enthusiastically, bellowing their approval.

Dolores and Kitty found a small one-bedroom flat to share, with a put-u-up in the sitting-room. The furniture was not much, neither was the location by the railway line with an abattoir the other side which stank in the hot Italian sun. But it was a two-storey building with no cracks in the ceiling, an improvement on Kitty's original *albergo*.

Dolores had started an affair with Giorgio, a member of the chorus. Kitty would lie awake at night and hear their passion and she would ache with longing for a love of her own.

Then at Christmas Dolores was suddenly promoted, first from walking at the back of the chorus to being a stallholder in *Carmen*, and she was finally given a solo line to sing. Her attitude in the changing-room altered too. For six months she strutted about the place with a smug smile on her face, ignoring Maria completely. Giorgio was a less frequent visitor to the apartment now, and when he came he was far more subdued than before.

Over a period of time things began to happen to Dolores.

Her make-up frequently disappeared. A large spider was found in her locker, which Dolores was convinced had not got there by accident, followed by a mouse and dead cockroaches. Then one day her costume was missing when she arrived late and flustered for a performance.

'What have you done with it?' Dolores raced across the room to confront Maria.

'With what?'

'You know bloody well. Give it to me or I'll go straight to the manager.'

'Please yourself, lovey,' Maria drawled.

'I warn you.' Dolores stamped her foot, tears welling up in her eyes. 'I will. I will. He'll listen to me.'

'Oh, sod you. They're over there.' Maria pointed imperiously towards a bedraggled bundle of clothes in the corner.

Kitty had never met the manager, only the musical director when she had auditioned. She had seen him swaggering around, though, a fat, middle-aged man with a self-satisfied expression, who wore a thick, vulgar watch-chain across his stomach. He was famous for having as little to do with the singers as possible, so Kitty was surprised that Dolores had so confidently declared that he would listen to her.

The following month – Kitty's first anniversary with the company – there was great excitement, and trepidation too, among the tenors. The tenor Marcheso had agreed to sing Rodolfo for three performances. Once this news had been released, the booking office was besieged. Those three days were a complete sell-out.

Marcheso had been world-famous in the 1950s, but his deep interest in the whisky bottle in the sixties had meant that now, in the seventies, his voice was a shadow of its former self. But there was still an aura to his name, past triumphs still protected him from too much harsh criticism. The surprise was that he was coming at all, but a bad gambling debt made his acceptance, at a reduced rate for him, essential now that the Garden, the Met and La Scala no longer wanted him.

Kitty was interested to hear him, for Cellini, while deploring his present condition, had sung with him in his prime and had often spoken of his once great talent.

After his first performance, which was not too bad, all things considered, Kitty thought, Dolores rushed up to her in the dressing-room as she was removing her make-up.

'Kitty, do us a favour. Lend me your blue dress – the taffeta one. Please, please say yes.'

'What's all the excitement? Of course you can borrow it. You going out somewhere nice?'

'Yes. It's so exciting I could burst. Marcheso's invited me to the post-performance party and then out to dinner. And then? Well, anything could happen, couldn't it?' She was literally skipping from one foot to the other.

'But I thought . . . what about Giorgio?'

'Oh, bah! He'll understand. After all, Marcheso's a *principal*,' she said breathlessly and raced from the room.

Once she had removed her make-up and changed into her street clothes, Kitty picked up her bag to leave. Giorgio was slumped in the corner of the room, a look of abject misery on his face.

'Fancy some spaghetti, Giorgio?' she asked kindly. Later in the evening she was not so sure this had been a wise decision; she had endured his self-pity, only to have to deal with his advances later.

'Certainly not,' she said, affronted, slamming the door in his face.

The next week Dolores left with Marcheso. No argument from Kitty could persuade her that this was not a wise thing to do.

'He'll make me a star. I know he will,' Dolores said, eyes shining and hands together as if in prayer. She kissed Kitty

goodbye, promised she would write, and called a cab to
take her and her bags to Marcheso's hotel.

'Bloody fool. Marcheso gets through women at the rate
of knots. He only has to look once and he's in love – until
the next time. He'll have dropped her in a month,' Maria
announced.

'Poor Dolores,' said Kitty.

'Poor Dolores my arse – fancy a piece of chocolate,
Kitty?'

'Thanks,' Kitty managed to stammer, so great was her
surprise at being treated kindly by Maria. But then, two
new members of the chorus had been hired, and so Kitty
was pushed up the pecking order.

A few days later she was summoned to the general
manager's office.

3

The office of the general manager, Signor Giancarlo Baddino, was hot, stuffy and stank of stale cigar smoke that
did not blend happily with the heavy, musky smell of his
liberally applied aftershave.

'My dear Kitty,' he said effusively, waving her towards
a chair opposite his cluttered desk. He did not bother to
stand for her, not that she had really expected him to.

'Signor,' she said simply, as she sat on the overstuffed
armchair, wishing it were not so hot. The past month had
been trying – too hot to work, to sleep, to think even.
Certainly too hot for opera but, with money short and in
the tourist season, there was no question of closing for the
hottest months. There were no handy Roman amphi-

theatres in the locality, so the company had to grin and bear the temperatures of the theatre. Kitty had often found herself longing for a damp and miserable English summer.

'Are you happy here?'

'Sometimes.'

'Only sometimes. How sad for us,' he said, expansively waving his arms in a gesture of despair. 'Our little friend, you're missing her?'

'Dolores? Not particularly,' she answered honestly. She had thought she would, but in the three weeks since Dolores had been gone she had found she hadn't – the heat, she presumed.

'So, what is wrong?' Signor Baddino asked, giving her an oily smile.

'I've been here a year now and I'm still at the back of the chorus. I had at least hoped to be given the odd chance.' Kitty surprised herself at her boldness, but she had become so disillusioned she felt she really did not care any more.

'But you can't expect to run before you can walk.'

'Signor Baddino, I've spent over four years studying, and have worked for two years as a professional. I've built a repertoire over the years but now I find myself already forgetting what I have learned.'

'Then you should practise. What am I told by those who know? That it is those who are dedicated who practise the most. If you don't, then the fault lies with you.'

'And when would I find the time? Where would I find the facilities? We work so hard, and in this heat, it's exhausting. We're performing six nights a week. What rehearsals we have are sparse. We are not allowed the practice-room, we are not allowed to ask any of the musicians to play for us. Of course I practise, when and how I can – my neighbours are sick to death of me already. Don't you lecture me, Signor!'

'You know, Kitty, you are very beautiful when angry.'

'Oh, really!' Kitty shook her head with anger.

'I didn't ask you here to lecture you. I asked you here because I thought it was time that you were given a chance.'

'Oh!' Kitty exclaimed, kicking herself now for being so outspoken. 'Oh, I see.'

'I've spoken to the musical director, he says you have a fine voice.'

'Thank you,' she said.

'So we thought to give you a chance. We thought perhaps, at one of the performances, that you might sing Frasquita in *Carmen* – do you know her role?'

'That would be wonderful.' Kitty pressed her hands together, unable to believe her luck. 'Yes, of course I know it. I can't thank you enough.'

'Now, now. Not so fast. I said *might*. It depends . . .' Signor Baddino rubbed his chin with one of his podgy, heavily jewelled hands.

'Yes?'

'You sleep with me.'

Kitty sat rigid in her chair.

'I beg your pardon?'

'I think you heard.'

'I couldn't do that. Never.' She shook her head and shuddered at the very idea.

'Of course, the choice is yours.' Signor Baddino splayed his hands on the desk, hands which Kitty was finding more and more repulsive. 'If you choose to, I can't promise you that your career will advance any further – that, in the end, is up to you. But I can assure you that if you refuse, then at the back of the chorus you will stay. *Comprendi?*' He smiled in a friendly manner.

'But . . . I . . .' The very thought of this man's hands exploring her body was anathema to her. His breath on her, disgusting. She could not even bring herself to think further about what it would be like. But then . . . how else was she to get anywhere? 'When?' she said firmly.

'What's wrong with now?' He lumbered to his feet and

walked round to her side of the desk. He half-sat, half-leaned on it, bent forward and gently stroked her cheek. '*Bellissima*,' he said softly.

She closed her eyes; perhaps if she kept them closed she could imagine it was Slim. She felt his fingers stroke her cheek, her neck, slide towards her breasts. His touch was soft and clammy on her skin.

'No!' Her eyes snapped open, full of anger. She slapped his hand away. 'No! Is this how you helped Dolores? You creep.' She jumped to her feet. 'I'm getting out of here.'

'You'll regret this, Miss Lawrence,' Signor Baddino said unpleasantly.

'Oh, no, I won't. I'm quitting – now!'

'And you won't get work at any house, if I can prevent it.'

'But you won't. You see, Signor, I've waited too long in this crummy place. I'm going home. I'm going to the top and when I'm there I'll tell the world all about you.' She was shaking as she spoke, and he laughed. She could not blame him for laughing at her bravado, what chance had she now? She turned abruptly and stalked from the room.

Outside in the corridor she slumped against the wall, her heart was racing, she felt sick, she gulped hungrily for air. She covered her face with her hands. How could she? How could she have even thought of allowing him to make love to her? How could she have let him even touch her? She shuddered with disgust. She pushed herself away from the wall and began to run along the carpeted corridor – down the main stairs, through a door and into the warren of corridors backstage. In the chorus changing-room she put her key into her locker but could not open it. Angrily she kicked it and tried again. The metal door flew open. In the bottom was her holdall. She began to sweep her possessions into it carelessly.

'Ha!' She heard a raucous laugh behind her. 'Turned the fat old pig down, did you?'

She swung round to see Maria standing behind her, hands on hips and grinning from ear to ear.

'Good on yer, cobber.'

'How do you know?' Kitty asked indignantly, blushing. She brushed her cheek with irritation at her colour.

'He never speaks to any of the girls until he wants to screw her. Once Dolores had gone it was only a matter of time. Mind you, I thought it would be that new girl, Rosa – but there you go, I can't be right all the time.'

'He's disgusting. I'm leaving.'

'Just as well – your life wouldn't be worth living after turning him down. I admire you for that, few of us do.'

'You too?'

'How do you think I came out top dog here – not my voice, I know that. But it's a living and I'd never be anything but a member of the chorus anywhere else. The climate suits me, and I like Italian men and they seem to like me – big arse and all. Where are you going?'

'I don't know. Home, I suppose, if I can face everyone.'

'Got enough money?'

'If I take the bus.'

'I'm glad you're going. You're too good for this dump. I never did understand how you ended up here in the first place.'

'It's a long story.'

'Usually is. Well, good luck, Kitty. And if you ever make it – don't forget us.'

'No, I won't. I promise.' And she meant it. Maria might have scared her in the beginning but she had begun to like the brusque Australian, at least she was always straight.

There was no one about to say goodbye to, so she asked Maria to say it for her. She walked out of the theatre and did not look back.

Once outside she crossed the square, and sat down in a pavement café and ordered a *limonada*. . . . Now what? She did have the fare but what then? Where would she go? Would Jenny, whom she hadn't seen for years and to whom she hadn't written since Paris, even though she had meant to, take her in? Could she expect her to? Ah, well, she told herself with an inward smile, there was always Selfridges.

'Kitty? It is Kitty Lawrence, isn't it?'

She looked up. Standing by her table was a smartly dressed man. He lifted the panama on his head in salute and she saw his blond hair. She recognized him and yet in her emotional state could not place him.

'Felix Masters.' He bowed slightly. 'I've heard you sing many times at the Hampstead Conservatoire.' He smiled.

'Of course, Mr Masters. Forgive me.'

'May I?'

'Please. Please do,' she said, although she would much rather have been left alone. Politely she moved her bag from the chair beside her.

'I was at the opera last night. I thought it was you but I couldn't be too sure . . .'

'I was a long way back.' She managed a small laugh.

'An interesting place, but surprisingly . . .' He moved his shoulders expressively.

'I know, it's a dump but the company is quite good, no thanks to the management,' she said bitterly.

'But why, Kitty? Cellini had such faith in you, we all did. But the chorus, in a place like this?' He shook his head in disbelief.

'It's gone, whatever I had – it's gone. Oh, I can sing, of course I can, but not as I used to. There's something missing and I don't know what it is.' She looked away miserably.

'Parma.'

'You were there?' She shuddered at the thought that he had witnessed her lacklustre performance.

'Yes. You sang well, I thought. But I would be lying if I

did not tell you I have heard you sing better. You lacked expression, warmth.'

'Exactly.'

'But after that you disappeared. We looked for you —'

'We?'

'Max Leitman, Ben, Cellini. It was Cellini. She met Marcheso, they sang together years ago. She asked if on his tours he'd met a Kitty – apparently he has a reputation for pretty young women.'

'My friend Dolores ran away with him.'

'So that was how he knew about you – we wondered. But we never dreamed you'd be in the chorus . . .'

'A long way back!' She smiled at her joke.

'I was coming to Italy for a holiday anyway so I promised to see if I could find you. You know, I haven't found a first-class restaurant yet.'

'I don't think you will, either.'

'I was hoping, if there was one, I could take you out for dinner tonight, after the performance.'

'I quit . . .' And to her horror she burst into tears and before she could stop herself the whole sorry tale spilled out.

Felix looked discomfited, unused to being in the company of weeping young women, and in public too. So he ordered a bottle of wine in the hope that would cheer her up.

'What do you want to do?' he asked eventually after he had expressed his shock and anger. He made a mental note to use whatever influence he had to have Baddino removed.

'To go home. I've got the fare.'

'And your singing?'

'Mr Masters, I don't know. I'm so afraid.'

'Miss Lawrence, I have a rented villa near Florence. Perhaps you would join me there for a short holiday? And you are welcome to come back with me in my car, if you like.'

'I'd like that very much,' she said, relief flowing over her in great waves.

'Perhaps when we are there you should go and see Cellini?'

'I don't know if I could face her. I feel so ashamed, the opportunities I've been given and appear to have thrown away.'

'It sounds to me as if you need time, Miss Lawrence. Time to get your confidence back and time to restore your beautiful voice.'

4

During the two weeks Kitty spent at Felix's villa she felt cocooned in comfort. It was not until she arrived that she realized how tired she was. During the months she had been working to survive both physically and mentally, something in her brain must have prevented her from knowing the extent of her fatigue and depression. But now, cosseted, comfortable, with wonderful food cooked by the maid of all work, Sophia, with little to think about except how to fill the long day with inconsequential activities, now the layers of the mind peeled back and she could not remember when she had last felt so tired.

'Shall we go into Firenze to the Uffizi?'

'Please, Felix, I just want to sleep.'

And another day: 'We could make an excursion to Pisa if you like?'

'Please, Felix, I just want to sleep.'

Felix's idea of a holiday, Kitty learned, was to fill each waking moment with these excursions. He could not rest until every church, every fresco, every monument, every sculpture, every painting of any significance in his area had been visited, revisited and duly studied. His passion for food, too, drove him to travel far and wide to find the perfect meal. Given that his companion wanted only to sleep and laze by the pool, he was remarkably patient, but he did not like to leave her on her own.

'Please, Felix, you go. I'll be fine here. Sophia's an angel and will look after me,' she said most days.

'No, I'd rather stay,' he always replied.

She could not remember when she had begun to call him Felix or when he said Kitty for the first time. She thought that neither had suggested it but that they had slipped into being less formal as they learned to relax with each other.

Felix was surprised at how easy it was to be with Kitty. He normally did not like house guests, finding having to consider other people's wants and fancies irksome. If guests were coming he made a point of inviting them for only three days or two nights. Any longer, he found, put a strain not only on the house but, more importantly, on his tolerance.

Living alone, he did not seek, or need, companionship when on holiday. He liked his own company, he always had done. He was rigid in his rituals, he knew, and was fully aware that he would not be a relaxing travelling companion nor a totally successful host.

Kitty was different, although she too, he noticed, appeared to enjoy her own company. He would watch her by the pool, reading or just staring into space, and he would see that she was totally contented. He did not need to rush out to talk to her, entertain her. When he was reading she never interrupted but, if she had something to say, waited until he closed his book. He had never met that level of consideration in a woman before. All those he knew, including his mother, thought nothing of demanding his attention even when it was obvious he was deeply engrossed in a book.

Although normally Felix would choose to play opera
from the large number of records he always brought with
him on these holidays, he sensed that perhaps this was not
a good idea for Kitty at the moment. So he restricted his
listening to Bach and Mozart and the rediscovery of the
delights of Scarlatti, and even further back, of Tallis.

The enjoyment of music, he felt strongly, was an
intensely personal thing and he would refrain from the
pursuit of his own pleasure when others were around for
fear of it being tedious for them. With Kitty this was not a
problem. To his joy he discovered that he was teaching her
the pleasures of music new to her. She might be the trained
musician of the two but he soon discovered her field of
knowledge was a narrow one.

He learned how limited her education had been – a
private school of dubious standards, which in any case she
had left at the too early age of sixteen. Her parents had no
doubt made sacrifices to send her there, thinking they were
doing the best for her but themselves lacking the education
that would have enabled them to judge the school's academic standing. It saddened Felix, for he discovered that
Kitty was highly intelligent and hungry to learn.

She had read a great deal, but in a haphazard manner,
with no order to it, and it amused him to make a concise
reading list for her, to choose from the fine collection of art
books in the villa. He enjoyed selecting reproductions of
paintings for them to study together, and rather fancied
himself in the role of Svengali. But Kitty's eagerness soon
made him honestly enjoy what he was doing.

She never spoke of her family, which pleased Felix. He
found people's obsessions with their childhood boring in
the extreme. He had noticed in life that those who failed
too frequently turned the blame on parents, invariably
dead, who could not defend themselves. Felix felt strongly
that one made of life what one could from one's own
endeavours. He would have no truck with the talk and

theory of psychiatrists and was convinced that Freud was nothing but a salacious meddler.

During the first few days at the villa Kitty had seemed to have little interest in anything except sleeping. But, rather like a small child, he thought indulgently, she would be enthusiastic to learn once she had slept her fill. This would have been the point when he would have expected to resume his exploration of the artistic splendours of Italy. However, he rarely suggested outings, he did not want to. He wanted to be here in this villa with Kitty, the world safely the other side of the high wall which surrounded the property. Indeed, he discovered he did not want this holiday to end and regretted the appointments he had waiting for him in London. He found Kitty soothing to be with. And he realized, perhaps for the first time in his life, that he could honestly say he had found a friend.

Felix wondered, once or twice, if this friendship was strong enough for him to confess that it was he who had financed Kitty's career. But then, given that she felt her voice was lost, that she felt such guilt towards Ben and Cellini and Max, he decided it was best not to tell her. For if he did, what would it do but add to the weight of her guilt?

He longed for her to sing for him – just him. But she made no mention of doing so, and he did not like to suggest it for fear of her reaction, for fear of burdening her.

It was their last full day at the villa. As he sat on the terrace of the house high in the hills above Florence, and waited for her to join him for champagne before dinner, he finally heard her sing. She was not singing a song but a scale, diffidently at first but then with more confidence. Then she tried a trill and then, as if satisfied with that, she sang with gusto. He smiled a smile of deep satisfaction.

They dined on the terrace by candlelight, with the lights of the city in the distance making a backdrop as pretty as anything in nature.

'Do you know, Felix, I don't want this holiday to end.'

'Neither do I. These past two weeks have been perfect, haven't they?'

'Totally. I can't ever remember feeling so relaxed with anyone. You're a wonderful companion, Felix.'

He did not reply but smiled broadly for he could not remember anyone ever saying that of him before. He would have liked to touch her at that moment, it would have been so easy to slide his hand across the glass-topped table and hold her hand. But Sophia appeared with the next course and the moment was lost.

'What now, Kitty?' he asked.

'I think I need time. I wish I could take a year off. A year to relearn, to get back to where I was. But that's impossible.'

'Why? It sounds a sensible decision to me.'

'I don't fancy starving, Felix.' She laughed. 'Maybe I can go back to Selfridges, live with my friend Jenny and hope to make enough to have the odd lesson with Cellini – if she'll have me,' she added doubtfully.

'Cellini would have you back. So would Ben Cooper.'

'Do you really think so?'

'Of course. A teacher gets the chance to coach a golden voice only once in a lifetime. Perhaps never.'

'Felix, you're kind, but you exaggerate. I've learned my lesson. I'm middle-rank, good enough to make a living – but a diva? Childish dreams, Felix.'

'We shall see.'

'You'd know if you'd seen me in Paris when I played the Countess – oh, my, the reviews. That's probably when I realized.' She shuddered at the memory for it had never gone away. She could have quoted the reviews word for word.

'That was an appalling production. The principal should have prevented the performance. The orchestra was useless, the conductor weak, you could barely move in that ridiculous costume, the –'

'You saw it?' she said in astonishment.

'Apart from your disappearance, I think I've seen every one of your too few public performances.'

'But why?'

'Because I love your voice. I decided to take an interest.'

'Ah, my voice. You know, there was a moment a few days ago when I thought it had left me and I was almost pleased that I would never be a professional singer again, but would just sing for my own amusement. I'm beginning to feel The Voice is a trap, it has a stranglehold on me. I'm not happy living with it but now I realize I could not be happy living without it – that's what I've learned.'

'Then I'm glad. For you not to sing would give me great sadness.'

'You haven't asked me to sing once in these past two weeks. Why, if you feel so strongly about my voice?'

'I didn't think it was fair. I sensed you were facing a crisis and needed to resolve it in your own time and way.'

'How kind you are, Felix.' She laid down her napkin. 'Would you like me to sing for you now?'

'Would you? Nothing could give me greater pleasure.' He stood up.

'No, you sit here,' she said, and moved quickly across the terrace and through the open french windows.

He heard her begin to play, falteringly at first, and then she began to sing a gentle, bitter-sweet Neapolitan love song. And it was there again in her voice, the warmth, the depth, the emotion – those things which had been lacking when he'd heard her last, singing solo in Parma.

He sat on the terrace in the dark, with only the guttering candles for light, the crickets a fitting chorus to Kitty's Italian song, and he found he was in tears. And as he wept, as he listened to her voice, he realized something. He wanted to care for her, protect her. He who had only ever thought of himself now found he wanted to devote his life to Kitty. He wanted nothing but the privilege of being the guardian of her voice.

After another song she allowed him to join her in the drawing-room and he sat and watched her as she sang again and again for him. Felix knew he had never been this happy in his life.

As he listened he wondered if he had always known that this was how it would be. Maybe that was why he'd agreed so readily to help Kitty. He had helped other students, but had never felt as involved as he did with her. He had not attended all their performances, yet he frequently put himself out to attend hers.

He sat and listened and marvelled at the sound he heard. In a way it was his creation, for had it not been for him, would she be as she was now? This was his voice too. To own such a thing of beauty, greater than any house or painting . . . her voice, his voice, their voice . . .

Inevitably she tired. She came and sat on the footstool before him.

'Well?' she asked anxiously.

'Well?' he repeated, but laughing, for he knew what she was asking.

'Can I do it?'

'I never doubted for a moment.'

'It's back, isn't it?' She was smiling at him, a smile of eager joy.

'It's back.' He nodded.

'I wonder why.'

'Perhaps . . .' He leaned forward and without thinking, stroked her cheek with one finger; such beautiful smooth skin, such a fine face, he thought. Kitty was surprised by the gentle caress, but it pleased her and instinctively she leaned forward. He bent down and placed his hands on either side of her face and kissed her tenderly. His touch, the kiss, were so unthreatening that she responded almost automatically. And then she realized what she was doing and where this could lead, but she was not sure she wanted to stop. He stroked her neck, his hand inching towards her breasts. Her body was responding to his touch, slipping down the path of no return. She tried to think. Did she want this?

Felix surprised himself. He so rarely made love, and never to someone he respected. Until now the only women he could bring himself to touch had been the women of the night with whom he did not need to be spiritually involved. Sexual contact might occasionally be necessary to him, but he had always found it slightly distasteful; now he found himself behaving in a totally different way.

She had enjoyed his kiss – it had been so long . . . But the rest? And then she thought, why not? He was kind, she was alone, he had helped restore her confidence and with it The Voice. And with him she could forget all thought of having to work for them both to survive – she and The Voice. So she opened her arms in welcome.

He made love gently – too gently. He did not arouse her as she ached to be aroused. But she pretended, for she did not want to hurt his feelings.

They lay on his bed and he looked down on her, a look of wonder in his eyes.

'Would you marry me, Kitty?'

'Yes,' she said, simply. It would have seemed wrong to say more, to gush and sigh. She would marry him because she would be safe with him – they both would, she and The Voice.

Lana, in a frilly nightdress, was leaning against lace-trimmed pillows in her beautiful bedroom. The drapes of the four-poster bed were sprigged with rosebuds which matched the curtains at the casement windows in front of which stood an elaborately skirted dressing-table.

Radio One was playing loudly and Lana had just finished eating her breakfast of Marmite toast, but was still sipping her orange juice which she had laced heavily with the vodka she kept in the bedside table and which she locked carefully after replacing the bottle.

She pushed the breakfast tray to the bottom of the bed and turned her attention to the pile of magazines and tabloid newspapers beside her. She dealt with the papers quickly for she read only the gossip and showbiz pages. She picked up the last one and tutted with annoyance. This was Slim's. She never read the *Telegraph*. It had been slipped in with hers by mistake – he'd be furious, he liked the crossword in this one. She leaned across to pick up the internal telephone to tell him she had it when a photograph on the front page caught her eye. She knew that face. Kitty!

'City financier weds opera singer'. She read the caption.

'Well, then, there's a turn-up,' Lana said aloud. Intently, she read that Felix Masters, millionaire financier, patron of the arts – 'Good one, Kitty,' she said aloud – had married Kitty Lawrence, rising opera star, yesterday. The report said that the quiet ceremony had been attended by a few friends. How odd, why didn't she let us know? Lana thought. Embarrassed about Slim, she supposed. She'd forgiven Kitty ages ago, why not? She had what she wanted – Slim was hers now. But there were times when she wondered if he had got Kitty out of his system, if he still hankered after her. It would explain everything that was wrong in their relationship.

Lana looked at the photograph again. It was Kitty, yet she was different. She was smartly dressed in a short-jacketed suit which might have been a Quant, Lana could not be certain. Her long hair was scraped back from her face into a severe bun, and she wore no hat. It was her face that bothered Lana. Her plain older sister looked beautiful. Lana was not sure if she liked that, she was the pretty one, she'd always been, she didn't want that to change.

'. . . rising opera star . . .' the newspaper said, and Lana liked the use of the word 'star' even less. It wasn't fair. She was supposed to be the star in the family, hadn't her mother always promised her and Cy, and then Slim? And what had happened? Nothing.

She wondered why Kitty had chosen to marry someone so old. She shuddered, she'd rather be in the muddle she was in now than sleep with *him*. That made her feel a bit better.

She pulled the external-line telephone to her and dialled a number. How would Slim react to this news, she wondered, as she waited for her call to connect.

'Mum, guess what?'

'What?'

'Kitty. She's married.'

There was silence the other end. Lana shook the receiver. 'You there?'

'Yes.'

'What do you think of that?'

'Not a lot.'

Lana could imagine her mother shrugging her shoulders. 'She *is* your daughter,' she said somewhat unnecessarily.

'So it says on her birth certificate. Not that you'd guess it the way she carries on. Maybe she's a changeling.'

'Don't be silly, we were both born at home.'

'It was a joke!'

'Sorry, I didn't recognize it as one.' Lana giggled. 'Don't you want to know who she's married?'

'Not particularly.'

'God, Mum, you're weird. *I* can't wait to meet him, find out what he's like. He's filthy rich, by the way.'

'How nice for her. Not that I'll see a penny of it.' Just for a second Lana could hear the whine in her mother's voice which she had used so adroitly in the past.

'Oh, come on, Mum. You don't need any of it. Don't Slim and I look after you well enough? Who paid off your overdraft – the one that creep Cy left you with when he closed your agency and left you with the bills? Who buys you nice presents?'

'Don't remind me of Cy whatever you do.' Amy sighed. 'A pretty penny he cost me and I thought he'd been straight with me. You're a good girl, though, and I'll never forget it. I just wish sometimes you didn't have to remind me at every available opportunity.' Amy spoke sharply.

Lana looked at the telephone, a hurt expression on her face. 'Oh, come on, Mum, don't be so crabby.'

'I'm not. Just stating the truth. If you see your sister you can tell her from me she needn't expect a wedding present!'

'OK, I will.' Lana laughed, she doubted if Kitty would expect one. 'What's wrong with your love life, Mum? You really sound as if you've got the hump.'

'It's none of your business, but if you must know, I'm fine in that quarter.' Amy sounded huffy.

'Who? That Vince bloke, the car dealer?'

'I'm not telling,' Amy said coyly.

'Then it is. Oh, go on, Mum, tell me. What's he like?'

Lana chatted with her mother for an hour, as she did most mornings. Sometimes when she talked to Amy she thought how much happier her mother seemed than she was. Certainly she had a more active sex life than Lana. The irony of the situation was not lost on her.

It was really her mother's fault that she was in this situation. When Slim had proposed to her less than a month after the crash, she was still in the hospital and none of the doctors would commit themselves to saying whether she would ever walk again. Lana had known Slim had proposed out of a combination of guilt and pity. She had turned him down.

Amy had hit the roof that night when she visited and Lana had told her about the scene with Slim.

'You bloody little fool, why on earth not?'

'I don't want anyone's pity, thank you very much. Look at me, I'm a wreck . . .'

'The bruising's getting better.'

'This scar will never go.' Lana touched her chin. 'No, he's feeling guilty. He knows it was his fault and is trying to make amends. I don't want his charity.'

'But you loved him so much. You were devoted to him.'

'I still love him, but nothing's altered – he doesn't love me. He didn't want to marry me before, so why now? What would I feel as his wife, knowing all the time he'd be wishing it was Kitty?'

'That little cow! When I think how she played him along, swiping him from under your nose. That was a vicious thing to do. If I was you I'd marry him just to get back at her.'

'But how would it? She doesn't want him. You never saw him, he was crazy about her – he'd have given her anything she wanted.'

'Then why did she turn him down? Has he told you?'

'Her career. She said it was too soon for her to settle down.'

'Then she didn't say she didn't love him, did she? She probably still does. I don't understand you, Lana. You love him. Marry him, make him love you, and at the same time you can spite her. You'd be mad not to.'

From the hospital bed Lana looked doubtfully at her

mother who was busily fiddling with one of the many vases
of flowers she had been sent – mostly from Slim.

'And what about your career? Think what Slim could do
for you there – he wanted to help you before all this. Think
what he would want to do now. With his contacts you
could do it, Lana, you could finally be a star.'

'What if I can't sing?' Lana looked sad.

Amy swung round. Clutching a long-stemmed yellow
rose in one hand she brandished it violently at her wan-
looking daughter.

'You can take that silly expression off your face, for a
start. What have the doctors told you until they must be
sick of repeating it? *There's no reason why you can't sing*. You
can talk, can't you? Then sing.'

'No. I'm afraid to.'

'God give me strength!' Amy said to the ceiling.

In June, seven months after the accident, Lana and Slim
were married.

She had no complaints about the wedding – it was
everything a girl could have dreamed of. A wonderful dress
and flowers, a reception for hundreds of people she hardly
knew at Slim's mansion. Enough wedding presents to stock
a store. And vintage champagne by the crate-load until she
had drunk so much she felt it would come out of her ears.
There had been no need for the wheelchair – she had been
only temporarily paralysed from the severe bruising to her
spine, and the use of her legs had returned. Not that Slim
knew. Amy had sworn Lana to secrecy, and she had not
taken much persuading – if he knew there was nothing
wrong with her he was just as likely to retract his offer of
marriage. Now that her mother had persuaded her what a
good idea it was, it was all Lana wanted. She intended to
take no risks.

Amy had discussed the matter with Tristan Riviera,

Slim's manager; both were aware of the publicity impact of Lana looking waif-like in the chair. Amy was certain the image of her pathetic daughter would remain in the public's mind for a long time to come and would make her a celebrity, which she could use later to help her career. Tristan knew that Slim could only come out of this as a kind and caring human being, marrying the poor crippled girl when he could have had anyone. Amy and Tristan were beside themselves with happiness at the mass-hysteria of the tabloid press over the touching scene.

They honeymooned in Florida where Slim wanted to consult a famous record producer about his still secret rock opera project. Toby went with them, which pleased Tristan, always the careful manager, inordinately, for now the whole honeymoon could be written down to expenses.

This honeymoon was the portent of what Lana's married life was to be – they had separate rooms, no sex, and she rarely saw Slim.

The days were long and empty spaces to be filled. But with what? Lana knew no one in Florida, and Slim, who did, had made no arrangements for her to meet anyone. At first the delight of the shops and the realization that she could buy whatever she wanted on Slim's more than generous allowance amused her. But after a few days even she found the excesses of her shopping were beginning to pall.

Slim had hired a villa for them, thoughtfully one-storey to accommodate Lana's wheelchair. She had servants, a pool and a wonderful large garden, although horticulture had never been one of Lana's interests and so she had not bothered to venture into it, nor was she expected to since everyone thought she could barely walk. Now, away from the prying eyes of the press, Lana had begun the charade of pretending she was learning to walk again – step by faltering step. She quite enjoyed her performance but only the servants saw her progress, for Slim was never there.

The luxury of her own pool amused her at first but the
loneliness made her discontented even with that. Slim laid
on a chauffeur-driven car to take her shopping and to the
beach, but sitting alone and watching others having fun
seemed only to accentuate her isolation. And then she
convinced herself that people were staring at her, so she
gave up the excursions to the beach.

Back at her luxurious villa she began what was soon to
become her routine. She awoke past noon and breakfasted
in bed. She would eke out her bath, dressing and making-
up to fill another hour or two. When finished she would
either sit by the pool or more often in the cool, cavernous
drawing-room and there she would listen to music by the
hour.

Once she had read all that month's magazines she
became restless. She had never been known to read a book,
so it had not crossed her mind to take one from the shelves
or to buy one.

That was when she began to drink again.

At first she did not need to drink much – the enforced
abstinence of her stay in hospital, and her convalescence,
ensured that the alcohol rushed to her head and made her
quickly euphoric. But this was not a situation that could
last, and every day the amount she drank spiralled.

Pretty, dressed always in white, with her blonde hair
caught in an Alice band, her face only lightly tanned – she
took care of that, sitting, when outside, under a frilly
parasol – she looked more like sixteen than her twenty-one
years. But she made a sad figure as she wandered aimlessly
about, stumbling occasionally in case a servant was watching. The servants debated her plight in the kitchen, the
gardeners in the greenhouse, the delivery men in their
vans. Any of the males would have given their souls to take
that one to bed, to make her happy, to make her smile.

And Slim? Slim appeared to be unaware of how unhappy

Lana was becoming. Before he left in the morning he might pop into her bedroom to say goodbye but often she was asleep. He did not see her drunk for she was more than likely asleep again when he returned from his meetings late at night.

The couple of times he did take her out to dinner and a club she clung to him like a grateful limpet and did not drink, not wanting to miss one moment of his company. But the wheelchair made these visits difficult to arrange and so they did not repeat them.

Lana told herself that when they returned home to England and Slim wasn't so busy, things would be different. Only they weren't, if anything they were worse, and it was her fault. She was drunk the day she made Slim angry, and she did not understand why she had behaved so stupidly. They were heading for the airport.

'You can leave that,' she said to the chauffeur, pointing to her wheelchair. Fuddled with drink, she had decided she'd had enough of this particular game.

'But you're not right yet, Lana,' Slim had said. 'Best we take it,' he ordered the chauffeur, who folded it up and carried it out. 'You must take things slowly, Lana, make sure the old pegs are given time,' he said kindly.

'Silly old Slim.' She giggled, more from the booze she had downed that morning than from any feelings of happiness. 'See what a wonderful actress I am? I've fooled you for over six weeks. Look, there's nothing wrong with me.' And she leaped to her feet and did a half-dozen high kicks to prove it to him.

'How long have you been able to do that?' he asked coldly.

'Weeks and weeks.'

'Before we were married?'

'Yes, before I left hospital.' She laughed at her own cleverness.

'You bitch!'

'No, I'm not, Slim, I'm not. I love you. Would you have married me if you had known I could walk?'

He did not answer but looked at her with such a bleak expression that she found herself sobering up with the speed of an express train as she realized what she had done.

'I'm sorry, Slim, I really am. I wanted you so badly.'

'Well, you haven't got me, matey, and you never will.' He turned on his heel, marched from the villa and didn't speak to her once on the long flight home.

At first Lana had thrown herself into the management of his house with enthusiasm. If this surprised her – she who had avoided boiling an egg in the past – she knew the reason why. It was something to do, and Slim loved this house. If he saw her taking such good care of it, perhaps he'd begin to look at her in a different light.

She wanted the followers out of the house. This was one of her first resolves. She mentioned them to Slim but he had said they could stay. So it was left to her to manipulate arguments and disagreements and to create such a difficult atmosphere that they left of their own accord. The last to go, since she had been the hardest to alienate, was Sam, Slim's housekeeper for all these years. Lana felt particularly pleased when she left, for she had convinced herself that Sam wasn't just here as an act of charity to an ex-drug addict groupie, but that she had once meant more to Slim and might again in the future.

Toby was allowed to stay since he did not live in the house and in any case was working with Slim on the rock opera which would make Lana a star. Tristan Riviera continued to visit and dine and sleep overnight since he was the one who controlled the career and the money that allowed her to live in such style. And the chauffeur remained, for Lana needed him since she still had not learned to drive.

Lana felt no guilt at the departure of the others. They had had to go. Without them there would only be her, and *then* Slim would be forced to pay her the attention she craved.

She polished and cleaned but he did not notice. She puzzled over cookbooks and toiled for hours to create meals that he would either eat without comment or, worse, say he didn't want at all. She re-employed staff, but of her choosing this time.

She kept herself pretty for Slim and she lost count of the times she had bathed, perfumed herself, and in pretty baby-doll pyjamas had crept into his room and attempted to seduce him. He'd rejected her so many times that finally she could not bear the humiliation any more. She stopped trying and bought herself a vibrator, which helped ease the ache of frustration.

So why, after three years, were they still together? She knew why she stayed and put up with the frustration and longing. She loved him, that had not changed, and she still hoped a day would dawn when he would want her. She was so much in love, despite his coolness, that she knew she could never leave. And in any case, how could she become a star without him? She needed him. She was old for the pop scene now at twenty-four – there were dozens of dolly-birds out there doing what she had once done. She couldn't face going back to the clubs, not now – how foolish it would make her appear with Slim as a husband, and, more than anything, would tell the world that all was not well in their marriage. He would finish his musical – opera – whatever – one day. It would be good, that she knew, for he was meticulous in his work, rejecting more than he kept, which was why it was taking so very long to compose. It would eventually make her a star.

But why did Slim stay with her? Lana had never worked that out. He could leave and divorce her – easy enough these days. But then, of course, maybe it was meanness. If he stayed married to her he wouldn't have to pay out a settlement – which with his fortune would be sizeable. The sad conclusion she had reached was that he did not care if he was married or not, and that was hardest of all.

She watched herself carefully these days. Her drinking was always in secret. The vibrator was often used, she would not make the easy mistake of taking a lover just to relieve her physical frustration. And, despite everything, she was always amicable. She had no intention of giving Slim any grounds for divorce.

The only time they had any communication was over their work. Every few weeks Lana would be summoned to the studio to sing a new song, or to sing an altered one again. At least, she comforted herself, this was one plan which remained firm, despite Slim's feelings for her. But for how long? Patient as she had been, she was beginning to wonder how much longer she could wait. She wanted a career, on her own if necessary. She felt she was not prepared to delay much longer for this star vehicle he was writing for her.

And now this – Kitty married. Maybe now he would look at her in a different light. Maybe?

6

Now to tell Slim that Kitty was married! That morning Lana had dressed quickly and set off with the newspaper to show Slim. But half-way along the corridor to his studio, she had changed her mind. She did not want to appear too obviously curious about his reaction or he might be cross with her, thinking she was gloating. She would have to come up with a subtle plan.

Instead, she retraced her steps and left the newspaper on the hall table. Then she went to the studio.

'How's tricks?' she asked as she entered the room where Slim was sitting at the piano, a synthesizer at one side and Toby at a table beside him.

'A good morning, wouldn't you say, Toby?'

'Right on. We've been working on the lyrics for "When Morning Comes". They're better, more moving.'

'And listen to this.' Slim's fingers ranged over the keys of the piano and Lana heard a haunting melody. She saw the happiness and animation on Slim's face and wished she could make him look like that.

'Slim, darling, that's wonderful. Is it for me?'

'Maybe. We haven't made up our own minds where it's to go – it came to me last night. I know it's called "April's Sadness".'

'There's no one in the opera called April,' Lana said, puzzled.

'It's the month.'

'What's sad about April?'

'Don't know yet but we'll work something out, won't we, Toby?'

'I wish you'd hurry up then. I sometimes think I'll be an old woman before I'm made a star in this one.'

'It's got to be right, Lana. I've a lot riding on this – my whole reputation. And it's got to be a real opera, not a fake, not a musical pretending to be one,' Slim said seriously.

'How do you know when it is?' she said very brightly, smiling broadly to hide the quick surge of jealousy she had felt. She knew only too well why it had to be a *real* opera, she knew who he was hoping to impress. 'Oh, by the way, I got given your *Telegraph* by mistake – I've left it in the hall for you.'

'Thanks,' Slim said, not even bothering to look up from the piano keys.

She never knew if he saw the paper, he never said. By

evening it was not there any more, but one of the staff
might have moved it. She wished now that she had told
him, to gauge his reaction. It would look odd if she
mentioned it now, hours later.

One advantage of Slim's fame was that Lana knew a
couple of journalists well enough to call and ask them for
help in tracking down Kitty. It had not crossed her mind
that this might be easily done, simply by using the telephone directory. She certainly was not so stupid as to trust
all the journalists she knew, but she had liked Weston
Neams on sight, and liked him even more when he had
flirted with her discreetly. And she had often heard Slim
say that if one was straight with Connie Fox she was fair in
return.

Her first choice, Weston, was on an assignment in
Cannes. And so it was Connie she dealt with.

Connie Fox, known as the Vixen of Fleet Street, would
not have been most people's choice of confidante. She was
famous for her bitchy gossip column with its heavy showbiz
slant. Connie had seen and heard it all, and it showed. Her
face was a mask of cynicism beneath the heavy make-up
and double row of false lashes. She was successful, as
witness the heavy gold bracelets she wore and the large
number of equally heavy rings.

'Lana! This is a nice surprise.' Lana heard the husky,
chain-smoker's voice, aware of its sharp interest at mention
of her name.

'It's ages since we saw you, Connie. Too long,' Lana said
in a voice of pure saccharine, but first Cy and then Slim
had taught her the importance of being sweet to journalists.

'You two are such recluses – you never party these days.
I suppose the world will have to wait until that Slim of yours
finishes his rock opera. Any sign of that, Lana darling?'

'You know what a perfectionist Slim is. I tell him I'll be
drawing my old age pension before I get to sing the *starring*
role.'

'You should be working, Lana. Building a public.'

'Oh, I couldn't, Connie. Slim needs me by his side, we work together you see – he seeks my advice on everything,' she lied effortlessly. It was something she often said, to the point where she almost believed it herself.

'As it should be, of course. No doubt the reason you're so happy together.'

Lana wasn't sure how to answer that one. It wasn't really a question, nor was it said kindly, she was sure she had heard a modicum of sarcasm there. So, not knowing how to answer, she felt it safer to say nothing.

'You are happy, aren't you?' Now that was a question pure and simple, fired at her like grapeshot.

'Delirious.'

'When are you going to produce, Lana?'

'I told you, I can't work . . .'

'Babies, I meant, Lana. Think how the readers would like news of a Slim junior.'

'Oh, plenty of time for that.' Lana laughed gaily to cover the hurt that there could never be a baby, at least not Slim's. 'Actually I need some help,' she said, wanting to stop this line of interrogation before she became totally bogged down – she could see now why Slim never spoke to any journalist without Tristan in tow.

'Anything,' Connie said expansively.

'It's my sister. I'm trying to find her. She's just got married and I'd like to get in touch but I don't know how.'

'Hang on, Lana. Where's my pad? Let me make a note. Do you know her married name?'

'He's a financier, somebody Marshall I think . . . or was it Masters or Mortimer?' Lana giggled. 'Silly me. I forgot to write it down. Her name's Kitty, if it's any help.'

'Felix Masters, was that the name?'

'Why, yes! How clever of you, Connie.'

'It's my job to read the papers,' she said smoothly. This was exciting news, Felix Masters was one of those mystery men of the City – rich, ruthless and remote. Patron of the arts, though invariably anonymously, and he had never been known to give an interview. The *Telegraph* had been lucky to get the photograph when no one else had. They obviously had a sharp-eyed contact on the local paper in the back of beyond where the wedding had taken place, to recognize the name – hardly a household one – posted in the Register Office. Interesting, too, that his bride was an opera singer – unknown, but not for long. If Felix Masters had taken the trouble to marry her she must be good, for he was only interested in the best. And now, an even better slant and the one which would make a good story for Connie – this Kitty, budding diva, was related to Slim, one of the greatest rock stars of them all. Most interesting.

'So you lost touch with your sister? And even your mother didn't know she was getting married? And now you would like to find her and have a reconciliation?'

'Well, yes, if possible,' Lana replied innocently, in one answer giving Connie access to all that information.

'Did you row?'

'No . . . I . . . I'd rather not . . .'

'Families!' Connie said with feeling. 'Mine's just the same. I've two sisters and we seem to have drifted apart – silly. Life's too short.'

'It is, isn't it?'

'And one of them, I pinched her boyfriend. I guess we'll never be friends now.'

'Oh, don't say that, Connie,' Lana said urgently.

Connie smiled into the telephone.

'Look, Lana darling. Obviously there's a story here. If I find your sister for you can I have an exclusive?'

'Of course, Connie – not that there's any story to tell. As you say, families drift.'

'Leave it with me, Lana. I'll get back to you.'

Within three minutes, simply by pulling the relevant directory towards her, Connie had dialled Felix Masters' house – he was not ex-directory, no need to be – and the housekeeper had told her he was returning from his honeymoon in two weeks. No, she could not say where they were, for the simple reason that Mr Masters had told no one where he was going.

Connie didn't call Lana back for two days. She didn't want her to know how easy it had been. Lana was gushingly grateful as she took down Felix's address and telephone number, told Connie she was a genius, and promised to let her have the whole story – not that there was one. But Connie knew better – there always was.

Lana, though impatient with curiosity, waited a full three weeks after their return from their honeymoon before telephoning.

'Felix Masters,' a deep voice answered. Lana hated people who answered calls like that, it always made them sound rude and arrogant, she thought.

'Lana Fletcher,' she said shortly, not to be outdone.

'Yes?' he asked, equally shortly. Obviously her name meant nothing to him.

'I'm Kitty's sister.'

There was a silence as Felix assimilated this information. Strange, he thought, now why hadn't Kitty told him she had a sister?

'Are you still there?'

'I am. I'm afraid Kitty's not available at the moment. If you would like to leave me your number I'll get her to call you back should she so wish.'

Stuck-up fart, thought Lana as she recited her number, and then had to force herself to wait for Kitty's return call.

The warm welcome that Kitty received from Cellini made her feel angry with herself that she had stayed away so long. How could she have doubted the older woman's sincerity? How wrong she had been, she thought, as she watched Cellini burst into tears.

'I thought we had lost you. I thought some wretched man had got you and you had given up,' Cellini said, noisily blowing her nose.

'He has.'

'Ah, but Felix is different. He is a jewel. He understands opera and the sacrifices needed better even than you do. He is a match made in heaven for you. And what is more, he will never let you give up – never,' she said dramatically.

'I want children one day, I've decided.'

'One day is a long way away. What are you, now, twenty-six? A good ten years of singing before risking so much for a brat.'

'I thought all Italians loved children.' Kitty laughed.

'Not all Italians are divas,' Cellini said, drawing herself up proudly to her full height. 'But I *am* Italian. I love children – other people's. I never wanted any, nor will I like yours, *if* you have them too soon. Now tell me why you disappeared.'

'I didn't really. You can't have tried too hard to find me – I was still in the opera world.'

'You call that flea-pit the opera world? My dear child, you had gone to the moon in professional terms. I couldn't believe it when Marcheso told me you were there. Thank God for Felix charging off like a medieval knight to rescue you.'

'He was going on holiday. He often goes to Italy at this time of year,' Kitty said pragmatically.

'Bah! Don't spoil it. My version is better.' Cellini laughed and then looked serious. 'Tell me, my child, what was wrong? We must discuss it so that it can never recur.'

'I thought I'd lost the quality in my voice. It lacked *cantabile*. I felt empty, my voice did too.'

'And why?'

'I'm not sure. I think it happened because I was low. When I'm afraid, when I don't have anyone to tell me that it's all right, that I will be fine, that the voice is just having an off-day – that's when it happens. I can't be alone, you see. I need constant reassurance or else I can't sing.'

'And calmness . . . you, my dear, must reserve your passion for the stage and not for your life. Are you happy with Felix?'

'Very much so.'

'Do you love him?' Cellini shot the question at her, and Kitty felt herself blush. She looked about the room as if searching for an escape route.

'It's quite a simple question,' Cellini persisted.

'I like him enormously. But love? No, not as I've understood love to be,' Kitty finally answered.

'Thanks be!' Cellini clasped her hands in mock prayer. 'Now, shall we sing, shall we see what damage the dramas of these past two years have wrought?'

Felix was waiting anxiously for Kitty's return from her lesson with Cellini. He felt that all would be well – hadn't he heard the quality of Kitty's voice return, the warmth, the dramatic tone, that indefinable something she had that others didn't and which always reminded him of liquid gold? But there was that lingering fear that those years of neglect – for that was what her time in Italy and at the opera house amounted to – had left her damaged in some way that he, the gifted amateur, could not hear but which Cellini with her perfect ear would swoop upon. And he felt he knew Kitty well enough now to know that if Cellini of all people said her voice was nothing, then something inside her would die and her voice would change irreparably.

He could tell from the way she walked up the short drive through the November gloom that it had gone well. He heard her key in the door and when she entered the drawing-room he was already pouring the champagne.

'How did you know?' She smiled at him.

'You have a happy walk.' He kissed the tip of her nose as he handed her a glass. 'To The Voice,' he toasted, and she too raised her glass. For the toast was not to her but to that other being who lived within her.

'So, what is Cellini's verdict?'

'A year of intense study. I need practice and then more and more – I know that. We never had time, you see – there were always so many other jobs to do. And the heat made me lazy. I'm forcing the upper register, I know that – panic, I suppose. But the rest is fine. I think, and so does she, that my problems were mainly psychological. I need supporting, Felix. So much. I fear I may bore you with my insecurities.'

'You need someone to care for you. And that you will never be without, I promise you. I've made many decisions in the past few weeks, I was waiting for Cellini's verdict to put them into practice. I am retiring in six months' time.'

'From business?'

'Yes. From all my directorships. It doesn't seem to matter any more.'

'But won't you be bored with nothing to do?'

'I shall have plenty to do. I'm going to become your manager – I don't trust anyone else. When you are performing you will never be alone again. I shall travel the world with you.'

'But Felix . . . What if I . . .'

'Don't even say it.' He held up his hand to silence her and smiled kindly at her. 'You will succeed. I know it, I've always known it.'

'But what if I can't make enough money for the two of us? Look at your lifestyle.' Her face was creased with an anxious frown.

'I have money enough for two lifetimes together. I shall still keep my portfolio of shares and I shall invest. All I shall need is my briefcase and a telephone, it matters little where I am in the world.'

'I'm so lucky to have found you, Felix.'

'No, no. It is I who am the lucky one.' He lifted her hand and kissed the air a centimetre above it. 'To help you – that will be a privilege.'

Kitty brushed a tear away from her cheek and looked at her handsome husband with grateful affection. She was truly fortunate, but she felt a small shiver of guilt . . . if only she could love him. Maybe she would one day, maybe it was possible to grow to love someone.

'Shall we dine out tonight?' he asked.

'That would be lovely. Then I must bath and change.' She walked towards the door, and her hand was on it when he said, 'My dear, I quite forgot. You never told me you had a sister.'

'Lana? Oh, I'm sure I did.' She swung round to face him.

'No. I would remember – I remember everything you say to me.'

'I haven't seen or heard from her in four years. We had an argument.'

'What about?'

'Do you know, I can't even remember. You know what sisters are like.' She lied again.

'No, I'm afraid I don't. It must have been a very big argument to lead to such a long break.'

'We were never close, we've nothing in common. She's – or, rather, she was – a pop singer.'

'Was she famous?'

'Not really. She had begun to be noticed, and then . . .'

'And then what?'

'She was in a bad car crash. She was paralysed and lost the use of her voice.'

'How tragic. And you didn't rush to her side?'

'Yes, I did. I was not welcome.'

'Why not?'

'Felix, really, I'd rather not talk about it. It was painful – let's leave it at that.'

'I would like to know,' he persisted.

'And I don't want to tell,' she said coldly. She opened the door. Perhaps she had better explain a little more and then hopefully he would drop the subject. 'She's fine now, I gather, and very happily married to another pop star, Slim Fletcher – he's world-famous. But his name would mean nothing to you, would it?' She tried to smile but found it difficult, that must have been the first time she had spoken Slim's name in years and it had been hard to say without emotion.

'How very strange,' Felix said, as if to himself. 'Well, anyhow,' he said more loudly, 'I can ask her myself. She called today. She left her number. She wants to see you. It would be churlish not to respond, surely?'

Kitty turned away from him to face the hall, her mind racing. How could she ever explain that it was not her sister she did not wish to see, it was Slim? It was one thing to force herself to forget him when separated from him by miles. She did not know how she would react if she found herself in a room with him again.

'You wouldn't like them, I'm sure,' she said emphatically.

'But they are your family. I should like to meet them. If you won't call and fix up an appointment, I will.'

'Where's the number?' she said wearily, and held her hand out for it.

When she had left the room Felix sat for some time deep in thought. His wife's reaction had been, as he said, strange. She was too emphatic that he would not like her family, her answers to his questions were too controlled. He picked up the telephone and called his secretary.

'Betty, call our cuttings service and ask them to find me anything on a Slim Fletcher and his wife, Lana.'

The following Sunday the two sisters were nervous for very similar reasons and over the same man – Slim.

Lana had chosen Sunday for Kitty and her husband to visit since that was the one day Slim did not work. Instead, he had nearly every newspaper delivered and spent the whole day wading through them, an occupation which drove Lana almost to screaming-pitch with boredom. She had invited them to Sunday lunch *en famille*, like old times. The idea amused her. And she did not tell Slim anyone was coming, for then he might have locked himself away, declaring he did not wish to see anyone. She simply said she had asked the cook to make roast beef and Yorkshire pudding followed by lemon meringue pie – his favourite meal of all, and one she was almost sure he would not miss.

She knew she could get away with the surprise, as she had begun to think of it, since Slim would be in his den at the back of the house. Kitty would arrive at the front and thus he would never hear their arrival.

'Your brother-in-law is obviously highly successful,' Felix said, as they rounded the bend in the drive and he saw Slim's magnificent house for the first time.

'It is beautiful, isn't it? He loves it, almost as if it were a person.'

'So you know Slim?'

'Oh, yes. Not very well,' she said, and felt the palms of her hands moisten. Why on earth she hadn't told him the whole truth at the beginning she did not know. She wished she had, maybe then he wouldn't have been so insistent about coming here. She was a fool. She had told him about Henri and Martin and he hadn't minded hearing of those loves. Quite the opposite, he had wanted to know everything, even what sort of lovers they had been. She often resented his curiosity, not aware that Felix asked because he feared any secrets.

'It's all in the past,' he had reassured her. 'Nothing to do with me.'

So what was different about Slim? Why could she not bring herself to be as open about this love affair? She looked out of the car window, preferring not to analyse the answer to that question too deeply. And while Lana had been pleasant enough to her on the telephone, she wondered how much her sister knew about her and Slim, and whether she did not have an ulterior motive for this reunion. 'I should think these rhododendrons must be a picture in spring, don't you?' she said to distract herself.

Lana had been watching for them and was already on the front steps as the large Mercedes ground to a halt.

'Is that your sister? How pretty she looks,' Felix said as he switched off the engine.

Kitty looked up at Lana – she certainly looked better than the last time she had seen her but she wasn't as pretty as she once had been. There was a puffiness to her face and a tiredness in her eyes that had not been there before, and Kitty thought her far too old for the clothes she wore.

Lana jumped down the short flight of steps one at a time, her long white skirt over white stockings and shoes swirling as she did so to show the mass of frilled petticoats beneath. Her blonde hair, held in place by a band of white silk daisies, lifted each time she jumped.

'Kitty, oh, darling Kitty, I can't believe you're here.' Lana swooped on Kitty as soon as she was out of the car, and to her intense surprise hugged her tight. 'Oh, I'm so happy. And this handsome man is Felix?'

Felix held out his hand in greeting.

'Oh, boo to that, you're my brother-in-law, aren't you?' And to Felix's surprise Lana kissed him too and then, linking arms with both of them, led them up the steps and into the house. 'Slim will be so excited when he knows you're here,' she said, making sure she sounded blithe.

'He doesn't *know* we're coming?' Kitty stopped walking.

'No, it's to be a lovely surprise for him,' Lana said as she opened the door to the long, beamed drawing-room, the most beautiful room in the house. She poured them drinks, all the while chattering to them of nothing of any consequence, and Kitty sat on the edge of the sofa and wished she was anywhere else but there.

Felix nursed his sherry and reflected. If these two had had a row then it was a minor one – Lana's welcome had been warm after such a long absence from each other's lives. And Lana had such an air of innocence to her – quite charming – that he was sure she was not playing a charade.

'How's Mother?' Kitty asked, to stop the flow of chatter about roses and chintz and chandelier-cleaning with which Lana had been regaling them.

'She's fine. Got a bloke – used-car dealer,' she said airily, and Felix shuddered inwardly at the very thought. 'She says you're not to expect a present from her.' Lana laughed, and Felix looked up to see Kitty's reaction.

'She's the last person I'd expect one from.' He saw Kitty was smiling – another mystery here, then, he thought. It would seem there were many things his bride had not told him. 'So she knows I'm married?'

'Yes, I told her.'

'She's managing all right?'

'Why, yes. Slim's an angel to her. You don't have to worry about Mum and money, Kitty.'

'I don't,' Kitty said sharply, and Felix found himself feeling relieved he wasn't going to be called upon to help support the woman too.

'Do I gather you've had a slight disagreement with your mother, Kitty?' Felix asked blandly.

'Hasn't she told you? Mum can't stand Kitty. Never could, could she?'

'No,' Kitty said and looked away, but not before Felix had noticed the pain in her eyes.

'What a strange woman,' he said loyally. 'Who could not love Kitty?'

'Ah!' said Lana, and Felix thought how sweet she was. But Kitty looked at her with suspicion; was she being sarcastic?

A young girl in a flower-printed smock appeared to tell Lana that lunch would be ready in ten minutes. Lana picked up one of two phones on a side-table and punched in a single number. 'Slim, my darling. Your lunch is ready,' she cooed. 'He'll be here like a long dog – he loves his Sunday roast.' She beamed at the other two and spoke as if she was imparting a great secret.

Kitty felt the room was about to fall in on her. She closed her eyes to stop the feeling but it would not go away, so she took a large swig of her gin and tonic instead and felt the alcohol rushing through her system.

The door opened and Felix saw a tall, slim man dressed entirely in black, with a mass of black curly hair cascading to his shoulders. He had eyes as dark as molasses and a fine, sculpted face. Felix saw his expression and suddenly felt very threatened and jealous.

'Kitty!' Slim said, his voice rising with pleasure, and rushed across the room towards her. Then he stopped dead in his tracks as he saw the distinguished man sitting to one side of her. 'Kitty,' he said more softly.

'Surprise! Surprise!' Lana was clapping her hands with excitement.

'How are you, Slim?' Kitty said, forcing herself to sound normal while her heart was leaping all ways.

'This is Kitty's husband, Felix,' Lana said quickly.

'I didn't know.' Slim did not even look at Felix but was staring at Kitty.

'It was very sudden – no one knew,' Kitty said, feeling flustered.

'I'd like to have known,' Slim said softly.

'I'm sorry,' Kitty replied.

And Felix knew in that instant. Knew that Kitty had loved this man who had married her sister and found himself afraid to think too far into what it could all mean. It must mean something, for why had Kitty not chosen to tell him?

7

On the journey home Felix said how good he thought the meal had been, how excellent the wine, how lovely the home, but not a word about Slim. Kitty did not know how to interpret this. Did it mean Felix had not liked him? But then he hadn't mentioned Lana either and he certainly liked her, sickeningly so. Did it mean he had guessed about herself and Slim? But how? She was sure they had not given anything away. They had behaved with circumspection, she was positive. Perhaps Slim's reaction to seeing her had let the cat out of the bag. But then, what was more normal than for an old friend to welcome her warmly, to be hurt she had not told him of her marriage? They had not even touched, she had made sure of that, and what agony that had been when she had wanted to hurl herself into his arms.

She had forgotten him, expunged him, she had told herself. Ha! All the old feelings had resurged, she loved him still, and what was she to do? She was married now; even though she did not love Felix as she wanted to love him, she liked and respected him. She could never hurt him. Slim was married too, and she had seen how affectionate Lana was with him. She was going to have to forget

Slim all over again. Maybe she would even confess the past to Felix to ensure she did not have to endure another lunch like today.

'You're quiet, what are you thinking?' Felix asked as they approached the outskirts of London.

'Cellini asked me what roles I would like to prepare this year. I was wondering about Lucia,' she said hurriedly.

'Not yet. I wouldn't have thought it was time for that particular role.'

'Why? Don't you think I could sing it?'

'No, I didn't say that,' he answered patiently. 'But . . .' he lapsed into silence.

'But what?'

'It's so taxing, so dramatic a role that perhaps it would be better to delay until you have more confidence in your ability. Of course you said Mimi?'

'I already know Mimi,' she snapped.

'To Cellini's exacting standards?' he laughed, but she did not respond. Instead she turned away and looked out at the passing streets of suburban houses; she was breathing deeply, controlling herself.

'Felix, there's just one thing I'd like to say.'

'Yes?'

'I'm happy for you to be my manager but I must point out – *I* decide what I sing.'

'Of course, but would it not be wise to listen to the opinion of those who care for you?' he said in a stilted tone.

'At the end of the day it's my voice, my reputation at stake.'

'Quite.' He glanced at her and saw an irritated expression he had never seen before. He wondered if this little spat was her way of dealing with seeing this Slim chap – the meeting had upset her, he was sure of that. 'Amazing how someone who writes his type of music can live in such style. I wonder what he earns,' he said, deciding to test the water.

'Are you referring to Slim?'

'Who else do I know who moves in such exotic worlds?'

'You needn't sound so pompous.'

'I wasn't aware I did – I'm sorry, I didn't mean to. I was curious.'

'He earns more than you ever will,' she said sharply.

'And you know how much I earn then, do you?' There was laughter in his voice which made her irritation even more intense.

'In fact Slim is a wonderful musician, he sings well too. He was classically trained, if you must know.'

'I see,' Felix said. He had been right, she was angry with him because of Slim. The newspaper cuttings which he had read on Friday had told him nothing of the two of them together, only of Slim's mega-success – but now he knew. He drove on in silence.

Kitty sat beside him, glad he wasn't speaking but, at the same time, wishing he had continued talking about Slim, and so allowed them to have a full-scale row about him. Then she could have told him everything and got it off her chest. She felt guilty now, illogically so, she told herself, since all this had happened long ago. But was it so irrational, this guilt? She could not get away from the recurring question. Why? Why had she chosen not to tell him about her love for Slim?

'What did you think of him, then?' Lana asked Slim, who lowered the *Observer* to stare at her long and hard. 'What are you looking at me like that for?'

'You did that on purpose, didn't you?'

'What?' Lana widened her innocent blue eyes.

'You know damn well what. Invited them here without telling me.'

'I did it that way because you always hide yourself away if anybody I like comes here. I know very well if I'd said

Kitty's back in England, she's coming to lunch, you'd have run for the hills.' She bent down to pick up one of the colour supplements off the floor where Slim had thrown them, and idly leafed through it.

'Then you'd have been wrong. I was pleased to see her, I wish I'd had a bit of warning, that's all.'

'Surprise she was married, wasn't it?'

'To me, but evidently not to you.' He returned to his newspaper.

'What does that mean?'

He ignored her. She rattled the back of his newspaper.

'Speak to me, even if it's only "goodbye",' she said tartly.

Slim once again stared at her. 'You knew all along. You wanted to rattle me, that's all.'

'Why should I want to do a thing like that?'

'God knows.' His laugh was ruthless.

'Well, it's done now, isn't it? Her married off and to such a nice man – I really liked him, didn't you?'

'He's OK,' Slim said, while wondering how Kitty could have given herself to such a cold fish.

'He's a bit old though, isn't he?'

'Maybe she's looking for a father figure.'

'Could be. She always preferred Dad to Mum.'

'Sensible of her.'

'What's my mum ever done to you?'

'Tricked me into marrying you, for a start.'

'She never did.'

'Didn't she? Odd that you had turned my honourable offer down and after a session with your mum, you accepted. And whose idea was it not to let me know you could walk? Why, dear Amy's, of course.'

'Tristan knew.'

'And presumed I knew. She tricked him too.'

'What a clever mum I've got,' she said airily. 'I did you a favour today, getting Kitty here, I laid her ghost for you,' she said, brimming with confidence, for she had watched them like a hawk and, apart from Slim's initial reaction – and that she could put down to surprise – she had seen nothing going on between them.

'Thanks a bunch,' he said, with an irony which was completely lost on her.

She balanced herself on the arm of his chair and ruffled his hair.

'Don't do that.' He shook his head in irritation at the gesture.

'I love your hair, let me touch it, please,' she wheedled, pressing up against him.

'You drunk already?'

'No!'

'Well, there's a surprise.'

'Why are you always such a shit to me?' She leaped to her feet.

'Because I don't like you.' He looked at her coldly.

'Don't say that.' She raised her hands as though to push his words away from her. 'Why hurt me all the time? I love you so much.'

'I can't imagine why.'

'Then if you loathe me so, why do you stay with me?'

'My accountant advises it.' He picked up the newspaper again.

'No, you don't.' She tore it from his hands and threw it across the room. 'You're going to talk to me – you never do. I could leave you, sue you for divorce.'

'Why don't you, then?'

'You know why. Because I love you, because I don't think I could live without you.'

'Oh, shit!' He stood up, collected his paper together and walked across to the door.

'Where are you going?' she shouted.

'To get some peace,' he replied.

'Don't leave me, Slim. I'm so lonely. I'm so unhappy. I

want you to make love to me. I want your baby,' she wailed desperately.

'Why don't you go out and find someone to impregnate you? *I've* no intention of screwing you.'

'God, you're a bastard! A stinking bastard! I hate you!' she screamed. 'It's not me, is it? You can't, that's why you never touch me. You're a raving poofter, that's what you are,' she sobbed.

'You reckon?' He laughed. 'Do me a favour, Lana, cut the histrionics.'

Lana picked up a small statuette and hurled it at him, missing by an inch.

'Thanks.' He bowed and opened the door. Lana hurled herself on to the sofa and cried uncontrollably.

Work was the solution to this problem, Kitty told herself, and when she found it difficult to concentrate, lectured herself more severely.

She had her own studio. It was her wedding present from Felix and had been the surprise he had hinted at on their honeymoon. How the work had been done in the short time they were away was a miracle, but two rooms at the back of Felix's large Hampstead house had been knocked into one. One end was decorated as a sitting-room with a chaise longue and bookcases which he had filled with books on opera, biographies of singers and scores by the dozen. The rest of the books were on other subjects Felix thought Kitty might enjoy. A painting of Nellie Melba hung over the fireplace. To one side was the latest in hi-fi equipment and a wonderful collection of records. He had purchased a beautiful Queen Anne bureau for her to write at, and covering the oak block floor was an exquisite Aubusson carpet. The other end of the room had french windows which opened on to a balcony. In front of them was a grand piano and beside it a rosewood music-stand

which, he proudly told Kitty, he had designed himself. The
height was perfect for her, it had a small reading lamp,
which illuminated the slanting top, and beneath it were
shelves for scores. It was so practical and so well thought
out that in a way it was more precious than the piano. Both
rooms were decorated in yellow – the walls palest yellow,
the curtains and upholstery a richer tone which exactly
matched the yellow in the patterned carpet.

'Felix, what a wonderful room. How can I thank you?'

'Yellow, you see – the colour of inspiration.'

'You think of everything. It was my lucky day for sure
when you asked me to be your wife.' She had laughed as
she spoke. And she had meant it. Yet now, just a few
weeks later, she was pacing this room which had given her
so much pleasure, berating herself for her inability to
concentrate.

There was a knock at the door and Felix popped his head
round it – he always knocked, so punctilious were his
manners.

'My sweet, I'm going to the City. I should be back by
six. Is there anything you need?' he asked.

'No, nothing.'

'You need plants and flowers in here – why didn't I
think of that?'

'It's perfect.'

'No, it's not. Leave it to me. I shall see to it.'

When he had gone Kitty sat on her piano stool and her
fingers played idly across the keys. And then her posture
slumped. Felix was perfect. So kind, so considerate, so
caring. She must make herself love him, make herself want
him.

And then a scrap of last night's wonderful dream, in
which she and Slim were making love, treacherously inched
into her mind. She had woken still happy until she realized
it was only a dream, and then she had turned her head into
the pillow and wept.

She was grateful then that she and Felix had separate rooms. At first when he had insisted she had felt strange about it, hurt in a silly way.

'My dear sweet one, I'm too old to change the habits of a lifetime. It would drive me to distraction to share a room, and my neatness and tidiness would soon drive you the same way. This is better,' he had explained, the first night they had returned home.

After her initial reaction, she had decided it wasn't so bad. It was rather exciting sitting in bed wondering if this was to be one of the nights he visited her. It made it seem illicit in a way, romantic when there was no romance.

She looked forward to those nights. She might not be in love but she had learned that that was no stumbling-block to enjoying being made love to. Felix was a considerate lover, if sometimes a bit too gentle. He made love to her as if he was afraid of damaging her, as if she was a piece of delicate china – she longed for a little more passion, a little more roughness on his part. And, if she was honest, for it to happen a little more often.

The sound of the telephone ringing made her jump. She crossed to the sitting-room end of her studio to answer it.

'Kitty, I've got to see you.'

Her heart lurched at the sound of his voice.

'Slim, I can't.'

'You must, Kitty. I'm going bonkers knowing you're back. Please, we've got to talk.'

'There's nothing to say.'

'There is. You know there is. You're suffering too, aren't you? I know you are. I saw your eyes the other day.'

'Please, Slim . . .'

'I've tried not to call, Kitty. It's a month since I've seen you. I've fought with myself every day since then.'

'But . . . Felix . . .'

'He's out. I know he's out. I've been sitting in my car since early this morning waiting for him to go.'

'Not here,' she heard herself say. 'No, I can't,' she added quickly.

'You remember that flat I wanted you to have? There, in half an hour.' And before she could argue further the line went dead.

Of course she wouldn't go, she couldn't go. There was absolutely nothing to discuss with him. She was still having the same argument with herself as she changed into jeans and a sweater and she continued it in the taxi she hailed five minutes later.

'I knew you'd come,' Slim said, holding the door of the flat wide open for her.

'I shouldn't be here . . .'

'But you couldn't help yourself, I know.'

She followed him along the corridor and into the sitting-room, which had not changed in a single detail from when she had last stood here four years ago and he had proposed to her. The clock she thought had stopped still stood ticking on the mantelshelf.

'Drink? Coffee? Tea?'

'No, thanks,' she said, relieved that he had made no move towards her, or attempt to touch her. 'Flat's still the same.' She glanced about her.

'Still unused.' He shrugged.

'It's wicked really, being empty . . .'

'Suppose so. Are you going to sit down?'

She purposely sat on an armchair rather than the long sofa.

'You don't have to worry, Kitty. I won't do anything you don't want me to. I honestly asked you here to talk.'

'Yes?' She looked at him inquiringly.

'Why him? Why Felix and not me?'

'I was older, it was the right time. It seemed the right thing to do. I was lonely.'

'Is he into music? I mean, is that his job?'

'No, he's a businessman, actually. But his passion is

opera. He plans to manage me – I'd like that. If and when I'm on tour' – her laugh was almost inaudible as she leaned over to touch a wooden coffee table – 'I won't be alone, you see.'

'Sounds more like a companion than a husband.'

She looked down at her hands.

'Do you love him?'

'Of course,' she said, without looking at him.

'I don't believe you.'

'Well, it's true.'

They sat in silence for a moment, she wondering what he wanted to talk about and he trying to think of something to say.

'I was surprised when I saw in the papers that you had married Lana.'

'Then you knew?'

'Oh, yes. When I was in Paris.'

'Were you upset?'

'No, why should I have been?'

'I wondered. I don't love her, you know.'

'Then why did you marry her?'

'I thought that she was paralysed because of me. I felt responsible for her.'

'How noble of you.'

'Don't be bitter, Kitty.'

'Me? Bitter? Don't be silly. We were finished, I was living with someone else at the time – blissfully happy too.'

'Felix?'

'No . . . someone else . . .'

'Who?'

'It doesn't matter who, does it? Not now.'

'I'm glad you were happy. I haven't been. I've not forgotten you, Kitty. There's never been a day when I don't think of you and what might have been.'

'There was never any "what might have been", Slim. It could never be, I explained to you at the time.'

'This other bloke, did you ditch him too?'

'Yes.'

'For the same reason?'

'Yes. He couldn't understand that I couldn't have children. That my career came before kids, before anything.'

'Well, I must say that makes me feel a bit better.' He laughed. 'So there's two poor sods in the world who lost you to a bit of warbling.'

She laughed too at his choice of words.

'And how's it going?'

'Disastrously for a while. But I'm on the right tracks again, I'm back with my old teacher and Felix is a tower of strength – I know I shall always be grateful to him.'

'Gratitude isn't much to build a marriage on.'

She looked intently at the palms of her hands.

'How's the pop opera?'

'Rock opera, if you don't mind. It comes, very slowly. I'd like you to hear it.'

'I'd like to very much.' She smiled at him.

'That's better. I've remembered your smile.' He stood up and crossed to a large tape-deck and flicked a switch, keeping his finger on it. 'You will say if you don't like it, won't you?'

'Of course.'

He let the switch go and music began to pour out of the great speakers on either side of the farthest wall. For so many years' work there was little to hear, but what there was surprised her. She had known it would be good, but not this good – it was a masterly mix of traditional rock and avant-garde electronic-sounding music, laced with a couple of beautiful ballads.

'That was wonderful, Slim. Truly. Is that all there is?'

'No. I've masses more at home – this is the stuff both Toby and I think is spot-on.'

'When will it be finished?'

'In six months, I hope.'

'It's an amazing achievement. It's so different to any-thing else I've heard – all those styles. And Lana will be the star – that's nice.'

'If she's still speaking to me.'

'Oh, Slim.'

'Don't worry, it doesn't bother me, in fact I prefer it when she isn't. Look, Kitty, there's nothing there. We've never even slept together. I married her because I felt sorry for her.'

'Poor Lana.'

'Poor Lana, my arse. She's done well out of the arrange-ment – she has everything she wants.'

'Except you.'

Slim shrugged his shoulders.

'I should be going.' Kitty stood up and bent down to pick up her handbag. When she straightened up again it was to find Slim standing close to her, dangerously close. 'Slim, I –'

She did not finish the sentence for he had taken her in his arms and his mouth was on hers, his tongue searching hers, his hands caressing her as if to make sure he was really holding her. She leaned her body into his. She closed her eyes and allowed herself to enjoy the sensations speed-ing through her. Then she pushed him away.

'I can't, Slim. Don't make me, please.'

'I'm sorry. I had to.' His eyes were full of longing for her.

'I'm going.'

'I'll see you again?'

'I don't know. Perhaps. No.'

She ran from the room, but even as she raced down the stairs she knew she would be back. Knew she would know no peace until they were one again.

*

When Felix said he would be home at six, he was. Even as the clock was chiming she heard his key in the door.

'My dear.' He kissed her cheek. 'Had a good day?'

'Yes. I think I'm getting to grips with Lucia,' she said, a little defiantly.

'Good. Cellini will be pleased,' was his single uncritical response.

'I hope so.'

He poured them both a drink.

'I've a little surprise for you,' he said as he handed her the glass. 'My day has been intensely boring. Now I know my future is with you and your glorious career I don't find my work interesting. I've suggested to Cellini that we go to France for a couple of months in the New Year – just the three of us. We can make a little tour, if you like, before your lessons begin in earnest.'

'What about her other pupils? She can't let them down.'

'Didn't I tell you? I've arranged with her that she has only one pupil – you.'

'Cellini?'

'The one and only.' He smiled at her.

'Felix, you're too generous to me.'

'So you haven't said, do you like my little plan?'

'It sounds marvellous,' she answered, but her mind was reeling with disappointment that she wouldn't be able to see Slim for so long.

8

There was so much that Kitty did not know about her husband. When he went to work in the City she did not know where he went or where his office was. She had asked once and had requested to have his office telephone number 'in case'.

'In case of what?'

'Should I need to get hold of you in the day.'

'But you won't need to, will you?'

'I might.'

'Very doubtful. You have your routine and I have mine.'

Since he evidently did not want her to know, she never asked again, but it did not stop her wondering why.

There were evenings when he would go out and not tell her where he was going or with whom. Had she loved him, she supposed such behaviour would have driven her wild with jealousy. Instead she found that she quite enjoyed these evenings alone. Their life together was formal – they changed for dinner even when it was just the two of them, he was considerate and obviously felt it was his duty to talk to her, entertain her. So it was pleasant to have evenings to herself when she could curl up with a book – not necessarily the sort of book he would approve of her reading – or watch television – something he thought a waste of time – or she simply did nothing, which Felix could never do. If he needed to entertain in relation to his business then he did it outside the home and without her. The only entertaining they had enjoyed in the three months since their marriage were a couple of dinner-parties, and their guests never varied – Ben and Frieda Cooper, Max Leitman and Cellini.

She began to think that Felix preferred to live his life in separate boxes and that the inhabitants of each box never overlapped, never met. It was a strange way to live and one that puzzled her. But it amused her to think she resided in the musical box.

She had become used to the thought of the planned trip to France and now found she welcomed it. It would take her away from close proximity to Slim, and the temptation to see him, and the fear of what that would lead to. She never thought it *might* lead to her sleeping with him, she just knew it would. She was sure that in another country she could forget him again, as she had once before when a student in Paris, although this thought did make her have a flash of worry, wondering if being in France might raise the ghost of Henri too. But she also wanted to go because she felt she needed a break from the iron routine her life had become – study, practice and then more – every hour of the day. Of course Cellini would be with them and she would still be working, but surely Cellini would also appreciate a bit of a holiday?

Felix enjoyed the fine things in life so much that it was natural for Kitty to expect the house in which they would stay to be an elegant villa in the south of France – if not on the Côte d'Azur, at least in the hills behind. Instead, after a journey of a month's duration, stopping and seeing virtually tourist-free sights, they travelled to the Auvergne, the wildly beautiful, unspoilt, almost secret centre of that great country.

The car pulled up in front of a long traditional farm-house. It was built of stone, some of it the black volcanic stone of the region. The shutters were green and in need of painting. The creeper covering the house had died back for the winter, yet with snow still on the ground, small green shoots were already appearing. The house was high on a *col* on the southern slopes of the Massif mountains, overlooking a valley of lush vegetation. Far below them flowed the Loire river, as yet small compared to the mighty waterway it would become, the late winter sun glinting on its surface making it look like a thread of mercury sliding through the lush water-meadows.

A short, plump woman with a pleasant, open face bustled out to greet them. She welcomed Felix warmly and he introduced her as Annette. Kitty's French was good but she had difficulty understanding the thick Auvergnat accent, although Felix appeared to have no problem.

A log fire was blazing in a large fireplace. Comfortable chintz-covered sofas, highly polished oak furniture, a profusion of potted plants, books and paintings furnished the huge beamed sitting-room.

'Such a lovely room,' Cellini said, sinking gratefully into the comfort of one of the sofas. 'If we had had to travel another mile I would have succumbed to exhaustion.' Her eyes lit up as the Frenchwoman appeared with a tray of coffee, liqueurs and a cherry cake.

'This is a traditional concoction,' Felix informed them.

'Whose house is it?' Kitty asked as she explored the cases of books, surprised to see so many in English.

'Why, mine, of course.'

'But . . .' she began, and then preferred not to continue, not to ask why he had never told her, not in front of Cellini – it made her feel foolish, not knowing.

'It belonged to my mother's family – she was French – and so it came to me. I restored it, but I come very infrequently, this area is too remote.'

'But ideal for work – few distractions here, Kitty, my child.' Cellini accepted a second slice of cake.

As the other two chatted Kitty sat with her coffee and wondered why her husband was so secretive with her. What did it achieve? He had spoken of his mother, who had been dead for five years, with obvious warmth and affection, but hadn't even thought to mention that she was French. But then an uncomfortable thought wormed its way into Kitty's mind. Who was she to criticize? Had she told him about Lana? About Slim? She had secrets too. She could not be sure why she chose not to discuss her sister, but she knew very well why she had not revealed her relationship with Slim. She had secrets for a reason, maybe Felix did too. She did not like this idea, and it surprised her that she didn't.

In the following weeks, as winter became spring, Kitty was happy. She worked as she had never worked before; Cellini had always been a strict teacher but now, with only one pupil to concentrate on, she surpassed herself. Kitty was woken at seven and was at work by eight. That lasted until lunchtime which was on the dot of twelve. After lunch she was allowed two hours for rest and siesta, and then at three work began again and carried on until eight. The books she had seen and hoped to read went unread. The walks she had planned never took place. The sightseeing trips that she had longed for Felix to suggest never materialized.

Music. It was her life. When work was finished the conversation was of music, of opera, of singers dead, of singers living, of rivals-to-be. There were endless discussions of the roles Kitty must learn, of the roles she must wait to learn. Her repertoire was being built. The parts – studied, analysed, memorized and filed away – were like building-bricks for her career. When Cellini pronounced that a role was learned, that near-perfection had been reached, Kitty's confidence in herself grew. She was being prepared for the day when she would be asked, 'Can you sing such and such?' and she could honestly answer, 'Of course.' Added to this she now had a repertoire of concert music which was practised as carefully as any *bel canto* role; she enjoyed learning *lieder* and folk-songs – English, Italian, Spanish – on top of the operas.

She still thought of Slim with longing, but she knew what to do when images of him appeared in her mind – she worked harder and the thoughts dissolved. To keep Slim at bay she concentrated on her first love and obsession – The Voice.

Her singing also distracted her from the lack of sexual passion in her life. Felix's visits to her room were becoming even less frequent. At first she had blamed herself, thinking he did not find her attractive. He confused her. When alone with her as well as in company he was the most loving and proud of husbands. She was slowly reaching the conclusion that she had married a man to whom sex was unimportant. And sometimes when he was in her bed she found herself wondering if he was there out of a sense of duty only, not of need. Weeks could pass without any intimacy between them so that she had begun to wonder when the visits would cease completely. The thought of a future without sexual love was bleak, but as she threw herself into concentrating on her voice, the physical need in her lessened too.

The two months had become three. And then one morning Felix and Cellini told her the reason for the trip, the need for the isolation. A concert had been arranged for her in two months' time in Lyon, where she was to make her proper début. Felix was adamant that her Italian concert tour with the 'American crook', as he referred to Jason Erikson, did not count. And Felix had been busy while she worked, he had arranged a second tour for her. She would be working in France and Italy for three months.

They had not told her before because they did not want to pressure her, to have her too frightened, too soon, at the prospect. Frightened? Kitty wasn't frightened, she was elated! Her time had come.

Slim had always been moody; he was worse now. He had started drinking heavily again and, worse, he had taken to snorting cocaine, something he had not done for years, which only exacerbated his depression. Even Toby, so patient and sensitive to Slim's moods, began to wonder whether he wasn't wasting his time, whether the rock opera would ever be finished, whether he should pack up and move on. He had once suggested to Slim that perhaps he needed a doctor. But he was unceremoniously told to 'fuck off'.

'What's the matter with him, Lana?' Toby asked one evening when Slim, in a particularly foul mood, had destroyed the past week's entire output. 'Honestly, I think I've had enough.'

'Don't go, Toby. I'd hate that.' She pushed a glass towards him and poured him a drink from the bottle of vodka she had in front of her.

'You see the position I'm in, Lana? I mean, it's not the money – Slim's generous – but I don't want to be paid for doing nothing. I want to create.'

'Of course you do, Toby. And I want to sing, and a fat chance I've got of doing that at the moment.'

'Why wait? Why not branch out on your own?'

'I've thought of that possibility, but I don't think I could face going back to all those dismal gigs. With Slim I'll be an instant star.' She looked at him, eyes shining at the prospect.

'Or an instant flop,' he said, as gently as he could.

'What do you mean?'

'Look, Lana, don't say anything to Slim, he'll scalp me but it's . . . well . . . we started off writing a rock opera, right? No problem, he knows that world, he's one of the all-time greats. But it's changed, it's not like that any more. We had some bloody good stuff – rock, lyrical, some quite good innovative electronics. What's he done? Scrapped the lot. Now he's trying to write like bloody Verdi.'

Lana sat bolt upright in her chair. 'He's doing what?'

'He's trying to write a right-on opera – fat ladies, the lot.'

'No, they're not all fat,' she said bitterly, and looked out of the window at the setting summer sun dappling the lawn.

'Aren't they? Thought they were.' Toby laughed.

'My sister isn't.' She faced him.

'Oh, my God, Lana. I'm sorry. I forgot.'

'He hasn't though, has he?' There was a slight catch in her voice. Toby put his hand out and touched hers.

'Why do you stay, Lana? Why?'

''Cause I love the creep. That's why. Though sometimes I wonder what there is to love.'

'Sure you're not in love with the idea of being in love with him? You know, the great rock star and all that?'

'He doesn't want me, you know. He's told me to go. He'd like to divorce me only he's too fucking mean – scared I'll go after him for all I can get – I wouldn't, I'm not like that. We've never made love, you know. Not once. Why? I'm pretty enough, I've got a good figure, haven't I?'

''Course you have,' Toby said, embarrassed by these confessions.

'He's told me I'm a scrubber, doesn't want to touch me. That's not fair. I played around, back in the beginning, but not since I met him – not once. Well . . .' She remembered her one slip with Tristan, the only one – she wondered now if that had been a trap Slim had set up for her to see if she was capable of resisting sex as she had pretended when she first came here. 'There have been plenty of opportunities,' she added proudly instead.

'I'm sure there have, Lana.'

'I mean, do you fancy me?'

'You ask?' He laughed, acutely embarrassed now. And he lied too, he didn't fancy her one little bit. The long blonde hair, the Alice band, the pretty flower-printed dress – it would be like shagging his kid sister, he thought.

'What's he do? I mean, do you know if he's screwing anyone? I sometimes wonder if he goes out at night – he used to, you know, in the past, when the house was full of people. He used to drive off into the night to get away from everyone.'

'I don't know, Lana. I've always thought with Slim that he didn't rate sex very highly. He's happier with his music than with a woman.'

'I could accept that if it was true. But there's one woman, isn't there? My bloody sister, he's bloody obsessed with her, isn't he?'

'Well, she doesn't want him. She's made that clear enough.'

'Has she?' Lana leaned forward eagerly. 'Tell me, tell me what you know.'

'Not a lot. Just odd things Slim's said. He's got some tapes of her singing – he plays them quite often . . . once he said how she didn't want any man, only her singing. He said he doubted if she'd ever marry, that her voice was her child in a strange way.'

Lana laughed. 'But she did get married, didn't she? Good old Felix has obviously got something that rock star Slim is lacking – maybe it's a prick!' She shrieked hysterically at her joke. Toby looked away, he'd never liked vulgarity in women. But Lana was right, Kitty had married and no doubt that was the reason for this prolonged depression of Slim's. It had been going on for nearly six months now. Yes, she must be right, it was about six months ago that Lana had given her ill-fated lunch.

After Toby had left her, Lana opened another bottle of vodka. Sometimes the loneliness of her life made her want to weep with despair, but she didn't, she couldn't afford to. If she let go she didn't know where her despair would lead.

She had been low before, but never this low. Toby had asked her why she was here. She had said because she loved Slim but now, drunk, she could look at the situation honestly. She *did* love him but not as much as she once had. How could she? All the rejections, knowing how irritable she made him, the isolated way they lived, together yet apart, all this had chipped away at her love. No, what had kept her here more than anything was that dream, that stupid, ridiculous dream instilled in her so long ago, that she would be a star. A star! It had been the motivation of her life for as long as she could remember, and Slim was to be the vehicle to make it all possible. And now?

She shook her head slowly from side to side, picked up the bottle and, focusing with difficulty, poured another tumbler of vodka.

And now? she repeated to herself. Slim was going to drop her from his opera, she could see that quite clearly. Perhaps he had never intended to make her a star. Maybe he had used her just to try out his songs in the studio. Maybe he always hoped Kitty would sing for him. Maybe when they had met six months ago he had asked her, perhaps it was Kitty who had persuaded him to change the music, the complete style of the piece. There, she had been relying on him making her a star, and now Kitty was thinking the same. It had to be. An opera! For Kitty!

'We'll see,' she said aloud, and got unsteadily to her feet. Clutching her glass and the bottle, she weaved her way along the corridor to Slim's studio, bumping from one wall to the other. She pushed open the door – the place was in darkness. She flicked on the lights.

'Where are you, you shit?' she screamed, but there was no reply.

Carefully now she placed the glass and the bottle on a table. She crossed to the shelf of tapes, lined up neatly, each carefully labelled. She ran her finger along the boxes. One by one she withdrew every tape with Kitty's name on it.

She opened the boxes. Unwinding the spools, she jumbled them into a pile on the floor, the brown tape snaking this way and that.

Then she went berserk. She snatched Slim's precious collection of instruments from the walls; she smashed them one by one against a large marble coffee table, then added them to the pile of tapes. She wrenched equipment from their sockets, and with superhuman strength, for some were heavy, she turned them over, dragging them towards her growing pile.

'You bastard, you bitch! I'll show you,' she kept repeating in a flat, monotonous voice. She was laughing now, a harsh, hysterical laugh, as microphones and a synthesizer joined her creation. She tore up music sheets, stuffing them on to the bottom of the pile. From her pocket she took a lighter and lit the bottom of her bonfire.

The tapes caught instantly and flames shot quickly into the air. Soon the whole pile was alight and Lana was dancing in a circle around the fire, her bottle in her hand, screaming obscenities between slugs of vodka. And the fire took hold.

9

Kitty was working in her music-room. It had once been a barn which Felix had converted into a library, and was now Kitty's domain. It was a lovely room, with a red tiled floor, white walls and a large porte-fenêtre open into the garden. The fine white Swiss lawn curtains lifted on the breeze, which was one of the things that made this house such a delight to live in; it was cool in even the most intense heat.

It was a week before Kitty's concert. She had worked so hard that she was ready, but she was leaving nothing to chance. She continued to practise, even though Cellini had suggested that a few days' rest might be a good idea. But rest was out of the question, indeed Kitty felt she would never enjoy rest again.

Her dress was upstairs. It was new, and Felix had helped her choose it when they had gone to Lyon to inspect the concert hall.

'Always blue,' he had smiled at her as she rejected all the others in the smart dress shop to which he had taken her.

'Because that was the colour I wore the first time I sang in public,' she explained. 'I feel it's my lucky colour.'

'You've worked too hard to need luck.'

'Insurance, then,' she'd laughed in reply.

Shoes had been purchased too, and new underwear in the softest silk, and Felix had taken her to a beauty salon where her hair had been styled in a sophisticated chignon, and her face made up dramatically. Liking the result, they had made an appointment for her to return on the day of the concert.

The manager of the pretty Théâtre des Célestins welcomed them as if Kitty were already a star. Ticket sales were surprisingly good, he told them. The programme had been printed and delivered, the posters pasted up. She fingered her name on the programme with disbelief and asked if she could have one, and a poster too, as souvenirs. Both men had smiled benignly at her simple request. Kitty did not know that the treatment she was receiving was not because of her voice, or because she had honoured the theatre with her début, but because Felix had paid a large sum to hire it, with the promise of a donation if the manager could fill it at least two-thirds full.

While Kitty was at the hairdresser's Felix had called on the editor of the local newspaper to finalize the arrangements for the photographer he had booked to be present. Back at the hotel he inspected the suites he had reserved for the music critics from all the major newspapers in

France, England, Germany and Italy. He was flying them in at his own expense. He was leaving nothing to chance.

With a week to go all was ready. In Kitty's room, washed and pressed, was the red chiffon scarf given to her so long ago by Camilla de Souza. At first Felix had objected at her insistence that she should carry it; Kitty refused to comply. She had decided that things had previously not worked out for her because she had forgotten to use the scarf as a talisman. No, she had to carry it.

'Superstitious angel.' He kissed her cheek gently. 'Happy?'

'Delirious. My dream's about to come true.'

With everything prepared, all that remained was for her to keep her voice ready. Cellini was resting, her job done. Then Felix interrupted Kitty at her practice.

'My darling, your mother is on the telephone.'

'My mother?' Kitty asked incredulously.

'Yes. My housekeeper in London gave her this number.'

'I don't want to speak to her.'

'But, my darling, you should, she *is* your mother,' said Felix, who had worshipped his.

'She hates me. She wished me dead.'

'She was not herself when she said it, I'm sure.'

'You don't know my mother,' Kitty said, only half-laughing, for the memory was still one that pained her. 'Oh, I suppose you're right . . .' She followed him out of the music-room to the study where the telephone receiver lay on the desk. Her hand wavered over it for a moment, resisting picking it up. She grabbed it quickly as if forcing her hand to act.

'Yes?' she said shortly.

'Kitty? Thank God I've got hold of you.' She heard her mother's familiar voice. 'It's Lana.'

'What about her?'

'There's been a dreadful accident. The house, it burned down . . .'

'Is Slim all right?' Kitty clenched the telephone, her heart plummeting with shock.

'Charming! You ask after Slim and not Lana.'

'I meant both of them,' she said quickly, aware that Felix was standing beside her.

'Slim rescued her – real hero he was. Dragged her out of the inferno just in time.'

'Is she burned?'

'No, thank God. But I nearly lost her, Kitty. The smoke, it nearly killed her.'

'And?'

'She's in hospital. She wants to see you and Felix.'

'Me? Felix? Why?'

'She's in trouble, Kitty. The fire, they're saying it was all her fault. I mean, that's wicked, isn't it?'

'The whole house went?'

'All of it.'

'How sad. Such a lovely place, and Slim had such beautiful things. His music-room, has that gone?'

'Everything.'

'Oh, my God, the poor man, all that work.'

'And what about Lana?'

'Did she do it, Mum?'

There was a long silence.

'Mum? Did she?'

'She says she might have, she can't remember. When are you coming?'

'I can't come.'

'What the hell do you mean, you can't?'

'I've got a concert in a few days, I'm preparing for that – I can't interrupt my schedule.'

'Not for Lana? What do you mean, can't? More like *won't*.'

'If you like. If I remember, the last time I visited Lana in hospital I didn't get much of a welcome from you.'

'What the hell are you talking about?'

'You remember.'

'I don't know what you're going on about. That's typical of you, isn't it? Your poor sister lying in hospital, every breath agony, and you won't go to see her and help her out of this mess.'

'What mess?'

'Slim's suing her for malicious damage and divorce. She's no money, she wondered if Felix could help.'

'I don't blame Slim, he loved that house. No wonder he's angry.'

'If you won't come, what about that husband of yours?'

'No, he can't either. I need him.'

'You selfish cow.'

'Thank you, Mother.'

'It's always the same with you, isn't it – think only of yourself. You're selfish, Kitty, I've always maintained that you are. You're jealous too – jealous of Lana. Oh, I hear your husband's rich, but I bet Slim could buy and sell him. You've always hated your sister, haven't you, having what you can't have? All her life she had the looks, the better voice – she was always better at everything. And then she got Slim and you needn't lie to me, I know the whole story, Lana told me . . .'

Kitty listened as her mother ranted at her down the telephone. Why had she answered the damned thing?

'. . . and now poor Lana might have damaged her voice.'

'Quite honestly, Mother, the way Lana's looked after it she doesn't even deserve a voice. Goodbye, Mother,' Kitty said, and slammed the phone down.

'Dear, dear. And what was all that about? Am I right in assuming Lana burned Slim's house down?'

'Apparently, but they're all right.'

'Good God, what on earth for? What a tragedy! He had that particularly fine Rossetti.'

'She wants us to help her.'

'I'll go if you like – you have Cellini.'

'No . . . don't . . . you mustn't.' She grabbed hold of his arm as if he was about to leave her there and then.

'My sweet, if you don't want me to, of course I'll stay. My place is with you, I've no desire to go.'

'Can Slim sue her for malicious damage when she's his wife?'

'I don't know, I'm not a lawyer. But if she has nothing, there would seem little point.'

'It doesn't sound like Slim – he must be very angry.'

'And with reason. Kitty, I couldn't help but notice that your first concern was for him and not your sister. Is there something I should know, something you haven't told me?'

Kitty looked at his placid expression. Nothing ever seemed to ruffle Felix's calmness, something she was finding valuable for her own equilibrium. Did it matter now if he knew? She had proved to herself it was over. Her reaction just then on the telephone was, after all, perfectly normal, that she should be concerned for a friend, even though she could see that it was somewhat odd not to be immediately concerned for her sister.

'It was a long time ago, Felix. It was a crazy thing – we barely knew each other – we only went out together for three weeks.'

'What went wrong?' he asked kindly.

'He asked me to marry him and I couldn't, it wasn't the right time for me.'

'Like Henri?'

'Yes, just like Henri.'

'My poor child. How sad for you. A voice such as yours can be a great burden, can't it? But then you made the right choice – and I don't mean that simply because it allowed me to be your husband. No, someone like Slim would be wrong for you – too volatile, too depressive. You need support in your life, not drama. But it's dangerous, I think, that it ended not in rancour but in sacrifice.'

'No, no. It's over now, I promise you.'

'Are you sure?'

'I saw him in London just before we left for France. It was dead, any feelings were gone.' She lied, even though she hated herself for it. But then, she reasoned, what point was there in hurting him?

'I know you don't love me, Kitty.'

'Felix . . . what a thing to say . . .'

He touched her lips to stop her saying more. 'I have always known. And I don't love you in the way a man usually loves a woman. To be honest, I don't think I have it in my nature to have a grand passion, but I love what you are, what you are to become. I love your voice with all my body and soul. I would kill to protect your voice.'

Kitty stood silent, not knowing what to say. His words sent a shiver down her spine, and she bit her lip to stop herself from crying. Now she knew. She wanted him to love her, even if she could not reciprocate it. She needed to be loved, certainly she sang better if she was. Was that illogical, vain or just human nature? His words had sounded so cold, making her feel like an object. Did this mean that The Voice was more important than she?

10

Slim did not sue Lana. His anger dissipated eventually and he merely felt weary of her. Her spite had cost him dear since her deliberate actions had invalidated his insurance policy.

He went to his lawyer and began divorce proceedings against her. He had had enough and he'd be surprised if she hadn't too. He shopped for new clothes, since he had lost everything he owned, got into his car and headed for Dover.

Lana was quickly discharged from hospital. It was the press cluttering up the pavement who told her she was about to be divorced.

'What's your reaction to that, Lana?'

'Is there another woman?'

'What caused the fire?'

'Are you counter-suing?'

She said nothing, she felt sick with fear of the unknown, destroyed with hurt and pain. But she flashed a happy smile for the bunch of cameramen whose machines whirred and clicked at her bright image.

'What are you going to do now, Lana?'

'What I've been intending to do for ages – get back to the stage as soon as possible,' she said cheerfully, before diving into the back of a taxi and sobbing her heart out all the way to Victoria station.

'You've got nothing?' Amy asked with astonishment.

'Not a bean.' Lana shrugged, pretending to be unconcerned.

'That's ridiculous. He's as rich as Croesus. Mean sod.'

'No, he's not. I just never had any cash.' She sat at her mother's kitchen table and wished she hadn't come if her mother was going to interrogate her like this. But then, there was nowhere else she could go.

'Then what did you use when you shopped? When you bought clothes?'

'He has accounts everywhere . . . I used them. Or else I just asked for money and he gave it to me.'

'And you didn't save any of it?'

'No, but then I didn't know this was going to happen, did I?' Her mouth began to quiver.

'With men you must always expect anything to happen and filch what you can – that's what I did with your father.'

'I'm not like you.'

'More's the pity. So what do we do now?'

'Oh, Mum. I don't know.'

'Well, I know one thing. As soon as you're feeling better we're going to London and we shop like crazy on his accounts – get something out of the bugger.'

'I can't do that!'

'Of course you can, don't be so bloody wet.'

'Oh, Mum. What a mess I've made of everything. I love him so much.' She began to sob.

'Then why did you burn his house down? You did, didn't you?'

Lana looked everywhere but at her mother.

'Didn't you?'

'Yes.' Lana's voice was a whisper.

'What on earth for?'

'I went mad. I was jealous. I wanted to get at him.'

'Was he seeing another woman?'

'No. But he loves another one. And I couldn't cope with it. He'd got all these tapes of her voice – it was those I wanted to destroy, not the whole bloody house.'

'Who is she?'

'Kitty.'

'You did that over Kitty?' Amy said with disbelief. 'Oh, how stupid of you! I knew she'd been after him, you told me how upset you were, that's why you crashed that car – all her fault. But that was so long ago and I thought it was all over – why, she's safely married. You must have imagined that Slim's still crazy about her . . . Oh, surely not? She's hardly the sort men would go potty about.'

'Well, that's where you're wrong, Mum, they do – especially my husband. It was worse in a way, that it was her.'

'Of course it was. She's a sneaky bitch – I've always said

it. And you wanted to see her when you were in hospital? Allowed yourself to be humiliated when she refused to come? I don't understand you, Lana. I really don't.'

'But, Mum, I shouldn't have done it. I wanted to say sorry to her.' She spoke with difficulty between her sobs.

'Sorry to her? What for?'

'For destroying the tapes of her singing. That was wicked – I should never have done it.' And she put her head on her arms on the table and her shoulders shook as she cried.

'There, there, my love. Don't carry on so. It'll be all right. Who cares about her? Come on, let Mum take you up to bed, there's a good girl.' Lana stood up and her mother put her arm about her and led her to the stairs and up to her room as if she was a small child.

'That's better, isn't it?' Amy asked as she tucked Lana into her bed in the room that had always been waiting for her. 'Don't you worry about a thing. You don't need anyone but me. I'll make you a star, I promise.'

Four days later Lana thought she would go mad. It was her mother's fussing which was getting her down. Not that Amy was any different, she had probably always been like this, it was Lana who had changed. She did not need her mother's constant caring and, at twenty-five, she did not want to be told she was staying up too late and lying in bed too long.

She stuck it with mounting impatience for ten days but the last straw came one morning when her mother told her she wasn't eating enough roughage.

'That's it!' Lana jumped up and began to fold the few clothes she had with her into a holdall. She swept the make-up her mother had bought her into her handbag. 'I can't take this, I'm off.'

'What have I done?' Amy asked, perplexed.

'You treat me like I'm three years old, that's what you do.'

'But you're my baby.'

'No, I'm not. I'm twenty-five years old, Mother. I'm a woman – or haven't you noticed? I've been married. Now I'm getting divorced. And you treat me as if I'd just got out of nappies. Do me a favour, just shut up.'

'Well, really! What a way to speak to your mother. After all I've done for you—'

'Ah, I knew that would come up sooner or later. It's your favourite refrain, isn't it? We'd best put it on your tombstone.'

'Why are you being like this to me? Why are you hurting me?'

'Because I've had everything up to here, Mother.' She patted the underside of her chin. 'I've got to have time on my own without you clucking about me.'

'But I thought you'd come home, I thought you'd come back to me,' Amy began to whine.

'No such luck, Mum. I could no more live here again than I could in a cage in the zoo.' She walked towards the door.

'Lana, you don't mean this—'

'I do, Mum, I do. Please understand that.'

'Where will you go?'

'I don't know.' She opened the door.

'You'll let me know where you are?'

'I might.'

'Lana, please . . .'

But Lana had gone. Amy heard her run down the stairs and slam the front door. She sat on Lana's bed, smoothing the coverlet down as if stroking it.

'Why?' she said to the empty room. 'All I did was love her.'

*

Once she was on the train to London Lana calmed down and wondered if she hadn't acted stupidly. She really had no idea where to go – she had no mates, for her years with Slim had isolated her, and the people he knew had been her only friends. Well, calling them friends was perhaps stretching it a bit far, she thought. They had all been self-obsessed to the exclusion of friendship, or stoned out of their minds. She had lost touch with her school chums – not that she had ever wanted to maintain contact, but perhaps it would have been better for her now if she had. She had no home, only this one set of clothes and the underwear and nightwear her mother had bought her. No money, other than the change from the fiver Amy had given her once she had bought her ticket. So what was she to do?

Clothes were no problem, she would simply go to Harrods and Harvey Nichols where Slim had accounts and book up a whole wardrobe. She smiled at the thought. Her mother had been right. Why shouldn't she? She liked clothes, it would be nice to have new everything. At least it was summer and she could sleep in the park if necessary. But then . . .

Quickly she delved into her handbag which, oddly, the fire had missed and which had been delivered to the hospital the day after she had been admitted. She hadn't even checked out what was in there. Her smile was even broader when she found a small black wallet containing her Access and American Express cards – or, rather, Slim's, with her as an additional holder. She'd use them, then she could eat and sleep in comfort.

The receptionist at the hotel looked somewhat askance at Lana and her lack of luggage when she asked for a room, but changed her expression when she announced she was Mrs Slim Fletcher. She booked a suite just to make doubly sure the woman took her seriously.

That afternoon she went shopping for clothes, had her

hair done and, in case Slim stopped her use of his cards and accounts – always a possibility – bought a stack of jewellery on account and then some more on his cards. She felt more relaxed and secure after this. She could always sell it bit by bit if the going got tough.

In the evening she ventured into a bar and was pleased by how quickly she attracted attention. The only problem was that every man who tried to pick her up was middle-aged and paunchy. Judging by their indignation when she told them to 'piss off', she assumed they thought she was on the game.

She did not enjoy eating alone in the crowded hotel restaurant where everyone else seemed to be having such fun. She ate as quickly as she could and then scuttled back to her suite, ordered a bottle of champagne from room service and sat watching television while she drank the lot.

It was not being on her own that bothered her, she was used to that – no, her loneliness had been the isolated kind, which was much harder to deal with when surrounded by other people. From then on she took her meals in her room.

She shopped frenetically, amassing clothes and jewellery. She had had to buy several suitcases to hold it all and a lovely fitted make-up case for all the new creams and lotions she had bought.

She had been in the hotel for two weeks when she returned to find a bill, for her stay so far, on the coffee table. There was also a note from the management to say that it was normal for long-stay guests to settle at intervals. She giggled when she saw the size of the account and ignored it.

Two days later the management was more pressing. Lana was visited by the manager himself.

'Sorry, I forgot,' she said gaily, flicking open her new Chanel handbag and handing over the American Express card.

He was sombre-faced when he returned ten minutes later.

'I'm sorry, Mrs Fletcher, but it would appear that this card is no longer valid.'

'Don't be silly, of course it is.'

'Have you another, perhaps?'

She gave him her Access.

Ten minutes later he reappeared, handed her the card and shook his head dolefully.

'This is a joke, isn't it?'

'I'm sorry, Mrs Fletcher, I wish it was. Have you a cheque, perhaps?'

'I don't have an account – it's never been necessary.'

'Well, then, where do we go from here?'

'Leave it with me,' she said airily. He bowed, a small nod of his head which barely involved his shoulders. 'And by the way, get some champagne sent up, there's a pet.' She flashed a broad smile at him, but judging from his lack of response, it seemed to have fallen on stony ground.

Alone, she dialled directory inquiries and then the number she was given.

'Tristan, it's me, Lana,' she said, when she had finally shrieked her way past what seemed to be an army of stalling secretaries. 'What the hell's going on?'

'Slim's not prepared to pay your bills.'

'But he's got to.'

'He doesn't have to do any such thing, my dear.'

'But a husband's responsible for a wife's debts.'

'Up until this morning, he was. But he's now posted a disclaimer – it was in this morning's papers.'

'What's that?'

'A notice to the public that he is no longer willing to pay your bills.'

'How could he do that to me without telling me? I don't understand . . .'

'Evidently not, my dear. But then you've had a good run

this past couple of weeks, haven't you, judging by the size of the charge accounts which arrived yesterday?'

Lana tried another tack. 'The problem is, Tristan, there's the small matter of my hotel bill here. They want it paid and I don't have a bean. You've got to pay it for me.'

'I don't think Slim would like me to.'

'Oh, Tristan, please. It's *so* embarrassing, you've no idea. I'll get out, I will – promise. I'll go somewhere cheaper – honest.'

'Just this, then, but no more. You do understand, don't you, Lana?'

'Yes. I'll get a job. I'll go right now and find one . . . perhaps you could help me, get me a gig – I'll go anywhere, pubs, clubs. You know I can sing, Tristan, don't you?'

'I can't help you, Lana. Slim would hit the roof. He's my client, I can't afford to upset him.'

'Please, Tristan – please. I'll go to bed with you –'

'No, Lana.'

'Please, Tristan, I'm so afraid.' She burst into tears.

'I expect you are, Lana,' she heard him say before the line went dead.

Lana was shaking, tears pouring down her cheeks. She went into the bathroom and surveyed her wrecked make-up. 'This won't do,' she said aloud. She splashed her face with cold water and even though she was still sobbing, redid her face. She changed, packed, called for a porter and, with head held high, swept down to reception and knocked on the manager's door.

'You send the bill to him,' she said abruptly, writing Tristan's name and number on a piece of paper. 'You'll have to look up the address, I've forgotten it,' she added unhelpfully.

'Hang on a minute. How do I know he'll pay?'

'Call him. Ask him.'

It was five minutes before the manager was put through to Tristan. Lana sat in front of his desk, twisting her hands anxiously and feeling sick. She had to fight back the desire to cry.

'Thank you, Mr Riviera. That's most understanding of you,' he said obsequiously into the receiver.

'See? I told you so.' Lana jumped to her feet and had an almost uncontrollable urge to stick her tongue out at him as she flounced from the room and out into the long reception hall.

'Lana? It is Lana, isn't it?'

She swung round. She couldn't see very well; the tears she had fought back in the manager's office were now blurring her vision.

'Avril! Avril Kepple! Oh, am I glad to see you . . .' And then she really cried.

11

'You've done well for yourself,' Lana said, looking around the beautiful sitting-room in the penthouse flat. 'Very well,' she added, a shade wistfully.

'My film contract helped pay for this.' Avril waved her hand to encompass the room. 'And being on Broadway for so long bought the rest.'

'Broadway,' Lana repeated breathlessly. 'Imagine, I know a Broadway star!'

'And a Broadway producer and writer . . . Don't forget darling Portman.'

'Portman, how is he?'

'Oh, he's fine. We're about to go into rehearsal on his new musical. We open in the New Year – gives us time to settle in before the tourists come.'

'Lucky you,' Lana said with feeling, perhaps a little too

much, she decided, and thought it might be better to change the subject. 'How was the film? I never saw it.'

'You didn't? Gracious, where have you been, Outer Mongolia? I thought everyone I know had seen it.' Avril laughed. Lana would have liked to say she hadn't seen it on purpose, but managed to control herself. She needed a bed for the night, and longer if she played her cards right.

'But you saw the show?' Avril fussed about, plumping up cushions which had no need of her attention.

'No.'

'No?' Avril found herself clutching a beige satin cushion which exactly matched the slub silk upholstery of the sofa. 'Couldn't you get tickets? They were hard to come by . . . but I'd have thought—'

'Oh, that was no problem – Slim gets whatever he wants. No, we rarely went anywhere. He's so famous it made going out impossible! But presumably you have the same problem.' Lana smiled sweetly.

'Not on Slim's scale, thank heaven! It must have made your life very difficult. I mean, how did you cope with it, all those groupies throwing themselves at him?'

'They never bothered me. Slim isn't interested in little scrubbers, he always came home to me.' Lana flicked her long hair off her shoulders as a gesture of defiance.

'Then what went wrong, if it wasn't another woman?' Avril sat down opposite Lana and looked at her with an expression of deep concern.

'Children. I wanted them desperately and he didn't. He's so insanely jealous of me, you see. He always said he couldn't share me, not even with kids. We had this dreadful row about it and the house burned down and now he's blaming me and wants a divorce.' Lana's pretty blue eyes filled with tears. This was the story she had decided to tell people, she was too proud for anyone to know the truth, but the tale sounded so sad it made her want to cry.

'Oh, my poor friend. How you must be suffering, and

I've been jabbering on about my career and not a thought for you! What must you be thinking of me?'

'No, I like to hear, it's so interesting. I feel I'm out of touch.'

'But what about you? Back in our school-days I always thought you would make it.' Avril said this as if reluctant to admit to Lana's talent.

'I fell in love, didn't I? Slim, of course. He didn't want me to pursue my career.' She smiled at this new embellishment.

'No! How selfish.'

'Oh, I didn't mind. I wanted to dedicate my life to him.' She took a hankie from her pocket and dabbed at her eyes.

'A drink?' Avril jumped to her feet. 'Let me get you a drink, maybe it will cheer you up.'

'Thanks, vodka on the rocks,' Lana said, a little too quickly, she realized. 'I need it. It's been a real pitsville of a day.' She looked down sadly.

'Poor Lana,' Avril said. 'Would you like to stay here with me for a few days until you sort yourself out?' she asked once she had served Lana with her drink. Lana wished it had been larger but she comforted herself with the thought that she had three-quarters of a bottle of vodka from the hotel in her case.

'Could I? Oh, Avril, that would be wonderful – I'm at my wits' end. You're so kind.'

'What are friends for?' Avril put an arm round Lana's slim shoulders and patted her. 'It'll be just like old times – you, me and Portman.'

'Portman?' Lana looked up sharply from her glass.

'Yes, we live together, didn't I tell you? We're getting married – when we can fit it in – we're both so busy.'

'Congratulations,' Lana forced herself to say, though she found she was seething with jealousy and could not be sure for what reason. Was it because Avril was so happy, or was it her success? Or maybe, and this was a thought that surprised Lana, for she thought she cared nothing for him, was it because she was with Portman? Most probably, she decided, it was because Avril had found love.

'Let me show you your room, then, if that's decided. I've got to go out for a couple of hours – my hair.' She picked up the ends of her pale blonde hair. 'It needs help with the colour these days,' she laughed.

'Really?' Lana said, eyes wide and innocent and patting her own hair as if to say, 'I don't', which was not true. And then she wondered why she was behaving like this.

Her room was furnished completely in beige and white, as was most of the flat, and had large windows and a small balcony which overlooked Hyde Park.

Avril looked at Lana's pile of cases. 'If you don't have enough room in these cupboards, there's another one across the hall. Well,' she looked about the room checking all was right for her guest, 'I shan't be long. Help yourself to drinks or whatever you want.'

Half an hour later, her clothes on the racks and folded away in drawers, Lana went off to explore the rest of the flat. It was a lovely apartment, ruined by dull and boring furnishings. Safe, she decided. And it was curious, too, for in her opinion it showed that Avril was not nearly as confident as she would like people to think.

A pretty Queen Anne bureau stood in the drawing-room – a woman's desk. Lana stroked the fine walnut wood, looking thoughtful. 'I can't do that,' she said aloud, but then a voice within her seemed to say, 'Go on, do it!' She ran into the hall and put the chain on the door.

'Better to be safe than sorry,' she said, and skipped back to her task. Instinctively she looked over her shoulder to check she was alone before opening the desk. She flicked through the drawers, not even sure why she was doing this or what she was looking for.

'Well, that is interesting. Just look at that.' She was studying a bank statement. 'Tut! Tut! Some overdraft! So

our Avril isn't as well off as she'd like me to think. Good!'
She talked aloud to herself, a habit she had started during
the silent years with Slim and was not even aware of.

She was soon reading a half-finished letter from Avril to
her mother that was even more illuminating. In it she
confessed how afraid she was, that she felt the pressures
were wearing her down, and she had nightmares that her
voice had gone.

'Better and better.' Lana grinned as she carefully
replaced everything as she had found it.

Having taken the plunge and searched the desk it
seemed logical to continue to pry. The clothes in Avril's
wardrobe were good – all designer labels, Lana noted. She
held a couple up against herself, they were too long, of
course, and they were big, especially round the hips. Avril
must be putting on weight, although Lana hadn't noticed –
good clothes could hide a multitude of sins, of course.
She'd certainly have a good look when Avril came back.

After the clothes, the rest of Lana's search proved
disappointingly fruitless. The books were boring, she had
read the magazines. The choice of music was middle-of-
the-road and old-fashioned – far too much Nelson Riddell
for her taste. Both Avril and Portman appeared to have
become very middle-aged in their tastes, was her studied
opinion.

When Avril returned, Lana, well fortified with vodka,
was sitting innocently looking at *Vogue*, dressed in a pretty
pair of psychedelic-patterned, flared silk trousers and a
skin-tight top with no bra beneath it.

Avril popped her head round the door and signalled
with finger on lip to Lana to be silent. She pushed the door
open and led Portman, his eyes firmly shut, into the room.

'You can open your eyes now, Portman.'

'Good God – Lana!' he said.

'Hello, Portman.' Lana uncurled her legs and smiled up
at him, and held out a languid hand.

'Isn't she a heavenly surprise, Porty, darling?'

'Aren't I, *Porty*, sweetheart?' Lana's voice bubbled with laughter and Portman looked uncomfortable.

'Drinks?' he asked.

'I'm gasping.'

'Lana, you should have helped yourself,' Avril admonished gently.

'Oh, I couldn't do that, Avril. What would you have thought of me?' she said, certain that she managed to sound shocked at the very idea.

'What are you doing these days, Lana?' Portman asked politely as he sat down opposite them.

'Nothing. Being accused of fire-raising and getting divorced,' she replied glibly but with a look of sorrow, which did the trick.

'Oh, how awful for you. I'm really sorry, Lana.'

'I'm not,' she lied. 'How's *darling* Portia?' she asked, preferring to change the subject. It was Avril's turn to look uncomfortable and she studied her hands a little too intently. Portman coughed. Lana looked from one to the other. 'So, how is she?'

'She's dead,' Portman announced flatly.

'Portia? I don't believe it. When? How?'

'It's something I prefer not to talk about, Lana.'

'Of course, Portman, silly old me, always wanted to know everything. I'm sorry.' Portman acknowledged her apology with a slight bow of the head. 'What's the new show about?' she asked brightly.

'Hamlet,' he said.

'*Hamlet!* You're joking. *Hamlet!*' And she began to laugh.

'I don't see what's funny,' Portman said stiffly. 'It's a good plot with a strong dramatic and tragic line.'

'Sure, sure. It's just the idea.'

'Have you ever read *Hamlet*, Lana?'

'Well . . . no . . . but . . .'

'Exactly. Perhaps you should. If you'll excuse me, I have

work to do.' He stood and walked with cold dignity from the room.

'Oops! I put my little foot in it there, didn't I?' She giggled.

'He feels very strongly about it. It really is lovely – the music is wonderful. We're doing the record first before the show opens – that's the new way, you know.'

'Oh, really? And who are you playing?'

'Why, Ophelia, of course. It's a wonderfully dramatic role, especially when she goes mad. And we're having this amazing river actually on the stage for me to float in. It's going to be absolutely fab!'

'Any chance of a part for me?' Lana asked, injecting as much longing into her voice as possible.

'I don't know . . . I mean the main parts have been cast.' Avril was flustered, she always was when hopefuls asked for her help.

'I'll sing in the chorus if need be.'

'It's nothing to do with me, you understand. I have no say. But I tell you what, I'll speak to Portman . . . there's my handmaiden . . .' She stopped speaking abruptly, she shouldn't have mentioned that part, not without speaking to Portman first, and the last thing she wanted was Lana muscling in.

'Would you, Avril? Would you really? I'd die to be back on the stage.' Lana seized Avril's hand and held on to it urgently, a hungry expression on her face.

'I can't promise anything.'

'Should I apologize about laughing at his idea?'

'No, best leave it. He's dreadfully moody at the moment – there's the worry of the show, getting backers, and of course Portia.'

'What happened?' Lana was leaning forward eagerly.

'She killed herself.'

'No!'

'Drove her car out into the Fens, stuck a tube on the exhaust-pipe and put it through the window.'

'How awful! Why?'

'Me. She hated me. While Portman and I were having an affair she put up with me, but when we moved in together she went right off us. And there was the most awful scene, apparently, when Porty told her we were getting married.'

'There would have been.' Lana nodded sagely.

'Why? Do you know something? Lana, you must tell me.'

'It's nothing.'

'What is it? I need to know,' Avril asked quite sharply. She had to find out just how much Lana knew from the past. She could so easily damage Portman, might even stoop to blackmailing him. She remembered Lana of old and how ambitious she had been, she was sure she would do anything to reach her goal. 'Maybe it's something that will help Portman out of his depression. He blames himself, you see.' She changed the tone of her voice to one brimming with concern and worry.

'Well, he would have to, wouldn't he?' Lana said tartly.

'Then you do know something. Please, please, Lana.'

Lana looked at Avril, fighting with her conscience, wondering whether she should tell her or not. Part of her felt it was wrong but another part wanted to hurt Avril now that she had so much and Lana so little.

'I shouldn't. It's none of my business . . .'

'Please . . .' Avril implored, hunching on the sofa before her.

'He was screwing her – his own sister.'

Avril's hand shot to her mouth. 'Portia? Oh, surely not.'

'No doubt about it. I saw them doing it at school. Remember how they let us think they were married? Not surprising, is it? They were potty about each other.'

'Lana, please, please say you're making this up!' Avril wailed.

'Sorry – no can do. And why should I be fibbing?' She sounded affronted at this. 'Mind you, there's something else . . .' The words were out and she could not take them back now. She was not even sure if she wanted to, she was confused at her muddled feelings. She was jealous, she knew that. Not like the insane jealousy she had suffered over Slim and Kitty, but an uncomfortable feeling all the same.

'What?'

'I can't.' Lana looked away, she regretted starting this conversation now.

'Please!'

Lana took a deep breath. Still, maybe she *should* tell Avril – it *was* something she herself would want to know about a man she was living with.

'I'm surprised he wants to marry you, he prefers little girls usually,' she said. 'I should keep an eye on him if I were you.'

'I will. God, this is dreadful. Little girls? Ghastly! I'm glad I know. Thank you, Lana, it can't have been easy telling me that – I know how *extremely* fond of Portman you always were.'

Lana looked at her closely, certain she had heard a tinge of sarcasm in her voice. Did Avril know about her and Portman? Surely not, they had always been careful. Then Avril smiled at her so innocently that Lana concluded she had imagined it. 'Do me a favour though, Avril, don't let him know I told you,' she said, a little scared of the possible consequences of her gossiping.

'I won't breathe a word.'

Later, when Avril was taking a bath prior to the two of them being taken out for dinner by Portman, Lana sought him out. She had been working one or two things out in her mind. She hadn't meant to blurt things out to Avril but now she had, she felt almost a sense of relief that she had told her about Portman. In a way she wished she had come out with the whole story – it was a secret which had lain deep inside her for a long time, one that would never go away completely, no matter how hard she tried to forget. A secret that always made her feel ashamed when she thought of it and one which perhaps should have been released. Even so, she had not been able to admit to Avril that she had been the 'little girl'. But now she began to see that perhaps she could use that past to her own advantage. She was hungry for that moment in the spotlight; she had not realized how much she still longed for it until she had talked to Avril who was bathed in it. Portman and Portia should not have done what they had to her. Why, she reasoned, they had stolen part of her childhood from her, and what was wrong in her asking for something in return now?

'Can I come in?' she asked from the door of his study.

'Please.' He was smiling but he didn't sound very pleased. She walked straight up to his desk.

'I want a part in your new musical, Portman.'

'It's been cast.' He didn't look up from his papers.

'That's odd, Avril said it hadn't. She said something about my being her handmaiden.'

'Your voice would be wrong.'

'It's changed. I can sing as sweetly innocent as I want, now. Slim suggested it. You know, sexy child–woman. But you'd know all about that, wouldn't you, Portman?' She smiled sweetly at him.

'I've someone else in mind. In fact, I've promised the part to her.'

'Then break your promise,' she said firmly.

'I couldn't do that. Put yourself in her shoes. How would she feel?'

'I don't care how she feels. I want that part.' She leaned forward, putting her hands flat on his desk.

'Impossible.' He turned away.

She felt a sudden urge of anger that he should dismiss her so easily. 'And you know what I'll do if you don't?' She looked at him steadily as he swung round to face her. 'I mean it,' she added, more to reassure herself than to threaten him.

'You wouldn't be such a bitch.'

'Try me.' She tossed her hair, her heart was pounding, but he was afraid, she was sure he was.

'I love Avril. Knowing about us would destroy her.'

'You reckon?'

'That was all a long time ago.'

'*I* was, but what about Portia? Bet you feel rotten about her, don't you? Poor cow.' She felt excited now, knowing she was in control, almost sure she would achieve what she wanted.

'Lana, I'm not going to beg. I've asked you to keep quiet, I can't make you. But Avril's a sweet girl and, as I said, I love her and don't want anything to hurt her.'

'What about me?'

Portman's expression was one of fear and sadness intermingled so that just for a second she almost relented.

'You, Lana? I don't think I know you any more, or if I want to. You used to be sweet, now you're hard. What happened?' he asked.

'You can sit there and ask me that?' She felt a sudden spurt of anger. 'I lost my virginity to an old man – yes, that's what you were to me. Followed by Portia. What effect do you think such an introduction to sex has had on me? Then out on the road being screwed by all and sundry and then Slim – who didn't give a fuck for me. Ha!' She laughed a hard and brittle laugh. 'That's truer than you know! All that and then you expect me to turn out like Avril who's had life handed to her on a bloody plate.'

'I'm sorry, Lana.'

'All my life I've been told I'll be a star. I grew to expect it. All I've had is a few years in stupid pubs and clubs with a fourth-rate band. And I'm good. I'm bloody good, and it's not fair.'

'No, you're right, it's not fair. I'm sorry, Lana, I wasn't thinking.' He looked at her, his face creased with what she thought might be concern. He didn't speak for what seemed an age. 'You'll have to audition for the director and musical director, of course – but I'll put a word in, I'll let them know it's you I want.'

'Portman, thank you.' Tears began to form in her eyes but, for once, tears of happiness.

'Lucilla has a couple of lovely songs.'

'Lucilla, is that her name? It's pretty.'

'Yes. She's Ophelia's confidante as well as maid, and she secretly fancies Hamlet, you see. It's quite a strong part.'

'Goody. When do we start?'

'I'll lead you through the part tomorrow and help you.'

'You're my angel, Portman. You won't regret this, ever. I promise you that.'

And she leaned over further and kissed him full on the mouth. But as she did so she knew that she had uncorked memories from the past that she should never have released – for her own sake. And facing them, she knew she would never forgive him, knew she wanted him to know unhappiness too, and if it touched Avril – so be it.

12

Back in London Kitty's favourite pastime was reading the reviews she had received during her concert tour in Europe. They were wonderful. Felix had bought her an expensive tooled-leather scrapbook with her initials and the number one in gold lettering on the spine.

'The day will come when these will fill a library,' he had said when he gave it to her.

'Not if La Scala has its way,' she said with feeling.

'Forget La Scala – there are plenty of other opera houses.'

But she couldn't forget La Scala, how could she? Wasn't it every singer's dream to sing there, to be the principal? And what had happened to her? She had arrived for her audition for a supporting role in *La Traviata* keyed up with excitement. The beautiful theatre had inspired her to sing better than she had ever sung – she knew it, she could feel it as the notes poured effortlessly and resonantly from her.

'Come back in a year, we'll hear you again then,' her unbelieving ears had heard.

She stormed from the theatre, Felix striding to keep up with her, Cellini puffing along some way behind.

'Come back next year? Never,' she said, standing outside and shaking with anger. 'They will have to beg me to sing for them.' She shook her head defiantly.

'That's my darling.' Felix had laughed. 'That's what I like to hear.'

'That was ridiculous.' An indignant Cellini had joined them. 'You've never sung better. Never.'

'I know. And they *invited* me. It's not as if I begged them to listen to me.'

'There, there! This sort of thing happens, Kitty. Sometimes one's face does not fit. Why, even the great Callas suffered the same humiliation. Of course . . .' Cellini smiled. 'I was accepted.' Felix glowered at her.

Cellini and Felix had clucked over Kitty, reassuring her, boosting the confidence that began to flag immediately. But it rankled, deep down inside her it rankled – she could take criticism of herself as a person but not of the voice. She was becoming as protective as a mother with her child for this creature within her.

That was weeks ago. Now she was in London, with an empty diary, past reviews, and the knowledge that she was still unknown here. She had a respectable repertoire, a fine, rich portfolio of parts she was able and ready to sing, but no one to sing them to. She worked as hard as ever with Cellini, who took her note by note and word by word through the scores, the only difference being that Cellini now came to her.

And then it happened.

Felix took the call, for Kitty was practising and the telephone in her studio was always disconnected when she was working.

'My darling! Tonight you sing!' He burst into the studio.

'Where? What?'

'Here in London. In *Carmen*, as Micaela.'

'Micaela? How? Why?'

'Conchita Fortuna has laryngitis.'

'Conchita! She's from Basildon.' Cellini snorted.

'But why me? They don't know me.'

'Do you have to ask?' Cellini laughed. 'Just do!'

'Ben Cooper happened to be in the theatre when the call came from Conchita's husband. He suggested you.'

'Dear, darling Ben. When do I go?'

'In two hours. They want you for a stage run-through.'

'Then we've two hours to work, Kitty. Out with you, Felix!' Cellini shooed him away.

The evening was wonderful. Kitty had known it was

going to be. She had stepped from the wings smelling that unique dusty smell of a large stage, and felt the wave of heat from the audience and lights. As she had tripped about in search of her lover, José, all nerves had gone, there was only Cellini's advice still ringing in her ears – 'Remember, sing from your heart and not your head' – and she began. And she triumphed.

The papers were full of her the next day. The singer plucked from obscurity, the singer no one in London knew, the singer for whom stardom beckoned.

And, best of all, the serious critics were full of praise for her performance.

There was a counter-side, there had tô be, she supposed. No one in the company would speak to her – the fact that Conchita's understudy, a member of the chorus, had been passed over ensured rampant jealousy. Kitty did not mind, though, she did not care what they thought. What was more important for her was that the star who sang José, and Carmen herself, went out of their way to congratulate her. It was their opinion that mattered to her more than anyone else's, except, perhaps, Cellini's. True to form, Cellini had said that Kitty was good, except she had noticed a phrase or two in Micaela's famous aria that could still be improved.

There were three performances before Conchita, still on antibiotics, but concerned by Kitty's notices, dragged herself back before the doctors had advised. Kitty gave her first interview to a newspaper and there was talk of a magazine being interested in her. But, more importantly, now other opera houses had heard of her.

'Could she do Norma?' the heavily accented voice on the other end of the telephone asked Felix.

'But of course. When?'

'In five weeks, here in Mexico City.'

'It's a long way to go for so few performances. I tell you what we'll do, Señor – you get her bookings in at least four other houses and she can open your season for you. Think, the new sensation in your first opera of the season – what publicity!'

It was Mexico, but it was a start. There was one problem, Norma was not in her repertoire. Cellini and Kitty worked even harder and longer hours as note by note, phrase by phrase, Kitty's retentive mind memorized the new opera.

She had no time for anything but music. She neither thought nor dreamed of Slim. Instead, she dreamed the part she was to sing. Her whole life, day and night, was consumed with this passion – one that was truer to her, she decided, than any other.

Slim, unknown to Kitty, had followed her every move. He had attended every concert and recital she had given and had been in the audience for her European operatic début in a professionally mounted *Carmen* in Italy.

He no longer dressed entirely in black, and he had had his long, curly hair cut. To his amusement, this acted as a total disguise – no one recognized him, not even Toby when he turned up on his doorstep one night. Not until he spoke, that is.

'Good God, man, what about your image?' Toby asked, once he had recovered from the shock.

'It's time for a new one, I've decided. Got any Scotch?'

'Sorry, come in,' Toby said, feeling rather foolish that he hadn't invited him in immediately. 'Where you been?'

'Around – trying to lay a ghost.'

'And have you?'

'Not really, but I'm learning to live with it.'

'Kitty?'

'Who else?'

'She's doing really well, I read.'

'Yes, her husband seems to be getting it right for her. It'll be the Met before we can blink. She made a wise choice

with him, I hate to admit. Ta.' He took the tumbler of
Scotch.

'So, what happened? Do you want to talk?'

'I listened to her sing, that was all. It was like listening
to another being – and I wanted to marry her, tie her down,
maybe help her lose that quality.' He shrugged. 'I don't
know. But I realized – painfully – that she was right, a voice
like hers has to come before all else, and certainly before
marriage to me.'

'But she married.'

'Ah, yes, but she doesn't love him, not as she loved me.
I could have been too much of a passion for her – he doesn't
count. He's her manager. Knowing that makes it all
bearable.'

'Christ, I'm sorry, mate,' Toby said. 'It's a real bitch,
isn't it?'

'It was. I'm OK now. In fact the reason I came to see you
was to discuss work.'

'Work?' Toby asked suspiciously, not wanting to get
bogged down in the rock opera again.

'Yeah. I've decided to go solo. I'd like us to work on a
few ideas I've had.'

'Now, that is good news. And the rock opera?'

'Even though I say it myself, there's some good stuff in
there but, let's face it, I wanted to do it for her – what a
nerve, eh? These past weeks I've listened to the music of
the gods – I can't compete. Best stick to what I know.'

'And the hair?'

'Oh, I think I'll keep it short, it's less hassle.'

The shoe buyer for Selfridges watched the start of Kitty's
rise to fame with a mixture of pride and sadness. Pride in
that Jenny could honestly say she had pushed her into
taking that first step, but sadness that she had not been
there to hear her triumph. She had not received a letter for

ages. Kitty was probably too busy studying, Jenny told herself for consolation. She did not like to think of the alternative – that Kitty had forgotten her.

Lana was working as hard as she knew how. She loved the rehearsals, in an old church hall in Camden. She was always up before Avril and Portman, egging them on so that they would be first there. Every morning she made them breakfast and cleared up before they left, washing up, tidying the flat, until Avril couldn't imagine what she would do without her.

She went to every rehearsal, even the ones where she was not needed and was not expected to attend. She sat quietly listening to every word, absorbing each and every instruction given to the others. Rapidly her knowledge of the musical became almost as expert as Portman's. In fact Portman often joked that he knew Lana remembered more of it than he did.

She was everywhere, helping. When the time came for costume fittings, she ran after the wardrobe mistress with needle, thread and pins, and she never minded helping out with the ironing. At night she helped Avril memorize her part, prompting her, reminding her of a phrase here, a complicated piece of melody there. It was only logical, then, that when the original choice had found she was pregnant and had had to leave the show, the director and Portman should have suggested Lana be Avril's understudy, for no one knew the part better. This upset Avril, who felt Lana was too talented for comfort, but she allowed only Portman to know how she felt. Because of the difference in height between Lana and Avril this meant a second set of costumes, but the expense was thought worthwhile since Lana was so reliable that everyone could relax.

Everyone was impressed with Lana's voice and her dedication. She liked the musical and was the first to admit that she had a couple of wonderful songs to sing. Well, one and a half really, she told herself, since one was a duet with Avril. But how she longed to play Ophelia – Avril had the best songs, and loads of them. She would sit watching her rehearse and knew that she could do it better, that her voice was more interesting, and – she couldn't help it – she longed for Avril to disappear off the face of the earth.

13

'Congratulations, Mrs Masters, you're definitely pregnant.'

The tastefully decorated walls of the Harley Street doctor's consulting-room seemed to wobble as if made of rubber, and the doctor himself appeared to recede and become minute.

'Mrs Masters, are you all right? You look faint. Some water?'

'I can't be pregnant.' Kitty looked at him with dismay.

He laughed. 'You know, I hear that expression so many times.'

'But I take the pill.'

'And perhaps there was one morning you forgot.'

'I can't have it,' she said in a voice which sounded as if she was barely in control of it.

'Undoubtedly, from your reaction, it's a shock. But I can assure you it is one you will rapidly come to terms with. When a baby isn't planned, then it can take time to adjust. But you will, Mrs Masters, I'm sure.'

'No, you don't understand, I *can't* have this baby. It's the wrong time for me. It would ruin my career.'

'Not necessarily, Mrs Masters.'

'It will! You know the human body better than I do – you must understand. It could weaken my pelvic floor . . .'

'We could make sure you had a programme of exercising after the baby's born – you'll be fine.'

'Haven't you been listening to me? I've just told you I can't – no, I *won't* – go ahead with this. I need a strong pelvic floor for my high notes. Without them I'm finished.' Her voice was rising with panic as she realized he did not understand.

'To destroy a baby is a —'

'Will you please stop talking about *a baby*? It isn't. It's just a collection of cells. Nothing. It means nothing to me. Nothing.' She kept repeating it for herself, this was the only way she could think of it, the only way she could deal with the situation.

'I'm afraid there's nothing I can do for you.'

She jumped to her feet. 'Then I'll find a doctor who will help me.'

'Please, Mrs Masters, sit down, try to calm yourself. You misunderstand me, I would have to refer you elsewhere, but we need to talk this through first. I have to be convinced there is a real need.' He looked at her with a quizzical expression which invited her to explain herself. She subsided into the chair, clutching her handbag in front of her like a drowning woman grasping a life-raft. She took a deep breath to calm herself, just as she did before walking on stage.

'Obviously, to someone outside my world my reaction must seem odd. I've a good husband, a lovely home, we could give a child a good life. But you see, doctor, I've studied so hard to reach where I am. Until I was seventeen I felt incomplete, and then I discovered I could sing and my life took on a new meaning. For years I have worked every waking hour to perfect my craft. I've sacrificed many things – a normal life, relationships – anything that would impede me. I am on the verge of attaining so many goals; I'm to fly to New York next month to audition at the Metropolitan Opera House. To a singer, doctor, to be invited to sing a principal role at Covent Garden, La Scala, the Vienna Staatsoper and the Met – these are our Mount Everests. If I sing at the Met the others will follow. I will have attained my life's ambition. And if I can't then I would rather be dead.'

The doctor looked down at the pad on his desk. The silence in the room felt oppressive to Kitty, the traffic outside the heavily curtained windows was muted. She felt isolated, alone, as she anxiously watched the doctor for a reaction. He picked up the telephone receiver and dialled a number.

'Paul, I have a patient here whom I think you should see immediately.'

Kitty's sigh of relief was clearly audible in the quiet room.

She had to lie to Felix. She had covered her visits to the doctor by saying she had a strained muscle in her shoulder, and all she had to do for a few days was to remember to move as if she were stiff.

To go to the clinic needed a more elaborate lie. She invented a telephone call from her mother asking her to visit.

'But I thought you never wished to see your mother again, my darling.'

'I know, but she's not well and it's nearly Christmas and, well . . . she is my mother after all . . .'

'I'll drive you. I'd like to meet her.'

'No, not this time, if you don't mind, Felix. It's likely to be strained after all this time – I'd rather be alone with her.'

'As you wish. But if she upsets you, call me immediately.'

'I will.'

It was more complicated than she had planned. Felix insisted on driving her to Victoria station and putting her on the train. She had to travel to the next stop and then back to London and so to the clinic.

The staff were icily efficient with her, she felt their naked disapproval of what she was about to do. If their attitude was supposed to make her change her mind, to test her, it had the opposite effect.

She sat in bed and felt angry – angry with herself for letting this happen, at the injustice of it. She and Felix made love so infrequently these days that for this to have happened was bad luck in the extreme.

The operation was unpleasant. She had refused a general anaesthetic for the sake of her voice and had asked for an epidural instead, and so she was conscious and aware as the life within her was destroyed.

They wheeled her back to her room and gave her a mild sedative to help her sleep. She wished she could get up and leave now. In the distance she could hear a choir – the nurses, perhaps – practising Christmas carols, and someone had put a miniature Christmas tree on the table in her room. Perhaps it was the sound of the familiar carols, or the sight of the tree, both symbols of that festival for children, that broke her resolve not to feel remorse. Now it was done, now it was too late, she longed for it to be undone.

'Oh, my baby!' she cried suddenly. 'What have I done?' And she put her hands on her stomach and felt an aching emptiness and a desperate loneliness.

She did not know how long she lay there. She wanted to be held, to be loved, to be told she had done the right thing. She wanted to be understood.

She buzzed for a nurse and asked for a telephone to be brought to her room. She did not have her address book with her but dredged a number from her memory and prayed she would be there.

'Jenny! It's Kitty. Oh, my friend, I need you . . .'

'I'd begun to think you'd forgotten me.' Jenny stood in the doorway of the hospital room, fatter than ever, but beaming at Kitty with the kind smile that always made her face look prettier.

'Jenny . . .' Kitty put up her arms towards her. Jenny sat on the bed and held her while Kitty cried again, this time not silently but great gasping sobs of grief.

'I thought I wouldn't care and I do, oh God, I do.'

'Of course you care. No woman has an abortion lightly.'

'Thanks for calling it that. They say termination here, as if to sanitize it. How can you?'

'Termination – sounds like a bus depot.'

Kitty grinned weakly.

'I had to do it, Jenny. I was so afraid for my voice. And it wasn't just that. It wasn't right. One day I'd like kids, but with someone I love.'

'So you don't love your husband?'

'Not in that way. He looks after me, he's good and he's kind. He loves my voice, not me.'

'Oh, poor Kitty. What a muddle there must be inside your head.'

'I'm sorry it's been so long, Jenny, and that my letters have been so infrequent. I don't know where the years have gone and it's been all work, you see. No time for anything else, and that means friends too.'

'Doesn't sound much of a life.'

'Oh, but it is. I don't mean to sound as if I'm complaining. When I perform, and it's gone well, I feel such elation – I don't think anything else could give me such happiness. When the audience applaud, and they stand and shout their appreciation – then I feel loved, truly washed over with love. I couldn't risk losing that, you see.'

'No. No one could expect you to lose that.' Jenny patted her hand.

Felix was angry when Kitty returned home from the clinic the following day.

'If you need to get away from me I would appreciate your being honest and telling me where you have been,' he said coldly. 'I called your mother's house last night and she informed me in no uncertain terms that she had not seen you, nor did she wish to.'

'I'm sorry, Felix.' Kitty suddenly felt very weary and sat down heavily in an armchair.

'So am I to be told where you've been?'

'I've been in hospital.'

'What's wrong with you?' His anger was replaced with genuine concern.

'I had an abortion,' she said in a hard voice, the only way she could both speak and control her seething emotions.

'But your voice? The anaesthetic—'

'I didn't have a general. I thought of that, don't worry.' She laughed a short, bitter laugh; of course he would ask after the voice first.

'This must have been dreadful for you. You should have told me.'

'Why? It was my decision to make.'

'I am your husband.'

'What would have been different? Would you have wanted me to have it?'

'Well, no. But then—'

'Exactly. I thought it was an easy decision to make but it transpired it wasn't. There would have been no point in our both being confused.'

'That was very considerate of you, my dear.'

'Wasn't it?' She smiled bleakly at him. 'I met an old friend at the hospital – Jenny – I doubt if you remember her, she worked at Selfridges with me and was at Ben's the first night I sang for you?'

'No . . . I can't say I do.'

'I've asked her to come and work for me. She's fed up with her job. She's very efficient, she could be my personal assistant, take some of the pressure off you. I can afford to pay her, can't I?' she said, aware he looked surprised, she never normally did anything without consulting him first.

'What a very sensible idea, and she'll be company for you. When is she joining us?'

'After Christmas. She's coming to New York with us.'

14

Lana had decided she shouldn't stay with Avril and Portman for Christmas, they had asked her to do so but she had seen how relieved they were when she declined. In any case, she wanted time away from them. She had arrived here suspicious of Avril's intentions and had been treated by her with nothing but kindness. But she could not stop the jealousy which still lurked in her – jealousy at Avril's success when she still felt she was the better performer; jealousy that Avril had Portman's love and she had no one; jealousy that Avril had security when Lana had none. Sometimes it was a strain not to let her true feelings out. Portman himself, as the opening of the show came nearer, was a bundle of nerves and bad temper. A break would do them all good.

She was faced with her perennial problem of where to

go. Considering how easy-going she was, it was odd how few friends she had, she thought. Slim was to blame, of course. She had hoped to make friends in the show but that hadn't happened, everyone seemed so jealous of her – for getting the part and living with Portman and Avril – that she had given up trying.

'Hello, Mum. Thought I'd surprise you.' Lana stood grinning on the steps of Number Fourteen. 'Am I a nice Christmas Eve present, then?'

'Oh, my baby! I knew you'd come back to me.' Amy fluttered about her favoured one, ushering her into the living-room.

'I love coming here, nothing ever changes. Makes me feel safe,' Lana said, looking round the familiar room where everything stood in the same place it had since the day she was born.

'Then why did you storm out last time? And you might come more often,' Amy replied tartly.

'Oh, go on, you know me.' Lana grinned. 'Put my little tantrum down to my artistic temperament.' She laughed. 'Honest, you've no idea what it's like, Mum, rushing about all the time – rehearsals, costume fittings, then there was the recording of the LP, that was exciting. Photo sessions, interviews. It's all go, Mum.'

'Oh, it sounds wonderful. My little star!' Amy clapped her hands together and leaned forward, watching Lana's face intently, following every word she said as she continued telling of her life in London – with a few embellishments. Amy listened in silence, filing away this information so that she could bring it all out again to mull over and enjoy when Lana had returned to London.

'You on your own this Christmas then, Mum? I won't be in your way? What about Vince – that was his name, wasn't it?' Lana smiled, confident in the knowledge that the love of Amy's life might be staying but that she would supersede him.

'Oh, Vince is old news. I'm going out with a bloke called Drew, he sells double glazing and he's rolling in it.'

'Good for you. You deserve the best. When's he coming?'

'He's not.' Amy looked edgy.

'He's married, isn't he?' Lana squealed. 'Oh, you naughty girl – cavorting around with a married man, whatever next?'

'His wife doesn't understand him,' Amy said defensively.

'You don't want to fall for that line, Mum, it's the oldest in the book. Don't get hurt, will you?'

'It doesn't bother me if she does or doesn't understand him. It suits me fine as it is. I get taken out, wined and dined something rotten. We go dancing, he brings me lovely presents. And I don't have to wash his socks or clean his mucky hair out of the bathroom basin. No, I like things as they are.'

'Good for you. So you're not looking to get married again?'

'Nope. And no bugger living here and sponging off me and me skivvying for him.'

'You're a real liberated woman of the seventies, Mum – who'd have thought it?' Lana laughed. 'Here's a little present for you.'

Eagerly Amy tore the wrapping of the slim parcel. 'Oh, my God! Oh, how wonderful! The show . . .' She held up the sleekly packaged record in its sleeve.

'Not even released yet, Mum. You'll be the first of your friends with that.'

'And there's your picture on it. Oh, Lana, I knew you'd do it. I just knew. Put it on. I don't want to hear it all – just your bits.'

Lana laughed at her mother's pride as she placed the glossy disc on the turntable.

'You haven't got much of a part, have you?' she said,

disappointed, when Lana had selected the two tracks she was on and had played two of Avril's songs for good measure.

'It's an important one. I've that solo and I'm rarely offstage.'

'Don't go much on that Avril's voice, it's weak and too sugary by half. You're much better.'

'Thanks. I think so too. Still, keep your fingers crossed – I'm her understudy, maybe she'll get just a little bit ill.'

'You want to put some senna pods in her tea.'

'Oh! What an idea!' Lana giggled.

They didn't bother with a cooked meal but opened some of the bottles Amy had got in and ate cheese on toast in front of the fire.

'I see that Slim of yours is building a new house,' Amy said through a mouthful of toast. 'It was in the *Sunday Express*. All modern, on the site of the old one.'

'He can afford it.'

'You divorced yet?'

'No, but all the papers have been served. Good riddance to bad rubbish,' she said, flicking her blonde hair defiantly. She wasn't planning to let on about the pain she had felt at receiving the documents, of knowing it would soon all be over for good.

'I hope you're going for the bugger. Screw him for every penny you can.'

'No go. He hasn't got any money I can get my hands on.'

'What do you mean? He's a millionaire several times over, and now he says he's going solo he'll make another fortune, I expect.'

'All in companies, the whole damn lot. The house was owned by one in Liechtenstein, he's got other trusts and companies in Jersey, Grand Cayman . . . All tied up, clever little sod.'

'You've had advice on this?'

'Portman took me to see his lawyer. Oh, he's supposed to be paying me maintenance but I haven't seen a penny.'

'Sue him.'

'You know, Mum, I can't be bothered. I'm all right now – I'm not earning a fortune but I will. I want to do it on my own. Make my own money. Be independent. I don't want to be beholden to him or any other man.'

'That's my girl. Oh, Lana, you'll never know how proud I am of you.' Lana grinned. 'Pity about that Avril, though,' Amy added, and Lana's grin disappeared.

As always when she was with Amy, after two days Lana felt she had had enough. The constraints were moving in, the pride was becoming suffocating. The day after Boxing Day she returned to London, leaving her mother two tickets for the opening night of *Prince of Darkness*: Portman had decided that calling it *Hamlet* might confuse people and put them off.

Kitty was watching *Top of the Pops* as she sometimes did, much to Felix's amusement. She usually said she felt she should have her mind open to all musical trends but she did not fool him. Felix knew she watched it in the hope that Slim might appear on the show one day.

She only half listened, the noise most of those groups made hurt her sensitive ears, but tonight she looked up from the tapestry cushion she was working on as music of a very different sort came out of the set. It was lyrical and easy on the ear, a ballad sung by an extremely pretty, tall girl.

'That's the new hit from that musical about Hamlet,' Jenny said from the depths of her armchair, where she was curled up with that week's *Woman's Own*.

'Hamlet? What will they think of next?' Felix laughed as he was about to leave the room – he did not have his wife's tolerance for certain music.

'Why not? We have Othello,' Kitty said defensively. These days she sometimes found Felix too pompous.

'That's different.' Felix left the room before she could think of a reply.

'Why is he always so intolerant of anything he doesn't like or doesn't understand?' Kitty turned to Jenny.

'He's very kind, though, and generous.'

'Yes, all of that,' Kitty said almost wearily. Jenny looked at her friend, she was still down and often got depressed. Jenny thought the trip to New York had come too soon after the abortion, that Kitty needed a rest. She hadn't said anything, for if they couldn't see it for themselves, there was little point in her putting her oar in. Still, she comforted herself, the trip had been a success. They were returning to New York soon for a three-month engagement. Other bookings were already coming in and Felix had bought an engagement diary for 1976 as well as for the present year. Kitty had always said she would never be a star before she was thirty. She'd been wrong. She was on her way and she wouldn't be twenty-eight until June.

'Crikey! Look, Kitty, isn't that your Lana?'

Kitty looked up at the television screen. There were three women now, standing behind the soloist, singing as a backing, and yes, she was almost sure one was Lana.

'This is a new show, you say?'

'Yes, the last one was lovely, Avril Kepple played a nun – The Angelus that was called, a smash hit. It made Avril a star,' Jenny recounted knowledgeably. It was nice to be informed on something musical that Kitty didn't know about.

'Of course I heard of it. Written by Portman Philbert. He used to teach Lana – she was potty about him.'

'Looks as if he's put her in his show, then.'

'That's nice. I wonder if we can get tickets, I'd like to see it, wouldn't you?'

'It's a sell-out.'

'Felix can get them for us. He can get anything. When does it open?'

'Three weeks, I think.'

'Fine, we can see it before we go back to America.'

Lana had spent the whole day being sick. Par for the course, she reassured Avril. But it was odd, she thought, when she'd been with the Mantras she was never sick.

She needed brandy, that would settle her stomach, she decided. She didn't think it would be a good idea to be seen drinking here in the flat – she'd laid off the stuff after Portman had given her a good talking to about her drinking habits. At the time she had thought his lecture a bit of a nerve, given the amount he had sunk in the past. But, like so many reformed drinkers, he was pious in his zeal to convert. She had not minded; she had found, to her surprise, that because of the rehearsals and the need to concentrate, she didn't need to drink.

This was an emergency, however. She'd ask one of the stage-hands to get her a bottle as soon as she arrived at the theatre.

It was a thrill, one that made her stomach dip even more alarmingly as they arrived at the stage door. The company had been rehearsing here for the past couple of weeks. The dress rehearsal yesterday to an audience of students and off-duty nurses had been dreadful, which had cheered everyone up. Theatre legend decreed that a disastrous dress rehearsal meant the first night would run smoothly and be a success. They hoped!

The atmosphere was electric, barely controlled panic seemed to have infected everyone. Mysteriously, costumes had become muddled or lost. Pieces of scenery which previously had worked perfectly chose to jam. Everyone was convinced they had sore throats and could not sing.

Tempers were frayed and tantrums common and Portman wondered what he was doing here.

Lana snatched the bottle of brandy gratefully from the stage-hand and carried it in a brown paper bag to the lavatory, where she locked herself in and gulped desperately. She immediately felt better. She took the bottle and hid it at the back of the wardrobe in the dressing-room she had to share with three other women.

Drew had been very impressed that Amy had tickets for the first night of *Prince of Darkness* – they were selling for a small fortune on the black market. He had treated Amy to a new dress, and as a special present for a special night, he had bought her a gold locket. He'd been a bit miffed when she'd cut up two snaps of Lana and put one on either side. It didn't matter now, though, he thought, as they got out of the taxi in front of the theatre – she looked great for someone her age. And best of all, he'd lied to his wife and said he was at a conference in Liverpool, so they could have a couple of days together in London.

Felix had managed to get Kitty two tickets, as she knew he would. He refused point-blank to come with them, so Jenny and she set off for the theatre together, arranging to meet Felix after the show in Fortnum's for a theatre supper.

Kitty was feeling better than she had for some time. She was well prepared for the Tosca she was to sing in New York – one of her favourite roles. Her packing was done and this was a nice way to relax before they flew out of Heathrow and the work began in earnest again.

She was in the foyer when she saw her mother. She stopped dead in her tracks and Jenny bumped into her.

'Christ, have you seen a ghost?' Jenny asked her as she saw her pale face, rigid with shock.

'It's my mother – look over there, in the red dress with that rather flashy man.'

'Go and speak to her.'

'I can't.'

'Of course you can. Family rows are just plain stupid, if you ask me,' Jenny said practically.

'She won't want to see me.'

'You want to bet? I'm sure she's as proud as punch at your success. What mother wouldn't be?'

'I don't know . . .' Kitty wavered. She was surprised by her reaction, she thought she had expunged all feelings for the woman, that Amy meant nothing to her. Instead she found she really wanted to rush over to her, put her arms about her, hear her say how proud she was. 'Yes, you're right.'

She eased her way through the crowd without difficulty, for Kitty was becoming a well-known face, even though some might not yet be able to put a name to her.

'Hallo, Mum,' she said simply.

Amy turned and looked through Kitty as if she was not there. 'Time we took our seats, Drew,' she said, and walked towards the stairs.

Kitty felt as though she had been slapped. She stood watching her mother chatting and laughing with her companion. All the happiness of the evening disappeared for her.

'Who was that? A stunning-looking woman,' asked Drew.

'My other daughter.'

'I didn't know you had another one.'

'I don't. She doesn't exist for me.'

'Christ, what did she do to you?' Drew grinned.

'She was born.'

Lana checked her make-up for the last time in the spotted mirror lit by a single bare bulb. In the corner she had taped her one telegram – from Amy.

'Break a leg,' she said gaily to the others.

She ran up the metal staircase to Avril's dressing-room. She had arranged to meet her there. Their entrance was together and they thought they could give each other moral support. She could hear the orchestra tuning up, the sound relayed through the speakers dotted about backstage so that everyone would know the point the show had reached.

She stopped at Avril's door, the door with a star on, and went in. Avril was sitting in front of her dressing-table, which had a spotless mirror with good lighting, Lana noticed. The room was full of flowers – vases on every surface and baskets of them on the floor. Good luck cards and telegrams were everywhere.

'This is it, Lana, my love.'

'This is it.'

'Five minutes, Miss Kepple,' a voice shouted with a bang on the door.

'Thanks, I'm ready,' Avril called back. 'Quick, here.' She handed Lana half a glass of champagne. 'Portman said we could have this for Dutch courage. To us and the show.' She raised her glass.

'To us. And thank you for everything, Avril.'

'It's been my pleasure, you deserve a break.' She took a sip of the champagne and put her glass back on the table. 'Listen – that's the overture starting. Shall we go?'

Lana drank her glass to the dregs and followed Avril out of the dressing-room, along the dreary corridor to the stairs. Avril began to descend. Lana looked at her back. It would be so easy . . . so very easy . . .

Avril turned to speak to her just as Lana, feeling suddenly dizzy from a mixture of excitement and brandy, tripped and caught her heel in the hem of her long dress. Avril put out her hand and grabbed Lana's arm to steady her, but it was too late. Screaming, they both tumbled down to the bottom.

The overture ended. The conductor stood, baton raised,

waiting for the twitch of the curtain, the signal to begin Act One. Nothing happened. He lowered his baton, the orchestra looked from one to the other. Arms that held bows in position relaxed. The audience began to whisper and rustle.

An official appeared from the wings and raised his hand for silence.

'Ladies and gentlemen, I regret that, due to an unfortunate accident to Miss Kepple, the show will be delayed for ten minutes. If you will bear with us . . .'

There was a muttering of disappointment from the audience.

'That's my girl!' Amy said, grinning broadly.

'What do you mean?' Drew asked.

'You'll see,' she replied.

Fifteen minutes later the curtain was raised, the orchestra played, and five minutes later Ophelia appeared, an incongruous sticking-plaster on her face. The entire audience save one – Amy – stood and cheered as Avril Kepple took her position centre-stage.

15

Lana was not an easy patient. Feeling she had lost everything, she had sunk into a deep depression compounded by an intense irritation which led to flashes of temper.

Every night when Avril and Portman left for the theatre she cried, which distressed Avril, which in turn worried Portman. If they had had a cat she would have kicked it.

'I know it's difficult for you, darling, but the doctor said you should be right as rain in a month,' Avril tried to comfort her.

'And back in the show?'

Avril did not look at her as she answered.

'That's up to Portman and the others, isn't it? My, what lovely flowers, who are they from, an admirer?'

'From the theatre management, to stop me suing them, no doubt. But maybe I will.'

'But Lana, it was an accident. If anyone's to blame it was me, grabbing at you as you fell towards me and probably making matters worse.'

'Then perhaps I'll sue you,' Lana snapped.

'Oh, you wouldn't, would you? I can't explain how miserable I feel for you, missing your big chance and on the first night too. But there will be others, I'm sure. And who caused who to fall I can't really remember, can you? It's all such a muddle, isn't it?' She smiled very sweetly.

She thinks I did it on purpose, Lana thought, that I wanted her to fall. She flicked her long hair over her shoulder at this idea for it was an uncomfortable one. She had *thought* it, but only for a moment, and hadn't she been punished enough just for wishing something could happen to Avril?

'How can I remember? I was the one who got concussed and came to in the hospital with my bloody mother weeping and wailing over me. And I missed everything – the opening, the party.' And her large blue eyes filled with tears.

'Poor Lana. Is there anything I can get you?' Avril fussed over her. 'Look, I'm not supposed to tell anyone this, but, to hell with it . . . I'm lunching with some film producers, they're keen to make a film of the show. Perhaps you'll be better for that. I'll mention you but don't let on I told you.'

This information cheered Lana immeasurably.

'Would you, Avril? You're so kind. A *film*.' Lana sighed the word, her eyes shining with excitement now, the tears forgotten. 'It will reach a much wider audience, won't it?

This silly old tendon will be completely healed long before that.' She sat up straight. 'I'll do my exercises now, I really will, and I won't breathe a word.'

Left alone in the evenings it was inevitable that, with only the television for company, she should begin to drink again. And she didn't pretend this time, she just helped herself, in any case, she had no money to buy any for herself.

Two weeks later she had been to the hospital for a check-up. Her ankle was mending faster than anyone had dared to predict. She let herself into the flat and dumped her bag on the floor – she felt tired from attending the hospital, even though Portman had laid on a car and driver for her. She started to call that she was back and then stopped. From their bedroom came the sound of Portman and Avril having a heated discussion. She tiptoed up to the closed door and stood listening.

'You tell her, I'm not,' she heard Avril say.

'She's your friend – supposedly,' Portman replied.

'What's that supposed to mean?'

'You know damn well, only we can't prove she tried to push you down the stairs – it's your word against hers.'

'Don't you believe me?'

'Of course I do. I wouldn't have thought it of Lana but if you say she did, then she did.'

'It still doesn't alter anything, how the hell am I supposed to tell a fellow artist that they're out? Oh, come on, Portman, that's your job not mine.'

'Well, do me a favour and tell her?' His voice had changed to one of cajoling. 'I don't understand why you can't, you've said often enough you wished she wasn't here, wished you'd never invited her. Why did you?'

'She was always so cocky, do you remember the way she just assumed she would be a star? I wanted her to see how important I'd become – not her.'

'Are you jealous of her?'

'Of Lana?' Avril laughed. 'Give me a break.'

'It's just that I think it would come better from another woman. And let's face it, it's mainly your fault. If you hadn't told the producers about her drinking they would probably have given her the role in the film.'

'I was only acting responsibly, they should be told how unreliable she can be when drinking. But I'm the last person to tell her that they said they think she's too old for the part. Heavens! I'm older than her.'

'Only just and you don't look it. You've taken care of yourself. But Lana, with all her drinking – the camera will pick that up so fast.

'I've been wondering,' Portman continued, 'whether to ask the others to let her back in the show when she's ready. Isn't being out of the film enough without losing the show as well?'

'I thought you said that decision's been made. That everyone was in agreement – her understudy is miles better. And in any case we don't want the rest of the cast upset with a reshuffle, do we? It's all going too well.'

'You bitch!' The door burst open and Lana stood there, shaking with anger. Avril stepped back involuntarily in the face of such fury. 'You can't do this to me. I've a contract—'

'Lana, I'm sorry.' Portman spread his hands wide.

'Sorry? You'll be bloody sorry. I'll sue you. I'll screw you for every penny.'

'It'll make a change from your normal screwing,' Avril said sharply.

'That's a foul thing to say.'

'You take her back, I leave, Portman, and that's a promise.'

'Read the contract, Lana, you'll see that if, for any reason, you're out of the show in excess of three weeks we have the right to replace you permanently,' Portman explained, an embarrassed expression on his face at this distasteful scene.

'It doesn't say that.'

'It does. I had it put in, I was concerned.'

'What about?'

'Your drinking, if you must know.'

'You're a fine one to talk – what a lush you were! Who nearly killed his sister? But you succeeded the second time, didn't you?'

'Lana!' Portman stepped towards her. 'Don't.'

'Don't what? Tell her about you and Portia? I already have, you dumb cluck. But I haven't told her the rest. Shall I? Or do I get my part back?'

'What else?' Avril asked looking at Portman.

'No, Lana, it's out of my hands. What she is longing to tell you, Avril, is that she and I had an affair a long time ago.'

'When I was fourteen. Don't forget to tell her that,' Lana shouted.

'Oh, that. I knew *that*. I thought you had something interesting to tell, Lana.' Avril smiled.

'What do you mean, you knew?'

'We all knew. But I bet Portman didn't tell you one thing – we all knew because he'd tried it on with the rest of us at the school, only we had more sense than you. You were the little scrubber he and Portia had been waiting for.' She laughed this time. 'Yes, I knew that too. I knew what game you were playing.'

'You bitch! I always said you were.'

'Yes, but look where it's got me! And where are you?'

'I'll tell the newspapers – they'll be interested in such a famous man's perversions,' Lana sneered.

'Do that and I'll sue them, and you, for libel. I shall deny it, and who's going to listen to you?' Portman said coldly.

'But she just said she knew.' Lana, her finger trembling, pointed at Avril.

'Oh, I'd deny that too, Lana, darling. So will the others, Portman's far too important for anyone in the business to cross. Surely you realize that, my sweet?'

'Don't you fucking well call me your sweet! I hate you, I hate both of you,' she screamed, screwing her fists into balls and hitting her thighs in impotent frustration.

Avril was now standing beside Portman, and she put her arm about him in a display of solidarity.

'Quite honestly, Lana, I think it best you leave, don't you? We don't want you staying where you hate everyone.'

'Why? Why did you invite me here?'

'You sure you want to know?' Avril laughed merrily. 'Because standing beside you I look so much better – that's why.'

'No!' Lana screamed. She limped from the room and into her own and slammed the door shut and locked it. She leaned on it, fighting for breath, shaking her head with disbelief. She pushed herself forward and looked in the mirror on the dressing-table. 'It's lies!' she shouted at the tear-blotched image that confronted her. There was a tap on her door. 'Fuck off!' The door handle was tried.

'Lana, perhaps it's best if you're gone by the time we return from the theatre,' she heard Portman say through the door.

'I've nowhere to go.'

'Oh, come on, everyone always has somewhere. What about your mother?'

'Portman, please . . .' she sobbed.

'I'm sorry, Lana. I'm sorry it should end this way.'

'I'll bet you are!' She hurled a hairbrush at the door and then, seeing her face in the mirror distorted and ugly with anger, she smashed at it with a bottle of perfume and her reflection divided in two, a great chasm down the middle where her nose should have been.

An hour later, after a long bath and a gigantic vodka, Lana was calmer but her anger remained. She felt cheated. She had allowed Avril to con her. She was convinced now that even if she had not fallen on the stairs Avril would have made her fail at some point. But why? What had she ever done to her? Perhaps Avril was jealous of her and her ability, frightened of her? That thought pleased her. Or maybe she really loved Portman and was jealous he'd once loved her.

As she sat in the bath she had mulled over what to do. Her first reaction was to smash the flat up as she had the mirror, but reason prevailed, she'd done that once before and look where that had got her. No, she'd be more subtle this time – well, relatively so, she grinned to herself.

Wrapped in her robe, she padded into the sitting-room. She crossed to an oil painting of a landscape and swung it back like a book. She looked at the safe behind it. Now, where would the number be? Avril had a dreadful memory, she couldn't even remember her phone number let alone the combination of a safe. She'd have written it down somewhere, Lana would put money on it.

'Chubb.' She said the name of the safemaker and crossed to Avril's desk. She opened it and took the bulky address book from one of the pigeon-holes. She leafed through it to the 'Cs'. Aha! There it was. Jamie Chubb.

'Bloody fool, Avril. A child could have worked that out,' she said.

She discarded the boxes of jewellery in the safe – she could get caught for taking them. But the money? That was a different matter. Lana had overheard Portman explaining to Avril that the cash was a kick-back from a vintage car he had sold for a good profit – half by cheque, half for cash. Now, wouldn't the Inland Revenue like to know about that? Judging by the pile of notes – there was a good £5,000 – it wasn't just a car he had done deals on. Should she take it all? No, better not. But then she remembered Avril's laugh. 'Sod her!' She scooped out the neat piles of money. From Avril's desk she took a sheet of paper and scrawled a note, put it into the safe and closed the door.

'*Ta! Love, Lana,*' the note said.

Two hours later Lana, with her expensive luggage and all her clothes, was booked into a modest hotel – she would not make the mistake of an expensive one again. She must make her money last until she could get a job singing somewhere. With a nail-file she unscrewed a small panel on the bath, left for plumbers to access the pipes, and carefully placed the money, less £500, and the boxes of jewellery she had bought with Slim's credit cards, safely into the space. Then she replaced the panel. Her ankle was really aching now, but ignoring the doctor's advice that she still rest it, she went out into the night. She had contacts to make.

Lana entered the darkness of the Blue Parrot, a club in Soho where she knew a lot of the groups hung out, and where she also knew Toby Evans often went. She had no trouble getting in – women on their own were welcomed by the management.

Most of the men were pawing the dolly-birds sitting beside them. One table of four men took an interest in her and invited her for a drink. Lana declined, recognizing the look in their eyes – dope-heads; she didn't need another group like the Mantras.

She sat alone, ordered champagne and waited. It was an easy hour, the groups were good. The Blue Parrot was famous for giving kids a chance and had developed a reputation for being a showcase for new talent. She might find a band here needing a vocalist and, she hoped, Toby; he was a good contact and he'd always liked her, and felt sorry for her, she was sure. Why, she might even end up with him. That was a thought, she hadn't had sex for so long, it was about time.

'Hi, Lana. This is a surprise.' Toby, with a beautiful

but vacant-eyed blonde on his arm, was standing at her table.

'I hoped you'd turn up, Toby. I need to talk to you.'

Even in the dim light she could see a guarded look come over Toby's face. Lana eyed the blonde. She was no competition – she looked drugged.

'Oh, yeah? What about?' Toby sat down. The blonde sat beside him.

'I need work, Toby.'

'What about the show? Sorry about your accident, but you got fab publicity over it.'

'I'm out.'

'Sacked? They can't do that. Get on to the union.'

'They screwed me on my contract – I didn't read the small-print.'

'The union will want to help, management are always screwing us.'

'I don't think I want to go back now. And I don't want the hassle. I couldn't work with them again. I feel my integrity has been damaged,' she said, quite pleased with this even if she wasn't sure what it meant, but mindful of the money back at the hotel. 'I want to go solo.'

'Difficult these days – the competition's fierce.'

'What competition? I could wipe the floor with them, you know that, Toby.'

'Once, yeah, Lana, but now? I don't want to hurt your feelings but it's a young chick's market.'

'Thanks, Toby. That makes me feel great.'

'I'm being honest with you, Lana. I don't want you hurt further along the line.'

'Slim's done it. I see his new one is heading for Number One and he's in his thirties now.'

'Oh, come on, Lana. Slim's a totally different kettle of fish.'

'Would he help me?'

At this the blonde snorted.

'You mind your own bloody business,' Lana swung round and spat out viciously.

Toby patted the blonde's thigh as if to stop her saying anything back. 'Quite honestly, Lana, I doubt if he would help, not the way he's thinking.'

'How is he?' She would have said she wanted to know because she still loved him, but not with that simpering blonde sitting so close.

'He's fine. You know about his successes. His new house is great, not as big as the last one, but you should see the studio – it's up to professional standards, we can do all our mixing there, so he's producing his own records.'

'And getting even richer,' she said, with a hint of bitterness.

'He's going to be a dad.' The blonde suddenly spoke.

Lana felt herself going cold, she fought from shivering.

'Really? You *do* surprise me. I didn't think he could get it up.'

'Depends who he's getting it up for, doesn't it?'

'Cow.'

'You asked for it.'

'Ladies, ladies.' Toby laughed nervously. 'Lana, this is Sal, my wife. There's not much point in sitting here if you're going to argue.'

'Toby . . . I didn't know . . .' Lana forced herself to smile at Sal who ignored her.

'I'll keep my ears open, Lana. If I hear of anyone looking for a vocalist—' He stood up.

'Don't go, Toby.'

'Sorry, Lana. I think it's best. Sal's an old friend of Slim's too, you see.'

She watched Toby guide his wife away from her table but they did not go to another one, instead they left the club.

Lana poured herself another glass of the very inferior champagne and sat looking at the bubbles dejectedly.

'Alone?'

She looked up to see a tall, rather gaunt young man, with an embroidered waistcoat, long hair and an engaging smile. Her initial reaction had been to tell him to buzz off, but looking at him again she saw there was something of Slim about him. Why not? she thought, so instead she smiled her most innocent smile.

He was Chris, twenty-two, not a musician, he told her, but into property. So she said her name was Carol and she was nineteen and worked as a beautician.

'Been stood up?'

'Oh, no. No one stands me up. I often come here alone.'

It was his insistence on paying for the champagne, expensive in a club like this, that made her decide to stick with him. They walked to another club, one she did not know and sleazier than this one, with a striptease and even more expensive champagne. She liked the striptease, she decided, she found it exciting to watch, so much so that she didn't mind in the least when Chris's hand inched up her thigh and manoeuvred her panties aside. She was drunk now – very – and happily invited him back to her hotel. He apologized for taking a taxi, but his Jaguar was having a service, he explained.

It was a wild night. She had never had sex like it in her life, in positions she hadn't known existed. Nor had she ever had an amyl-nitrate capsule broken under her nose so that she felt the strength of her orgasm would break her back.

It was noon when she awoke. Her head was splitting, the early spring sunshine pouring into the room blinded her, her mouth tasted dreadful. She stumbled to the window, pulled the curtains and inched her way to the bathroom to clean her teeth.

The panel was off the bath. Forgetting her aching head, she dropped on to one knee and with frantic fingers

searched the gap. Everything had gone. All that was there
was a note: *'Thanks, Lana. Brilliant night!'*

She slumped on the floor, blinking at the writing. So he
had recognized her, knew who she was all along. She'd
been set up. Had he picked her, presuming she would have
pickings worth taking, or had Portman put him on to her?
Was this meeting just a coincidence?

In the bedroom, she turned her handbag out on to the
bed. The wad of £50 notes thumped on to the soiled and
rumpled sheets. At least she had that.

She sat calculating in her head. Four and a half thousand
pounds, and the jewellery, when sold, must be worth
another five.

'Shit! Nine and a half thousand quid for a screw!' she
said, and began to laugh. There didn't seem much else she
could do.

16

It was a combination of factors over the next two years
which made Lana act as she did.

Her finances were soon in a perilous state. She had long
since moved out of the hotel and taken a small bed-sitting
room in Earl's Court. Even this was too expensive for her
but, if she moved further out of the city into cheaper
accommodation, she would never get work, she reasoned.

Most of her clothes had gone. She had taken them, over
the months, to a kindly woman who ran a 'nearly new'
shop. The main problem with this was she did not buy the
clothes from Lana but sold them for her and took a
commission, so Lana received no money until a sale had

been made. If the shop was well supplied when she visited then she knew her clothes would be put into stock and the wait would be even longer.

So far Lana had resisted applying for work in shops or as a waitress. She felt that if she did her career was over, she would be accepting defeat. No, she was destined to be a star, she still felt it, and so she could only survive by performing. She had used some of her precious money to buy a guitar and had patiently taught herself, if not to play expertly, to strum adequately.

Some mornings she awoke and this conviction of impending stardom was harder to hold on to than at other times. And sometimes, at a gig, when no one stopped talking and eating to listen to her, it almost disappeared completely, but a tiny spark of hope somehow remained.

The gigs were hard to find. London, it transpired, was full of young women with a guitar, who felt as she did about themselves.

Mainly she sang in pubs, but occasionally she managed to get a booking in a restaurant. She liked these best. They were quieter, and a meal was always part of her fee. She would go days without eating and so these restaurant bookings came as a godsend. By never saying no to one she managed to make a living of sorts.

She did not eat because she preferred to drink, not because she had no money for food. And vodka, her favourite tipple, was expensive to buy. The mental haze that the alcohol gave her made her situation better than bearable but it did little for her looks.

Lana never appeared down, this was her strength. She kept her bright, innocent smile, her face was still pretty, she was sure, even if the make-up she used was of necessity heavier these days to disguise the puffiness, the dark circles under her eyes, the spots that not eating properly made inevitable.

She was not lonely. She had friends among the other

performers and the buskers who all met in a café on the Earl's Court Road where they swapped information on jobs, loaned each other money and shared their reefers and gossip. Lana had had the odd affair but they never lasted long. This was what she wanted. She wasn't ready for a complicated relationship, one that would make demands upon her time and emotions. It was essential for her career that she concentrate upon herself, and a permanent man would not fit into her plan.

Perhaps she could have continued this way had it not been for one night. She was in a pub in Battersea, which was full to bursting. She was sharing the gig with a young girl, Ruby, who, she noted, could not stay in tune and avoided any high notes at all. Beside her Lana would sound wonderful. Who knows, she thought, tonight might be the night a talent scout was out there.

She took her place confidently on the small stage, no bigger than a box really. She stepped to the microphone to announce her first song.

'Get the old bag off,' a voice shouted from the crowd.

'We want Ruby,' shouted another.

And soon the chant of 'Ruby, Ruby' was too much for her to speak against. She stood holding the microphone and felt her legs give under her; but for the mike she would have fallen. She looked at the beery faces, the open mouths, the red flushed faces.

'Bugger the lot of you,' she yelled, and to a deafening cheer ringing in her ears she ran from the stage and into the back-room. She wanted to cry but did not have time, for she was soon embroiled in a noisy row with the landlord who was refusing to pay her. It was a heated exchange which ended in compromise; he gave her half the agreed fee.

She sat in a café, staring into the cup of pale coffee in front of her. 'Old bag': she could not get the words out of her mind. How, at not even twenty-eight, could she be called that? She glanced in the mirror that covered one wall but she did not see what others saw, only what she wanted to see. However, she was hurt and scared and she used her money to buy two bottles of vodka from an off-licence before going back to her bedsit from which she did not emerge for three days.

She felt rough as she made her way to a mini-market. Her stomach was giving her hell, as if someone had poured acid into it. She needed milk, she decided, lots of milk. She paused at a news-stand to buy some matches and her eye was caught by a magazine cover.

It was Kitty as Lana had never seen her. She looked wonderful. Her dark hair had been scraped back from her face, and that face was starkly arresting with its strong, chiselled bones and full, sensuous mouth. But what was most striking of all was the proud way she held her head.

Lana could not really afford the magazine but she bought it all the same and clutching her carton of milk returned to the small room.

She turned the pages for the article on Kitty. It was a long one. It detailed her career to date, her success, how much in demand she had become, and so quickly, by so many opera houses. She was compared to Callas, she was praised to the rooftops.

'Good God, who'd have thought it?' said Lana.

The article was illustrated with copious photographs by Bailey of Kitty in clothes by Givenchy and Saint-Laurent. She was wearing wonderful jewellery which, as the captions indicated, was her own.

'She's bloody rich!'

It wasn't the clothes or the jewellery she wanted, haute couture would never have been her style. 'Not tall enough.' She grinned to herself. No, it was the success. She felt envy build inside her that Kitty had succeeded where she had failed. She had never once felt jealous of any talent Kitty had. She did now.

She picked up a pen and scrawled all over the cover, and then to amuse herself went back through the article and drew moustaches and heavy spectacles on all the photos of her sister. She felt better when she had done that.

A sharp stab of pain from her stomach reminded her to drink her milk. Glass in hand, she returned to her magazine and idly began to read a couple of articles.

She turned the page and another photograph leaped out at her. Slim! A happy-looking Slim complete with new wife and baby! Seeing him with her hurt, hurt like nothing in her life had done before. Why? Why could he not have loved her, why could he not have given her that baby? Oh, why? And then she began to cry.

It was then that she went on a drinking binge like no other. She had a little money put by in a tea-caddy and she blew the lot on vodka. Then she sat alone in her little room and day after day she waded through it.

It was her stomach that saved her. One night she awoke with a pain so severe that it cut through the miasma of her drunken self-pity. She sat up in bed, a coat round her shoulders, and she shivered, not from cold but from fear. She knew as clearly as if any doctor had told her that she was killing herself, that if she went on like this, she would die. She had to eat.

In the morning, aware that her purse was empty but for a handful of small change, she knew she needed help. She dragged herself to the call-box in the hall.

It was a long shot but one that might just work. People often kept their old telephone numbers, perhaps even when the house had burned down.

A woman answered. Lana knew instinctively it was her, and nearly put the phone down.

'Slim, please.' She forced a brightness into her voice.

'Who's calling?'

'Tell him it's Kitty.'

She knew she would not have to wait long.

'Kitty. Is it really you? What a wonderful surprise,' she heard the oh-so-familiar voice, almost breathless with excitement, say. She felt new bitterness rise up in her.

'No, it's not, it's me, Lana.'

'That was a shitty thing to do.'

'I know. I'm sorry. I'm sorry about everything, Slim. I need help, I need money.'

'Get lost, Lana.'

'But you never paid me, Slim, you owe me. I need help desperately. I'm ill, Slim. Really ill.'

'Get stuffed, Lana.' The line went dead and she could imagine the force he used in his anger.

She dialled another number.

'Kitty Lawrence's secretary speaking. May I help you?'

'Could I speak to Kitty please? It's her sister, Lana.'

'Would you please hold on?' Jenny said, but she did not go to the studio where Kitty was, as always, practising. She went to Felix.

'Felix, I have Kitty's sister on the telephone. Should I tell her?'

'What does she want?'

'I didn't ask.'

Felix paused for a moment, deep in thought. 'Tell her she's not in. Best thing, really. I don't want her disturbed, with a performance tonight.'

Jenny returned to the telephone.

'I'm sorry, Miss Lawrence is not available.'

'Won't speak to me, you mean.'

'No. She cannot be disturbed. Can I help you?'

'Tell her I called, will you? Tell her I'm desperate. I need help. My number, I'll give you my number . . .'

When the call was completed Jenny returned to Felix, relayed the conversation and gave him the number. Felix pondered a while and then tore the piece of paper into little shreds. It will only upset her, she can't afford to be upset,

he assured himself, and threw the scraps into a waste-
paper bin.

Lana waited all day for Kitty's call and when it did not
come she went once more to the call-box.

'Is that Connie Fox? It's Lana here. You remember,
Slim's ex and Kitty Lawrence's sister?'

'Of course I remember you, Lana. But I'd quite given up
on you.' Connie smiled into the telephone and hauled her
engagement diary towards her.

'I want to talk to you, Connie.'

Connie ran her pencil decisively through her lunch
appointment.

'Today at noon suit you? I'll buy you lunch.'

'Thanks, Connie. I knew you wouldn't let me down.
Where?'

17

Kitty lived in a safe cocoon. Everything was done for her.
Felix arranged the performances, it was he who argued
with the financial and musical directors of the opera houses
around the world. She never knew about the many arguments he had as he negotiated to increase her fees, each
time succeeding. She did not know of the gambles he had
taken at the beginning, turning down reasonable offers
which he felt were not good enough.

'You insult my wife with this paltry fee. Come back to
me when you've learned some manners,' he'd been known
to say.

He knew that at that point in her career Kitty would
have sung for nothing, but if there was one thing Felix had

learned in his business life it was never to undersell, and that was the theory he used with his wife's voice. If they wanted her they would have to pay for her. Nor did he neglect the importance of exclusivity. He was careful in the choice of venues and he restricted the number of Kitty's engagements. His plan was that eventually they would be *begging* her to sing.

It was a gamble that had worked; these days he turned down more offers than he accepted. It was Felix who had negotiated Kitty's contract with Decca, her recording company. As soon as the music world woke up to the realization that a remarkable voice had emerged, Felix had been inundated with telephone calls from record companies. He had shrewdly talked to them all but it was Decca's marketing skills he opted for. Kitty's voice, he was determined, should not just be known to the elite few who could afford a seat at the opera, he wanted it to be heard by the world. As the royalties for her recordings came pouring in, Felix could congratulate himself on his choice.

As Kitty's fame increased and audiences clamoured to hear her, and performances were sell-outs the moment they were announced, Felix became even more demanding. He wanted new productions for her. Any opera house management, always fighting a deficit, preferred an old production, for new sets, new costumes cost small fortunes. But after one production of *La Bohème* where the sets needed painting, the costumes were darned and, in Kitty's case, held together with safety pins, he said, 'Enough. Only the best will do. If you want her then she will want a new production, or we go elsewhere.' Invariably they agreed.

All that Kitty knew about her finances was that they were healthy and growing. It delighted her, once a month, to be shown her bank statements or her portfolio of shares. She was rich in her own right. It had all happened so quickly, and it was all thanks to Felix, as she was at pains constantly to point out to him.

Wherever they were in the world it was Jenny who arranged her life for her. It was Jenny who booked them on to flights, checked that cars would be waiting for them. It was she who badgered the hotels to make sure the best suite was available, the temperature of the room just so, the air-conditioning turned off because it affected Kitty's voice. She telexed instructions that no lilies or mimosa should be amongst the flowers in the room – they made Kitty sneeze. But above all no dahlias, for they made Kitty depressed.

When Kitty arrived at a strange hotel she always found Malvern water waiting for her, no matter where they were; the four feather pillows without which she could not sit comfortably in bed to study her scores; the Floris soap and always a complimentary bottle of Calèche, the only perfume she wore. All faultlessly arranged by Jenny.

When they arrived, Jenny unpacked for her and it was she who pressed her clothes, for she would not trust anyone else to iron the beautiful clothes that were Kitty's only extravagance. Jenny had become indispensable, and Kitty showered her with presents and thanks, always afraid that she was not showing enough gratitude to her friend.

Kitty herself was treated like royalty and had adjusted quickly to this lifestyle. Half the time she did not know where she was or where she was going next. All that concerned her were the acoustics of the theatre, who she was to sing with, and the conductor.

Music, its study, the performances, filled every waking hour. Music filled her dreams. Apart from Jenny and Felix she had no friends, she had no time for them or the socializing they might demand of her, and she did not need them. She had a friend, a far more demanding one – The Voice, that creature within her who was the reason for her living.

Kitty's rise had been spectacular, manipulated as it had been by Felix. She had now, by the age of thirty, sung in the great opera houses that mattered to her. She had kept her promise, and had sung at La Scala only when they had begged her to and she had graciously accepted.

She was famous for her pursuit of perfection, not just in performance but in herself. She was never late for rehearsals and always knew the score by heart. She worked herself and the cast far harder than they thought possible.

The more celebrated she became, this insistence on such detailed rehearsals intensified, although she was no longer expected to rehearse – others rehearsed, not the principal soprano. 'I need to go,' she explained to Jenny, who, worried she might be overtiring herself, had suggested she cut a rehearsal. 'I have to know myself that I have done everything possible to make my performance as near perfect as I can make it.'

Things did go wrong. A conductor whose tempo was too fast and upset her phrasing regretted it later when she told him her opinion of his ability. A tenor who held a note almost imperceptibly too long was subjected to her anger when others had not even heard it. A fellow soprano in a lesser role who came unprepared was told to find another career. She did not laugh, like the rest of the cast, when in *Tosca* she lost her petticoat and the tenor rescued her from her predicament. When a wig slipped, a chair broke, a pen for a letter to be written was missing, a light bulb went, a flat wobbled and others were amused, Kitty could not be. How could it be amusing if the all-important performance was ruined?

When she came off stage, if she had made one mistake, missed one note, got one breath wrong, or sung below par, then Kitty was in a frenzy of rage and disappointment – with herself. She would forget how well she had sung that particular role before and would worry and nag away at what she saw as her failure.

None of this made her popular with other singers, with the chorus, with conductors, with the directors or the management. She could not understand why, she only wanted everything perfect. Why didn't they?

Reasonable divas were the fashion in the business at that time. But one like Kitty, who was so demanding, was manna from heaven to the press. They had no difficulty acquiring their stories, there were many in the companies who were only too happy to feed them the latest drama. Even to those who had never heard an opera in their lives, Kitty was becoming famous for being classically temperamental.

People felt sorry for Jenny and Felix for having to live with such a tyrant. They need not have been. Kitty's dramas and anger were reserved for the theatre where, she felt, they belonged. There were two Kittys. When at home or travelling she was always the same, good-natured, sweet-tempered and, others would have found hard to believe, with a sense of humour. And then there was the other Kitty, the one with the daunting responsibility of looking after The Voice. When she argued and complained it was not for herself, it was for that other part of her, the part which demanded only the best and which she knew deserved it.

What no one, not even Felix, understood was that Kitty was afraid. Her success, after all those years of study, had, by anybody's standards, been meteoric. But in that confused part of her where her lack of self-confidence lurked, always ready to emerge, lived also the fear that because she had become a success so quickly it could all disappear with equal speed.

Was she happy? She knew she was – hadn't she achieved everything she had strived for? Critical acclaim, adoration from her audiences, the knowledge that The Voice was getting better, richer, more dramatic and versatile, and that she had money and would never want for anything ever again. But still . . .

There were days, and she never admitted this to a soul,

when she felt trapped, when she thought it would be nice to go to a pub, to a coffee bar, to wander around Selfridges again. There was nothing but shyness to stop her doing any of this – she was well known now, the public recognized her – and her obsession with work. But more importantly, and this was the real reason, she feared exposing herself and the precious voice to any germs in the crowds.

There were days when she felt an emptiness inside her. She was cared for, cosseted, guarded with devotion by Felix. But it wasn't love, not as she had once known it, and which, if she allowed herself to pursue the thought, she longed for. On such days she would punish herself with extra scales, a new concert piece to learn.

Two years running on one particular day in mid-July, the day she had worked out should have been the birthday of her baby, Kitty awoke feeling deeply depressed. She had tried to avoid that date as it approached on the calendar, tried to forget it. But she had remembered. And to combat the guilt and depression there was only one thing to do – work.

She had one treacherous thought which she kept suppressed, but occasionally, when she was tired, or things were not going well, it would surface. There *would* come a day, she thought, when The Voice would leave her and she would be free. She could become herself and love as she wanted, be what she wanted. Treacherous it might be, but it always surprised her that she found this thought a comfort as well.

To maintain her regime it was vital that nothing trivial should bother her. Felix opened her mail, and he and Jenny answered the telephone. Jenny typed her letters and Kitty signed them, often barely skimming them first. She did not experience the loneliness that so many other singers suffer, away from family and friends, touring from one strange town and hotel room to another, for she was never alone. Felix and Jenny were always there, so she never had to return to an empty hotel room, or take dinner by herself. Although her earnings were rapidly increasing, her money was untouched, Felix financed everything. He was glad to, regarded it as a privilege, and felt that all his hard work and financial support in the years before had merely been towards this aim – to support a great voice.

It was not surprising that Kitty felt she was on a treadmill, but then, she would tell herself, it was of her own choosing.

The fact that her elder daughter was now a star had filtered through to Amy. She had fallen out with Drew and was alone again. Now in her fifties, she doubted whether she could replace him, or even if she wanted to. She longed for news of Lana, which never came. Reading an article about Kitty in her *Sunday Express*, Amy found to her surprise that she suddenly felt very proud. Maybe she'd made a mistake after all. She'd got on with Kitty when she was a child, she thought with sublime self-deception, maybe she could again. She wrote Kitty a letter in which she said she was sorry they had grown apart. She mentioned how, as she grew older, she realized the importance of family, how she found she missed Mike and now appreciated what a good husband and father he had been.

Felix opened the letter, remembered how upset Kitty had been when she had been ignored by Amy at the theatre, and threw it in the bin.

No matter what he did, however, Felix could not protect Kitty when Cellini retired.

He had done everything to persuade her to stay, offered her double the fee he was already paying her to stay on as Kitty's teacher. Cellini tearfully refused. She was seventy. She wanted to return home to Genoa and die amongst her family. She had done, with Kitty, what she had set out to do; she had failed only to give Kitty confidence in herself.

Kitty was beside herself with fear for the future when she was finally told that Cellini was leaving her.

'My child, I could have died, and what would you have done then?' Cellini asked her.

'Been no one,' Kitty replied.

'Oh, what rubbish you talk. The voice would still have been there, someone else would have come to help and guide you.'

'But no one as good as you, Cellini.'

'Probably not,' Cellini replied, without a wisp of conceit. 'It might have taken you longer but I believe you would still have succeeded.'

'Don't go.'

'No, my dear child, I need my family – we all, in the end, need our families. And I'm tired. I can't go on cavorting around the world with you and you are so rarely in London these days, so there is no point in my waiting here for you, is there?'

'I shall be lost.'

'Never. Remember always what I say to you – listen to the music, the composer tells you all you need to know. A gesture, a phrasing . . . listen with your soul and you will hear.'

Nor could Felix protect Kitty the day that Connie's newspaper started the serialization of 'My life with Slim by Lana Lea'.

The promotion for this particular serialization had been immense, with advertisements on television, posters, hoardings. Unfortunately they had arrived in London the morning it appeared and Kitty noticed a billboard beside a news-stand.

'Jenny, look.' She pointed out the headline in capital letters. 'Oh, we must get one.'

'Do you think that's wise?'

'Probably not, but I'd like to read it.'

Ten minutes later she sat in the back of the car ashen-faced and close to tears.

'Oh, Jenny. How could she do this to us?' She handed the paper to Jenny to read.

18

Lana had been paid a small fortune to lie. She hadn't set out to do so on quite such a grand scale but once she had started talking to Connie Fox, just answering the initial questions, Connie pointed out to her that such information was not going to pay as well as if she embroidered everything. And Connie had gone to so much trouble that Lana did not want to disappoint her.

'Did Slim take drugs – does he still?' was one question asked over lunch after Lana had failed to get the talk around to a fixed fee.

'There was everything a junkie could want in the house,' she'd answered truthfully, hopefully whetting Connie's appetite.

'And Slim?'

Lana winked at her. 'What do you think?' Well, she hadn't lied, she told herself.

'Did he deal?'

'Oh, come on, Connie, we've no agreement yet on what your paper is willing to pay me.'

'Ah! So he did.'

Lana made no denial but felt a mite uncomfortable.

'And sex, was he faithful? What's he like in bed?' Connie mentioning sex and reminding her of Slim's lack of interest in her, made the discomfort disappear.

'You mean you want stories about the orgies and things? Then that will cost you double whatever you think you are going to pay me.' No doubt of that, she thought. If she was going to have to lie, someone was going to have to pay her for it.

'If you've got stuff like that, we'll pay.'

'And cheating on the Wall Nuts?' She had always thought Slim had been unfair to the others in his group, leaving them as he had when none of the others, while good, had his many talents.

'This gets better and better.'

'And screwing the sainted Kitty Lawrence?' That piece of information she did want included – she was certain she would never forgive either of them for that.

'How much do you want?'

Connie took Lana away to a country house hotel for three days of luxury while Lana spilled the beans, in long sessions, into Connie's tape-recorder. She was surprised, once she got started, how easy it was to exaggerate everything and make things sound worse than they were.

With a clever use of pauses, and Connie's cleverer writing, it was easy to imply that Kitty had been part of the orgies in the den at Slim's mansion. And, by innuendo, that Kitty had also been part of the drug scene. She had to tell about Slim and Kitty, even though it still hurt, and she cried quite pathetically when she did, for this was a big part of the selling potential of the story. Still, she managed to make it sound as if it had happened after she and Slim were married. The biggest lie of all, however, was that she and Slim had enjoyed an idyllic love life until Kitty poked her nose in – pride would never let her tell the real truth on that one. Best of all, she rounded off the story by saying that Slim had set fire to his house in a drink- and drug-induced rage when Kitty left him for another man.

The newspaper made her sign a declaration that all she had said was true, and indemnifying them against any legal action. But Lana was pretty sure that if either Kitty or Slim sued for libel the newspaper would cough up, there would be no point in them pursuing her for she would spend the money the paper handed over the minute she signed – just in case. She rather hoped they would sue, for then she would appear in court and remain longer in the limelight. And surely all this would help her career?

She banked the cheque in a new account opened in the name of Lana Lawrence, which might take longer to trace should she not have spent everything. She withdrew a couple of thousand in cash and booked into the Dorchester in the knowledge that she could easily pay any bills she ran up. Then she went out and did what she enjoyed – shopped until she nearly dropped.

By the time Kitty's car pulled up in front of her home it was already under siege by reporters who had been there since early morning.

She and Jenny parked the car round the corner and walked down a lane which skirted the back entrance. But that too had been staked out.

'I have no comment to make at this time.' Kitty pushed past them.

'Did you really take part in orgies?'

'No comment.'

'And drugs?'

'I shall be issuing a statement through my solicitor,' she said, fixing one journalist with an angry stare.

'You'll sue?'

'No comment.'

Kitty and Jenny raced across the garden, aware that

cameras with zoom-lenses were clicking as they ran. They burst into the kitchen, startling the housekeeper, Mrs Moffat, who was red-faced with indignation at the impertinence of the gutter press. She had even taken the phone off the hook since it never stopped ringing.

As they reached the hall the front door opened and Felix, pursued by reporters, burst in and then had to push with all his strength on the door to shut them out.

'Animals!' he said angrily and then, seeing Kitty standing white-faced in the middle of the hall looking like a trapped animal, he walked quickly over to her and took both her hands in his. 'My poor darling. Tea, Jenny, with a shot of brandy in it, I think. Come, my darling. Come and sit down.' He led her to the drawing-room.

'Why?' Kitty looked at him with an anguished expression.

'I must know, Kitty. Is there any truth in these statements of your sister's?'

'Apart from the fact that Slim and I had an affair *before* they were married, no. I went to their house twice – once the first time I met Slim, the second time with you. And that's the truth, Felix.'

'If you say so, then it is so. I can hardly believe that sweet child Lana could do this,' Felix said sorrowfully.

'She hasn't been that for a long time,' Kitty said with feeling, as she accepted the tea from a concerned Jenny. 'No, this is typical. This is my family still getting at me. And she's angry with Slim for marrying someone else,' she said bleakly. The news that he had remarried had upset her too, so she knew how Lana had felt.

'As soon as my secretary showed me a copy of this example of the gutter press, I called our solicitor. He's on his way here now.'

The solicitor advised Kitty that she had very good grounds for a libel case, especially since she could prove she was in France at the time of the alleged affair. But still his advice was not to pursue it, that the hours in court and in the witness box would be a trying experience and, no doubt, a painful one. Felix and Jenny agreed with him. Kitty wanted to go to court and clear her name, but as the argument washed back and forth she finally gave in.

'But I want an out of court settlement from the newspaper and a printed apology. Otherwise, I sue.'

'And give the money to charity,' the solicitor suggested.

'No. Why? I'm the one who's had the upset – not some charity.'

'Quite,' the solicitor said, put firmly in his place.

The newspapers also sent reporters to Kitty's mother. There they had a better welcome, with tea and freshly made scones, no less. Amy was only too happy to talk about her ungrateful daughter, how she and her poor dead husband had worked so hard to provide for her, and to encourage her, and pay for lessons . . . Amy did not lie, she simply failed to mention they were dancing lessons, not singing. And why, she told her eager listeners, only last year she had written begging to see her and Kitty had not even replied.

The reporters left well satisfied, but one with even more zeal than the others and a sharp eye which had shown him there were no photographs of the dead husband in the house, went to the local newspaper offices and unearthed the truth. Next morning:

'Diva Kitty's Dad a Jailbird!' were the headlines.

Slim's reaction to the reporters was different. He was in the middle of recording his latest LP. He was furious at being interrupted.

'Are you suing?' the reporters shouted in unison.

'What's the point in suing a nutter? Lana needs sympathy and a straitjacket,' he said, before slamming the door shut and going back to work.

With no libel actions pending, the story soon fizzled out.

Felix took Kitty for two weeks' rest at the farmhouse in the Auvergne. There were half a dozen millionaires' yachts on which they would have been fêted guests, a dozen millionaires' villas in which they would have been welcome. But Kitty had never understood the sort of people who enjoyed collecting the famous, and always refused. What little spare time they had they always spent in the Auvergne, for this was the only place, Felix noticed, that Kitty truly relaxed.

Slim's LP was released, plus a single, and both went to Number One, which coincided with the announcement that his wife was pregnant again.

Amy spent many happy hours updating Lana's scrapbook which she had kept over the years, and even if these latest cuttings were not about her being a star, at least it was her name in the newspaper, and that was what mattered to Amy.

Lana, furious that she had spent so much money so quickly when she need not have done, was horrified to see so little was left. She booked out of the Dorchester after calling a friend she had met on the pub circuit who often knew of available work.

'Could you get up to Cambridge by tonight? They need a girl singer – silly cow who was to have done it has OD'd.'

'Sure. Where, when?'

'Queens'. It's for three forty-minute sets at a May Ball –
but the pay's good.'

'How odd,' Lana said quietly.

'What's odd about it?'

'It's a long story.'

19

Cambridge, Lana found on her return after nine years, was
one of those places that never changes. There were new
buildings, and more building societies had opened, ruining
pretty Victorian façades with plate glass windows and
mosaic panels, but the atmosphere of the city was the same
and the people appeared not to have changed either.
Perhaps the types who became undergraduates all looked
similar down the years, Lana thought, as the taxi she had
taken from the station wove perilously close to the cyclists.
They seemed to be more in control of the streets than the
cars were.

Knowing no one here, she had decided to take a chance
and see if Paula, Cy's wife, still took lodgers in her house
across town in Chesterton. But Paula had moved, the new
owners told her, to outside the city, Madingley way. Lana
had kept the taxi, just in case, and asked the driver to take
her to the new address.

Paula lived in a farm set in what, for this flat countryside,
was a wooded valley. Anywhere else, it would have been
called a dip in the terrain.

It was not a working farm, that was obvious from the
lack of machinery and the overgrown state of the farmyard.
The one long barn, with its sagging roof, was littered with
cars from which various parts had been cannibalized. A

few chickens pecked around optimistically; a goat was tethered on a small patch of grass; and Lana could see a donkey and pony in an adjacent field. There were more children than livestock running about. But to one side was a surprisingly neat, fenced off vegetable garden.

The farmhouse was rather ugly, built of unpleasant yellow-coloured brick, with metal windows not graced by curtains. Merrybank Farm seemed an acute misnomer for such a place.

'Does Paula live here?' she asked a boy of about ten who was playing football with five other children of varying sizes and both sexes.

'Who wants to know?' he asked, suspicious beyond his years.

'An old friend. Tell her Lana Lea is here.'

Five minutes later the taxi was paid off and over camomile tea Lana was filling Paula in on the intervening years.

'I've followed your progress with interest, you know. From the papers, of course, and Cy used to have odd bits of news.'

'Some progress!' Lana shrugged. 'So you still hear from Cy?'

'Bless him, yes.' Paula smiled indulgently at the memory of the man. 'He's in America, didn't you know? He's doing really well for himself. He's in real estate now but he still manages a couple of groups.'

'Screws them, more like.' Lana laughed.

'He was always a bad 'un, that one, but you couldn't help but love him, could you? He could charm the birds out of the trees if he felt like it. And what a prick!' Paula and Lana shrieked happily at that particular memory. 'Still, he's done it,' Paula continued. 'He's done what few of us manage, fulfilled his dream. He lives in his spiritual home – America.'

'Are you still married to him?'

'Yes, but don't tell his wife, will you?' They both giggled

helplessly. 'Here, tell me,' Paula said, patting the tears of laughter from her eyes with a piece of kitchen roll, 'all the stuff in the newspapers a few weeks back, was that all true?'

'Nah. I made most of it up. I'm afraid I got a bit carried away. Mind you, I felt a lot better once I'd let it out and they paid me well for my fibs.'

'Still got it?'

'No, I blew the lot.'

'Best thing to do with money – it only leads to grief if it's hanging around. So what will you do now?'

'I don't know – try and scrape some work together, I suppose.'

'You could stay here for a bit if you wanted. I'd have to put it to the others but I can't see any of them disagreeing.'

'What others?'

'This is one of the last communes going, didn't you realize? Even we are petering out. There used to be a dozen adults here, now we're down to six and the kids . . . it's not really enough to make it work.'

'Why did the others go?'

'Loads of reasons . . . personality conflicts, usually with Dan – this is his house. Or they became disillusioned or the call of Mammon was too strong.'

'How long have you been here, then?'

'Oh, I don't know, what's time? I suppose it must be getting on for five years, the longest I've ever managed to stay anywhere. But I love it, we take turns with the boring chores and cooking and that gives me plenty of time in my vegetable garden. We share what we have, which is useful when you've got bugger-all. You're never lonely – if you've a problem then there's always someone around to help see you through. Do you know what I mean?'

'Slim's house was a bit like a commune except no one did anything but smoke pot and screw and no one was the least interested in other people's problems.'

'Oh, we've had folks like that here, but they never last, Dan sees to that.'

'Do you really think they'd have me? I'd like this for a while.' She looked about the untidy kitchen, at the food-spotted Rayburn, at the dirty crocks and empty milk bottles on the table and thought she'd quite like to tidy it up.

'I'll put it to them tonight over supper. You won't be back until early morning, I'll leave the key under the doormat for you. Let me show you where you're sleeping so you can find it when you come in.'

'You didn't seem in the least bit surprised to see me walk in,' Lana said, as she climbed the steep uncarpeted stairs behind Paula.

'I wasn't. Cambridge is like that – everybody comes back sooner or later.'

Lana didn't enjoy the May Ball, not like last time. She thought the behaviour of the undergraduates was infantile. With distaste she watched them spraying champagne and hurling bread rolls at each other. She thought them noisy and their partners shrill and silly. She didn't like the music or the clothes. And there were no decent fellows, they all looked like schoolboys. She had three sets to play, in a cloister, which was a pretty setting except that hardly anyone bothered to listen to her. It had all been so different last time. Better by far – elegant, amusing, great music, fab clothes and, of course, Slim. Ah well, she thought, as she packed her guitar away after her last piece, maybe I'm getting old. And she smiled, for she realized she'd never even thought it of herself before.

She had worried about finding a taxi at this early hour of the morning but she need not have, the streets were full of revellers self-consciously having a good time, and in the Market Square a long line of weary and bored-looking drivers sat waiting in their taxis.

When she arrived back at Merrybank at five-thirty she had expected to tiptoe up to her bed, that no one would be around. So she was startled when she quietly opened the kitchen door to find a man sitting at the table, pensively drinking a mug of tea.

'Hello, you must be Lana. I'm Dan.' He scraped out a chair for her as an invitation to join him. 'Are you tired?'

'A bit. Thanks, I'd love one, two sugars,' she answered, as he waved the tin pot.

'Has Paula explained how we work here?'

'Yes, she did.' She opened her purse and took that night's fee out and laid it on the table.

He laughed. 'That's generous of you.'

'She said you share everything.'

'That's the theory but it rarely happens – people tend to keep a bit back for themselves. Fancy bacon and eggs?'

'Wonderful idea. Can I help?'

'No. I like cooking breakfast.'

She watched him as he collected the ingredients. He was not what she had expected and she didn't know whether she was disappointed or not. He looked so old – fifty at least, she decided. His hair was brown, speckled with grey, but his beard was white which, she thought, looked really odd. He was very tanned, which was why his eyes looked so blue, she reckoned. His face was interesting rather than handsome, with a fine network of wrinkles around his eyes and deep laughter lines running from beside his nose and disappearing into his whiskers. She thought he was too old to be handsome, though he might have been once. He wore a singlet and shorts from which his somewhat pendulous stomach had escaped, but she liked his legs, strong and muscular like tree trunks, and his hands, capable and strong too.

'What, apart from money, do you think you could contribute?'

'I'd enjoy cleaning this up for a start.' She waved her hand around the messy kitchen.

'Good Lord – an angel, no less.' He smiled at her warmly, and returned to his sizzling bacon, the smell of which made her realize how hungry she was.

'You're not vegetarians, then?'

'No way. You get the odd one but they never last, they can't stand it when they see my gnashers sinking into a juicy rare steak.'

'How did it all come about?' she asked. Perhaps, for her own sake, she should ask some questions too.

'My wife had left me for someone else – more exciting than me, as she explained. The kids had grown up and were off my hands. I was bored rigid with the environment I lived in and so I sold up and bought this. I was at Cambridge, so it seemed natural to come back here. Then I gave shelter to one young couple and it grew from there. It suits me: I get fed, there's company and sex when I feel like it.'

'What were you?'

'Before I dropped out? A bank manager.' He grinned at her.

'I don't believe it!' She laughed.

'Nobody ever does. Here you go . . .' And he placed in front of her a plate of bacon, eggs and fried bread which she felt was the best meal she had seen in ages.

In theory, living in this quasi-commune had sounded wonderful, in practice it was not that easy. The mutual sharing of tasks, to which they all paid lip-service, rarely worked, and the carefully constructed work-rota was frequently ignored. This was all very well when it was housework or washing which was not done, but far more serious when that day's cook went walkabout.

The children, who were everybody's responsibility so

that there was always someone to look after them and an adult for them to turn to, should have been blissfully happy. In fact they were a neglected, scrawny and warring crew. The six adults to love them were too often the six adults screaming at them, so that they were totally maladjusted and resentful of any authority.

It should have been a selfless group, instead everyone was completely selfish. They collected their social security payments, the family allowance, but the sums put on the table never matched what the government had handed out. There were private stashes of pot, alcohol and chocolate secreted about the house. And, of course, their labour was the last thing to be shared when they had more important things to do.

Bongo, a failed drummer, had music to write. Doreen, who had once been a pretty blonde suburban housewife, had left her insurance salesman husband and had run away with Bongo, taking her four children with her.

Steph was intense and mystical and made jewellery from wooden beads which she sold to the market stall-holders in Cambridge. She was fiercely protective of her son, Offa, who was fat, and the bully amongst the kids.

Stu was the youngest male and had dropped out of college after an acid trip from which he had never fully returned. He claimed to write poetry. The sixth child, Dom, had latched on to Stu for reasons known only to himself; who he belonged to no one could be totally sure of any more. He had arrived the year before with a mainlining heroin addict called Crystal who had gone out one night and never returned. Paula, with her gardening, and Dan, with the book he was writing, were the only relatively stable influences in the house.

Lana was not to know that her acceptance had not been straightforward. The meeting the night she had played at the May Ball had been quite heated. They were six, and introducing a seventh could unbalance everything, Dan had pointed out, and the others had agreed. It was only when she had walked in, smiled at him, and put her money on the table that Dan had changed his mind.

He had been right, though, her arrival was disruptive. Before, they had amicably practised their free love, coupling with each other as and when the mood took them. But Lana, the youngest and by far the prettiest of the women, set the three men against each other like rutting stags. And the women were discontented for it did not take a degree in mathematics to work out that if no one felt like a threesome, one woman would be left out in the cold.

They need not have worried unduly. Within twenty-four hours the oddest thing had happened to Lana – she had fallen in love. For the first time in years she was no longer obsessed with thinking of Slim; he had faded away to where he belonged, her past. She was not interested in free love. She wanted no other man, and the very idea of sex with another was anathema to her.

She even knew the moment it had happened. He had singled her out that first night and in front of everyone had said he wanted her. The bald way he had said it, as if it was a fait accompli, as if she had no say in the matter, had strangely excited her. She went willingly with him, even if it surprised her. He had led her to bed and had sat a long time just holding her, and she had felt so safe. And when he began to kiss her she had felt a strange awakening of her body which she thought had gone for ever. And when he laid her down and she felt his weight on her she felt secure. And when he had made love to her and again held her tight and talked to her she felt loved and not used.

'I think I love you, Dan,' she whispered.

'That's nice,' he replied.

The others were going to have to go, Lana had decided within a week. She wanted to be alone with Dan to build a new life, and the others would get in the way of this goal. And they were using Dan, and she who knew so much about being used had resolved she would protect him.

It took her a long time to realize this ambition, however, for she had forgotten the tenacity of those who have nothing, to stay with those who have something they want. Nor was she alone in loving Dan – Paula did too, but she had made the mistake of believing herself entrenched. Paula liked to think she was the chief concubine in his little harem, that others might come and go but she would stay for ever.

When Dan was with one of the other women Lana suffered agonies of jealousy, but she never made the mistake of showing it to anyone, least of all him. Nor did she then pop into bed with one of the other men – she did not want to, but more importantly, she wanted Dan to realize she was sleeping only with him.

So those nights she had him she made sure that she pleased him every way she knew how and every way he invited. She had finally found out he was fifty-four, older than she had first thought, but he was a lot lustier than men she knew over twenty years younger, and far more considerate to her needs. And he never turned over and went to sleep but lay in the darkness talking to her and finding out about her.

She used this time to find out about him too, and, as she had hoped she would, discovered the key to getting him all to herself. He was a sham! This dropping out, this communal living he had fallen into, didn't really suit him at all.

But having gone along that path it was as if he'd lost his way and did not know how to get back to the mainstream.

He often talked of meals he had enjoyed – traditional English food like steak and kidney pudding, spotted dick, treacle tart. He reminisced about the smell of wax polish. One night he mentioned linen sheets. And Lana came to the conclusion that although he might have been happy to leave the restrictive life he had led, he regretted leaving behind the creature comforts of a well-ordered, middle-class house.

So Lana, who had never been a model housewife, decided to become one. Many times she thanked Amy for what she had taught her, and was grateful for her clean and polished upbringing. When it was her turn to cook she made the sort of dishes she knew Dan longed for. She cleaned up the kitchen, which he appreciated, and the communal sitting-room, which he admired. And then she left both rooms for a couple of weeks to be wrecked by the others.

Personal hygiene was not high on the others' agenda but Lana made sure she was always spruce and sweet-smelling herself, and that her lightly made-up face – no heavy make-up here – made the contrast between her and the other women more pronounced. One day she found an iron and, after washing and ironing her own clothes, she did Dan's for him, and his sigh of pleasure as he slipped on a pair of fresh underpants was an indication to her that she had almost won.

Her day came in September when Dan had gone into Cambridge in his old car. It was so unreliable that they never knew when he would be back, and it was that day the others chose to get rid of Lana.

'We were fine until you came, you interfering bitch,' Paula spat at her before Dan's car could have reached the main road. 'And to think you're only here because of me.'

The others muttered their agreement.

'You're a selfish bitch, Lana, don't you see you're cocking it up for everyone else?'

'What can you possibly mean, Paula?' Lana asked calmly, though her heart was racing. This was not what she had meant to happen, she did not want a row, she just wanted them to slope off quietly.

'You bloody well know – I see what you're up to, sucking up to the old boy, pretending to be so perfect,' Steph joined in.

'You make it impossible for the rest of us,' Bongo added. 'We had a good thing going here. So why don't you just go now, nice and quietly, before the old sod gets back?'

And then they were away, shouting at her, verbally abusing her, all in chorus suggesting she piss off. She felt herself close to tears.

The door opened violently and Dan stood in the doorway, shaking with rage.

'Leave her alone!' he shouted. 'Look how you're upsetting her!'

'But Dan . . . don't you see . . .'

'Shut up, Paula. Shut up all of you. In fact, do better than that, do me a favour, get out, all of you. Now!' he roared, like a bull, and, intimidated by his voice and size, they did his bidding.

'Dan, thank goodness you came back,' Lana said tearfully, as she flung herself into his arms. 'What made you?'

'Bloody car broke down a mile up the road – for once, thank goodness.'

September 1977 was also a momentous month for Kitty, but not a happy one.

She knew from Felix's expression, when he entered her bedroom where she was resting, that something dreadful had happened.

'What's the matter?' she asked anxiously.

'My dear, I'm sorry. It's sad news. Callas has died.' He sat on the bed and took her hand.

'Who?' she asked stupidly and then shook her head. 'Oh, no! It can't be.'

'I'm afraid it is so. I've just heard on the radio.'

'Where?'

'In Paris. In her apartment.'

'She was alone, wasn't she?' She shuddered. She did not have to wait for his answer, she knew how it had been for the greatest singer of them all. She had lost her lover and her voice, what could there have been left for her to live for? That was how it had to be. She shuddered again and clutched at her throat. She had forfeited love but at least she had The Voice.

Strangely, she began to cry. Strange because she did not know the woman and had not even met her. She had never heard her sing live, not because there had been no opportunity but because she feared to hear such excellence in another and, in the fearing, to feel that she herself would fail. She wept for the woman whose voice, alone, had set her on this weary path. She grieved for, in an even stranger way, she felt completely alone.

If falling in love with Dan, a man so much older and less like any other man in her life had surprised Lana, what followed probably surprised her even more.

When the last of the group had grudgingly left, she had started at the top of the house and scrubbed and cleaned and polished until she could hardly stand, her muscles ached so much. And she kept on, not just to please Dan but because she found she loved to do it.

'What about a new stair carpet?' Dan asked her one day, as he watched the very pleasant sight of Lana's rear moving down the stairs towards him as she swept them.

'Can we afford it?'

'Of course we can. I've a bit put by and a good pension.'

'You couldn't run to a vacuum-cleaner, could you?'

'Whatever you want, my little one.' He always called her that and she liked it.

Soon they had new curtains, carpets, a three-piece suite and a bed – she'd never fancied lying where Dan made love to other women.

Lana had found contentment.

And, slowly, she began to find a modicum of success. In the evening she often got out her guitar and played for Dan. He didn't much care for pop music but he liked folk songs and Country and Western, so she learned some just to please him. It was a small step towards starting to play professionally again.

She began in pubs and then an open air pop festival and suddenly she was in demand. And the demand grew further away from Cambridge, at summer fairs and other festivals, and she got write-ups in the local papers.

Dan drove her everywhere so she was never alone. They had had to use money from his savings to buy a new car to transport her from gig to gig. But it was not long before she realized that with the money she was earning she could pay him back. He was gratefully surprised and made jokes that, at this rate, he would soon fulfil his dream of being a kept man.

She looked a picture as she sang in her flower-sprigged dresses, her long fine hair falling about her pretty face. She drank less now – her desire to drink had diminished. She was easy to live with for she had become sunny-natured again. Living with Dan she felt safe and like a little girl once more, just like when her daddy had been alive.

Dan and Lana had been together for two idyllic years when Lana discovered she was pregnant. She was appalled, and travelled back from the doctor's surgery with her mind in a turmoil. What would Dan say? He'd had children and they had left home, he wouldn't want to start another family at his age. It would come between them, it would change everything and not for the better. They were so happy, just the two of them, she didn't want anything to intrude on their life – and what could be more disruptive than a baby? She didn't like babies, she could never remember crooning over one, she walked past prams in the street with total detachment.

It could not have happened at a worse time. An agent in Cambridge was taking an interest in her and had suggested she do a demo tape. They were waiting to hear if a record company was interested. The agent felt that her soft, husky, bitter-sweet voice was just right for now, an antidote to the raucous music which had taken over the young. Lana's appeal, he was convinced, would be to the older generation, the over-thirty-fives who could still remember what a song should sound like. But now this. Who'd sign a pregnant woman? And she was too old, she'd be nearly thirty-one when it was born. How could she be Dan's little girl any more?

He knew something was amiss, he always knew. A sorcerer, she'd jokingly called him when, in the past, he'd read her thoughts. This time she was determined not to tell him. She had worked it all out while she cooked the supper. She would pretend her mother was ill and say she had to visit her. Then she'd go to London and get an abortion, she had the money now, mounting up nicely in her bank account.

'Nothing's wrong,' she kept saying in answer to his query.

'You're pregnant, aren't you?'

'What makes you say that?'

'I can tell, you've got a look about you.'

'That's an old wives' tale.'

'Is it?'

'Oh, Dan, don't keep going on. There's nothing wrong.'

'Please say you're pregnant – please.'

She stopped peeling the potatoes and looked at him sitting at the kitchen table and she saw he had tears in his eyes.

'Why would you want me to say I was?' she asked cautiously.

'Because I love you so much, my little one, that I want you to have my baby.'

At that she burst into tears and he was up in a trice and hugging her and kissing the top of her head as he pressed her to him.

'But I don't want to be pregnant.' She sobbed into his shirt. 'I want to get rid of it.'

'You what?' He put his hand under her chin and tilted her head the better to see her face.

'If I have a baby I won't be your little one any more.'

'Of course you will. I'll have two of you.'

'It's the wrong time – what about my career?'

'What's more important? A career or a child? There's no contest.'

'But all my life I've wanted to be a star.'

'You are. You're mine.'

'Oh, Dan, I love you so much.'

'Of course you do and I love you and we'll both love our baby, now won't we? And no more talk of doing away with it, promise?'

He won.

Seven months later, just before her thirty-first birthday, Lana was safely delivered of a baby girl in the upstairs bedroom of the farm, with just a midwife and Dan in attendance.

'What shall we call her, then?' Dan sat on the bed after the midwife had packed up her paraphernalia and had long since gone. 'Lana, after her pretty mum?'

'Me a mum! Silly, isn't it?' She giggled. 'But isn't she the sweetest thing you ever saw. She's so dark, though.'

'All new babies are.'

'Dan, she's so beautiful.'

'And who didn't want her?'

'I was afraid of losing you.'

'Silly goose.'

'But no, I don't want to call her Lana – I've never liked the name myself. I know. . .' She looked up at him from adoring the baby. 'I know, we'll call her Cilla, after Cilla Black. It'll be fine for her when she's a star!'

INTERMISSION

Kitty had just completed a concert tour in Scandinavia that had been a sell-out success. She did more concerts these days – they were less draining than a full opera; the fees were good, and in any case, she liked doing them.

Her programme was carefully chosen and invariably the same, so she had the comfort of knowing she would rarely make mistakes and so was less at risk. Now she was a success the critics were harder on her. It only needed one bad operatic performance from her and the knives would be out. They had been waiting their chance: build them up and knock them down seemed to be their delight, as Felix was always sure to tell Kitty if a review was even remotely negative.

She was due to fly to Chicago in a fortnight to start discussions on a new production of *Madam Butterfly*. Oddly, she had never been asked to do this opera and yet it still remained one of her favourites – she always sang 'One fine day' at her concerts, it was her lucky aria – but whenever she and Felix had suggested it there was always some reason why the opera was rejected. But now, at last, she was to sing the part, and not before time she had joked, she was thirty-five in June, if they left it much longer she'd be too old. She was a fine-looking woman, in her prime, and could confidently afford such jokes against herself.

She felt harassed as Jenny packed for them to leave Stockholm. They should have done this tour at some other time, not mid-winter, it had been bitterly cold and now Felix was ill with a heavy cold that had turned into bronchitis. He had never been ill in all the time she had known him and she was worried. But what had really frightened her was that her dream had returned, the dream when she stood on stage with a bouquet of dead dahlias. But this time when she turned her father was not there, just a shadow, and she was so afraid it was Felix.

She felt an overwhelming sense of relief when Mrs Moffat telephoned from London to say that Kitty's mother was seriously ill in hospital: so the dream had meant her, not Felix.

'Don't go, Kitty. What's she ever done for you?' Jenny asked when the news came.

'I feel I should, even though I don't want to, even though I think it'll be a waste of time.'

'Then fly to France with Felix – he needs you.'

'He says he's feeling a lot better. I think I should go, she asked for me, you know.'

'Probably wants something, ' Jenny said pragmatically.

'There's that chance, certainly,' Kitty laughed. 'No, I must go. I want to see her. I need to know if I can feel differently.'

'Do you want to?'

'Maybe.'

The flight was late and at the airport she and Jenny separated. Kitty took the chauffeur-driven car that Felix always hired with the same driver, if possible, when they were in London. They were rarely in England these days since they lived mainly in Switzerland for tax purposes and holidayed in their house in France. Jenny took a taxi to the apartment run by Mrs Moffat now that the house had been sold.

Kitty was shown to her mother's bedside by a bustling and rather officious night sister. She stood in the darkened ward and looked at the woman lying in the bed, and as she had feared felt nothing, only an annoyance at the disruption to her schedule – at least, that was what she told herself.

ACT FOUR

1982–1983

1

Kitty emerged from the bathroom wrapped in a towel to find Jenny, fully dressed, tidying away the shoes and underclothes she had carelessly dropped on the bedroom floor. It wasn't like Kitty to be untidy.

'Don't do that – don't act like a maid, please!' Kitty was embarrassed. 'I thought you'd gone to bed.'

'No, I was reading in my room. You didn't think I'd go to sleep until you came back?' Jenny sounded mildly affronted. 'You look bloody awful.'

'Thanks, I feel it. It's not much fun, you know . . . seeing . . .'

'Love, I'm sorry. I didn't mean to upset you. Look, have a drink – a whisky?' Jenny was concerned by Kitty's gaunt expression. 'Do you want to talk?'

'I don't know what I want. I stood looking at my mother willing her to die, but I was pretending to myself. You know, say I didn't care and then it wouldn't hurt. Can you understand that? But I found I wanted to feel something, Jenny. I wanted to think she'd asked to see me . . . because . . . oh, hell, because she loved me. Then perhaps I'd love her too – or maybe I do.' Kitty shook her head with puzzlement at her confused feelings.

'How could you be expected to love her? She's hardly been the ideal mother, now has she?'

'I know . . . I know all that. But she's still my mother and I discovered it counts. But Jenny, there's something dreadfully wrong with me. I didn't want to touch her. I shuddered when I had to. I felt unclean – my own mother made me feel dirty. Hell, what does that mean?'

'It means you're tired, you've had a shock, you're working too hard and you were expecting too much. So on top of everything else you're deeply disappointed,' Jenny said compassionately. 'Come on, let's go into the other room – I'll fix that drink.'

Kitty curled up on the sofa while Jenny, incapable of doing anything quietly, clattered about amongst the bottles and brought the ice.

'There you are. Down that and I'll pour you another. I'm a great believer in getting drunk in situations like this.'

'She wanted Lana. That's why she got me there. She wants me to find her. She did want something, you were right.'

'And you said you would?'

'Yes.'

'I'd have told her to get stuffed.'

'She wants to be moved to a private room – I've told them to do it. Could you call Peter Greenmarket in the morning for me, tell him to pay all her bills for me?' she asked, referring to the agent who organized the London side of things for her these days. Not the bookings nor the negotiations, Felix would never let anyone else do that, but Greenmarket handled the other arrangements for her.

'Sucker,' Jenny said with feeling.

'What else am I to do? You should have felt the icicles from the nursing staff as it was.'

'Your mother was always good at fluttering her eyelashes when it suited her. Is she as ill as . . . you know . . . is she . . .?' Jenny's voice trailed off.

'Is she going to die? They couldn't say. She won't until Lana appears on the scene, of that I'm sure.'

'How do we find her?'

'It shouldn't be too difficult. Ask Peter if he knows of a good detective agency. Did Felix call?'

'Yes, and you're not to worry, he's feeling a million times better back in one of his own beds. Kitty, you look

done in; come on, Jenny'll tuck you up.' She put her arm
round Kitty as she stood up. 'I am sorry, you know, truly
so.'

'I know. I'm so confused.' Kitty looked away, she didn't
want even Jenny to see the hurt in her eyes.

'I suppose it's silly, a grown woman wanting to be loved.'

'Don't we all? You've got more than most.'

'Me? Don't be silly. Who?'

'Felix for a start, your fans, me.'

'Yes, you. I believe that, but no one else – they just love
my bloody voice.'

'Gracious, you are feeling sorry for yourself, aren't you?'
Jenny grinned at her. 'Bed, I think, it'll all look better in the
morning as my nan used to say.'

She did not expect to sleep but she did, fitfully – no
doubt the whisky, she told herself, when she finally awoke
with a headache.

'Do you really think this is such a good idea?' Jenny
asked from the foot of her bed, waving a bulging black
plastic bin-liner. 'Bit extreme, isn't it?' She tipped the bag
up and the mink coat which Kitty had been wearing when
she visited her mother tumbled out on to the carpet.

'Maybe I overreacted, I had to throw it away, and the
dress. Don't ask me why but I don't think I could wear
them again. They'd always remind me of last night. You
have it.'

'Don't be silly, it's too small for me.'

'Then give it to Oxfam.'

'I don't think they're too keen on accepting furs any
more, people aren't wearing them much now in England.'

'Why?'

'Cruelty to animals.'

'Perfect. I can use that as an excuse not to wear the damn
thing and then I won't hurt Felix's feelings.'

'Pity,' Jenny said, stroking the sleek pelts. 'Maybe I can
make a bedcover or something.'

'If it won't fit you then it certainly won't fit a bed.' Kitty was laughing.

'I don't know,' Jenny said, patting her backside and peering at it in the mirror. 'You sound brighter,' she said in a more gentle tone.

'Yes. Everything last night was an overreaction – you were probably right, I've been doing too much. I was dead tired.'

'You still going to find Lana?'

'Yes. She's had all the love so now she can have the responsibility.'

'Now that's what I call a sensible notion,' Jenny said, stuffing the mink coat back in the bag.

It took the detective agency which Peter Greenmarket had recommended just over twenty-four hours to locate Lana. Wanting to get everything settled so that she could return to Felix for a few days' rest before going to Chicago, Kitty set off immediately, with Jenny driving.

'Don't you think it would have been a good idea to telephone to say we were coming?' Jenny asked as they drove along the A10.

'No. She might refuse to see me and I've one or two things I want to straighten out with her.'

'Help! You sound very determined.' Jenny laughed.

Since the address was a farm Kitty had dressed in slacks and flat shoes for the country, but all the same, she quite expected to find the farm to be a modern estate in a town built on what once had been farmland. The very idea of Lana living in the countryside was difficult to comprehend – she was a city animal and always had been.

Kitty refused Jenny's offer to come with her to the house.

'No, it's better I see her alone. I'll meet you in the village. I'll probably need a walk after this,' she said, getting out of the car.

It was a farm, and in countryside, and although it was a rather ugly house it was well looked after; the garden in front was tended and the gate was newly painted. On a lawn were a child's swing and slide, a pedal car and a ball. Was she an aunt, then, and didn't even know it?

She knocked on the front door and realized she felt nervous as she waited for a reply. How long had it been since she'd seen her sister? It must be getting on for eight years. Then Lana had been in a hospital bed and they had not spoken.

'Oh, hello. I wonder if you can help me?' She smiled at the large and kindly-faced man who answered the door. 'I'm looking for my sister – Lana.'

'Then you've come to the right place. You must be Kitty – your voice has given me great pleasure over the years.'

'Why, thank you.' She smiled, but it wasn't the usual professional smile she turned on when accepting compliments. She had expected a frigid reception, not a warm one.

'Come in, do. We're in the kitchen, if you don't mind informality? Here's a surprise for you, Lana,' he called as he opened the door.

Lana was sitting at the table patiently feeding a baby its bottle. Her hair was still blonde, but it was a changed Lana. She was plumper, which suited her, but what was most striking was the contented expression on her face as she concentrated on her task. It disappeared the moment she looked up and saw Kitty.

'What are you doing here?' was her welcoming remark. It was not said aggressively but, Kitty thought, almost suspiciously, as if she was wary of her.

'I've come to see you.' Kitty smiled but was aware that she felt shy and a little awkward. She might have been planning to be cool, to tell Lana what she thought about her dealings with the tabloid press, but upon seeing her sister with the baby, all such plans disappeared. What was the point? That was in the past and it was best forgotten. 'It's been too long,' she added.

'Why now and after so long?' Lana said guardedly, as if she was expecting Kitty to make trouble.

'Tea, Kitty? Or something stronger?' Dan asked.

'Tea would be fine. How old's the baby?' Kitty asked, knowing that was the sort of question mothers liked to hear, and the best way to make contact and stop feeling a stranger with her own sister.

'Six months. He's called Michael, after Dad,' Lana said unnecessarily.

'That's nice.'

'You got any kids?' Dan asked from the stove where he was putting on the kettle and warming a teapot.

'No, not yet. There's been no time – I'm always so busy.'

'Leaving it a bit late, aren't you?' Lana said sharply, and then looked embarrassed. 'I'm sorry, I shouldn't have said that, I didn't think.' Then she laughed. 'I sounded like Mum, too.'

Kitty joined in the laughter. 'Don't apologize, it's true. Even if more women have babies in their forties these days, I can't keep postponing it, putting my career first.' But as she spoke she did not look at her sister, it wasn't that simple, one needed a man to conceive, and with Felix's lack of interest, the chance was even more remote. 'But then sometimes I wonder if I really want children, maybe we are just programmed to think we do.'

'Lana didn't want our two, did you, my little one? But now she's the most devoted of mothers, aren't you?'

'I enjoy being with them,' Lana said simply and Kitty envied her such contentment and felt a moment of jealousy.

'That's a surprise. I mean . . . well, you never seemed the maternal type,' Kitty said, flustered by the time she had reached the end of the sentence, and wishing she had not said it.

'Did you ever know what type I was?' Lana retorted.

'Here you are. Sugar, Kitty?' Dan placed the mug in front of her. She wondered if he kept interrupting because he too was aware of the tension in the room and was trying to defuse it.

'Two children, you said?'

'Yes, we've a little girl – Cilla. She's eighteen months old . . . she's having her nap.' Dan nodded to the ceiling above.

'My, that's a handful, both so close together. I don't envy you, Lana.' She smiled kindly enough.

'But then you never have envied me, there's never been any need for you to, has there?' Lana's pretty face looked shrewish.

Kitty took a long time stirring her tea. She looked up. 'Look, Lana, I haven't come here to fight with you. I'm sorry I haven't been in touch before, maybe I should have, but hell . . . a lot has happened between us . . . I'm willing to forget if you are.'

'I notice you didn't say *forgive*.' Lana moved the baby so that he rested on her shoulder, and proceeded to pat his back. As the baby was moved Kitty was aware of the warm sweet smell of an infant and felt a deep longing to hold him and an even deeper one to hold her own. Tentatively she put out her hand and gently stroked the soft down on the baby's head. 'Did you?' Lana interrupted Kitty's joy in the moment.

'Of course I forgive, it goes without saying.'

'I'm not sure if I can, though.' The baby belched and Lana lowered him on to her lap.

Kitty's mouth dropped open at Lana's audacity. 'Quite honestly,' she began and then stopped speaking. No, she had not come here to rake over the past. 'How's your singing?' she said instead.

'Oh, I've given that up. This is more important.' She nodded at her baby.

'You have such a pretty voice, it seems a shame,' Kitty said, unaware how patronizing she sounded.

'I keep telling her perhaps she should think about going back to it when the children are older.' Dan smiled at his wife proudly.

'It wouldn't be that easy. My type of music doesn't stand still, fashions change. Not like Kitty's music which is always the same: she can drop out any old time and go back to it.'

'It's a little more complicated than that.' Kitty smiled. 'But I expect Mum would like you to,' she added, thinking she must get round to discussing their mother.

Lana laughed. 'Poor old Mum, I suppose I've let her flaming dreams down. To be honest she was really more of a hindrance than a help.'

'That's hardly fair, Lana. You were her life,' Kitty admonished.

'How would you know? You scarpered off fast enough when you were eighteen – how often did you go back to see her?'

'Not often. But then she has made it clear she doesn't want to see me. Even now . . .'

'What do you mean?' Lana looked up from tying the baby's matinée jacket.

'Mum's ill in hospital and she wants to see you. She had a bad viral infection and, you know Mum, she didn't go to the doctor when she should have. It got really bad and has left her with a weakened heart.'

'Is she dying?'

'Maybe . . .'

'Then let her die.'

'You don't mean that, Lana.' Dan spoke softly.

'Yes, I do. What do I care? She lied to me, all my life she lied, "You'll be a star, Lana", "I'll make you a star, Lana, I promise". It was all lies!' Lana banged the table and the baby began to cry. 'I don't want anything to do with this. You visit her, you take care of her, you're the star.'

'Oh, come on, Lana, this isn't on. All you've ever had is her love – I had none and I envied you so much. And you treat her like this when she needs you?'

'Balls! You never liked her.'

'Maybe I didn't. Perhaps I didn't like her as a defence against all that love you were getting – don't you understand? Liking and loving, they're two different things.' Kitty leaned across the table and put her hand out, wanting to touch her sister, needing to make things right between them.

'If she doesn't care about you, then why did she contact you and not me?' Lana moved her position in the chair so that Kitty could not touch her.

'Because I was easier to find than you . . . that's why. And when I got there what was it for? To be told to find you.'

'Bet you hoped she'd gone before you got there. Don't give me all this crap – quite honestly, Kitty, I don't think you're capable of loving anybody.'

'Lana, that's not true.' Kitty moved uncomfortably in her chair – how close Lana had got to how she had been feeling in the hospital. 'There's my husband.' As she spoke she wondered why she said that; she undoubtedly loved Felix as a friend, but as a husband? How could she when he didn't love her as a wife? Convention, she supposed.

'Oh, yeah? You didn't feel enough for Slim, though, did you? Thought of yourself first and fucked him up good and proper.'

'Lana . . .' But Dan was ignored.

'I don't have to listen to this.' Kitty stood up.

'You always did run away from anything unpleasant.'

'You always were spoilt, Lana, and you haven't changed one iota. You've got so much, don't you see? A good husband, kids. And I . . .?'

'What were you going to say? "And what have I got?" I'll tell you what you've got, everything I always wanted –

fame, stardom, money! And you stand there whining at me, saying it's not fair that Mum loved me more. She did, for the simple reason that I was easier to love, because I gave back to her – you, you were always distant. What's not fair is I didn't have the same breaks – that you messed everything up for me with Slim. That I wasn't given a chance! You who've got everything, don't you bloody well tell me what's fucking fair or not.'

As Lana shouted the baby began to scream and from upstairs small footsteps could be heard pattering across the floor.

'I'd best be going, Dan. My mother's in her local hospital in the private wing. Should Lana decide —'

'I won't change my mind.'

'Bye, Dan. Bye, Lana.' Kitty moved to the door.

'I'll see you out.' Dan held the door open for her.

Kitty stood in the hall.

'I'm sorry, Dan. I don't know why I came or what I was trying to achieve. I don't even know why I wanted to see her – but I did.'

'When a parent is dying it's a lonely experience to face alone. You've obviously had a complicated relationship with your mother. No doubt you hoped to patch things up with Lana so you could face it together.'

'I suppose I did. I hoped certain things had been forgotten.' Kitty looked at the floor, unsure how much Dan knew.

'Most of the time it is, seeing you has brought the memories back.' Kitty looked up at his words. 'Yes, she's told me everything. She's very ashamed about the newspaper thing, you know.'

'Has she really given up all idea of the stage?'

'I'm not sure. She says she is happy and I've no reason to disbelieve her. But sometimes she seems sad and distant as if she's remembering another time. Maybe it's for her career which had just begun to lift off again before Cilla was born. Or maybe she dreams and longs for Slim . . .'

At this Kitty put her hand over her mouth to suppress her gasp of surprise.

'Don't be shocked, Kitty. He was probably the love of her life, I'm aware of that. But I know she cares for me too, even if it is in a different way. It is possible to love more than one person, you know – there's nothing wrong in that.'

'Isn't there? I wonder.' Kitty looked thoughtful. 'She's lucky to have you, Dan.'

'No, I'm the lucky one. And what are you doing up, young miss?'

On the stairs stood a small child. Kitty had expected her to be blonde and blue-eyed, being Lana's daughter. Instead she was tall for her age, dark-haired, with dark eyes. Kitty found herself looking at the mirror image of herself.

'And this is Cilla?' She approached the child quietly and knelt down on the floor. 'Hello, I'm Kitty.'

'Yes. Lana's got great hopes for her – she loves listening to music, you know. She says she's really going to be a star.'

Kitty looked up at Dan.

'Oh, Dan, don't let her. Stop her, please!'

Having shown Kitty the short cut to the village, Dan returned to the kitchen to find Lana, her head resting against the baby, sobbing quietly. Cilla was standing beside her, her thumb in her mouth and crying.

'My poor ladies, what's all this, then?' Dan sat down and swung Cilla on to his lap and hugged her to him. He stroked Lana's hair. 'What's the matter, little one?'

'Oh, Dan, why did she come here? We were so happy . . . everything's changed . . . she's spoiled things again.'

'How can she? Nothing has changed.'

'I want it as it was. I don't want to remember, to think about it. I want us to stay as we were.'

'And so we shall.'

'You can't be sure of that, Dan. The outside has come in. I'm frightened.' And she clutched at his arm as if afraid he was going to leave her.

2

The Voice dominated Kitty's life. She must care for it, nurture it above all else. The Voice was all that mattered.

Kitty knew this. She had willingly grasped at the role fate had given her. To maintain it, to be its custodian, to allow it to give pleasure, had once been her only goals and aims. And she had achieved both beyond her dreams. But now, something had changed and at first Kitty could not understand what it was or how it had happened.

She found herself wishing she could take that voice out of herself, place it in a box, put the box away and become someone else. And then she could return to it and replace it – but when she wanted. Just as the voice was trapped within her body, she was trapped by this voice inside her. They were victims, both of them, but she was the weaker of the two. Whenever she felt like a rest, a change, she did nothing about it for The Voice always won.

Kitty had occasionally thought like this before – she knew most singers did. The difference, in the past year, was that she constantly thought it, and finding it uncomfortable, she decided not to analyse the why and the how too closely for fear of what she might find. She did what she always did, she concentrated on her work, but she was finding even that more difficult to do, the thoughts refused to go away.

Everything was harder. Kitty had achieved so much. She

was fêted and applauded, she was admired by many and
worshipped by some. She had sung every role she had ever
wanted and there were still others to learn. Her reviews
were good, and the few bad ones she had had she could
explain away to herself, putting them down to jealousy or
spite on the part of people she had inadvertently offended.
They still hurt and angered her but her damage-limitation
technique helped her to deal with them better.

They had houses in Switzerland and France and a flat in
London, all fully staffed and equipped. She had a wardrobe
full of clothes in each home so she could travel between
them with just an overnight bag if she chose. When touring
she stayed only in the best hotels, was driven in the best
cars, and only flew first class or in private jets which were
gladly offered her by wealthy fans.

Kitty had never been a classic beauty, but now that she
was dressed and styled by experts she appeared beautiful.
Her success had given her a second blessing in that she
carried herself with pride. She was rich in her own right.
She could retire if she chose and would still have money
for the rest of her life. She could buy anything she cared
for, go wherever she desired, do what she wanted as a
wealthy, independent woman, but she did not. She could
have eased up a little, but she did not.

Instead, she worked even harder than before. She had
to. She was at the pinnacle, there was nowhere else to go
but down. She worked herself into stupors of fatigue from
fear. Already there were other, younger singers beginning
the climb she had made. There was one young Italian in
particular who was too good for comfort. The reviews, the
mounting hysteria now targeted someone else. She heard
this girl compared to her as she had once been compared to
Callas, and it sent shock-waves through her to think that
others were racing up behind her. So she strove and she
practised and she repeated relentlessly to keep the top
position to which she had become accustomed.

Why? It was simple. There was nothing else. For over sixteen years music had been Kitty's life. She was surrounded by people who shared her passion. Performing one role, she was learning another. Each lesson she studied as seriously as any novice, more so, as she polished her voice and maintained its splendour. There was never a day when she did not exercise her voice – even when she was resting, time had to be set aside for it. She was never without a teacher to advise her, to encourage her, in every city she had a favoured one to call on now that Cellini was no longer with her.

There was no small-talk at her tables, in her drawing-rooms, she and her few guests talked music. For her obsession was theirs too – they found it infectious when they were with her, as if it would be wrong to talk of other things.

Apart from the tapestry cushion covers that Kitty sewed between acts in all the opera houses of the world, she had no hobbies. She might have enjoyed gardening, but was never anywhere long enough for that pursuit; consequently her gardens were left to professionals to tend. She would like to have read books again, but she did not seem to have the time – there were scores and librettos to be studied on planes, in cars, on trains. She might have watched television once, long ago, but if she tried now she felt guilty, felt she should be studying more.

She was never ill. She guarded her health like a hypochondriac. She ate sensibly, she took walks for health and not for pleasure. She avoided crowds and germs. She knew no one who smoked for they would have been banned from her presence. She took vitamins and she consulted osteopaths, kinesiologists, homoeopaths, anyone who would keep her body healthy to enable her to sing.

She *was* her voice; without it she was nothing. She knew this, and had once been content with the bargain. The mistake she had made, and did not realize for some time, the one that made her question her life and fear an empty future, was that at the time of her mother's illness, she had allowed reality into her ordered and guarded musical cell, and the result was havoc as repressed thoughts and emotions resurfaced.

Why, at her age, should she suddenly become so upset at her mother's coldness towards her? Hadn't she always known Lana was the favourite? She had coped with it when young, when it should have hurt more, and yet it tore her apart now. The answer came: her husband did not love her, only her voice; if her mother did not either, then she was loveless. Perhaps she had always thought that there was still time to win Amy's love, but now she was ill, possibly dying. It could be too late.

When she had visited Lana she had watched Dan, only a few years younger than Felix, deal with Lana patiently and with concern. The house was ugly, they obviously had little money, but how she envied her sister the love of that good man!

Lana had taunted her over Slim, that ghost so successfully laid. Or was he? She thought of him constantly now but, sadly, never of what might still be but only of what might have been. She tormented herself with the thought that, had she not been so ambitious, so obsessed with the need for fame, she too would have a man who loved *her*.

Meeting her niece had affected her more than she had at first realized. If the child had been blonde and blue-eyed she knew she would not have been so acutely knocked off her mental balance. It was Cilla looking so like herself which had upset her – Cilla should have been hers. She should have had such a child to love and to love her. But she had killed that choice.

At first she resisted these intruders but when work, which had always been her saviour in the past, did not help and her concentration repeatedly failed, she allowed them back into her thoughts.

She wondered where Slim was now, where he lived and whether he was happy. What was it about his wife that had made him choose her? And, most important, had he forgotten her? She kept a folded press photograph of him in her handbag and often looked at it surreptitiously.

She wrote a long and involved letter to Lana, trying, as best she could, to explain her confused thoughts, asking to be kept informed about her mother and if she could have some photographs of Cilla and Michael. Lana did not reply, but Dan did. He wrote to say he would be happy to keep Kitty informed about her nephew and niece and he enclosed a few photographs. Kitty had them enlarged and duplicated and framed in silver. They stood on her pianos in the work-rooms in Switzerland and France.

Perhaps it was writing to Dan that made Kitty think of others she had lost touch with. She wrote to Max Leitman, someone in whom she felt she could confide her discontent. And she wrote to Camilla de Souza, the woman who, more than anyone, had set her on this path. She wasn't quite sure why she did. She had allowed friends to disappear, saying she did not have the time. She must make the time. And perhaps she just wanted to touch her own past to remind herself that she had existed once in a different form. She began to correspond with Max and Camilla and she looked forward to their letters.

Kitty had hoped this would make her more contented; but in fact the opposite happened. She realized, as she looked at the photographs, that time was rushing by, that her life had been one-dimensional for too long, that she did not live as others did.

3

Amy did not die.

For several days after Kitty's visit Lana loudly proclaimed she did not care about her mother and had no intention of visiting her, why should she? But then a mixture of guilt and fear and happy memories overwhelmed her. What if her mother should die and she had ignored her, how would she be able to live with herself then? But what if she was dying, what then? Lana feared death and her reaction to it. And then she thought of the good times when she had been a child and her mother had had such faith in her, had made her feel so important, the way her mother had pushed her, given her confidence, when she herself would have preferred to give up. She remembered the good laughs they had had together, the chats – they had been more like sisters. Then she relented and made the long journey to the hospital, leaving Dan at home to look after the children.

When she saw Amy sleeping and looking so frail and wan in the large hospital bed, Lana burst into tears. Amy's eyes opened. At sight of Lana she smiled.

'Well, this is a pretty kettle of fish and no mistake. Hospital visitors are supposed to cheer patients up.' Amy smiled again at Lana as she wearily brushed a tear away from her own eyes.

'Mum, I'm sorry. I'm so sorry . . .'

'Nothing to apologize about, Lana. You're here now and that's what counts.' Amy patted Lana's hand reassuringly. 'You and me, we've had our ups and downs but we'll always love each other, we'll always get back together.' And Amy began to haul herself up in the bed.

'That's right, Mum.'

'No one and nothing can ever break us up.' She settled back on the pillows, a satisfied expression on her face.

'I was so confused, Mum. And miserable.'

'I know, love.' Amy smiled.

'And when I lost my part and everything I was so depressed . . .'

'I understand. You don't have to explain yourself to your old mum. That's all past now. Water under the bridge . . .'

A nurse entered the room, the flowers Lana had brought with her arranged in a vase.

'Now, we don't want to tire our patient, do we?' she said fussily.

'This is my daughter, nurse,' Amy said proudly. 'She's like a tonic to me, don't you make her scarper yet.'

'You've certainly got more colour in your cheeks already, Mrs Lawrence, and that's a fact. And sitting up too, that's good.' The nurse plumped up the pillows and helped lift Amy further up the bed.

'Isn't she beautiful?' Amy asked the nurse, nodding at her daughter.

'Oh, Mum!' Lana giggled with embarrassment.

'You should hear her sing, she's like an angel.'

'Both daughters singers, you must be proud of them.' The nurse folded the top sheet down expertly. 'I'm quite partial to a bit of opera, you know, the nice arias . . .'

'I'm proud of my Lana,' Amy said with such a defiant look that the nurse decided not to inquire further of the other daughter.

'Ten more minutes, then.' She bustled from the room.

'Mum, you must stop going on like this. Kitty's been good to you, just look at this room, it's lovely. It must be costing an arm and a leg.'

'She can afford it.'

'That's not the point, she need not pay for it unless she wanted to. She loves you, you know.'

'No, I don't know. Funny way of showing it, if you ask

me,' Amy said sharply. 'And I don't want to waste the next
ten minutes talking about her. I knew you'd come, I just
knew it. They thought I was going to die . . . not until I've
seen my Lana, I thought to myself.'

'Mum, don't talk like that. You're going to be fine.'

'I know I am, especially now.' She extended an emaciated hand to Lana. 'Now, tell me all about yourself and
the kids – I can't get over the idea of me being a granny.
Brought any pics?'

'You don't look much like a granny.'

'No need to fib to me, Lana. I look like a bloody old
crone. But once I'm out of here . . .' She laughed, and
Lana was amazed at the difference in her since she had
entered the room. 'And this Dan of yours, tell me all about
him.'

And Lana did, her face glowing with pride and love as
she explained how safe and happy she was with Dan. And
as she watched the pleasure on her mother's face she felt
guilty that she had shut her out of her life for so long – she
had not had the right to do that.

'And what about your singing?' Amy asked suddenly.

'What with the kids —'

'You're not going to tell me you've given up?' Amy was
bolt upright now.

'I don't need it, Mum. I'm happy as I am – happier,
probably.'

'Was this your idea or that Dan's?'

'Mine. The need to sing just isn't there any more.'

'I've never heard such a load of cod's-wallop in my life.
Why can't you sing and be happy as well? I'll have to see
about this . . .'

Amy was in the hospital for a further two weeks. Lana
visited as often as she could get away, but it was a long and
tiring journey. It was Amy who suggested that she be

moved to a private hospital in Cambridge, closer to Lana. An ambulance was hired, Kitty was billed for it, and Amy settled happily into the Evelyn Nursing Home in a downstairs room which overlooked the pleasant gardens. Now Lana could visit every day.

Amy's rate of recovery amazed everyone, including the doctors. It was as if she was willing her tired heart to recover, as if once reunited with her daughter she was determined to live for her sake. She found being treated as an invalid restricting and she whined, cajoled and begged the doctors to let her out.

'But Mrs Lawrence, you're not strong enough to manage on your own,' her doctor counselled.

'I won't be on my own. I'll be at my daughter's, she'll take care of me.'

She said this with total confidence, even though she had not consulted Lana about the plan. The first Lana knew was when, on a visit, she was asked to wait to see the doctor.

'She'll have to be kept quiet, you do understand?' he said.

'My mother? Quiet?' Lana smiled.

'It's imperative. She's had a very nasty infection which, untreated, has led to the weakening of the heart muscle.' The doctor looked sternly at Lana as if her mother not going to her GP when ill with the initial infection was her fault. 'She will have to take things easy for a good six months or so.'

'Six months?' Lana repeated inanely, reeling inwardly at the thought of having her mother to stay for that length of time.

'Quite so, and even then her dancing days will be over. She tells me she loves to go dancing but . . .' The doctor spread his hands expressively. 'Such a character, your mother. Such an indomitable spirit. The nurses tell me they'll miss her.'

'Yes, she's quite something, isn't she?' She was already wondering how she was going to break the news to Dan.

Lana need not have worried about Dan's reaction, she should have known he would welcome his mother-in-law into his home, that he would regard it as his duty to care for her as long as necessary. And in any case, he announced, he liked her, she amused him. Certainly Amy went out of her way to charm him, fluttering her eyelashes at him at every opportunity, thanking him effusively for everything he did, constantly telling him how grateful she was for her daughter's happiness and contentment, and never, ever whining.

Having her mother in the house was not nearly as bad as Lana had anticipated. She turned out to be a surprisingly good patient, pacing herself sensibly.

'I'm determined to get better quickly, so I've got to follow the doctor's orders,' she said as she swallowed the first of the many pills prescribed her during the day. 'I've things to do.'

'Like what?' Lana asked idly as she dusted her mother's bedroom for her.

'Get you back on course.'

'Me?' Lana stood holding a yellow duster limply in her hand. 'What do you mean?'

'Your singing. You've got to start again.'

'That's over, Mum. It was fun but it's in the past. I've got a family now.'

'Nonsense. You must sing. A talent like yours, it's wicked not to be doing something with it.'

'Dan and the kids are more important than that.'

Amy leaned forward and grabbed Lana's hand. 'Listen to me, my darling. You were born to be a star, why else would I have *known* to give you a star's name? You *will* be a star. I know it. I've always known it,' she said urgently.

'Oh, Mum, you are funny. You never give up. I've told you, I'm not interested any more.'

And Amy did not give up.

Her campaign was subtle and insidious for she had had plenty of time to plan it in the days when she was allowed little activity. First, as a thank-you present for caring for her, she used her savings to buy Lana and Dan – she was at pains to point out it was for him too – a brand-new hi-fi with fine matt black speakers and a couple of records of Country and Western music which she knew Dan liked. It sat proudly in the small sitting-room and they would sit and listen to it of an evening when there was nothing to watch on the television.

Then, on each of her trips to Cambridge to see her doctor, Amy would pop into Miller's record shop and buy a couple of records. Jazz, Country and Western, pop, and then, one day, the music for *Prince of Darkness*.

She waited until Dan was out to play that particular record. When she put it on and the so-familiar notes of the overture pounded into the room, Lana sat rigid in her chair, her children neglected, looking as if she was not breathing, silent tears beginning to roll down her cheeks. Despite her condition, Amy was across the room in a flash.

'Don't take on, my sweet. Don't cry. It won't be long, you'll be back there slugging it to them, that's a promise.'

Lana looked at her mother, her face tear-streaked. 'Oh, Mum. I miss it so.'

One day Amy just happened to mention that Dan did not seem to help Lana much. Lana defended him but then she did notice that perhaps after supper he moved to his chair by the fire a little quickly these days.

'What is it about men that they never think to thank you for cooking them supper?' Amy said one evening as she helped with the drying up. And it was she who queried what Dan got up to on his many trips to Cambridge.

'Perhaps he's got a bird,' she joked and laughed loudly, but Lana didn't.

She followed this up with remarks on how dowdy Lana was looking in her old clothes, asking when had she bought anything new. And when Lana told her that she could not afford it, Amy opened her purse and they embarked on a shopping spree.

'Just like the old days, Mum,' Lana said gaily.

And it was Amy who paid for Lana's hair to be done, for the kitchen to be painted, and finally for a little red Mini and a course of driving lessons.

'You should have your own wheels in this day and age. Gives you a bit of freedom,' Amy advised when she handed over the keys.

'But Mum, can you afford it?'

''Course I can. Living on my own I put a tidy sum by. I'm not like your sister, I'm generous with my money,' she said with a sniff. Lana, despite thinking this an unfair comment, did not defend Kitty.

It was not necessary to be so subtle with the children. Amy was horrible to them so that they played up, occasionally pinching them to make them cry, certain this would give Lana a headache.

4

Unusually for Kitty she was travelling alone – in fact, it was the first time since she had become a professional singer that she could remember this happening. She wasn't supposed to be on her own but circumstances had intervened.

Felix was at home in Switzerland. He had a worrying recurrence of the bronchitis which had laid him low last winter and this time the doctors had forbidden any travel and had insisted he stay in bed.

Kitty and Jenny had flown to Milan for a performance of *Tosca* which was well received although Kitty was far from pleased with it. She hadn't liked the conductor who, she felt, had little respect for the singers and had objected strongly when she had wanted to rehearse for a longer time than he had allotted. She disliked the tenor who was past his prime and sloppy in his approach. And she felt her voice was lacking the dramatic quality – normally her *forte* – that *Tosca* demanded.

'I didn't notice,' Jenny said, holding her cheek. 'You sounded as good as usual.'

'You say that when I sing in the bath,' Kitty said, a shade sharply for her, but she was irritated that she did not have Felix here to discuss with him what had gone wrong.

'And you do.'

'What's wrong with your cheek?'

'I've got this tooth which keeps twingeing.'

'You eat too many chocolates,' Kitty said unsympathetically. 'I want to go back to Switzerland tonight – do you think you can arrange it?'

'But this hotel's fine . . . I'm sure Felix is all right, Kitty. You need a good night's sleep.'

'No, I have to see him.' She knew she was being unreasonable, she could not help herself. The Voice and she needed reassurance.

'Why, for heaven's sake? Let the poor man rest. We'll have to be away tomorrow morning to Paris.'

'Jenny, just for once, be a pet, do as I say, will you? Book us on a flight . . .'

It was only the use of Kitty's name that got them on the last flight to Geneva. And it was two in the morning before they arrived at their chalet in the mountains. Snow was falling.

'It'll serve you right if we get snowed in.'

'Oh, shut up, Jenny.'

Felix had heard the car and was at the top of the stairs peering down anxiously as, stamping the snow off their shoes, the two women entered the pine-panelled hallway.

'What's wrong? Why are you here?' he asked anxiously.

'It was a disaster. Oh, Felix, why weren't you there? I shall never sing when Zoffi conducts again – ever! The tempo was all over the place. I think he was drunk.'

'Never!'

'I do.'

'Honestly, Felix, she was fine,' Jenny interrupted.

'Fine!' Kitty said shrilly. 'That buffoon Rincini can't sing – he was transposing all over the place. He constantly placed himself in front of me. And he kept missing his cue . . . and he's finished. Why should I be expected to sing with has-beens like that? He's hanging on to my coat tails, Felix. I won't have it!' She spoke as one in a panic does.

'Nor shall you, my sweet,' Felix said, coming down the stairs towards them. 'Let's have a drink and talk this over, shall we?' He put out his hand and took hers and led her towards the study.

'Felix, you don't look well, you should be in bed,' Jenny fretted.

'This is more important than any cold, Jenny. Could you warm me some milk with honey? I fancy that with a touch of brandy. Now, my dear one. Tell me what was really wrong?' he asked, when Jenny had left the room.

Kitty's shoulders slumped. She looked dejected. 'It was me, Felix. The Voice – I felt as if only half of it was working.'

'Half of it?' He looked quizzically at her.

'Well, a bit of it. I lost my depth, I felt I was losing the dramatic quality – it was plain, boring, no texture.'

'Did the audience think so? The others?'

'No, but I did. I could feel it. My soul wasn't in it and I don't know why.'

'Shush.' He put his arm around her shoulders. 'Do you think perhaps you are working too hard? That the freshness is harder to maintain?'

'Then you've heard it . . . you didn't tell me.' She moved from his arms and looked at him accusingly.

'No, I've heard no such thing. If anything, I think you're in better voice than ever before. But if you think it then something is wrong. I believe you are tired. I believe you need a rest. We should cancel Paris and Chicago and you should see a doctor.'

'Cancel! I couldn't do that. I've never cancelled, not once in my whole career.' She sounded appalled at the suggestion.

'So, this once you would be forgiven. Other singers do . . .'

'I'm not other singers, I'm me!'

'Oh, Kitty, I knew that would be your answer.' He laughed. 'I love you when you talk like that. My dear, darling Diva.' He smiled at her.

'You mean you love my voice . . .'

'No, I didn't say that . . .' But Jenny entered the room and the conversation ceased.

It was five before Kitty felt sufficiently reassured and they went to bed.

The next day she and Jenny flew to Paris. Two days later Jenny had an abscess on her tooth and Kitty insisted she go to their dentist in London.

That night she felt sick with nervousness as she faced going on alone. Normally she was not nervous – she knew she was well prepared, knew her role, knew her voice was in good shape and, equally importantly, that Felix would be standing in the wings, willing her success. That night, surrounded by the rest of the cast, she felt completely

isolated. She willed herself to step on to the stage, moved
to her position, acknowledged the applause of the audience
at her appearance, nodded almost imperceptibly to the
conductor, opened her mouth to sing, and no sound
emerged!

She recovered quickly, even if she felt dizzy with fear.
She held up her hands and apologized, smiling as if totally
unconcerned. She took a deep breath and sang. At the end
of the aria the audience stood and roared their approval
and their thanks. But Kitty was shattered; nothing like that
had happened to her before on any stage.

How could Felix let her down? Why was he ill now of all
times? Why was he not here when she needed him? she
asked herself illogically later in her dressing-room before
she allowed in the many admirers of her voice who liked to
come to see her after a performance. Normally she did not
mind but tonight she could have done without them.

Now she was sitting in the VIP lounge of the airport
waiting for her delayed flight to New York and then to
Chicago. She was reading *Paris Match* – she should begin to
read other things beside scores, she had begun to tell
herself, she should relax more.

The tension inside her was almost intolerable. After the
scare on the Paris stage she was flying off to Chicago alone
to face God knew what in the long-planned production of
Madam Butterfly. Her Paris agent should have been with
her, but the fog that was holding up her aeroplane was also
delaying him – he was stuck somewhere near Versailles.

She had called Felix, fortunately after she had calmed
down. He sounded very depressed. She had assured him
all was well and that she was looking forward to Chicago
and singing Madam Butterfly for the very first time. Looking forward! She felt terrified, she felt like a novice again.

A young and very beautiful woman with long blonde
hair and long legs, smartly and expensively dressed, who
had been sitting across the room with two noisy children

and a harassed-looking nanny, jumped to her feet as the airport hostess appeared.

'Any news?' she asked, in a flat Boston drawl. Kitty glanced up. There was something familiar about her but she could not place her.

'I'm sorry, Mrs Fletcher. The fog is getting worse.'

Kitty ducked back behind her magazine. Slim's wife! She felt her heart thudding, her palms dampen. She wanted to look at the woman, study her, and, at the same time, she couldn't.

'Oh, dear. I'm not sure what to do. I arranged to meet my husband here and this God-awful fog must have delayed him. My children are exhausted.'

Kitty could not help but smile, the children certainly did not sound exhausted.

'We could put you up in the airport hotel, Mrs Fletcher – at our expense, of course.'

'No, thanks. I think I'd better go back to the Ritz – he might be there. He'll be worried.'

'I'm sure he'd have called to check, Mrs Fletcher.'

'No, you don't know my husband . . . he wouldn't think . . . Emma, collect the children's bags, please,' she said to the nanny. 'Thanks so much.' She smiled at the ground hostess and Kitty found herself almost wishing she had been rude and vulgar, not charming and nice.

'Miss Lawrence, I very much regret . . .' The hostess was standing over her. 'The met report looks bad. Do you want me to book you into a hotel?'

'When's the next weather report?'

'In half an hour.'

'I'll wait, just on the off-chance we can fly.'

'Is there anything I can get you?'

'No, thanks, I'm fine.' Kitty settled back to her magazine and the hostess continued on her round of apologies.

'Excuse me, I wonder, have you seen my wife with two children? We're booked on the New York flight.'

Kitty's heart lurched as she recognized the voice – it was Slim. She did not dare look up, was afraid to see him, afraid to see a polite expression where once there had been longing. She raised the magazine to cover her face entirely and sat in turmoil – he was booked on her flight. She could not avoid him if they were on the same plane. She got quickly to her feet, the hostess was at her side in seconds.

'Changed your mind, Miss Lawrence?'

'Yes, I'm tired . . . I think . . .'

'Kitty! It's Kitty.' And Slim bounded across on his long legs, his face alight with pleasure. He hugged her and kissed her cheek, which gave her a guilty feeling of pleasure. 'This is a fabulous surprise.'

'It's amazing we haven't bumped into each other before,' she said prosaically.

'Isn't it? You're not going?'

'I was. I don't think this fog –'

'Stay, Kitty, just a while, just for old times' sake.' He put his arm out to restrain her.

'Well, just five minutes,' she said, sinking back into her chair, and knowing she should run.

'You look wonderful, Kitty.'

'Thanks. I like your hair.'

'I couldn't go around looking like a rock rebel for ever.' He laughed. 'This suits my solo image better.'

'You're doing well, then?'

He laughed loudly and several heads turned in their direction. 'Dear Kitty, when you met me you had no idea who I was, remember? And now you still don't know. I'm a big success – Number One in both the UK and America and here in France.'

'I'm so pleased. I'm sorry – not much of the outside filters into my world.'

'Oh, I'm a phenomenon,' he said, but she heard a tinge of bitterness.

'It's certainly an achievement to still be up there after all this time . . .'

'You mean at my age?' He was laughing again.

'I remember you once saying you never heard of middle-aged rock stars.' She smiled.

'Times change. I think now maybe I can go on until I've had enough.'

'You haven't yet, then?'

'It's my life. Isn't singing yours?'

'I begin to wonder. I sometimes think maybe I've sacrificed too much for too long.' She was surprised how easy it was to talk to him, to tell him the unthinkable, but should she have been, she thought.

'Now she tells me!' He hit his head in mock despair and grinned at her. 'But then you've got a loving husband, that makes a difference, something to go home to.'

'And you?' She longed to reach out and touch him, but stopped herself.

'Fancy some dinner? We could be hours yet before we know about flights.'

'You're going to New York too?'

'Yes. We can sit together too, fabulous.'

'I'm sure they'll get us something to eat here.'

'Here? You're joking. Come on – I know a great little place. Nothing'll leave here tonight – have you seen the weather? We can leave the number of the restaurant.'

'But your wife—'

'Oh, she's used to me not being where I'm supposed to be.'

Slim was right, it was a great little place. It had taken them some time to reach it, in the countryside outside Paris, and an enormous tip to the taxi driver to brave the fog and take them there at a crawling pace. The proprietor of the restaurant was quite surprised to see clients on such a night, they were the only ones.

'We'll never get back tonight,' she said, as they waited

for their aperitifs to arrive. 'We're miles out in the back of beyond.'

'Who cares? I don't, do you?' He looked at her intently.

'No, not really.' She laughed, feeling quite lightheaded at the stupidity of it all.

'There's a river out there.' He pointed out of the window where they could see nothing. 'I love it here in summer. It's got rooms too, if we decide not to try to venture back.'

'Really?' she said noncommittally.

Over the meal he seduced her and she allowed him to. They had picked up their conversation so easily, as if all these years in between had not happened, and so it seemed to her the most natural thing that he should flirt with her, gently at first, then more obviously, and then blatantly make his intentions clear.

'Shall I ask the proprietor for a room?'

'Before you do, there's just one thing. You're married – what about your wife?'

'What about your husband?'

'He would understand, I think . . . we've never had a deep relationship. But I have no children. You're not answering my question. If we go upstairs and make love, Slim, I couldn't just walk away from you, not this time, I'd have to see you again and I don't think we've the right to hurt others.'

'I won't hurt Penelope. She need not know. She's a good kid and a devoted mother but, you know how it is, we've been together a long time. She's used to my ways – she's allowed me a long lead. Maybe that's why we're still together. She knows I'll look after her, I could never leave my kids – but I have my freedom.'

'How dreadfully sad . . . I'd hoped for you . . .' But she did not finish the sentence.

'Aren't we both?' He looked away from her, fearing she had misunderstood, afraid she might have changed her mind.

Kitty gestured to the waiter.

'Do you have a double room free? The weather . . .' She smiled at the waiter and touched Slim's hand across the table.

5

Once she had succumbed to the feel of Slim's body against hers in the large feather-mattressed bed, it was as if all the frustrations of the past years were released in a great passionate wave. The lack of love in her life, the infrequent and inadequate gentle sex with Felix, had dammed up in her a great, primeval need. At Slim's first kiss all guilt disappeared. She thought of no one but them and this moment. As he entered her she knew this was where she belonged, in his arms, his body upon her thrusting deep into hers and deep into her soul.

They did not return to Paris the next morning but ordered breakfast in bed – great cups of steaming coffee, croissants oozing butter. And afterwards, giggling in the way of lovers, they licked the crumbs from each other. The fog persisted, cocooning them in the small inn – Kitty had no idea where she was. They ordered food and wine. They left the tiny, flower-papered room to bathe and then returned to their domain – the bed. They ventured downstairs for dinner, having the restaurant still to themselves and enduring the knowing look of the *patron*. And then, replete, they returned upstairs for another night of love.

The next morning they awoke to the same thick blanket of fog and stayed where they were – and the next day. The day after that, the fog began to lift.

'I should go,' she said, peering out of the window, regretting the fog's passing.

'Why?' Slim said from the bed.

'Why indeed? By the time I arrive in Chicago I'll be too late to rehearse, and—'

'They'll have substituted you by now.'

'No doubt.'

'Then come back to bed.'

'Maybe I was never meant to sing the Butterfly!' She laughed as she joined him.

It was amazing how they still felt about each other – as if they had never been apart. If anything, they loved each other more. Kitty found she could talk to Slim in a way she could not to others. He was told of her fears, of her feelings. To him she confided that she sometimes hated The Voice, that she felt it was a monstrous gaoler of her life.

Bravely, they planned so much for their future together. They could not separate again, children or no, he said firmly. They had been fools to lose each other before – she by insisting she went and he for not stopping her. Kitty felt young again with the light-heartedness of youth in love.

On the fourth day, in the afternoon, they ventured out of the restaurant with rooms and ambled along the river-bank in the weak, fading winter sunshine. They returned, their arms about each other, engrossed in themselves.

'Miss Lawrence! Slim!'

They turned towards the voice, still smiling, still holding each other as a camera clicked and clicked again, recording their happiness.

'You bastard!' Slim dived at the cameraman who had appeared from behind a bush but who was already running as fast as his legs would carry him towards his parked car.

'I'm sorry,' Slim said, as he came back, puffing from exertion. 'The creep got away. I should have been more careful.'

'How did they find us?'

'The *patron*, no doubt – out for a fast buck.'

'Oh, no, surely not – he's been so kind. What do we do now?' She stood in the pathway looking dejected.

'Do you want to go?'

'No . . . not yet, one more night, please.'

'Then we'll stay – face the music tomorrow.'

It was her decision to grab one more day but perhaps it was a mistake: the world had intruded, they were both edgy, some of the magic had passed.

That night the dream returned. But there were no dahlias, instead her arms were full of mimosa that she smelt even in her sleep. Then the beautiful frothy yellow plumes began to change in her hands until they were a shrivelled black. She turned but there was no one beside her, just a black void, and she woke screaming.

'My darling, what the hell!' She heard Slim fumbling for the light-switch.

'I'm sorry, it's this dream . . . something bad is going to happen . . .' She clung to him, shivering with foreboding. He made her tell the dream.

'Go on . . . don't you know dreams mean opposites? That's what my mum always said.'

'Someone's going to die,' she announced dramatically.

'Bollocks,' said Slim, cradling her in his arms and rocking her back to sleep.

The scenes at the airport the following day were pandemonium. Enclosed in their own selfish little world, neither of them had thought of the consequences of their antics. They had disappeared, that had been the newspaper headlines, searches had been made for them. The photograph snatched of them yesterday was plastered over the papers. And, on the off-chance that they would appear at the airport, a posse of photographers had been sent.

'Christ, what a fool I am,' Slim said, as he saw the pack

descending upon them, cameras poised ready. 'We should have guessed.'

'Both of us have been foolish.' She squeezed his hand tight as the mob surrounded them and questions were fired from all sides. It took them twenty minutes to inch, tight-lipped, across the concourse to the protection of the VIP lounge, and once safely in the hands of the ever-attentive ground staff, Kitty felt she had been through a battle.

'You still wish to fly to New York, Miss Lawrence, Mr Fletcher?'

'No. Geneva,' said Kitty.

'London,' said Slim.

They sat huddled, holding each other's hand, as the arrangements were made for them.

'Call me the minute Felix knows. Tell me what he says.'

'He'll know now – you saw the newspapers.'

'Are you scared?'

'No. He'll be angry about my missing Chicago – that's work. As for me? No, as I told you, he never really loved me, more my voice – it's been a convenience of a marriage, really.'

'You'll come to me as soon as possible?'

'Need you ask?' She smiled at him, dreading this farewell but buoyed up by the thought that this time it was not for ever.

Felix was waiting for her.

'What the hell do you mean by behaving in this manner?'

To her surprise he was shouting at her, something he had never done before.

'I'm sorry, it was the fog . . . there were no planes, I could not have got to New York let alone Chicago in time.'

'Schiphol was open.'

'And how the hell was I supposed to get to Holland?'

'By car.'

'In that fog?'

'You got to your love-nest.'

'Felix, please.'

'How else could you describe it? For five days; are you mad? I've been worried out of my mind. I've had the police in three countries searching for you. Don't you understand the drama you have caused?'

'I didn't think, I'm sorry.'

'Kitty, you astound me. You stand there, returned from an adulterous trip that has made me the laughing-stock of Europe and you say "Sorry".'

'You needn't shout!'

'Needn't shout! Dear God, what has happened to you? I thought you were happy, that we were happy, I had no warning of this.' He began to cough.

'Felix, I'm so sorry – please. I didn't even ask, how are you? How's your poor chest?'

He waved his arm dismissively at her concern. 'How long has this been going on? I have to know. How often have you seen this Slim?'

'Felix, really! How could you ask?' It was Kitty's turn to sound indignant. 'It has not been "going on". We were fogbound in Paris, Slim invited me to dinner and then . . .' She did not know quite how to continue.

'And then you just happened to fall into bed together – what a sordid tale.'

'It was not sordid!' she flashed back at him. 'I love Slim, I've always loved him, and he me.'

Felix sat down suddenly on a chair, his face grey with fatigue.

'You told me it was finished.'

'I thought it was, but some things you can't finish. I want a divorce, I want to marry him.'

'Kitty, no!' Felix cried with anguish. 'You can't do this to me, we'll work something out.' He had jumped to his feet.

'There's nothing to work out. I'm tired of this sterile life we lead. I'm tired of my voice, of the regime, of life passing me by. I'm tired of not being loved . . .'

'Kitty, don't say this.' He held up his hand to ward off her words. 'You are loved, no one could love you more than me.'

'You don't love me, you never have.'

'How can you say that?'

'Because it's true. You told me right at the beginning you were not capable of loving me as a woman – that it was The Voice you loved.'

'At the beginning. But it changed. I learned to love you.'

'Don't talk rubbish. You never told me, never showed me.'

'Because you yourself were so undemonstrative – I thought it was how you wanted it to be. But my actions spoke for me, surely?'

'What actions? You hardly ever made love to me and now never.'

'But that was you, too. You were always so unresponsive to my advances, I didn't want to bother you unnecessarily. And now, I'm sorry, but I'm sixty-two, I don't know if I can any more.'

'How convenient. Now you tell me all these things when I tell you I want to go. You're afraid of losing me because you don't want to lose control of me – arranging my life, owning me and my voice.'

'This is not so. I love you, Kitty. I worship you, I always have.'

'Don't torture me!' she shrieked. 'Let me go! Let me find my happiness!'

'And how long will it last with a man like him? What have you in common with someone like that?'

'More than you'd think, more than I have with you.'

'No, that's not possible. We have everything together – our lives are intermeshed. I can't let you break it all apart, not after all I've done for you.'

'Stop it! Don't say that! Never say that to me!' she cried out, the words echoing those of Amy, so long ago. She backed away from him and the hateful words.

'Why should I not say it? I'm proud of all I've done. You wouldn't even be here if it was not for me.'

'I would. I'd have still had Ben and Cellini—'

'Would you? With no scholarship?'

'What do you mean?'

'There was no Willow Scholarship. I paid for you from the very beginning. I paid for all your fees, your tuition, Paris . . . everything. And this is my reward.'

'You think you bought me! Why didn't you tell me?'

'I didn't want you to know.'

'Until it was convenient for you that I did, you mean.'

She faced him, breathing deeply, fighting back a desire to hit him, not knowing what else to say, feeling spent.

'If you leave me you'll be finished.'

'Me? Never!' She shook her head defiantly. 'I don't need you.'

'Very well. As you wish,' he said, suddenly icy-calm. 'If you feel like this then I no longer wish to be part of your life either. You are right, it's better we should part. For tax purposes you may keep this house in Switzerland.'

'I don't want it.'

'Very well. I can't give you the house in France – it is my family property as you know. But you are happy there, you may use it.'

'Thank you, Felix. I knew you'd understand,' she said, calmer.

'I don't understand a thing, Kitty. But I recognize when I'm not wanted, nor needed.' He turned his back on her and with dignity left the room.

As soon as he had left, Kitty picked up the telephone to call Slim, realizing as she did so that she was shaking.

'How was it?' Slim asked immediately.

'It was dreadful. He made it so difficult. He said he loved me – after all this time.'

'Frightened of losing you and all the loot you bring in, more like.'

'No, it's not like that, he never touches my money.'

'Then perhaps he meant it?'

'Oh, no don't say that, if that were so . . .' but she did not finish for, if it were so, she had been unbelievably unkind. 'No. He just said it to be awkward.'

'Where're you going?'

'To his house in France, he's allowing me to use it – I love it there, you will too.'

'He won't like me being there.'

'Then we'll find something else in the same area. Oh, Slim, I'm missing you already.'

'Me you.'

'It won't be long, will it?'

'No. I've some work here to finish up. What about you?'

'I'll see my doctor tomorrow, get him to say I'm physically and mentally exhausted, then I can cancel everything for the next three to six months.'

'Won't it damage your career? You know what I said, I'll never stand in your way.'

'Oh, damn my career – it's us that's important now. And I've never cancelled even one concert in my whole career – not like some. And with a doctor's certificate . . . Have you told Penelope yet? What did she say?'

'She's not here, she pissed off to the Seychelles, presumably when she saw the newspapers. She left a note, she's angry.'

'I don't blame her. I'm as jealous of her as hell – all these years you had together that should have been mine. Slim, I can't wait. It won't be long, will it?'

'I'll be with you as soon as I can.'

6

The following day Kitty did not have to persuade her doctor into giving her an excuse to cancel her performances for the next three months.

'Not before time,' he said to her, after examining her. 'You are underweight, your blood pressure is too low, and if these blood tests say what I think they will, you are anaemic as well.'

'But I feel fine. I've always been fit – you can't contemplate being an opera singer unless you're as healthy as an athlete.'

'Tired?'

'Well, sometimes, but with my schedule it's to be expected, isn't it?'

'How tired?'

'Totally . . . but then it's always been like that. When you give a performance it takes everything out of you . . . you feel empty the next day, when the adrenalin has gone.'

'And you think you can keep on doing that to your body? Keep exposing it to that amount of stress without something giving? When did you last have a holiday – and I mean a real holiday, doing nothing?'

She laughed. 'When I was about twelve.'

'Then you can't go on like this, Kitty. You must begin to take it easy. Less performances, more holidays. If you don't, then you will collapse one day from total exhaustion. A three-month break is the minimum I recommend at the moment.'

'But it's not serious?' she asked, suddenly worried, realizing this was not a game.

'Not yet – but it could be.'

*

With the prospect of three months of total freedom stretching ahead of her, and with Slim arriving soon for company, Kitty travelled with Jenny to the Auvergne, to the long house on the hill which was swaddled in snow.

She took delight in not practising, in not even entering the beautiful music-room which Felix had fashioned for her. Instead she read, watched television, and listened to both orchestral music and Slim's.

'You'll never keep this up, you know,' Jenny said one evening, as they finished watching a mindless game show on French television, half of which they had not understood, so quick and glib was the repartee.

'You want to bet?' Kitty grinned back at her. 'I feel wonderful – almost liberated.'

'For a while, but you can't expect to give up totally.'

'I didn't say I wanted to.'

'Then how are you going to get back to it? You always told me you had to practise each day, that your voice would pack in if you didn't.'

'A week or two won't hurt – I'll have to work harder after a lay-off like that, admittedly. I'm a bit like a footballer who does nothing for a while. But it'll be all right. Promise. Remember what the doctor said.'

'Yes, but an hour a day wouldn't hurt.'

'I'll start when Slim comes.'

But the two weeks stretched into three, and Jenny worried. Felix had talked to her before they left Switzerland and had made Jenny promise that she would not let Kitty give up because of this sudden – to him – infatuation, that she would ensure Kitty practised. Jenny had promised but knew how Kitty could gladly give her whole life to a man. She had also agreed because she knew Kitty's life would be empty without her singing. There would be times when Slim would have to leave her for the sake of his career, and Jenny thought it wise if Kitty filled the time he was away

with concentrating on her own. And if it did not work out
with Slim, what then?

The telephone was Kitty's lifeline. Her days were punc-
tuated by the times she knew Slim would call her and she
him. They talked for hours.

Slim had been delayed by a production problem on his
new record. He never stopped working now, he told her;
since their meeting the music was tumbling out of him.
And he was still waiting for his wife to return so that he
could talk to her. Asking for a divorce had to be done face
to face, not by letter, he said, and Kitty agreed.

She had hoped he would come for Christmas but she
was the first to agree when he called to say his wife and
children were returning in time for the holiday and he
would like to spend this last Christmas with them. That
was right and proper, she said.

'We've waited so long for each other, what's another few
weeks?' she asked blithely.

During this winter of change there had been another
momentous upheaval.

Towards the end of Amy's initial six-month stay, Dan
had begun to feel edgy. There was nothing he could put a
finger on, he just felt that Lana was slipping away from
him, that a barrier had been erected and that it was Amy's
doing.

Amy had not wanted to leave, and as he feared, Lana
did not want her to go, either. That was odd since she had
been full of doubts when it had first been suggested, and it
was Dan himself who had reassured her.

Seeing how the situation was developing, Dan put his
foot down with Lana.

'She's got to learn to stand on her own two feet – she's
fine now, the doctors have said,' he had argued with his
wife, of necessity in a whisper since every word could be

heard upstairs in Amy's room where, tearfully, she was packing.

'What if she gets ill again?'

'She won't if she looks after herself and if she does, well, then she can come back.'

'You promise?' Lana had asked.

So, it was a happy Dan who had driven a rather silent Amy home.

Things did not work out quite as he had hoped, however. Lana was moody when he returned and often bad-tempered – she hadn't been like that before. There was an edgy restlessness to her that was also new.

'Would you like me to see if we can get you a few gigs in the pubs?' he asked one day, presuming it was her longing to sing again which had emerged and was causing the problem.

'I'm never going to sing in a pub again as long as I live.'

'Fine by me. How about getting hold of that bloke who organizes the open-air concert on Midsummer Common? Or the May Ball committees?'

'Maybe. I'll let you know,' she had replied vaguely.

Dan mourned for the past but he was not surprised by what was happening. He'd been half-expecting it ever since Lana had entered his life. How could he, a man of sixty, expect a thirty-four-year-old woman to stay contented with him? He adjusted to this shift in their relationship but what he could not so readily excuse was the change in Lana with the children.

She had always been a good mother, now she was a sorely impatient one. It seemed that everything about the children irritated her: the noise they made when they played; the work they created for her; even brushing Cilla's hair had become an annoyance to the extent that Dan, angry that Cilla yet again was crying at her mother's roughness with the hairbrush, had taken the child to have her long dark hair cut short.

Lana had once taken pride in the children's appearance, but no longer. Dan wondered if the irritation was because she saw the children as a trap. She could, he supposed, easily leave him, but she loved the children too much to desert them, hence her frustration.

He was not angry with her, nor disappointed. He felt sorry things were as they were and treated her with patience, which only seemed to make her edgier. She once more took to spending more time in her room, strumming on her guitar, occasionally singing. And she had frequent headaches now, which were used as an excuse when she snapped at the children, and to spurn Dan's sexual advances.

It was Dan himself, desperate to cheer Lana, who suggested Amy should come for Christmas. He was soon regretting it, however. He began to feel he was in the way. Amy and Lana seemed to be more like sisters, giggling and gossiping together; they would shut themselves upstairs in Amy's room and chat for hours at a time. He was sure that if he left they would not even notice he had gone.

Amy had given up all pretence with Lana, her motives were out in the open. Up in her room, with her daughter, she began a relentless campaign.

'You're wasting your life here with that man.'

'Dan's been good to me.'

'Oh, he's nice enough, but ineffectual. He'll never make anything of himself, he's left it too late.'

'He doesn't want to do anything – he's done it. After all, Mum, he was a bank manager.'

'I bet it was only a small branch,' Amy replied sniffily.

Expertly Amy revitalized Lana's dreams.

'It's not too late for you, my darling. The talent's still there and you've kept your looks. You can do it, girl, you *can* be a star.'

Relentlessly Amy kept on, reassuring, inspiring, adding to her daughter's discontent.

'How could I start again? I'd need to go to London, what about the kids?' Lana argued.

'Dan's a good dad, he could care for them. Think of the better life you could give them with all the money you'll earn,' Amy countered.

Lana shrieked with laughter. 'God, Mum, always the optimist.'

'One of us has got to be.'

'And how are we to finance my restart? Have you got any money? I haven't a bean.' Lana grinned.

'Something'll turn up, it always does.'

Amongst the stack of Christmas cards delivered one day was a letter.

'Who's that from?' Lana asked. 'You don't get letters, only bills.'

'It's from your sister,' Dan replied.

'To you?'

'To both of us.'

'Then why wasn't it addressed to both of us?'

'I don't know.' He hadn't told Lana about their exchange of letters, he had sensed she wouldn't like it.

'My, you are honoured, Dan. She's never written to me,' Amy said from the other end of the table.

'What's she want?'

'Nothing – she's giving. See, a cheque for the children for Christmas presents.' He waved the cheque in the air.

'How much is it?'

'£500.'

'You're joking!' Lana laughed and glanced quickly at her mother.

'About time too. She's always been so mean. I've never seen a penny.'

'Oh, come on, Mum, she paid for your hospital care and the private ambulance.'

'From guilt. She's never given me a present as such – well, not for years, not since she could afford to give me little luxuries.'

'She seemed a nice enough woman to me,' Dan said.

'She would, she's got charm when she wants to use it. But don't be taken in by it, Dan, she's a cold woman, always has been. All she can think about is herself and her career.'

'Aren't you proud of her, Amy, international star that she is?' Dan asked, curious.

Amy thought for a moment. 'Quite honestly, Dan, no. It's as if she's nothing to do with me – I've never felt she was mine, even when she was little she was all for her father, not me. Now, if it was my Lana here, I'd be as proud as punch.' She smiled adoringly at her daughter.

'She seems to have taken a shine to Cilla. Her letter's full of her. Hopes when she's older she can holiday with her. And she adds that anything we need for the kids to let her know. Look . . .' he handed the letter to Lana who glanced at it.

'I should watch her with Cilla if I were you. Women with no children can go a bit funny in the head. You don't want her pinching her now, do you? She's done enough of that to Lana,' Amy said darkly.

'I'm going to go and feed the rabbits,' Dan said, weary with the bitterness he was hearing.

The cheque remained on the mantelshelf until after Christmas.

'I'll bank that for you, shall I? Mum and I thought we'd like to look at the January sales, and then I'll drive her to the station,' Lana offered.

'I've said I don't mind driving her all the way home.'

'No, she's said she'd rather go by train.'

Dan helped load Amy's cases into the little red Mini she had given Lana. It was odd, she seemed to have a lot more baggage than when she had arrived. He could not keep the smile from his face as with Cilla beside him and Mike in his arms he waved goodbye to his mother-in-law.

By seven he had fed the children, bathed them, read them a story and tucked them up. By eight he had his and Lana's supper ready. By nine he was worried.

Before calling the police he had the sense to check their bedroom. Lana's wardrobe had only half her clothes hanging in it, and her drawers were only half full. On his pillow was a letter addressed to him.

She had gone! The note was quite short. She wrote that she loved him, knew he would care for the children, but she had to go, she had to give herself this one last chance. She explained that it was Kitty coming into their lives again which had made her long to return. Her sister was a star and she wanted to be one too, it was that simple. She promised to be in touch.

Dan sat on the bed, holding the letter. On the one hand he felt a sense of release that the tensions had been removed from the house. On the other he felt overwhelmed by a sadness that it was all over. At least he had the kids, he could not have borne it if she had taken them too. But he wished she had looked sadder this morning, not as happy as she had as she drove off. Surely she owed him a sad glance. Evidently not, he sighed to himself, and folded the note back into its envelope.

He doubted if Kitty was totally to blame. Maybe seeing her again had roused jealousy in Lana but he was pretty certain that Amy was the culprit. He could imagine her fanning that little jealousy into a roaring fire, could almost hear her persuading Lana she could become a star and was wasting her life as a wife and mother.

He decided not to make a fuss. Perhaps it was best to let

Lana try to get this lust for fame out of her system. He doubted if she would achieve it, it was too late for her. She'd be back, he consoled himself.

7

Lana had not left on a whim. She and Amy had planned carefully what they were to do during the many hours they spent closeted in Amy's room.

Kitty's gift to the children could not have come at a better time for Lana. She had no intention of banking it in Dan's account, she would forge his signature as endorsement – an easy thing to do – and put it in her own account. She knew Dan, he would not make trouble for her. The £500 would finance her for the first few weeks of her bid for fame, she would pay it back later when she could afford to.

Lana had left with more than the cheque and some of her clothes. She had in her possession something of inestimable value for a singer. In her head she had the memory of two of Slim Fletcher's songs, ones which had never been sung, never published.

The songs were from the old rock opera, all of which had gone up in flames. But Lana had sung the two songs Slim had written for a female voice so often that she knew them by heart and would never forget them. Now that she could play an instrument, she could pick them out on her guitar and someone else could notate them. It was a gamble Amy and Lana were about to take – would Slim object and refuse to allow the record company to record them?

They decided it was best if Amy went to see Slim.

'You're sure you're not doing too much, Mum?' Lana asked as they drove along in her Mini. They were going to

Oxford, where Lana would wait in the hotel while Amy took a taxi to Slim's.

'Me? I've never felt better. Honest, love, I can tell you I bet I'd be in my box now if you hadn't come to visit me. All this has given me a new lease of life.'

'Don't get over-excited, will you?'

'I reckon the doctors don't know what they're talking about. I reckon excitement's good for my old ticker.'

Amy's initial plan was just to turn up at Slim's and with force of personality, tenacity and her large handbag, get herself past the guards.

'No, Mum. Call him first. Make an appointment. He's not an ogre and he's polite – he'll see you, you never did him any wrong.'

Amy was none too sure, but to her surprise Lana was right and she drove up to the gates of the mansion in her taxi and was admitted with no problem.

The modern house excited Amy. She much preferred the new to the old and could never understand the fuss when the other house had burned down – 'nasty, musty place full of dry rot', was her opinion of the architectural gem her daughter had destroyed. This large-windowed, wide-patioed, parquet-floored and spacious-roomed residence suited her down to the ground.

Slim seemed pleased to see her, had tea made for her, was concerned over her news of her heart trouble, and even asked after Lana in a kind and interested way. In fact, Amy related later to Lana, he was happier than she had ever seen him before. Both Amy and Lana were glad that Kitty's name did not come up.

Amy launched straight into the reason for her visit.

'Good for Lana, I wish her well,' Slim said, all smiles.

'So you don't mind if she sings your songs? I mean, money's a bit short and she could not afford to pay you anything . . .' Amy refrained from offering to pay in the future.

'Tell you what. Tell Lana she can have them as a present, just so long as she attributes them to me. Back-alimony if you like.'

'Slim, you're so kind,' Amy gushed, and then asked more guardedly, 'No royalties?'

'Nothing, Amy, she can have the lot.'

'Well, I never. She'll be overjoyed.' She sipped her tea thoughtfully. 'I couldn't have that in writing, could I, Slim? You know . . . . life's odd . . .'

Slim burst out laughing. 'Are you going to be her manager this time?'

'Yes. I don't trust none of them buggers out there in this rat race.'

'Good on yer, Amy. She'll be all right with you. Of course you can have it in writing.'

No politician ever returned from the negotiating table with such a sense of achievement as Amy did that day. So elated were the two of them that they pushed the boat out, ignored Amy's doctor's orders, and bought a bottle of champagne.

Lana had wanted to make a demo tape of Slim's songs.

'No way,' Amy said. 'Someone might hear them and nick them and not listen to you. No, this is a package deal – if they want Slim's songs, you record them or there's no deal.'

Amy set off for the offices of Silverside Records without an appointment. But this was no barrier for Amy. Sweetly dressed in a dusky-pink wool suit, wearing her gold locket and sensible shoes, and with her hair newly permed and set and less make-up than she would normally wear, she turned on the charm. Sweet, middle-aged grannies were rare in these offices, so she stood out immediately from the trendily dressed crowd milling around in reception. She charmed her way past the receptionist, past several secre-

taries and a couple of personal assistants until she was in
the office of a somewhat surprised Bart Melody, the cur-
rently most successful record producer of them all.

'Let me get this straight, Mrs Lawrence,' a rather confused Bart said five minutes later, swinging his Reeboks off
his desk and slipping off his Ray Ban sunglasses the better
to see this charming little lady who reminded him of his
mum. 'Your daughter is Slim's ex and has two songs of his.
And she wants to sell them?'

'No, no, you've got it all wrong,' Amy said tetchily,
which she could not know reminded Bart even more of his
mum. 'She's a singer, she wants you to record her and
launch her.'

'Got a demo?'

'No. We want you to hear her in person – no tapes.'

'Wasn't he married to Lana Lea – sang with the Mantras
years ago?'

'That's right. Wonderful she was then, but you should
hear her now.'

'Bit long in the tooth, isn't she?'

'Not a bit of it. How old are you?' Amy said as sharply
as if he had queried her age.

'OK, then. You win!' He flicked open his big engagement
diary. 'I've got a space on Tuesday. Do you?'

'It will be a pleasure, Mr Melody.'

'Oh, please call me Bart.'

'Only if you call me Amy,' she said, so coquettishly that
Bart was amazed to find himself flirting with someone as
old as his mother.

Lana sang her heart out that day. At the end of 'When
Morning Comes', Amy, allowed into the control-room, was
dabbing at her eyes with a tissue.

'And Slim says this song is yours, Lana?' Bart asked her
suspiciously.

'Absolutely, it was a present from him. I've got it in
writing if you want to see. It's all legally mine.'

'And you never thought of doing it before?'

'I forgot about it.' She giggled, flashing her blue eyes and looking years younger than her age.

'Jeeze!' the record executives said in unison. This was the next best thing to finding an unpublished Lennon and McCartney number.

This was the beginning. The record producers got to work on Slim's beautiful ballads – though they would record both, only one would be released immediately. For the recording the London Symphony Orchestra was booked to provide the best backing money could buy. A world-class flautist was brought in and Lana sang the hauntingly beautiful songs with more heart than she had ever sung before. Even Bart Melody, who had heard it all before, was in tears.

Bart's interest in Lana was soon apparently more than as her record producer. He took her out to dinner, to rock concerts, to Stringfellows. Lana's name once more appeared in the gossip columns.

She liked Bart but she had decided she didn't want to get involved, not yet. She'd had enough of being too close to the men in her career to make the mistake again. What if they had a row? Then Bart could destroy her career overnight. This way, with him lusting after her, his interest in her and her career were guaranteed.

Image-makers – unheard of when Lana had started in the business – were brought in. Everyone, even Amy, agreed that Lana's previous trademark of the innocent child-woman was pushing it a bit – she would be thirty-four next birthday. Instead, her hair was cut into a very short, gamine style. Though still blonde, her hair was more faded now, so highlights were added. The make-up evolved for her was pale, with dark accentuated eye make-up, and they dressed her entirely in black. She looked

stunning, like a modern equivalent of an existentialist of
the 1950s, and since that was a period coming into fashion
her appearance was all the more sensational and avant-
garde.

The record was released. As Slim's ex she was news,
and appeared on *Wogan* and *The Gloria Hunniford Show*. She
entered the charts at 102 and within two weeks was in the
top twenty. After *Top of the Pops* Lana was Number One.

Amy thought she would die of pride as she looked at the
listings.

'It's thanks to you, Mum.' Lana kissed her, dizzy with
excitement and still too dazed at the speed of her success
even to have had time to miss Dan and her children.

'I always said leave it to me – and if you had, you'd have
been up there, a star, years ago.'

8

Slim did not come to Kitty.

Every word he had said in that final telephone call was
branded on Kitty's mind and would, she knew, never leave
her.

'It's my kids, Kitty. I can't leave them.' He was breathing
heavily as if having difficulty speaking.

'I see,' she said, in a quiet, controlled voice.

'It was this last Christmas – I knew then. I've been
making excuses about coming ever since.'

'I'm sorry,' she said with quiet dignity.

'They're so small and vulnerable and they'd never understand.' There was a catch in his voice.

'Of course.'

'And my wife – she doesn't deserve this treatment. All

she's ever done is love and support me, I've made her ill with grief. I couldn't live with myself, Kitty. I can't hurt them.'

'Of course.' Her voice sounded calm when inside she was screaming, 'What about me? What about my pain?'

'Please understand me, Kitty. This has been the hardest decision of my life. I love you, I'll never love another. I'll never forget you – ever.'

'Are we not to see each other?'

'It's better we don't.' There was a long pause. 'I promised Penelope . . .'

'Ah!'

'I've been to hell and back these past weeks. I haven't known what to say to you . . .'

'That there are some things more important than me and our own happiness,' she stated calmly, automatically.

'Yes, yes. That's it. How did you know?'

'Because I said it once, a long time ago, and to you.'

'Kitty!'

'Goodbye, Slim.' She replaced the receiver and sat in the darkening room looking into nothing and feeling she was empty and lonelier than she had ever been before in her whole life. She sat rigid in the way that those suffering from shock sit. It was too soon to assimilate this, too soon to analyse, to excuse, to understand . . .

'What are you sitting in the dark for?' Jenny bustled in and switched on the lights. 'We've got Auvergne sausage with green lentils tonight – yum . . . What on earth's the matter, Kitty? What's happened?'

'Slim isn't coming.'

'Oh, my poor darling.' Jenny clattered across the room and took hold of Kitty's hands. 'The shit!'

'Shush. Don't say that. No, he's not. He was faced with an intolerable decision . . . if he had decided otherwise he could not have been the man I loved.'

'The kids?'

Kitty nodded. Pride would not let her admit that Slim's wife had played a part too.

'I did wonder about them. Maybe when they've grown up, then he'll come.'

'Maybe . . . Oh, Jenny, to find love twice and to lose it twice.' A tear rolled unchecked down Kitty's cheek. 'How long?' she repeated. 'If you don't mind, Jenny, I'll skip your sausage. I think I'll go to bed.'

'You all right?'

'Yes, I'm all right.' She stood and walked to the door. 'Don't worry, Jenny, I'm not going to do anything silly.'

'Over a bloody man, I should hope not.' Jenny forced herself to laugh.

'No, not over a man – never.' Kitty closed the door.

Kitty was not all right. She withdrew into herself. She spent hours sitting looking at the view which had once given her such pleasure and which now, even as she looked at it, she didn't seem to see. She didn't talk with Jenny, she would answer her questions but she never instigated a conversation. Nothing interested her. Jenny put on records of her singing, Kitty would take them off. Books were started but not finished and letters piled up and went unanswered. Dutifully she ate what was put in front of her without enjoyment.

'Kitty, you're going to have to pull yourself together. You're supposed to be singing in Verona in April.'

'Don't you understand, Jenny? I can't sing, not any more, it's finished. Cancel it.'

'I've never heard such rubbish. Of course you'll sing again. You'll get over this.'

'Will I?'

'How can one man destroy your voice?'

'He hasn't. It's The Voice, it's . . . tired . . .' she said vaguely, not even sure herself what was happening to her.

Jenny, frantic with the responsibility that was now hers, called Felix and begged him to come.

'She says she can't sing.'

'She would know.'

'But it's like she's in some sort of zombie state. I'm at my wits' end with her. I can't shake her out of herself.'

'I'm sorry you should have this burden, Jenny.'

'I don't mind, it's just that I don't know how to deal with her. She's having a breakdown, I'm sure she is. I think if she just started to sing again, it would be all right. She'd have that – at the moment she has nothing. You might persuade her.'

'I will come but only if Kitty asks me to.' Felix was adamant.

When Jenny suggested this to Kitty she refused.

'After the way I've treated him how could you even ask him? No, it's not fair . . .'

As the spring came and the fields burst blood-red with poppies, still Kitty did nothing.

'Look, Kitty, I'm getting pissed off with this. You're behaving stupidly. Snap out of it.' Jenny tried a new tack.

'I'm sorry, Jenny. I'd be sad if you went, but if you're that fed up perhaps you should.'

'Oh, don't be wet, of course I'm not going to leave you. I just hate to see you like this.'

'I'm sorry,' Kitty said like an apologetic child. 'I don't seem able to do anything about it.'

Jenny, without telling Kitty, wrote to Cellini begging her to come and help her, but most importantly to help Kitty.

The reply when it came was from Cellini's sister. Cellini had had a stroke and could not speak, let alone be moved. Jenny didn't tell Kitty for fear of what effect the news might have upon her.

And then Jenny remembered Max Leitman, the teacher who had built the foundations for Kitty's great voice. She telephoned him and Max immediately agreed to come.

He arrived with a huge bouquet of mimosa.

'Oh, no, not you,' Kitty said, backing away with a look of horror on her face, to both Max and Jenny's surprise.

'I know I'm not the most popular of people but I did hope you'd be pleased to see me.' He smiled.

'I'm sorry, Max, not you. It's the flowers I meant,' Kitty said, flustered.

'They make her sneeze,' Jenny explained, and Kitty allowed this explanation to pass for the real one.

'I should have remembered.'

'I'm so happy to see you, Max. I can't think of anyone I'd rather see.' And she put up her arms and hugged him so tight that he felt alarmed at the intensity.

He was so patient with her. He spent hours talking to her, walking in the countryside, never mentioning her voice, never saying she should sing.

She finally started to talk one evening as they sat with a log fire burning, for the evenings were still chill.

'You see, Max, I understand myself better, I have to have someone who cares for me above everything else. Someone to support me and tell me it's all going to be all right. Someone who is always there for us. I've lost my anchor. I *know* I can't sing.'

'Felix, you mean?'

'Yes.'

'But you sang before he came into your life.'

'But never as well as when he did. I had a lover years ago in Paris, he supported me, loved me, and when we finished my voice went,' she said in simple explanation.

'Then it's fear that's stopping you.'

'Yes. Fear of the sound that will emerge. And also . . .' She stopped speaking and gazed at the flames, her expression showing she was unsure whether to continue or not. The others waited patiently. 'Oh, I know I've been a dreadful bore to poor Jenny here these past months, and stupidly depressed. But in an odd way I've felt very peaceful, you know. Not singing. Not having to dance to the monster's tune.' And she hit her chest quite violently. 'And yet without it I feel empty – I feel I am nothing.'

'Don't you miss anything?' Jenny asked gently.

'The adulation, oh, yes, that's dreadful. When they applauded, when I felt their appreciation coming in great waves from the auditorium then I *knew* I was loved. Yes, I miss that.'

'And wouldn't you like it back?' Max asked as gently as Jenny.

'Oh, yes, but not with everything else. Not the prison my life had become.'

'Why don't we approach things gently? Why not let's try, you and me, for a few weeks to see what you can do, and then maybe a concert, what about that?'

'Perhaps. You see, I don't want to be like Cellini, my voice gone and teaching others half as good as she was. Oh, no, that would be a living death to me.'

They talked a little more and when Jenny left them to see about some supper, Max looked at Kitty sitting in the firelight, more beautiful now, if possible, than when he had first met her. He longed to have the courage to tell her he loved her and always would. That he would care for and support her emotionally, that she need never feel isolated with her talent. That he would be happy to take Felix's place. But he couldn't quite bring himself to do so, it seemed so presumptuous of him even to dream that she might want his love.

Max was surprised by what he heard; he had expected a weakness and a diminution of range after this time of inactivity. Physically the damage was far less than he had anticipated but the voice was colourless, the dramatic warmth had disappeared. It was a shadow of its former self. This was a psychological problem he was facing, it was as if something in Kitty had died and the voice reflected it.

'That's not nearly as bad as I thought it was going to be. You've been lucky. We'll soon build the voice back up. The voice is still there, don't forget it's you who are weaker around it,' he forced himself to sound encouraging.

'You're telling me the truth?' She looked at him anxiously, desperate for approval. 'You think it's still there?'

'When have you ever known me to lie to you?' he replied.

FINALE

The whole atmosphere of the house changed as the lessons progressed, the muscles were built, the range recovered. But it took long weeks and spring had drifted into summer and the heat intensified so that they could only work in the cool of the early morning, even the evenings were too hot. This slowed their progress.

Ben Cooper was receiving weekly reports from Max. It was only because it was Kitty, and Ben feared her glorious voice might be lost to the world, that Max was given a sabbatical from the Conservatoire and allowed to stay with her.

They worked on her old recital repertoire – maybe one day she would return to the opera, but not that year. And Max agreed that *slowly* should be their watchword. They were aiming for November; Kitty had requested Lyon, where she had held her first concert, and Max was pleased with the choice. Paris or London might have been too critical of her, and if they were not informed, the big-gun critics might not turn up. It was all a confidence-boosting exercise.

It was almost a year since Kitty had sung in public and she was nervous in a way she had never been before. Three things were rattling her: first, she had lost her red chiffon scarf; it had been mislaid in the move, Jenny had looked high and low for it, and Kitty became convinced that without the scarf she could not sing. Jenny thought her soft in the head but loving her, she patiently began to search again. Then Kitty had called Cellini to ask her to come but without telling the others of her plan. It was a dreadful shock for her when she had finally heard of Cellini's plight. No scarf, no Cellini – she felt everything was collapsing about her. The third and, as Kitty sat in her dressing-room, still unresolved matter was that she had written to Felix begging him to come, so that he would be standing in the wings as he had always done. But as she waited for his reply, she was not to know that Felix was out of the country and had not received her letter.

Max was unhappy when he saw the audience begin to arrive: he knew many of the faces – opera buffs from Paris and London and several big-time critics – rumours spread quickly in the musical world. But at least Kitty, tucked safely in her dressing-room, need not know they were out front. She could go on stage contentedly thinking it was only the Lyonnais, they who had given her career such a rapturous send-off nearly ten years before.

'Ten years!' Max repeated softly to himself. He had not worked that out before. What did they say? Ten years to build a voice, ten years at the top, and ten years sliding – surely not, not Kitty.

He felt confident that Kitty was fit again, Jenny had seen to that. She was not quite as good as she once had been, but was not far off. All the same, he could not remember the last time he had felt this sick with nerves for anyone.

The applause was deafening as Kitty, dressed in an elegant, long and straight midnight-blue gown and holding a red chiffon scarf to please Jenny, who had bought it for her, walked on to the stage. She stood white-faced and transfixed for a moment, her expression one of surprise that the audience had forgiven her her long absence. Then she nodded to her accompanist and began.

She sang the first four songs to perfection, and Max felt himself begin to relax.

When Kitty came off stage for her first break, he beamed at her. 'You see. You were wonderful, didn't I tell you?'

'Why, thank you, Max,' she replied, but somewhat distantly, he thought.

Upon her return to the stage she sang two songs perfectly but then, half-way through the third, her voice wobbled precariously, she missed a note, and the next sound was hard and metallic. A man booed, and then another.

Max hit the wall with his hand in frustration. This was all she needed – she'd never been booed, this would destroy the confidence he had so patiently rebuilt. He heard the piano stop. He dared to look from the wings at Kitty.

She had her hands in the air and she was shrugging her shoulders and smiling apologetically at her audience. She crossed to the pianist and spoke a few words, then launched herself into the song again, starting from the beginning. This time she sang without a hitch and it was beautiful. She bowed.

The audience stood and applauded, shouting their appreciation, and did so again and again until the concert was over and they had thrown their bouquets. Kitty was back!

Kitty stood on the stage as the roars of appreciation rolled towards her – like the sea on shingle, she thought, and shuddered. She stood waiting for the great feeling of love which they always gave her and which helped her carry on.

'It's me they love, not you! It's me they're cheering.' She swung round, expecting to find someone standing beside her, but the stage was empty. The voice was inside her, it was The Voice speaking to her. Abruptly she turned, and without further acknowledgement of the audience, she left the stage.

Max had expected Kitty to be excited and elated on the journey home. Instead she was strangely quiet.

'I could have killed that bastard who booed,' Jenny said.

Max frowned, he would have preferred it if they had not mentioned the incident.

'They demand a lot,' Kitty said quietly.

'Too bloody much.'

'They paid their money, they have a right to expect the performer to perform,' Kitty argued.

'Yes, but just the once.'

'It isn't allowed,' Kitty said firmly.

'Still, you recovered brilliantly,' Max offered.

'We did,' Kitty replied flatly. In the dark Max could not be sure how she meant this to be taken, her voice gave nothing away and he could not see her expression.

'I think I'll go straight to bed, if you don't mind,' Kitty said as soon as they returned. 'Thank you both for all your tender help and concern.' She kissed them and lingered at the door as if she was going to say more, but she did not; she gave them a little wave of the red chiffon scarf she still clutched and was gone.

In her room Kitty sat for a long time thinking and then she went over to her desk and wrote a long letter – to Slim.

As the dawn broke she went downstairs quietly and let herself out into the early snow which covered the garden, pulling her coat about her in the chill November wind. The well-oiled garage door slid open and she free-wheeled the car down the slope and half-way down the hill, so as not to wake anyone, before starting the engine. And then she drove some way into the mountains.

She found her favourite place eventually. It had not been easy since many of the signs were obliterated with snow. Carrying a rug, she walked to a small copse of trees where at one time she had sat with Felix to admire the view and where she had once planned to bring Slim.

She stood for a long time looking down on the valley far below and at the mountains guarding it. Smooth, rounded mountains, more comforting than the craggy Alps. The view gave her strength and calmness as it always did.

And then she began to sing. Her beautiful voice, clear and perfect, carried far in the still winter air. She smiled to herself as she finished, that was how it should always have been, that was how it had once been, she thought, a pleasure, a joy, to sing for oneself and not as a performing animal.

For so long she had feared that without her voice she would be nothing. These past months without it, she had hoped she might not want it, might not need it. But with no voice she had felt empty. Now her voice was back with her, and she had sung to *them*, and she had stood on that stage and she had known. She might have her voice but even with it *she* was nothing, felt nothing, enjoyed nothing. It was The Voice they came for, The Voice that was worshipped and loved.

She touched her throat. She had always felt herself to be the captive of The Voice. But it was not so. The Voice was as much a prisoner as she.

'Go then, my beauty – let us both be free,' she said aloud, clearly and distinctly.

She opened her mouth and began to scream and scream and scream until she had no voice left.

Then, deliberately, she folded the blanket from the car into a form of pillow and she lay down in the deep fresh snow to sleep . . .

The obituary writers were kept busy that night for they were unprepared.

> Kitty Lawrence (36) born of humble parents is dead too soon. She was possessed of a voice of beautiful texture and colour, with accurate intonation and a remarkable evenness. It was a fearless and dramatic voice . . . Who of us privileged to hear her Norma and Tosca will ever forget the power of her performance? Her repertoire was still building and we had yet to hear her Lucia, but the many records she made encapsulate for all time the many other roles she sang to such perfection.

Some of the audience at Covent Garden wept openly when, at the end of that night's performance, the General Administrator announced the sad news.

Camilla de Souza was relaxing in her bath with her radio and cat for company. Her sadness and tears were genuine but she felt disappointed, too, that now she would never be on *This Is Your Life*.

A small, dark-haired child with expressive brown eyes, unable to sleep in a farmhouse near Cambridge, excitedly pointed at a face on the television, a face she remembered. And she wondered why her daddy looked so sad.

*

Felix was told on the aeroplane bringing him back from New York. A considerate pilot thought it best to inform him so that he could come to terms with the news before they landed to find the press waiting. Felix looked out at the star-studded sky and felt an intolerable emptiness, and knew for sure his own life was over.

Slim's wife Penelope had been distraught over his relationship with Kitty but she was not a malicious woman. She quietly entered his studio and as gently as she could told him the impossible. He said nothing but turned away from her. Through the night, feverishly, he composed – he wrote his requiem for his dead love.

Lana had just come off the stage at the London Palladium and was in her dressing-room – the one with a star – when her mother called to tell her.

'Do you think there's a will?' Amy asked, a shade excitedly.

'Oh, Mum!' Lana said, feeling suddenly chill and very alone. 'Oh, Mum.' Tears were streaming down her face and then she laughed. There didn't seem much else she could do.